CODENAME: *HELLBUG*

"You asked what she'll do that the others won't?"

As the men watched, the plane lifted into the air, and when its skids were fifteen feet above the concrete hangar floor the whole aircraft began to pivot . . . now it floated near one back wall of the hangar. The pilot lifted its nose slightly and began to parallel the wall. Backward.

"This is absolutely staggering," said Randolph, watching Black Stealth One as it began to parallel another wall.

After his path had described a "U" pattern, the pilot moved the craft as far from them as possible. "Watch," said Ben Ullmer.

"Jeeesus Christ," said the Director of Central Intelligence.

The aircraft, in an instant, had disappeared.

"A CLEVER TECHNO-THRILLER . . . Ing's combination of ultralight and stealth technologies is convincing."

—*Publishers Weekly*

"A HEADY MIXTURE OF SPY STORY AND ROMANCE. . . . The novel is tightly plotted, with interesting and attractive characters. In a season crammed with techno-thrillers, Ing reminds us of the poetry and joy of flight, which give this subject its enduring fascination."

—*Library Journal*

Tor books by Dean Ing

The Big Lifters
The Black Tide
Blood of Eagles
The Ransom of Black Stealth One
Single Combat
Wild Country

"Set aside six hours and appreciate this romance without interruption or distraction! It is not only thrilling, but subtle and fascinating. . . . the story is told largely in dialogue that would do credit to the hard boiled detective story. Those who find the 'techno-thriller' too difficult to be entertaining should not be put off reading Ing's great opus. . . ."

—West Coast Review of Books

"Has the reader hanging on to each page. . . ."

—Associated Press

"Readers familiar with Dean Ing's near future sf have long been wondering when he would produce a technothriller. . . . Ing knows his espionage, aviation, Mexico, pacing, and characterization, to name only the principal elements that make up this eminently successful book."

—Booklist

"This high-tech thriller is loaded with lots of suspenseful showdowns, double-crossing rats and stuff like that."

—New York *Daily News*

THE RANSOM OF BLACK STEALTH ONE

DEAN ING

A TOM DOHERTY ASSOCIATES BOOK
NEW YORK

This book is a work of fiction. All the characters and events portrayed in it are likewise fictional, and any resemblance to real people or incidents is purely coincidental.

THE RANSOM OF BLACK STEALTH ONE

A Tor Book
Published by Tom Doherty Associates, Inc.
49 West 24th Street
New York, N.Y. 10010

Cover design by Joe Curcio
Interior illustration by Dean Ing

ISBN: 0-812-50857-2

Library of Congress Catalog Card Number: 89-35078

First Tor edition: April 1990

Printed in the United States of America

0 9 8 7 6 5 4 3 2 1

For the women in other men's lives:
Elaine, Carole, Suz' and Suzanne.

ACKNOWLEDGMENTS

Because the very nature of stealth is ambiguity, we need not be surprised that the subject is both top secret and high profile. It was not my intent to ferret out and publish information that might compromise the security of existing programs. My advisors assure me that I did not. Those now active in aerospace programs did, however, help me focus on the better sources in open literature, and critiqued my preliminary design of Black Stealth One. Retired engineers free to swap brainstorms, and to critique my own fictional stealth techniques into something like feasibility, include Everett Elerath and Joseph Vasilik. William Brubaker made his library available and has my thanks for it. A few whose employments are more sensitive must remain, in their jargon, "low observable." To them I offer generic thanks.

ONE

WESTON, WHO WAS NOT A LIGHT SLEEPER, AT first sensed only a dull impact through his bedroom floor to the mattress. It did not shake him fully awake and he was unable, later, to testify how long it took him to become aware of the door buzzer. Too long, at any rate. He did recall that the digital clock downstairs in the living room read "02:51" when, conservative as always, he slipped a raincoat over his pajamas, his old .45 service automatic heavy as a curbstone in the right-hand pocket.

Although he had been a full-fledged member of the intelligence community for over forty years, the first thing that popped into Weston's head as he squinted through the peeper was: *some damn kid's prank.* He opened the door anyway. The rounded dark mass slumped against his alcove brickwork seemed about the size of those huge plastic mulch bags to a man whose sixty-three-year-old eyes were still full of sleep. The position of his alcove light and Potomac's country-lane street lamps in his face at three o'clock in the *morning,* for God's sake, didn't help. James Darlington Weston, a patient man, resisted the urge to kick that bag of mulch, sighed, took his right hand from the overcoat pocket and snapped the alcove light off.

Nothing had ever startled him more in his life than when the bag of mulch mumbled, "Thank you, Halcyon."

Dar Weston was suddenly, vibrantly, awake. He did not snap the light on again because as his awareness dilated, it included the sedan abandoned across his front walk and the fact that the car must have shaken him half awake as it slammed into the low brick pilaster flanking his carport. It included some faint familiarity with that voice, too, which had thanked him for plunging the alcove into darkness again, and used a code name he hadn't answered to since 1953. Weston had not even run agents as a case officer for many years, but nobody who'd been in that part of the business ever forgot as much of it as he would like to, and Weston's response was immediate.

He snapped off the living room valance light, then stepped out onto chill cement and squatted, sensing that the huddled figure needed help. By the time he got the man into the guest room, carrying more than guiding him, the man's attaché case banging shins at random, Weston knew the man needed that help very, very badly. His own hands were sticky, and blood does have a special smell when there is enough of it, and civilized men do not void their bladders or bowels while fully clothed except in the greatest physical extremity.

He swore as the reading lamp flooded the room, and lifted the man's legs onto the bed to save the carpet. The left trouser leg was already stiff with blood, which seemed to be coming from the man's lower left abdomen. The attaché case, with three feet of cable linking it to the man's wrist manacle, could wait. As Weston tugged at the man's windbreaker and sportshirt, he traded calm gazes with the stranger who did not seem to be in much pain. The face was sixtyish, clean-shaven, with the pallor of gray milk, and like the voice it was distantly familiar. Weston, hoping to find a knife wound, said, "Forgive me, but I don't recognize you." Then he saw the hole in the man's abdomen, slowly pulsing as fresh blood pumped out, and swore again. Inside that man was a metal slug.

"I was 'Sparrow' in the old days," the man said, sounding very tired. "You knew me well enough then." A pause, and a cough that must have hurt. "You were the only one whose address I knew tonight. Sorry."

Weston studied the gray face, seeing the strong, chiseled tawny face of the young hellion beneath thirty-six more years of disenchantment, and nodded. It was Sparrow, he was certain. *God damn an agency that sends old men to do boys' work!* Weston snatched at the telephone he had knocked askew near the lamp table, and began to dial with brisk, furious strokes. "I'm calling Company paramedics. You're filling up with blood, Sparrow."

The manacled wrist levitated as if by some outside power. "You will know who gets this," Sparrow said softly, his eyes closed now. "I was intercepted in Bethesda. Not your man's fault." He waited for Weston's rapid-fire telephoned instructions to cease, then added, "First combination: three one five. Second combination: seven four zero. Make certain—" A long pause, long enough for Weston to begin probing the free wrist for a pulse. Then, "—that you don't press the stud with any other combination."

The pulse was thready. Dar Weston had seen good men die before, and in the silence of his lonely house he felt that sense of loss again. "Hang on. We'll get you fixed up," he said, and squatted, frowning, his face near Sparrow's. "Is absolutely everybody else in your section on fucking vacation?" That famous note of command, which had stiffened the postures of two generations of intelligence people, seemed to wake Sparrow from light sleep.

"I asked for this courier job, Mr.—Weston. This"—again the jerk of that right wrist—"is from the Israelis. Open it."

"I didn't know of anything incoming from there," said Weston. "That means I haven't the need to know, yet. It can wait."

Struggling up, eyes blinking wide, Sparrow fell back to the coverlet with a sigh of mortal exhaustion. "You will have. It's the Red Book."

"My God," Weston said, glancing at the attaché case. The poor bastard was bleeding out on him right before his eyes, and Langley was a full twenty-five-minute drive from Potomac, and that damned Company paramedic van was probably still ten minutes away, even with an expert driving like Mark Donohue two laps down. But—the Red Book? Well, even that could wait. He and Sparrow had been close, once upon a time.

"Yes, the new Soviet shopping list." Sparrow was watching him now, licking gray lips with a gray tongue. "Take it. *Let me see you take it,"* he begged. "Three one five. Seven four zero. Be careful."

Shaking his head, Weston said the numbers aloud, setting the two combinations on the metal case. A sudden wild thought struck him that all this was window dressing, that some bright Sov case officer was waiting for him to press that stud and blow himself through the roof. *Paranoia. Which doesn't mean they aren't out to get you,* he finished the old gibe silently, and pressed the stud.

There must have been over a thousand pages in that stack, cunningly bound between the covers of a Sears catalog by some Flaps and Seals man—or more likely, woman. The Company had got its hands on an old one, back in 'eighty-five. The list of what the Soviet Union wanted its agents to steal had been a wonderful treatise on what they didn't yet have. Letting the pages fan beneath his thumb, Weston saw that this was a photocopy of a new list, which the other side might not know had been compromised. "Sparrow: do the Sovs know you have this?"

He had to lean nearer to hear Sparrow say, ". . . five. Seven four zero. Careful, Halcyon."

"I have it," Weston said gently, patting the bloody forearm, holding up the most valuable Sears catalog in existence. "See?"

Sparrow did not see, though his eyes were open. Sparrow was fading from 1989 back into the world of 1952 when all good things seemed possible, when Sparrow could drink to the future, when a man loosely connected to the U.S. State Department was buying every other round and answering to the name of Halcyon. Good days; days to remember as Sparrow lay dying.

TWO

AS THE LITTLE LEARJET WHISTLED SOFTLY PAST them on its landing rollout, Ben Ullmer and his assistant, Marie Duchaine, stood outside the Snake Pit and swiveled their heads in unison. "Oughta be a Model Thirty-Six, with all the heavy brass she's haulin'." Marie's expression said she didn't get it, though an aircraft freak would. Ben Ullmer knew airplanes the way some men knew batting averages, down to the third digit.

He knew top brass, too; the arrival of National Security Agency and Central Intelligence directors on the same flight was absolutely unprecedented. Those two might smile at each other across the table from the President, but each year their cooperation looked more like competition. Ullmer had heard of Dar Weston, CIA's top man for science

□□□

and technology, which added up to two CIA nabobs too many nosing around NSA's Snake Pit.

And a couple of other links in the daisy chain of command were tagging along too. That meant Ben Ullmer would have to make nice to the wing-tip oxford brigade. Now, as he often did in moments of stress or deep reflection, Ullmer chewed one of the cigars he never lit, standing near the aircraft fuel pumps and glowering into a bright spring afternoon. Ullmer glanced through the tangle of curly hair on his forearm at his old windup Breitling, the only kind of decoration he would allow his people in the secluded hangars and workshops near Elmira, New York, which NSA people called the Snake Pit. "On time, more's the pity." He readjusted the yellow baseball cap with the CATERPILLAR legend to cover his balding head. The cap was a joke: the Snake Pit's specialty was precisely the opposite of heavy equipment.

With years of Ben Ullmer's peeves behind her, Marie Duchaine knew that growl well enough to discount half of it. With her glasses pushed into her graying blond hair, Marie could not have read the schedule on the clipboard she carried. With Marie's memory, she did not need to. "Shall I send the Black Hangar crew home early, Ben?"

"Yeah, clear 'em out—all but Medina." He watched her, appreciating the fine hips and purposeful stride that could fool a man into thinking Marie was a long jump shy of fifty. Then, "Hold on! It'll look better if they're in the library. Won't kill that bunch to bone up on aircraft specs for an hour."

"Good idea," she said without breaking stride, smiling to herself because she knew how Ben hated to waste a single man-hour. He even made his vacations coincide with the annual Oshkosh fly-in, studying the experimental aircraft of amateurs because good ideas lurked in the damnedest places, and Ben's wife Lorraine had quit trying to change him before their kids left the nest. It was Marie Duchaine, not Ben Ullmer, who accompanied Ben's wife on her vacations. Small wonder that Marie was almost as much family as she was assistant by now.

Ullmer grunted in satisfaction to see the Lear taxiing toward him because, on the uneven taxiway at highway speed, it bobbed like a toy. *Shake 'em up a little; do 'em good.* "Damn stupid, is what it is," he said as he stumped out to the aircraft, talking to no one but his feet, the short arms swinging wide as a weight lifter's as he walked. Ben's crews liked to say Ben was built like a garbage can, but nobody had ever found a way to put a lid on him. "CIA thinks we're leaky, we know fuckin' well *they* are, but we let 'em in here. Call in the *National Enquirer* while they're at it . . ."

The first man out of the Lear was the DIRNSA, Director of the National Security Agency, Charles Foy. NSA folk called their director "Dernza," this one bending almost double to exit the Lear because of his immense height. Ullmer shook his hand, the hand that could fund or eliminate any project in the Snake Pit by a simple jiggle of a pen, and then offered his blunt paw to the others.

Abraham Randolph was DCI, Director of Central Intelligence, with the demeanor of old money and the face of an aging matinee idol, but Ullmer thought his handshake perfunctory. It was James Darlington Weston, CIA deputy for science and technology, who had the handshake of a C-clamp though he was at least Ullmer's age. Weston's brown tweeds and sober tie betrayed membership in the Old Boy network, but Dar Weston's face had the lines of a man who could laugh when it suited him.

Ullmer waved them toward the office, a two-story brick affair squeezed between windowless metal hangars, and responded to small talk as always—badly. He already knew Foy's deputy, Bill Sheppard, the country's top crypto man. A skinny little specimen who walked with quick, precise steps, Sheppard had a reputation for backing the right ideas. He had backed Ullmer's stealth programs to the hilt, and Ben figured the man must have a backbone of beta titanium.

Ben's direct superior, Malcolm Aldrich, walked beside him as if to cement a closeness that did not really exist. Aldrich smiled a lot, but behind his Rotarian cheer lay a festering resentment that his subordinate, Ben Ullmer, lay beyond his control. Well, the Snake Pit work and the autonomy it required were Bill Sheppard's doing, goddammit; let Mal Aldrich piss and moan to Sheppard. Ben had no ambition to rise above Aldrich, but try and convince *him* of that. Ambition, hell: no talent for it, either! Georgia Tech had pumped out a helluvan engineer in Ben Ullmer, but no politician. Ben proved it, standing in the hallway: "Mr. Foy, you flew these folks in over my Cyclone fence so I guess they have the need to know. Which tour do you want?"

It was Sheppard who said, softly, "Black Hangar, Ben. You know why we're here. You can start your briefing."

□□□

"It's your—" He knew Aldrich feared he would say, "funeral." He almost did. "—birds, Dr. Sheppard." Ben led them to the elevator, talking as they filed in, and inserted his ID card in a slot that seemed only a poor fit of the panelwork. "Okay: NSA's used CIA aircraft for over thirty years to gather data. U-2, SR-71, Quietstar, stuff from Lockheed's Skunk Works. I worked there awhile. Good bunch." The elevator door whispered shut. "A few years back, I was asked to develop some, uh, different delivery systems for NSA. They wanted something that could deliver and retrieve a man—or a suitcase nuke, or a sensor package—across continental distances without detection or landing strips." His glance toward Aldrich was bland, and Aldrich returned it the same way. Mal Aldrich had fought this project at its inception, and he had lost.

The elevator lurched, an addition to the sinking feeling these CIA people must have felt when they first realized NSA could build its own stealthy birds. When NSA no longer needed CIA aircraft, the locus of power would inevitably shift. Ullmer was unperturbed. "I was ex-Lockheed, and two of my crew in delivery system design were just plain nuts about aircraft: Medina and Corbett."

From Randolph: "Kyle Corbett?"

Ullmer: "That was the man. He and Medina fought like two cats in a sack but, dear God, how they could cobble up an airchine!"

"Friend of yours, wasn't he?" Randolph glanced at Weston, who only nodded with a faraway look.

"Hard to make friends with a guy like Corbett. Damn shame, to die at the peak of his abilities," Ullmer said.

□ □ □

"At least it must've been quick," Weston said. "And I gather he finished the job."

Ullmer shrugged. "The part that dealt with flying an airchine, yeah. First we built a series of stealth studies, flyin' breadboards, so to speak. The Blue Sky project." He saw Dar Weston's quizzical glance. "You know, invisible airplanes; nothin' but blue skies do I see." Ullmer sang it, evidently in the key of "Z," and saw pained smiles of recognition.

The elevator hunted a bit, and the door slid aside. The overhead fluorescents revealed an expanse twice the size of a basketball gym but with a flat ceiling thirty feet high, the floor of another hangar directly overhead. "This is Black Hangar," said Ullmer, leading the way with a gesture that was unnecessary because everyone was already staring. "We cannibalized Blue Sky One, so I can't show her to you, but there's Two and Three."

Murmurs of appreciation. Two slender shapes loomed silently against the wall, one suspended above the other by slender metal beams cantilevered from the wall. Those spidery supports suggested that the aircraft was feather-light, though it had sturdy wheels folded flush into the wing. Both craft sported canopies that bulged above the wings, and twin tails mounted on extension tubes that seemed slender as pencils. The wing of the lower craft was covered with fabric, painted blue below, mottled brown above. The two shapes were subtly different, but they looked more like sailplanes than powered craft.

"The lower one's Blue Sky Two, powered by a pair of little French turbo units." Ben strolled with his visitors, whose heads kept swinging to scan the sweep of those wings as they approached. "Wingspan's a tad over forty feet, crew of one. Engines buried in the fuselage, so the locals never paid much attention to her. Helluva lot of high-performance sailplanes around Elmira, you know."

Although the upward slope of the wing put its tip eight feet above concrete, Charles Foy reached it with ease, tapping gently with a finger. "Plastic?"

"And carbon fiber," Ullmer nodded with the squint of a critic. "The crew got experience with superstrength materials when we formed those tips. They're a little wonky," he added, "but we've done better since. A lot better. These were just practice for the materials and processes of the final bird."

Sheppard, whose memory rivaled Marie's, had evidently read every progress report on the craft. "Did you ever manage to lower its infrared signature?"

"No way," Ullmer admitted. "We got the exhaust spread enough so it's not visible, but on any good IR scope it's a goddamn beacon in the sky. Besides its heat signature, it's still vulnerable to radar, which just pokes right through fabric and plywood and spots the metal in the engines. Not so much on Number Three. For one thing, we put Schiff-base salts in her paint. Very high radar absorption, not as much of a signal. Basically, Two is a wood-and-fabric bird. It'd burn like a boxkite if you lit a match to it."

He ducked under the wing, motioning the others to follow, and pointed to the craft that hung above. "We built Blue Sky Three as a two-place with shrouded pusher props. A little heavy because of the skin heaters. Y'see, the skin of the entire airchine is stretched over a matrix of little electric heat strips. With heat-sensitive paint, this airchine can change color like a chameleon. We're talking more heat than you'd get from skin friction or sunlight, of course, so it carries a little weight penalty." Ullmer paused for one beat. "Not exactly the same as bein' invisible, but close. A long step in that direction. Naturally we had to uprate the engine power. Pair of little Rotax engines at first, but then we went to some air-cooled rotary jobs of our own—if anybody cares," he said, wondering if anybody but Sheppard gave a damn.

To his surprise, CIA's Randolph did too. He cocked his handsome profile over, nodding, and spoke as if to himself. "Thousand-mile range, low observables, two-man crew. Dr. Sheppard briefed us at last week's Security Council meeting," he said by way of explanation.

That must've been one bastard of a meeting for Foy and Sheppard, thought Ullmer, *with the President watching while they admitted how we tried an end-run around CIA.* "Well then. Any questions?"

"Several," Randolph assured him, "beginning with whether Blue Sky Three is fully operational."

"You betcha," Ullmer said. It was evident that the others awaited his answer with more than casual interest.

Abraham Randolph was not finished, however. "Could it, for example, fly a mission over Fort Meade without detection?"

Ben Ullmer stood perfectly still, considering the question of flight over NSA's own headquarters as if it were a reasonable scenario. Then: "Depends on whether Dr. Sheppard's boys were lookin' spe-

□□□

cifically for it, Mr. Randolph. If they weren't, it probably could. Little blip on a scope, maybe."

Now it was Weston, for the first time, who pressed the issue. "Is Blue Sky Three advanced very much beyond anything the Other Side is flying?"

Jesus, what a question! CIA itself controls the finest fleet of spy aircraft on earth. Of obsolete spy aircraft, some imp of ego reminded him. "All I know is what our guys and your guys tell me," Ullmer shrugged. "My guess is, the Sovs would wet their pants if they knew what this bird can do. As I understand it, they don't even know about the chameleon skin yet, never mind the range and the low IR and radar signal."

A subtle relaxing among his visitors, and a glance between Weston and Randolph. "Good enough," Randolph said as if it were of no importance; but Ben Ullmer knew, somehow, that it was very important. The CIA leader cleared his throat, with a glance at Charles Foy, and mixed a metaphor full of frosty humor: "And now, if we could see a bird of a different color . . ."

"Black Stealth One." It was Sheppard who said it, the phrase an incantation assuring Ben that it was all right, that these men too were priests of high technology, bowing before the same altars.

Ben Ullmer nodded his head toward the far wall, a towering partition with massive panels on caster wheels. "Right," he sighed, and led them to an ordinary metal-faced door in one of those panels.

Ben watched their faces as they stepped through into an expanse as great as the one they had left. He took no pleasure in their silent awe, feeling instead that he was giving up his virginity. They had murmured in excitement at the sight of the Blue Sky craft, but no one spoke as they stared at Black Stealth One.

Ben gave them time for it to sink in, expecting the reaction because he still felt it himself when gazing at this creature, a vast bird of passage crafted from filament and ceramic. Like your first sight of an albatross in flight or a perfect-bodied ballerina *en pointe,* every line seemed so natural, so *right,* you wondered why any other kind existed. And you smiled, and you let the goose bumps travel over your skin until that magical moment of pure pleasure had passed.

It had no ordinary wheels; only tiny casters on skids. No fuselage to speak of and no tail at all, only slender swept wings subtly twisted at their tips, spanning fully sixty feet with low rudders, canted inward, far out on the wings. In repose, the wings sagged as if the bird were exhausted.

Its surface was not black, but a dull gray, glass-smooth and absorbent of light though pinpoints of sheen glistened like dew on its hide. A huge duct yawned like a manta ray's gullet in front of the wing, and it extended back to a circular exhaust vent behind the wings. A two-seat cockpit pod was suspended inside that duct, protruding aggressively forward like the head and neck of a live thing. The pod's shape was that of a flat-nosed bullet, and its canopy bulged on each side, resembling the multifaceted eyes of some enormous alien insect. Once you were near it, you could not escape the feeling that it was watching *you* for the slightest mistake, for a chance to inhale you through that gullet that seemed to have half swallowed its pod. An immense, all-seeing winged predator, waiting for an excuse to hunt—or for unwary prey to come nearer.

"Some of the crew call it the hellbug," Ben said to break the spell, and then raised his voice, "Medina! You asleep in there?"

Even before the muffled reply, Black Stealth One rocked slightly on its skids, a monster flexing mighty wings. Aldrich took a step backward, startled. "Yo," a voice called from inside the creature. "In the port wing fairing, Ben." Only a slender man could fit inside that wing.

"I know where the hell you are. Come out and meet your betters," Ben called with gruff good humor.

Chuckles from Sheppard and Weston, and more of that rocking motion from Black Stealth One. Ben led them nearer with, "You see how a man's weight affects it; you won't believe it but this bird weighs under five hundred pounds empty."

Over someone's soft whistle he said, "And her radar cross-section is just about nonexistent, God's truth."

"Similar to the B-2?"

"The stealth bomber is low observable," Ben agreed, "but its signature is the size of a hawk's. The hellbug? More like a hummingbird. We're talking *non*observable here. Structure's almost entirely kapton, carbon, and polymer, which damn near floats, and the rotary engine's mostly ceramic. Even the nuts and bolts are polymers loaded with quartz filament. We've only got test-hop tanks in her so far, but her wings are thick enough to carry fuel for four thousand miles. They wouldn't be tanks, exactly; we call it 'wet wings.' "

□□□

"How long would it take to install wet wings, Ben?" Sheppard's gaze held the same keen interest that Randolph's had.

"Couple of months. Have to move her upstairs into Blue Hangar for that. She can't vertol with that much fuel, though. She'd need a short run, maybe a hundred feet. Medina's logged about ten hours of test flights."

"Nobody mentioned that," Weston blurted. "This thing can take off vertically?"

"And land the same way." Ben Ullmer squatted at the sleek nose of the craft, tapping a rounded opening beneath, the diameter of a basketball and thin as stovepipe. "This is an exhaust for the diverter waste gates. Another one under each wing. When you swap an external propeller for an impeller *inside* the airplane, and bolt it to a couple of hundred horsepower, you get a ducted fan that'll pump air like God's own vacuum cleaner. When you deflect the exhaust through these big suckers, the whole airchine will rise straight up."

"That, I must see," said Dar Weston, risking the knees of a five-hundred-dollar suit as he knelt. Then, perceiving that a man's head had just popped from a hatch where the wing joined that yawning duct, the CIA man chuckled. "Well, hello there." He turned back to Ben. "What else will this bird do that the others won't?"

Ullmer watched as the man eased himself from the hatch, a sweat-covered wiry fellow wearing spotless coveralls and cloth gloves, with the dark eyes and blue-black hair of a latino. Fine squint lines hinted that the man was older than he at first looked. Ben introduced the visitors to Raoul Medina.

□□□

"You flew for us awhile," said Randolph when Medina had emerged barefooted to sit on a protective pad. "I believe you have a jockstrap medal back at Langley." CIA men joked that Company medals could be worn only on your jockstrap, and the medals rarely left Company headquarters at Langley, Virginia.

"Yessir," Medina agreed, smiling, wiping sweat from his face, moving from the wing root to a nearby inspection stand. "Before you were DCI."

"Some passes in a U-2R over 'Nam and China, against stuff that might've brought you down," Randolph persisted.

"Yessir," Medina repeated, the smile unchanged as he folded the blanket-sized pad.

"But it didn't, and here you are with NSA," Randolph said, smiling back, supplying words for a man who seemed to lack them.

"That was then. This is now," said Raoul Medina, with an easy candor that avoided insolence by a millimeter. He began to position the hatch cover with loving care. As if to atone for his earlier brevity, Medina kissed his fingertips and placed them on the wing. "And this, as they say, is the most fun you can have with your clothes on. She's a handful when hovering but compared to anything else that hovers, she's quiet as mice."

"How many people can fly it?"

"Only him, so far," Ben Ullmer put in. "Raoul got his A and P ticket after he left you. Pilot first, master mechanic second. A lot of Black Stealth One is his doing; his and Corbett's."

"That means you must've designed it before, um, 'eighty-five," Weston mused.

"Right," said Ben. "You have to quit changing

and start building at some point, or you'd never finish." Medina studied the CIA man for a moment, but said nothing. Ben went on, "I s'pose you folks want to see what else the hellbug can do. You won't believe it unless you see it. Raoul: need a preflight?"

Medina shook his head. "What's the drill?" Pulling the gloves off with his teeth, he tugged at a flush latch below the creature's bulging left eye, which raised in gullwing fashion for his entry. He shoved his toes into a spring-loaded niche to step up. Again, the entire aircraft flexed as if shrugging. Medina snapped a five-element harness, flicking switches, scanning dials.

"Make a circuit around us at five meters. Then back off near the wall and go to chameleon mode. Set her down in her plumage." Ben was almost smiling, an expression he had never shown to Aldrich before.

Medina nodded and latched the canopy. Ben Ullmer led the way back to the wall where they had entered, said, "Might get a little breezy in here," folded his arms and waited.

A faint smoky chuffing from the exhaust vent caused the craft to shake perceptibly for a moment, but as the engine's whirr sped up, the shaking ceased and the smoke disappeared. Ben said to Weston, who stood next to him, "You asked what she'll do that the others won't? Well, we pass the engine exhaust through finned mufflers behind the impeller blades; no IR signature because the exhaust jet is just cool air. And all hovercraft make a hell of a racket. Except this one." Now, Ben was definitely smiling.

"No louder than a stiff breeze," Weston noted.

□□□

The engine noise was not even as loud as that multiblade impeller, whirling inside the duct, gulping air around the pod and flinging it out behind. A man did not have to shout to be heard. "Don't impeller blades return a radar signal?"

"Not if they're plastic," Ben replied. "And blades are way up inside the inlet duct; adds to the muffler effect."

As he spoke, the hollow rush of air took on a different note, the wings rising almost as if to flap. "Diverters working for vertol," Ben said. And then Black Stealth One was rising steadily on three invisible columns of air.

The watchers blinked away dust motes in the breeze that eddied around them, and when its skids were fifteen feet above the concrete the whole aircraft began to pivot. Ullmer shook his fist. The pivot motion stopped and Medina backed the ship away. "Just tellin' Medina what he'd get if he gave us a zap of exhaust. Blow us all flat. You want to watch his sense of humor, gents." But Medina had manipulated the craft so that it now floated near one back wall of the hangar. He lifted its nose slightly and began to parallel the wall. Backward.

"This is absolutely staggering," said Randolph, watching Black Stealth One as it began to parallel another wall.

After his path had described a "U" pattern, Medina moved the craft as far from them as possible. "Watch," said Ben Ullmer.

"Jeeesus Christ," said the Director of Central Intelligence.

The aircraft, in an instant, seemed to become transparent and virtually disappeared. Where the background was cream-tinted wall, the skin of Black Stealth One was cream. A hangar air duct, blocked by the wing, suddenly appeared to be visible through the wing. Even the vertical wall seams were reproduced, but with the faithfulness of a wayward lover, not quite perfect. The canopy, however, remained a canopy and the fidelity of the illusion was not exact for anyone but Foy, whom Medina had evidently chosen as the focus.

When Medina caused the craft to begin rotating, more than one man exclaimed aloud; the illusion remained. The skin of Black Stealth One was changing its patterns as it rotated, to fool a watcher only a hundred feet away. Ben had learned to look slightly away from it while the craft was in chameleon mode, but the others were staring hard, trying to blink the fuzziness from their vision.

Enjoying the slack jaws despite himself, Ben said, "From this distance it's not very convincing but put 'er a thousand feet up and, mister, she is flat fuckin' invisible. Dr. Sheppard's boys ran across the fact that the colors of some liquid crystals are voltage sensitive, and we figured out how to embed some in a skin. 'Bout a thirty-pound weight penalty for the entire skin area. Medina just gives the computer a focus viewpoint it has to fool. Its video looks in the opposite direction and paints the skin with the liquid crystal display to match the backdrop. Kinda like the pixels of a big TV screen; as she moves, she compensates."

Aldrich, who knew the answer: "And if I move?"

"If the computer's IR scanner is locked onto you, it compensates. It only fools one viewpoint, but the pilot can select it."

□□□

"Another team is working on the canopy problem," Sheppard assured the audience. "If the pilot can trust video displays completely, the next version won't have a canopy."

Weston: "Let me see if I understand this. The skin only seems transparent because the skin facing the chosen observer takes the appearance of what that observer *would* see, if the aircraft weren't there. And the videos on the side facing away from the observer—the back side—are in effect filming the obscured view and projecting it onto the observer's side."

"Yeah," said Ullmer. "In effect. Goddamn little computer's got some smart parts; it even recognizes when the hellbug's own shadow is impinging on the backdrop, like when it's just above the ground. It won't let its own shadow screw up the projection. That's *smart,*" he winked.

By now, Black Stealth One had slid back near its original position, still two stories above them. Ben Ullmer held up his hands, linked their thumbs, and mimed a flapping with his open fingers. Medina nodded and made a console adjustment. Instantly, the Snake Pit's guests were laughing, for the wing display had become an almost-perfect replica of a bird's plumage, even to the splayed pinion feathers at the wingtips. A sixty-foot buzzard hung almost silent above them.

"We programmed that in just for fun," Ben said. "But when she's soaring over our runway, and you've got nothing to scale 'er against—well, it'll fool these old eyes." With that, he gestured a thumbs-down and Medina let the craft settle on its skids, the soft rush of air quickly dying as Medina busied himself with a clipboard inside.

□□□

"Now, just for your opinion, Abe." One of Charles Foy's elegant brows elevated slightly. "You agree that hiding this is worth the sacrifice?"

"I do, Charles," Randolph said. His tone had a matching cool elegance, but in fact the air almost hummed with heightened anticipations. "Given how advanced this is over Blue Sky Three, it seems little sacrifice at all."

They stood in momentary silence gazing at the craft. "Just consider," Foy said as though thinking aloud, "what one could do with only a hundred of these. It's invisible, it can land in any pasture, delivering men or devices, or bringing them back. It could hover unseen over the very Kremlin. Goodbye to all security in the most tightly controlled nation on earth."

"That shopping list wasn't very specific." The Director of Central Intelligence pulled at his chin, noting that Black Stealth One was now a dull gray again, and turned back to the Dernza. "They specify when they can. I don't think they have a clue about what they're after, except that it's a third generation stealth program—and that's enough to make it Priority One for them."

"My thoughts exactly," said Charles Foy. "Ben says he'll need two months to install the long-range tanks. That won't be the final product. The new canopy won't be ready, for example. But, still, it will be able to play its part in our flim-flam." He noticed a faint frown on Ullmer's face. "Excuse me, Ben, we're talking gibberish to you. Is the other side of Black Hangar secure?"

Ullmer nodded. He got Medina's attention, mimed a throat-cut and pointed to his Breitling—

□□□

"kill it; quitting time"—then led the way back through the door.

"It's almost five," Aldrich reminded no one in particular as, without apparent intent, the men formed a loose ring near the center of the expanse.

Foy stuck his hand out to be shaken again. "Ben, the reports don't do this thing justice. You've outdone yourselves; tell your crews I said so."

Ullmer shifted that dead cigar. "But," he prompted.

"No buts. It's unbelievable. Still, sooner or later we had to share the news."

"Depends on how wide we share it," Ullmer said darkly, looking down at his feet.

Randolph, with a sad smile: "Still need-to-know only, but don't worry that the Soviets will find out about it." He paused.

It was Dar Weston who dropped the bomb: "They already have, Mr. Ullmer."

"Hell and damnation! How could we leak?" The pain on Ben's face was so real he seemed in danger of bursting into tears. "And what the GOD-damned hell do we do now?"

"We've already talked that over. Had to," Foy said ruefully, "after a man died placing a copy of the new Sov shopping list in Mr. Weston's hands. CIA saw that the Other Side is uncommonly interested in something CIA itself was unaware of, until we told them; something called Black Stealth aircraft. Sovs even know it's not CIA, or Lockheed or Northrop—but they don't know any of its technical tricks. They just figure that if it's stealth they must have it."

"And they'll keep coming after it until they have one for themselves," Foy ended.

□□□

"Like our side felt about that MiG that Belenko stole," Ben said. "Yeah, I know how it works. So what do we do about it?"

Randolph looked at Foy, who looked at Sheppard, who said, "Uhm, well," and took a breath. "Well, Ben, we have to convince them to go back to sleep; to quit sniffing around. In short, to relax."

Ben shifted his cigar, bit it hard, and snarled, "I wish I had the foggiest fuckin' idea how we might manage *that,* by God I do."

"Simplest thing in the world," Sheppard said gently. "We let the Sovs steal Black Stealth One."

THREE

BEN ULLMER CAUGHT MOST OF HIS CIGAR BEFORE it hit the floor, glaring speechless at NSA's top cryptographer. He removed a wet mass from his mouth, the part of the stogie he'd bitten off, and crammed the fragments into a pocket. Then his features began to relax. "That is the dirtiest joke I have *ever* heard," he said, hoping someone would smile to endorse the idea.

"You understand," said Sheppard, "that the joke will be on the other side. We *will* let them have Blue Sky Three, suitably fudged with a dummy flight log. You mentioned that we might be able to spot it? Believe me, Ben: we can. So, they can have it. Instead of having KGB people seeking the real thing, we'd much rather lull them to sleep by letting them steal the sacrifice. If they don't know

□□□

what Black Stealth One can do, they won't know we're delivering a substitute."

"This decision is already cast in concrete, I suppose," Ullmer growled.

Charles Foy: "I'm afraid so. This is damage control, cutting something adrift to save the crucial bits. It would be hard to overstate the tremendous loss this country would suffer if the other side ferreted out the facts of the real Black Stealth One. Their next strategic bomber wouldn't have to be fast, or heavily armored."

"No shit," said Ulmer, whose political sense seemed to have shattered in the shock wave of this thunderbolt his superiors had trained on him. "We couldn't spot a hellbug any easier than they could."

"I'm afraid you're right," Sheppard admitted, staring away at nothing, "though it *can* be spotted, Ben."

"Maybe, but it'd be a two-ton brindle bitch of a job," Ullmer insisted. He saw Mal Aldrich gazing heavenward at this colorful metaphor and did not give a shit. Might as well dive headlong into matters for which his need to know might be arguable, so he did. "However you work this out, too damn many people in the intelligence community will know about it. One little leak and the Russkis will have Blue Sky Three AND an itch for the hellbug."

Dar Weston had been leading Greeks near Khalkidiki in 'forty-four, behind German lines, at the age of nineteen. He had mastered the use of voice tones before he could vote. Ullmer, of course, was not in his agency, so the CIA man's timbre carried both firm assurance and persuasion. "Mr. Ullmer, eight men on earth know what we intend to do, including you and the President. It will be nine when your pilot is told—or ten if he declines the mission. Without prejudice, I might add. We will simply have one of our people train in the airplanes so that he can steal them."

Weston stopped because Ben was shaking his head. "Them? He only has to steal Blue Sky Three, you said."

"The scenario is for that one to be flown to a location near the exchange site, after it's agreed, and soon. Our man really *will* take Black Stealth One, when the time comes. He'll just land and make a switch before he meets the Sovs with their ransom money," Weston explained.

Ben scuffed one brogan at a hard coin of chewing gum some idiot had dropped on his clean floor. "Why take the hellbug at all?"

Charles Foy, with the abused patience of a man who was justifying something he didn't like himself, answered brusquely. "Ullmer, this operation *has* to ring true, else the other side won't buy it. You know the Sovs listen in to everything, and if they hear every weekend warrior on the hunt, in addition to the Coast Guard, FBI, Air Force, and God knows who else, we think they'll be persuaded that something genuine—and very big—is going down."

"But why not just *say* the thing has been stolen," Ullmer still protested. "You could press the alarm anyway. If it's invisible who can tell it's not up there?"

"Three reasons," Foy said, and he turned to Sheppard. Foy knew that if Ullmer trusted anyone to have Black Stealth's best interests at heart, it was Sheppard.

"First, Ben," said Sheppard, "we have to move her anyway. This whole gambit will expose Snake Pit, so we have to put the craft elsewhere. Second, we don't think we can fake the theft convincingly if we never actually put her in the air. If she's actually up there, there *will* be some fleeting sightings, but of course no one will catch her—which will make her seem all the bigger prize to the Sovs. And, third, Ben, what better way to test your handiwork than to see how she does with the whole Air Force after her?"

"Where are you going to bring her?" Ullmer asked grimly.

"Let's say, the southwest," Sheppard answered. "Of course she'll never go anywhere near the border."

A long moment of silence; then Ben sighed. He began to smile, a hard rictus that was not benign, as he added, "I know how far I am down the scrotum pole, gents, but I can tell you this: if it doesn't work, you have my resignation. I love the Snake Pit, and I'll do everything in my power to make this work. But if it doesn't, gentlemen"—the smile fading as he looked at each of his visitors in turn—"I'm out of here."

"An emotional decision, Ben," said Aldrich, with what seemed to be real concern.

"Damn right," Ben replied. "But if you think I'm emotional now, try me if this operation goes down the tubes."

"Well"—Dar Weston sighed—"we'll just have to see that you stay employed." His hand on Ben's shoulder was gentle.

"That means you'll be shuttling back to Meade during the coming weeks," Sheppard said, nodding at Ben. "Lots of details to work out, beginning with how much we can tell Medina, and when we tell him."

Ben dry-washed his face and grimaced. "There's gotta be an extra man in this. The guy who contacts those fuckin' thieves to make the deal."

"No extra man," said Randolph. "It's got to be the same man who flies the plane."

"He's expendable," said Ben, stating it as a fact, hoping for a denial.

The reply was silence.

FOUR

"JESU MARIA, I THINK MY ARM'S ASLEEP," SAID Medina. He shifted his weight, his forehead pressing against the Toyota's headrest.

"That's not all that's asleep," was the reply into his right ear. Not angry, but philosophical.

He longed to tell her that if, instead of getting philosophical, she would get *busy,* maybe all his parts would stay awake; but he didn't. For one thing, it had been her languid grace that attracted him a year before, and the other word for languid was lazy. Most times, that didn't bother him but these times weren't most times. For another thing, you didn't get just a whole lot of mileage out of criticizing her or even hinting at criticism. For a third, it really wouldn't have made much difference what she did, he was so *chingada* preoccu-

□□□

pied with that *chingada* business in the Snake Pit, he was in no mood to ching.

It suddenly occurred to Raoul Medina that he was getting a cramp, suspended dickless above someone else's wife while he silently listed good reasons why. A moment later he said, "I guess this just wasn't the night for it, Arlene. Maybe I'm getting a cold," he added quickly, attaching the blame to himself.

She sighed and turned her head so that she could deliver one of those long, deep, languid kisses that were easily the best things she did. "Then I'll have it too," she said. Arlene had a great throaty voice. She could give you a hand job over the phone.

He managed to wriggle back across the shift lever without tearing his chinos, which tended to rip because he liked to wear them tight to show off his butt, still taut and lean, especially for a man in his forties. She took his right hand and they lay silent in their reclined bucket seats for a few minutes, watching clouds drift across a bomber's moon through the Toyota's open sunroof. After flying RB-66 recon, then U-2's for the Company, and now for fifteen years one of NSA's elves, even a well-conditioned macho in his forties should know better than to play the games he'd been playing. But those games heightened his awareness, made him greet each day with a tingle. And were now beginning to steal perfectly good, serviceable erections. Well, too late to back out now.

"Peso for your thoughts," Arlene said at last, and listened to him laugh.

Medina wasn't laughing for the reason she thought; if women liked his latin looks, why tease him about them? He was laughing because a peso was worth a hell of a lot less than a penny, and his thoughts were worth—well—at least five million dollars' worth of Swiss francs. Or so Dar Weston had told him, a week before when they'd made their pitch and he'd said yes. Not that CIA intended him to get anywhere near the money, much less spend any of it, but that's the kind of price the KGB would expect him to negotiate. And Dar Weston, whose hobby was spy-catching above and beyond his normal duties, had studied a lot of spy-for-profit cases.

Why the hell had he agreed to do it? Maybe to prove he still could, including that jazzy SCUBA stuff they wanted him to use. And maybe CIA had discovered his own hidden agenda, maybe they were trying to see if he'd "go private," the spook phrase for an employee who made himself disappear. If so, they'd be ready for it—might even have a couple of bozos staked out with a starlight scope on the Toyota right this minute. So the only sensible thing was to keep up ordinary appearances, but with this kind of pressure there was at least one thing he could not keep up. *Mierda* . . . "I was just thinking," he improvised, "our anniversary was last week and I plain forgot."

"You mean," said Arlene with a nice hand squeeze, "you forgot that you didn't forget. We celebrated me raw, darling, on the couch in your living room." Pause. Then, genuinely mystified: "What was that thing with all the rivets in it that looked like Darth Vader's armor? You never did say."

He chuckled, returning the squeeze. "Now I remember. Bless that couch. The thing you call armor was a piece of ducting. Six-oh-six-one alloy.

□□□

Just something for the house," he lied. Actually it was the new boundary-layer duct for the Mini-Imp, a single-place sportplane with the potential to outrun anything in its class and land like dandelion fluff, given the mods he'd sketched for Kyle Corbett four years ago in the Snake Pit library. Arlene had never seen the little screamer under those tarps in his garage, and would never see it until he'd towed the finished product to Ithaca and bolted the wings on for test flights. Maybe not then, either. He and Corbett had barely begun the extracurricular project, starting to cobble the whole thing together in Medina's garage two nights a week, before Corbett's accident.

For a long time now, Medina had wondered if it *was* an accident. It could've been an on-purpose. A deliberate bug-out. If so, it was just possible that CIA knew, meaning Weston. And now, of course, there was no way to find out what had really happened to Corbett. Long ago, he had given Medina the number of that post office box in Depew, near Buffalo, but two months after the accident Medina had driven to Depew. Through the little window Medina had seen that the only letter in that post office box had been the one he'd sent, with no return address. It had been there three months later, too. Corbett had never picked it up, so the chances were the man was dead. If only there were some way to send a message without being obvious!

Arlene sighed, a sound full of contentment. Nice girl, really, with a sharp mind that belied the impression she gave of being always half asleep. "Why don't I come to your place again next week, Raoul? I could park in your garage," she said. "God knows who might spot my car, everybody in Elmira knows George."

She couldn't know it, but there was no room in that garage for a car. "Oh, I almost forgot," he said; "The company's sending me down south next week, honey. Something about floppy-disk drives, pain in the ass but I'll be back in ten days. Less, maybe." The good people of Elmira still bought the legend that the Snake Pit manufactured components for home computers. And yes, he was going south, all right! All the way to the decommissioned strip near Regocijo, in Mexico's state of Durango. The people in the Bulgarian trade mission, Weston had assured him, were a direct pipeline to the KGB; and of the three swap sites he would offer in Mexico, no matter which one they chose, he could get there from Regocijo in one hop. Which was why he would be flying Blue Sky Three down there as soon as she was all gussied up to masquerade as Black Stealth One. Pretty sharp thinking on somebody's part to have the craft in place two months ahead of time, even before he had anything worked out with the so-called Bulgarians.

His flight in the hellbug to the secure hangar near Los Alamos in New Mexico would take several days, of course, slow as these birds were. Plenty of time to think this all over. Presently he sat up, yawning, and they racked the seats upright, Arlene touching up her face and hair as he drove her back to the Mart parking lot. She stroked his neck, both to tease and to remind him, but was careful not to do anything dumb as he dropped her off because, as she often said, you never knew who might be watching. Man, if she only knew!

Medina got back home before the Carson show,

turning the audio up so he could hear it in the garage. The Imp was practically ready for trials, lacking only the boundary-layer ducts and it would fly fine without those, but with them it could take off at a speed hardly faster than a man could run—maybe. Staring at his handiwork from the doorway, he realized that he'd been putting off those final touches. He should rent hangar space at Ithaca or Binghamton and trailer the little sucker up there right away, clean out the garage, give Arlene a place to park.

Because when he got into this Bulgarian bullshit, sure as hell someone would be sniffing around his house. He didn't want Ben Ullmer to know he'd been shaving the Imp's hardware so close to outright Snake Pit specs. And it was important to remember that Ben was NSA, whatever else he might be. If Medina ever had to go private, an Imp that could take off on a dime might just be his only hole card. Keeping it here, with spooks flitting around, would be like sending them an open signal.

It was at that moment when Medina realized what he had to do. Not much time to compose the message, and it had to say exactly the right things without saying too much, and it might not be taken seriously even if it was received. It would take a while, the delay was built in, but perhaps he could force a delay in the preparation of those wet wings for the hellbug. Screw it up when the work was half done, maybe; buy a week or so that way. It would be easy enough to do, everybody pulled a fumducker now and then, even a master

□□□

A and P mechanic. But there was another word for doing it deliberately, especially when CIA folks were breathing down his neck.

The word was sabotage.

FIVE

"FROM ANY OTHER SOURCE," PYOTR KAROTKIN muttered, "I should discount this as a ruse. In some ways, Sasha is a complete *shavki."* The term meant "shit-eating dog," and was reserved in the KGB for low-level incompetents. It was true that few professionals would send vital intelligence by way of embassy groundskeepers. As Karotkin spoke, he nodded toward the object on his desk, and a pale reflection of the overhead fluorescents gleamed from the skin stretched like rawhide over his hairless skull.

Leonid Suslov, watching the rawhide gleam, hated those fluorescents. Perhaps, he thought, Karotkin hated them too. But no one in Washington's Soviet Embassy harbored more suspicions of windows than Karotkin, *rezident* for the KGB's Intelligence Directorate. This windowless room had been Karotkin's own choice, between other rooms crammed with data collection equipment.

Suslov, *rezident* for Directorate "T" which handled scientific data collection, greatly preferred the view from his own office. From there he could see down Massachusetts Avenue with the White House and other sensitive buildings clearly visible in the near distance. Since the Americans had been such idiots as to permit the new embassy compound to be built on high ground, they should have expected thickets of Suslov's electronic ears to sprout from the embassy roof.

But Sasha's bombshell had not trickled in by coaxial cable from the roof. It had come, as always, over the wall; the act of a *shavki,* indeed; but an astonishingly successful one. Suslov reached for the object, which lay in a sealed bag on Karotkin's desk, and shifted his bifocals to study it closely. Suslov ran field-grade agents to satisfy the shopping list, but he did not run Sasha. Sasha ran himself, and did it in a manner unique in Suslov's experience.

"In any case, this is not ours to discount, Pyotr Borisovitch," Suslov replied, noting that Sasha had not sprayed crimson paint evenly over the object in the bag. Enough to be seen, however, in daylight, though crimson looked black at night. It was perfectly round, of high-impact plastic, with the appearance of a borscht jar lid. Its center portion, unlike Sasha's earlier missiles of information, was hinged. "I see Sasha has gone high-tech."

"It is called a Flutterbird," Karotkin said, "a new device which does not shatter when struck by shotgun pellets as clay targets do. Instead, its center pops open and it falls." A sigh. "Readily obtained

□□□

at sporting shops." Karotkin's fingers danced as if anxious to pluck the object back, yet he remained polite. He could well afford to, while the little devices continued to sail anonymously over embassy walls with startling messages. So long as Sasha operated without contacts, Karotkin's directorate would remain Sasha's pipeline to Dzerzhinski Square in Moscow. And Sasha's pipeline pumped in only one direction.

"One day we shall trace him," Suslov said wistfully.

"If we did, Lenya, I would not be able to tell you." Karotkin rarely used diminutive forms of address, and never before to Suslov. It suggested—not friendship, for Karotkin avoided closeness—perhaps something akin to pity for a fellow *rezident* denied his fondest desire.

Suslov nodded without rancor. The rigid constraints on exactly who may know what was even more strict in Soviet intelligence agencies—KGB, GRU, and the party secretariat's own spooks as well—than in those of the United States. No one above field-grade operatives gave it a moment's thought; it had always been thus, and would only intensify in the future. Suslov passed a hand through his curly black hair, dyed assiduously to maintain his youthful appearance, and laid down the bag with care. He would know, in any case, that Sasha had not been smoked out so long as his clay pigeons kept sailing in every year or so. Once the KGB was running him, Sasha would damned well report when, how, and on what he was told.

Karotkin had not bothered to hide the stack of three-by-five cards, his favored method of arranging pieces of a puzzle, that lay on his blotter. His habit was to sit erect, shuffling and arranging the cards feverishly with fingers that scuttled like white tarantulas, as he pondered the meanings hidden in each set of cards, like a blind man with a tarot deck. This deck was pink, with dates scribbled on upper right-hand corners. The top card, Suslov saw, read "99" because he was reading it upside down. Therefore, 'sixty-six. The year of their first message from Sasha. Suslov could infer the data his colleague had scribbled on those cards.

In 1966, Leonid Suslov had been in Moscow when Sasha's first clay pigeon soared onto the old embassy grounds in Washington, to be found by a guard. According to the printed message in clear English, CIA was coordinating data from new American spy aircraft and ferret satellites for early missile warnings. If true, this could give Americans an edge so tempting that they might grow more bellicose, more reckless in their demands. Once they knew where to focus their antennae, Soviet science had found it *was* true. The USSR had taken certain steps to equalize that situation. Suslov still did not know exactly what steps.

1967: Sasha had warned of CIA-run "Phoenix" recon teams in Vietnam, small hit teams of *boyevaya* as murderous as the GRU's. Sasha said they were targeting Viet Cong nurses and doctors for assassination. Destabilizing, and true again.

1971: CIA stealth aircraft had progressed far beyond the Helio Courier, the Windecker Eagle, and Lockheed's Quietships, said Sasha. The long-winged, turbojet "Cope" had no pilot and could find its way home after a full day of mapping at high altitudes. The shopping list had brought con-

□□□

firmation, finally, with photographed blueprints from a paid *schpick*, a rank novice.

1974: According to Sasha, NSA found unexpected success in Wisconsin with a low-frequency antenna rig that could permit direct communication between submerged Poseidon subs and command locations. Some American hawks were already whispering that this provided a first-strike advantage that should be used before the Soviets equalized the situation. The most stabilizing response, Sasha added, would be a crash program by the Soviets in the same technology.

1977: A secret Nevada air base was soon to receive its first production-type stealth aircraft from Lockheed's supersecret "Skunk Works" in Burbank. If they could be refueled in flight—and they could, Sasha warned—such aircraft could blind radars or lay a nuclear weapon on any given acre in Libya, China, or the Soviet Union with relatively low danger of detection. It must have been a tremendous temptation for Americans, who might think they could vaporize a Soviet nuclear power plant undetected and then offer regrets about the nuclear "accident."

1981: Sasha claimed that, with NSA equipment and CIA operational help, Americans were tapping Soviet undersea cables to verify the accuracy of Soviet test missiles. Such knowledge generated a dangerous power imbalance. An American traitor named Pelton said so, too. This problem was remedied immediately by the Soviet Navy.

1984: A devilish device built by NSA and air-dropped by CIA near East German air bases looked exactly like shrubs, said Sasha. But they recorded and eventually transmitted MiG radar

□□□

signals, until a counterintelligence team found and destroyed this fake foliage.

1988: Similar shrubbery had been air-dropped near the Nicaraguan coast, which gave warning when Ortega's people tried to ship arms to certain other communist forces. With such precise information, an unidentified aircraft had sunk two boatloads of arms. It was very possible that the aircraft in question was some new experimental stealth model, one of the so-called "black," or unmentionable, U.S. programs.

Eight clay pigeons. Eight crucial messages, all accurate as far as could be determined. And now another, the longest yet, in some ways the most detailed. And easily the most galvanizing, if Moscow reacted as Suslov knew they would.

Tapping those pink cards on his blotter, Karotkin said, "I am even more certain, now, that Sasha is either CIA in a middle-echelon technical post, or NSA. If he is NSA, he could be in a minor position."

"Or somewhere above," Suslov said. "But you had concluded that already." He gave his colleague a thoughtful glance. "If CIA, be glad that their man Weston is only a few years from retirement. The technical man could be on his staff, and Weston has shut down two efforts to penetrate CIA already."

Karotkin's shrug suggested that James D. Weston was not all that unbeatable, and the pursing of his lips said he was considering a new idea. "Weston's tendency to play spy-catcher, when his job lies in other areas, has bought him some enemies among his counterintelligence colleagues," Karotkin said dreamily. "No matter how adept, a man with too many enemies—" He gestured as if to say the outcome was predictable. In the KGB, it certainly was. "Like their spy-catcher Angleton, in the old days," he added, "ultimately forced to resign. We could help Weston make more enemies, perhaps."

Suslov put his head back and laughed. "An exquisite irony! Anonymous tips from us, which let him unmask a low-level *schpick* or two of ours. More long faces and new enemies for Weston in his own agency, eh? Eh?" Suslov was nodding as he asked.

"A man can be too successful for his own good," was Karotkin's only response, but the heavy-lidded smile endorsed Suslov's guess. Even at the *rezident* level, KGB colleagues were wise to avoid brainstorming freely even in matters of mutual concern. Both men knew and accepted the rules. You sought subtle colleagues with a creative bent, and you swapped ideas as necessary, but you did not divulge your decisions beyond gestures and innuendo.

As their smiles faded, Karotkin snapped a finger against the crimson Flutterbird in its bag. "It was necessary to pass the message across my desk before you saw it. If I can be of use—"

"We're turning up the heat to verify it," Suslov said, "and I suspect a major covert operation will be demanded from your people by Moscow's *papakhas.*" The word meant "big hats," and implied only faint disdain between equals for the top decision-makers.

"Then you believe Moscow will want us to make a deal with this turncoat who contacted the Bulgarians," said Karotkin. His colleague's un-

□□□

changed expression was as good as a nod and Karotkin continued, "Which implies that Moscow believes it *is* possible to build a truly undetectable aircraft. I had hoped that was an exaggeration."

"Perhaps it is. The first that we knew of it, we learned from a few moments of conversation by two NSA men when the window laser scrambler failed in their limousine. Almost any price would not be too steep for such a craft." It was a veiled query: how high was that price? Karotkin would reply if he could. Suslov went on, "If they alone have it, the thing could upset delicate balances of force, worldwide." In this, Soviet spymasters agreed with their counterparts in the West. Men who failed to understand delicate balances failed to rise very far. Of course, each side viewed proper balance as a slight slope in its favor. Even a small fleet of truly undetectable aircraft would tend to shift that slope against the player who relied most on secrecy.

"I cannot divulge the turncoat pilot's asking price," Karotkin said. But he pointed at the ceiling.

"If it is high enough, it could tempt good men into a high jump." Suslov's phrase for an agent who took his booty and disappeared had its counterpart among U.S. agents. A Soviet agent took the high jump; an American agent went private. Each side knew the other's jargon, with a few exceptions. There was no jargon phrase in Russian for the hidden packet, including a great sum of money, some agents kept in readiness for the day when they might, for personal reasons, opt for abrupt retirement. Alcoholics had supplied the word when hiding that emergency pint of booze: it was called a "spooker." Perhaps no phrase in

□□□

spookspeak had ever been borrowed more appropriately.

"The man who steals a stealth aircraft," said Karotkin darkly, "is a fool if he asks for less than enough for a lifetime in, say, Paraguay."

Suslov checked the Omega on his wrist. "He is a fool anyway. Moscow would never give your people the sanction to offer such a price without some means of getting it back," he said, getting up with a sigh. "We rely too much on ideology, and not enough on the charm of money."

Karotkin stood companionably, toying with his cards, walking with Suslov toward the door. "Ask yourself, Lenya, how they would get it back, and what damp sanctions they would have. My people may not get the entire task."

Suslov nodded and walked out. The simplest way to avoid payment was to kill the American turncoat pilot—wet work, in Soviet parlance. And that meant the job would probably go not to KGB, but to the violent men of GRU, Soviet Military Intelligence.

Suslov was not a man who believed in unnecessary violence. Like Karotkin, he felt that wet work only escalated until the *boyevayas* on both sides had turned the world's great cities into travesties of dusty streets in Wild West movies. It had happened in Vienna, for a time.

And wherever the turncoat pilot chose to deliver that stealth aircraft, he could not be so stupid as to forget that—for a sufficiently high price—the West could get wild again.

SIX

ON A LATE SPRING AFTERNOON IN THE MILE-HIGH altitude of San Luis Potosi, the Mexican sun is fierce enough to fade paint, and the windburned man in stained coveralls found a triangular blotch of shadow near Morales's rickety hangar. He fingered a pack of Alas from a breast pocket and lit one, idly watching the tail of a Mexicana jet shimmer as it taxied to the distant terminal. The yanqui tourists on that plane were only a mile away. And a world apart. He had almost ceased envying them.

The Mexican youth finished buttoning the cowl on the AgriCat, still one of the best craft around for crop dusting, and shuffled toward that triangle of shade. The older man, whose dark hair was sun-blotched and graying, wished he had some of the kid's *Indio* blood, maybe some of his youth, too, to help fight the ravages of sun and wind in the central highlands of Mexico. Evidently this was going to be one of those days when envy drove him early to a cantina. Well, *no hay problema,* no problem. The Negro Modelo was cold and cheap, and better than Dos Equis. At least he could afford a few of the finer things in life. Good beer, a restored Borgward coupe, and a small whitewashed place with a patio near town, yes; safe travel and young bones, no.

He offered the pack to the youth, who shook his head. *"Tómalo,* Enrique," the older man insisted, but the youth was already lighting a Winston. He pocketed the pack, thinking the kid was right, the little unfiltered Alas were strong as dynamite fuse and burned just about as fast. Winstons were a luxury. He felt good, knowing Enrique could afford them.

He squinted at the reflection off Morales's Agri-Cat, glad that they'd finished the overhaul early because a man could fry petrified eggs on that aluminum by now. Morales, a man who knew how to keep good help, would probably spring for a bonus, and the middle-aged mechanic would share it with Enrique because that kid already had two kids of his own.

The windburned mechanic would have gladly traded his bonus for a chance to test-hop the Agri-Cat, or for that matter anything else with enough power to make a cinch of a hammerhead stall, but knew Morales would never allow it. The rancher, a better than average pilot with several aircraft in addition to the AgriCat, had good reason for his view. He'd seen his mechanic flying his own fabric-winged MX, an ultralight that was half hang

□ □ □

glider and half go-kart which had been sold cheap to Morales and which the rancher had sold more cheaply still. Some pilots were deadly mechanics, some mechanics deadly pilots. Morales watched his excellent mechanic falling around the sky in that damned MX and then, good man that he was, tried to buy it back at a higher price. He'd rather have a live mechanic, he'd said, than a dead pilot. But Mexicans, even rich ones, know how to let a man go to hell as he likes and Morales hadn't insisted.

It evidently never occurred to the rancher that it took an exceptional pilot to make an ultralight flounder like that, year after year, with never a bent spar. So Morales helped spread the legend: fine mechanic, awful pilot.

Enrique was idly flipping the pages of a new copy of *Sport Aviation* magazine which Morales subscribed to, though the text was in English and the youth could understand only the pictures. Knowing the older mechanic always kept them, Enrique borrowed it first. The semiofficial magazine of the Experimental Aircraft Association, *Sport Aviation*'s tattered remnants could be found in hangars all over the world. Presently the youth finished, handing it silently to his companion, and strolled off to douse his head in tepid water. The older man spent ten minutes on a first cursory survey of the articles, which might save lives, and then turned to the Marketplace section which could only lose him in further hopeless envy.

Well, this was a day for it. A Long-EZ with all the trick stuff in the cockpit, only $14,000; a steal, but not on his pay. One of Molt Taylor's little Imps, half completed; he noted the seller's address and

□□□

forgot it. And, near the bottom of the ultralight category, felt gooseflesh in hundred-degree heat, sliding his backside down the hangar wall to squat, his knees trembling.

> DEPEW Humongous—complete. IT'S SPEEDY. URGENT, must sacrifice but no foreign sale, please! (607) 734-5137 eves.

His hands did not tremble, but they sweated as he checked the instructions for classified ads. That ad had been placed only two months before, but a lot can happen in sixty days. He did not doubt for a millisecond that the ad was intended to be read by a dead man, but by now the man who had that telephone number might be dead, too; dead, or turned. If so, the ad was as neat a trap as a man could devise.

He read the ad again, moving into the sunlight to soak up warmth which had suddenly fled his body. He had absolutely no doubt about most of the ad, but foreign sale? That seemed wildly unlikely, but a hell of a bunch of unlikely things had happened since he and Speedy began their little games. The ad itself was roughly as likely as tits on a lizard. And nobody on God's earth could have devised that ad but Speedy, whether or not somebody had held a gun at his head while he did it.

Probably that was the truth of it: caught and turned, and once the mechanic called that telephone number he would be on the shit list again, and that would mean *he* was half caught already. But only half, and he'd escaped worse odds. *But you were younger then,* his demon critic whispered.

Fuck it, he answered it; *nobody lives forever.* He knew what he was going to do, as surely as if he had already done it, but there were ways to do it half smart, and ways exceedingly *estúpido.* He could fire up the MX and be in Aguascalientes in two hours, not that he needed more than a cow pasture but there was a jet-rated strip there too, and that might make them hunt Lears, not MX's. Or they might not.

There was a chance, no bigger than a needle roller but still a faint chance, that Speedy was running clear on this. And besides himself there were only two men on Earth, if that many, who had reason to become inextricably tangled in the fate of the "complete Humongous." *Oh, that was cute, Speedy.* To any other EAA reader that would be plain gibberish, easily forgotten, especially when there was no ultralight designer named Depew. But there was a place.

If he intended to be back from Aguascalientes before dark, he knew it was time to pray for tailwinds both ways. He walked behind the hangar and tossed the magazine into the Borgward, then told Enrique to go home to his kids. He needed only a few minutes to fuel the MX alone, and pushed it out of the hangar as a man would push a kite. A humongous kite . . .

SEVEN

TWO THOUSAND MILES TO THE NORTHEAST OF THE aircraft buzzing toward Aguascalientes, the blue vintage Javelin of Dar Weston thrummed onto the Connecticut Turnpike at roughly half of its potential speed. Dar enjoyed the old brute but would have denied he loved it, with its firm ride, whopping semirace engine and fat tires to match. Weston had thought auto racing a singularly senseless pastime until his sister Andrea married Philip Leigh.

Who would have thought a no-nonsense New Haven stockbroker like Phil, with more serious money than the Westons, would take up such a sport? Dar had turned over the family portfolio to Philip Leigh, his sister's husband, in 1960 after returning from a Turkish U-2 base. Now *that* had been a fiasco! A sweet bird of high passage, the U-

□□□

2 had scanned millions of square miles of Soviet turf before the Sovs, with an SA-2 missile the size of a telephone pole, managed to shoot one down—on May Day, of all days. Dar, dividing his time between base personnel and the handling of the U-2's crucial spy equipment, had listened to the vacillations of his own leadership, including Dwight Eisenhower, with growing disappointment and then alarm. You didn't offer transparent lies to the Sovs, let alone switch stories in public, if you wanted the bastards to respect you. If they didn't respect you, sooner or later they would eat you alive. The trick to living with a murderous paranoid, Dar's father used to say, was to keep him respectfully worried but not terrified. Old Farley Weston had made a lot of mistakes with his stony conservatism, but Dar had found that particular adage more apt with every passing year.

Reposted to Langley after the U-2 incident, Dar had found that he'd lost a pile of Weston money because you couldn't simultaneously watch a stock portfolio and fight a cold war from an outpost. As executor of his father's estate, Dar took his responsibilities as seriously as Farley Weston had expected. His mother, already in failing health then, needed expensive care until her death some years later. His sister, Andrea, would never go hungry so long as young Philip earned a six-figure income; but even if Andrea did not feel her paper losses, Dar had felt them deeply. The solution was simple: turn the Weston portfolio over to Phil, then pursue his career. It had been Farley Weston's assumption that his son Dar could do both: husband the family fortune, and become the kind of cold warrior who protected and served his country in important ways.

Dar apologized to his father's memory, relinquished the portfolio, and pursued his career with the kind of quiet, balanced zeal that marked him as a comer. Inside the Company, top posts were reserved for people who managed a fine balance between stolid conservatism and a willingness to consider the new, the offbeat, and the unthinkable. Dar Weston, year after year, worked to improve the delicate sense of balance that marked him as a cold warrior.

Still, he had learned when to hold another warrior's coat, and it was Kyle Corbett and Phil Leigh who'd taught him. When Phil's tiny roll-caged Cooper sedan showed up in 1966 at the Leigh estate in Old Lyme, Connecticut, Dar thought it was a joke. When he heard that Phil was racing the damned thing, he thought the joke had gone far enough. It was not until after the birth of Petra Leigh, when Phil graduated to a bellowing Mustang racer, that Dar tried to talk sense into his sister's husband.

And through two tours in Southeast Asia, overseeing the hardware security of U-2's and the prodigious "Blackbird" SR-71's, Dar Weston had continued to try talking sense to Phil.

Corbett, one of the Blackbird pilots, had become one of Dar's few close friends by 1968. Nursing their third round of San Miguel—"MacArthur specimens," as Corbett called them—on Luzon one night, Corbett had put the challenge to his friend. "Okay, your brother-in-law could buy a plot some Sunday, but this isn't exactly safe shit we're doing, Dar. Go on, tell me you didn't get a taste for living on the edge behind German lines in Greece. Or in Israel in the fifties, to hear you tell it."

"It's not the same," Dar had said. "I had a profession."

"Oh bullshit. You had an *excuse.*" The brown burr haircut bobbed as Corbett nodded to himself, hunching thick shoulders as he crossed those short, heavy forearms. "Leigh just doesn't have the excuses they gave you in Lipton Prep and Yale. What you've never done, and what you ought to do when you're stateside again, is go with Leigh some weekend. Check it out."

"Bloody likely," said Dar, pulling on his beer.

"Until you do, you'll never know what it is that he's really doing. For all you know the guy is just cruising around, keeping out of the way. Or maybe he's hanging it all out. Like we do."

"He doesn't have to. He's got a family," Dar countered.

"Your family. You've got to let go, you know," Corbett said. Dar had shared more of his history with Corbett than he had with anyone except, possibly, Phil Leigh. But while Phil said little until he had decided on a course of action, Kyle Corbett came at you straight ahead, right out of the starting gate. "Anyway, if he wasn't goosing Mustangs around he might be whoring or embezzling. It's an outlet, Dar, and you don't know as much about it as that year-old baby girl. Find out. Then at least you'll have a little credibility."

Dar had snorted at that, but he'd thought about it. And a year later, permanently posted to Langley, he had made his first appearance on Phil's pit crew, and by 1971 he could recognize Roger Pen-

□□□

ske's silver thatch from behind, or Mario Andretti's footprint in mud. And the tooth-loosening hammer of Mark Donohue's Javelin, a red-white-and-blue meteor, from any point on a track.

Dar Weston had known Donohue only as a nodding acquaintance in the pits, but as Phil often said, "There's nothing like him. He's not like the pointy-shoe Europeans or the playboys or the Foyt types. I bet the CIA could use fifty of him. He's a graduate engineer out of Brown, right here in New England, says 'sir,' and 'thank you'—and then he gets in that Javelin with the patriot's paint job and runs away and hides from the best. And waves every time he passes you."

Maybe it was that all-American paint job that did it for Dar. By 1971, Andrea Leigh was bringing tiny Petra along to northeastern tracks like Lime Rock and Watkins Glen to watch Daddy race, and Dar Weston no longer donned coveralls for credibility. He did it for fun, knowing Phil Leigh was enough the cautious broker to keep out of trouble, and not enough warrior to beat the likes of Jones or Revson—or Donohue.

Perhaps the death of Donohue, later and in a monstrous Porsche that related to a Javelin as an SR-71 relates to a lawn chair, motivated Phil to quit the sport. Phil never said. He just bought a blue Javelin with a few limited racing options, had it painted so that its red and white trim was subdued enough to be overlooked in New Haven, and drove it for a year. After that he slid into more comfortable ways, and Dar bought the Javelin.

Kyle Corbett, between tours, had been a houseguest in New Haven, then Old Lyme; had brought forbidden fireworks to the Leigh estate, had kidded Dar about that All-American Javelin. Something turned over in Dar's heart when he found that little Petra considered such jokes an affront to her daddy, to Uncle Dar, and to Mark Donohue, a legend she could not have remembered with any detail. What Petra could do, with Dar's support, was to take violin lessons and woodworking, to float wooden boats in New Haven's East Rock Park and, as she grew older, to rebel against her private school because it was long on etiquette and short on science.

A headmistress, citing Petra's "distressing tendencies," told Philip Leigh, "Petra seems always driven to *do* things, not content to *be* someone."

Dar had driven up for the family discussion on it because Petra, then fourteen, had begged him to. Phil had largely allowed the argument to eddy and swirl around him, saying little until he had thought it out. Andrea, grown soft but too proud to let herself gain weight, nibbled cress sandwiches and wondered aloud why Petra was not content to just *be* somebody.

"That's pointless," Petra had cried, reddening so that her freckles disappeared, her short honey-blonde hair bouncing. "Any idiot can do that, Mother! God, I wish I had some sisters who'd make you happy." It was the cruel outburst of a child; Petra knew her mother was unable to bear more children.

"I wish you had, too," Andrea had said, biting her lip, suddenly near tears.

From Dar: "Low blow, Petra."

"You want to do 'special' things," Andrea had said acidly.

□□□

"She wants to make a difference," Dar had said quietly.

Petra, impassioned: "Is that a crime?"

"It can be addictive," said Andrea, with a look that impaled both her husband and her brother.

"Evidently, you inherited it from your uncle," said Phil, patting the girl's hand. "No, it's not a crime, Pets, but it's a pain in our backsides. Tell you what: go ahead, finish high school in New Haven, take all the science courses you like. Then try, oh, Bryn Mawr or one of the others for a year." He saw the girl's mouth open, perhaps to negotiate on that year, and added, "For your mother. Deal?"

Petra knew that tone. It said she wasn't going to get a better deal; not from Phil, certainly not from Andrea. And not from Dar Weston, no matter what he felt, because Uncle Dar knew his place in these family arguments. But she saw Dar's almost infinitesimal nod. "Deal," she said, and hugged her mother first before Andrea could renege on an agreement she had never meant to allow.

The girl had done wonderfully well; even fidgeted through that obligatory year in a very posh school before announcing that it was either Brown or Cal Berkeley.

Dar felt the Javelin's steering grow heavy as he slowed, departing Route 95 near Old Lyme. Just mentioning Berkeley to Dar or either of the Leighs had been a stroke of genius on Petra's part. Dar grinned, remembering; hindsight told him it had been Brown she really wanted, with its safe traditions and solid engineering sciences, even though she had to start over as a freshman. Brown had been the carrot, Berkeley the stick, still tainted with its radical politics and lotusland mystique.

□□□

Dar could have kept tabs on her by then—the Company frowned on it officially, but the Old Boy net kept its avenues of recourse and CIA had developed a domestic presence to watch foreign students in Berkeley and elsewhere, including Brown. FBI complained that CIA should leave *all* domestic surveillance to the Feebs. No dice, Dar had argued in policy meetings. Dar's view was that CIA was needed as a balance against some excesses the FBI maintained, a legacy from America's own paranoid, Edgar Hoover. Dar had championed that view long before Petra's ultimatum; had been amused to find it might benefit his own family. James Darlington Weston considered himself simply incapable of subordinating the welfare of his country to his private interests. Not even family; not even Petra, wherever she went.

But Petra had gone to Brown, made her mistakes with the ponytailed playwright and the narcissist jock, and was nearly through her Junior year without getting drug-zonked or pregnant, and neither of the elder Leighs felt more throat-tightening pride in her progress than her Uncle Dar. This was the last weekend of the month when, by unspoken agreement, Petra usually drove the eighty miles from the campus in Providence to Old Lyme. Reason enough for Dar Weston to do the same from Langley. The Company's pace in the Black Stealth One matter was limited on one hand by progress in Elmira, and on the other by tentative and cagy responses to Medina from the other side. Had Weston felt any guilt about leaving Langley that weekend, he would not have budged.

He drove under a familiar canopy of sycamore and maple, now a dappled green summer sunshade that would become a palette of sweet-sad color in the fall, and turned left at the Leigh escutcheon on a stone wall. They would recognize the Javelin on sight, but on impulse he gunned its engine because even if she and Phil were playing tennis in back, Petra would know that exhaust rap. The loving camaraderie she shared with her Uncle Dar was something special, something with no sinister overtones, yet a thing to be brought off lightly because, as he grew middle-aged, Philip Leigh showed signs of resenting Dar.

He parked the Javelin near the carriage entrance, then crossed the pass-through into the quiet of a formal garden on the cusp of summer. He saw them then, sharing the gazebo swing as they often did on summer evenings, and tried not to show his disappointment.

"Heard your old honker," Philip Leigh called, getting up carefully to avoid spilling his martini. "We figured you'd be here about now."

Andrea did not rise, but waved as befitted a Weston and a Leigh who was content to *be* someone. It was unnecessary for her to be more specific when she called, "She's not coming, Dar."

Weston made himself smile and shrug as he took the proffered hand. "Fine with me. Who needs the little whippersnapper underfoot anyhow?" He bent to kiss Andrea, noting the fine squint lines, the good Weston bones that would photograph well through any number of wrinkles.

Phil picked up a third glass—evidently they had, indeed, been expecting him—and raised the pitcher from its bed of ice. "Dar: one lump or two?"

"No doubles, thanks. Just let me unwind," he

said, choosing a woven rattan chair that fairly hissed aloud as he settled into it.

He took the martini gratefully, stretching his long legs, sighing in contentment that was half real. "So what's the kid up to that's more important than us," he said at last.

"Finals project," said Phil. "Sends her love, as always."

"Ah, well," Dar said, and sipped again, conscious of the fact that a man should not feel depressed in such a lovely New England setting.

After a silence of perhaps two minutes, which seemed much longer, Andrea said, "I've been making out my will, Dar."

"What? What? Are you—?"

"Oh, I'm not sick or anything, but I've been thinking about it for weeks. And I didn't want to do it without you."

"I'd think Phil could handle it as well as," Dar began.

Her glance, not her words, cut him short. "Dar, I have only one reason to make out a will, and she's on a campus in Providence this weekend—or at least she'd better be. It's not what goods I leave her. It's what I'll have to tell her."

Phil Leigh nodded over his glass. "And I told Andrea that what she says just might be up to you, Dar."

EIGHT

IT HAD BEEN A BITCH OF A WEEK FOR MEDINA, A bitch for two months in fact, what with the trouble he'd had finding a hangar for the Imp's final assembly, not to mention trailering the goddamn thing at night. And a few blisters on his eardrums from Ben Ullmer when test patches of the hellbug's wing sealant showed serious "accidental" contamination, as Medina knew they would. It had set back the wet-wing mod for Black Stealth One at least ten days.

Medina had earmarked this Friday evening for a scouring of the garage, removing all traces of the project he'd begun with Corbett so long ago. He wondered, while stoking his fireplace with precious drawings, if someone was noting the smoke. Well, better for them to wonder than to know. If they did find out, they might not care much. Or they might blacklist him, or worse. They already had him on a tether with this fucking fake class ring, a real Captain Midnight gizmo that could record both ends of a phone call as long as he held the receiver right. He'd already used it twice for the Bulgarian connection, which seemed to be coming down as planned. The recorder's limitation was the tiny battery, they said, which was why he had to turn the bezel as an "on-off" switch. And if they were lying about that, if it was on all the time—but probably they weren't. Raoul Medina knew his energy cells as well as the next techie.

In fact, Medina grew more antsy as this operation progressed because knowing he was one of the few technical types who had worked for CIA *and* NSA, they had to know he could put two and two together. And because it kept adding up to exactly four, he was starting to wonder if he was missing something. He'd been over the scenario until it was leaking out his ears. The first part, flying Black Stealth One to a site in New Mexico and then continuing to Regocijo in a Cessna, hardly seemed worth worrying about. Or so CIA had implied, which made Medina think hard about it, though, try as he might, he could find no flaw.

CIA's worry was with the final exchange site, a useless stretch of coastal scrub called Llano Mojado. CIA had taken one good look at that site and said, flatly, they could not protect him there in a face-to-face against an unknown force of Russians without a full military squad, which would certainly have queered the exchange.

The alternative, they said, was simple: he must not show up for the money. He must make a low pass to demonstrate that heat-sensitive paint job;

screw up his mixture control to make a convincing show of an emergency; and then sweep out beyond the scrub to crash, a thousand yards offshore. Ullmer had agreed: even in pieces, Blue Sky Three would not sink and the water was shallow enough for free diving. The recovery team could gather up the wreckage and would simply have to wonder whether sharks had got Medina's body, if indeed they cared much when they still had their money and enough of the aircraft to gladden Muscovite hearts.

Medina's tough moment would come when trying to stall the bird into a breeze so it would pancake nicely. After that he would go over the side with that nifty compact SCUBA rig before anyone got close enough to see him do it. His own recovery team would be a pair of Mexican deniables, waiting a few miles up the coast.

On the face of it, CIA seemed to be saying Medina was worth more than the money. Medina had said "yes" to that face—and then found himself saying "yes, but" to himself. Ullmer had bought it. Sheppard had bought it. Neither of them had ever been CIA, themselves. Perhaps it was simply that, deep down, Raoul Medina knew you could never tell what those bastards really wanted until after they got it.

And still no reply to that ad, two weeks after the new issue of *Sport Aviation* showed up in his mailbox. Maybe there wouldn't be any. One thing for damn sure, he would never again deliberately botch a piece of work in the Snake Pit. Sure, that junketeering high-level spook Weston from Langley made him nervous, but it went deeper than that. Funny how a man's *cojones* could measure how deep he was in shit. Arlene had jumped to the predictable, and wrong, conclusions. He was tired of her; he had another girl; he was scared that George would find out. And calming her fears only added to his shitload.

His trip to Mexico in Blue Sky Three had been his only real enjoyment since April, and he still smiled to recall the expressions on faces when he taxied the bird after dark into Air Force hangars alerted for him. At Scott, east of St. Louis, they'd seemed almost afraid of him; no questions, not even good honest curious stares. At Laughlin, near Del Rio, the two maintenance officers had been just the opposite, plying him with sourmash at the OC, trying to steer his war stories toward that repainted velvet-black two-seater they'd locked up in an alert hangar. He stuck to his cover story—that he was testing the craft for drug interdiction along the border—and eased off after three drinks. It was roughly an even bet, those two spiffy bluesuiters were CIA, DIA, or some other bit of spookdom's alphabet soup, testing him in Air Force uniforms.

That last leg had been the real bastard, ghosting across Mexico to Culiacan over country that looked as hospitable as broken glass. In a U-2, a man could glide hundreds of miles on a dead engine from 80,000 feet. His bird couldn't get above the weather, and it was dead slow, and if he'd had to land short of his goal his orders had been to destroy it. Weston, his case officer, had used some doubletalk phrase about the climate of accommodation with Mexico at present. What it boiled down to was that the Mexicans were pissed about something else and would just love to catch an

□□□

NSA spookship in an overflight. That meant the Mex government still didn't know about the Regocijo strip, either. And Julio, the old caretaker at the reactivated strip, had seemed every inch a Mexican national, but Dar Weston had said he was a Company man. One more wedge between the two countries, if it became known.

When the kitchen phone shrilled, he jumped six inches, then decided it was probably Arlene. He was wrong.

The connection was lousy, but from the first few words he knew who it was. And he wasn't entirely sure his phone was secure.

"Medina here," he said.

From far away, years away: "Get me Speedy Gonzales," in that unforgettable dry, gruff whiskey baritone. Absolutely no doubt about it. Corbett, and only Corbett, had dared call him that at the Snake Pit because the insult underlined the antagonism they wanted to maintain in public. Kyle Corbett, HolyMarymotherofGod . . .

Medina switched hands, shoving the one with the ring into a hip pocket. " 'E's not 'ere, señor, I theenk." Not for any other man on earth had Raoul Medina ever played the pocho fool this way, but it was as if he'd opened an old book, fondly remembered, a book from whose faded pages he could still quote at length.

"You write a cute ad, Speedy. Talk to me."

"Just trying to sell a homebuilt," Medina said. "Call you back from a pay phone." If they *were* listening, he could show them the Imp; admit a little, hide a lot.

The silence was not true silence, but tiny squeals and white noise for a five-second eternity, the kind of delay a dead man might employ while deciding whether he trusted this spirit medium named Medina. Then, "You'll need a shitload of quarters. And if you can't call in fifteen minutes, don't bother."

"You wasteeng time," Medina said in his singsong fool voice. He took down the numbers, a string beginning with "011-52-491," and then another string. Not CONUS, continental U.S., for sure. Then, his voice husky, Medina said, "I knew it, I fucking *knew* it!" But he was talking into a dead phone.

Three miles away and thirteen minutes later, Medina ducked out of the Mart into the twilight with four rolls of quarters and sprinted for the phones that nested against the Mart's outside wall inside tiny shrines to Mammon. He knew he was cutting it close and a gangling youth with the complexion of a pizza slouched next to one phone, oblivious of the swarthy man who slammed a quarter into the other machine.

Nothing; out of service. "God DAMN," said Medina, and jerked the boy upright. "Life or death, young man. Hang up. Please!" He knew it didn't sound much like "please," it sounded more like "or else."

The boy wrenched himself loose, looking down at this slit-eyed latino, donning a mask of youthful outrage. "What the fuck, man; what the *fuck,*" he said, and turned away to resume talking.

The youth felt himself spun completely around, dropping the receiver, this time registering true shock at this sudden attack on a Friday evening by a madman in public. Medina cradled the boy's throat with his left hand, his right fist drawn back.

□□□

"This," he said, letting his fist vibrate, "or this." And he offered the roll of quarters. The boy blinked twice. Ten seconds later Medina was alone, stammering to the operator because his alloted fifteen minutes were up. And even after he got the international operator it took him twenty-six bongs, at three seconds per bong, to feed the damned machine.

But when he heard the connection go through, there was hardly any buzz at all. *"Digame, señor,"* said the voice he had already despaired of hearing again.

"JesusMary, I had to mug a fucking kid for this phone," Medina said shakily. "Sounds like amateur night, wherever you are."

"Cantina. Speedy, just one thing. If somebody's running you, remember: I won't get mad. You do remember?"

"Fuck you, Mr. Depew," Medina replied, letting the flash of anger steady him. "I'm not calling for anybody, but I feel a cold breeze blowing up my personal tailpipe. Something's coming down, and I checked out Mr. Depew's box a long time ago so I figured you might still be suckin' wind, and I don't know who else to turn to."

Laughter from Kyle Corbett, from the far distance and the distant past. "You seem to have something for sale. Something humongous."

Black Stealth One had spawned several pet names among the men who had designed and built her. Between Medina and Corbett, the word was "humongous" because of its great wingspan. Since both men were NSA, they knew that the agency's equipment was incredibly sophisticated and had been for years. Voice-coded, word identifier machines could monitor hundreds of thousands of telephone lines at once, especially those that used international trunk lines. A word like "stealth," or "CIA," or even "hellbug" could flag a conversation for recording—even tagging the locations of both phones. With this shared knowledge, they resorted to their own jargon. "The sale isn't kosher, but the bird is flying, and, man, it does everything we hoped."

Corbett: "You don't mean the Imp?"

Medina: "Oh hell, no. That's all assembled. Main ingredient of my own, uh, Depew kit, if I can ever get it flight-tested. I'm talking humongous, man. We made the target weight, it's stable as a table, and I'm the only one checked out to test it. But somehow, word has got out, and there's a buyer."

"Who's the buyer?"

"Nice people; they make flashlights that backfire." The NATO designations for Soviet aircraft included the MiG "Flashlight" and the "Backfire" bomber.

"If you think I'd help you sell, you can get stuffed."

"Not me, JesusChristno! It's from the very top, a scam to sell, uh, Number Three, and pass it off as humongous."

Another laugh, full-gutted and now more relaxed. "Sounds cute to me. Might even work."

"Yeah? Listen, it's already working for somebody, but I'm not sure it's us. The drill is for me to ferry Number Three and hide it near, uh, let's say Mazatlan. Then snatch our humongous bird when its wings are wet and while everybody in the country goes nuts to make it look good, I stash humongous in New Mexico, fly down and pick up the

□□□

fake, and then—you'll love this—ditch the fake offshore where they can see it and pick up the pieces. That way I don't have to face 'em, but I have a long swim. And I leave without even getting to see what five million worth of Swiss tickets looks like."

"Mazatlan, you said?" Corbett's tone was not pleasant.

"Please deposit five dollars and twenty-five cents for the next three minutes," said a disinterested female voice.

Medina told her to count the bongs and fed the quarters in. Then he spelled out "Regocijo" using the standard phonetic alphabet, "Romeo-Echo-Golf-Oscar-Charlie-India-Juliet-Oscar" because he could think of no other way to do it. "It doesn't smell right. It's not our turf."

"Plus, you could get popped, Speedy."

"That's crossed my mind," Medina admitted.

"What do you want from me, a backup?"

"Honest to God, I'm not sure what I want, or what you can give. Just advice, maybe."

"I'll tell you what doesn't smell right. It's too neat a coincidence, making the switch so near where I am already. And I don't believe in coincidence. What I do believe in is my hide. And I'm wondering whether somebody's running you without your knowledge, to get to me. Maybe they don't intend you to ferry Number Three down here."

"Wrong. I've already done it."

"No shit! Well, you can't blame me for a few suspicions," Corbett grumbled. "Right now I'm thinking the high-techs who could be listening in will already have figured out exactly where I am, but this isn't their turf and I'll be long gone before they could get here, so I'll tell you. I'm in Aguascalientes. See why I might worry about the coincidence? But if you've already stashed one bird, all I'd have to do is verify that. Maybe take it myself," he chuckled.

"I wouldn't. Old guy named Julio might just put some holes in you. And I'd kiss him for it. That's all I need, you fucking me over from that end and heavy brass from our old employer trying to run me from this end."

Medina wondered at the pause, because it was a long one. Then Corbett said, "Our previous employer, you mean?"

"You got it. They're coordinating this. Hell, my briefings are with a guy who'd probably love to know you're still mean as ever. Initials Delta Whiskey; is that enough?"

"Enough. I wish you could tell him, Speedy, but you can't. Guys like him absolutely cannot afford to take chances on guys like me. Neither can you, but it sounds like you're hung out to dry already."

"Feels that way, too. By the way, why did you fake that accident?"

"You mean, was I turned or just greedy? Neither. Maybe we can puzzle it out one day. Not now. Right now I need to get a feel for timing. When are you slated to start the real shitstorm blowing?"

"About a week, ten days. I'm already dealing with the buyers—and as soon as we wet down the humongous wings, I'm supposed to haul ass. That's the holdup, and I can't delay it." He wanted to say, My God, I've already done sabotage on Black Stealth One to buy this much time, what do you want from me. But if they were being monitored, that admission would have bought him twenty years in the slammer.

As if they were telepathically linked: "We've talked long enough," said Corbett, "but I have to know more, with exact map coordinates. I want you to call me in an hour from somewhere else. I won't be here but I've already got my alternate number. Only the last five digits are different. Got it?"

"On an open line? I'm not sure you should—"

"Just listen," said Corbett, maddeningly calm. "We take the last digit of Mr. Depew's old address number, if you remember it."

That post office box! "Ri-i-ight," said Medina, grinning in spite of himself. The number had been "six."

"I'm gonna give you some simple arithmetic using that last digit as a baseline. First number: subtract one. Second number: add three. What the hell are you laughing at?"

"This is *so* goddamn amateurish, man," Medina cackled, "I swear it's almost fun."

"Hold that thought," growled the dead man in Aguascalientes, and continued before the operator could cut them off. When the lank youth returned with a carload of friends a few minutes later, they found the telephone abandoned.

Medina had to write a check and talk like hell, but an hour later his jacket swayed with its load of quarters as he bought a ticket to see the only local movie that wasn't besieged by Friday night crowds. There would be no background noises around the pay phone in there, and the place had four exits. As he stuffed the first quarter in, he began to laugh. The reason the movie wasn't

□□□

mobbed was because the place showed old classics. Tonight's feature, with Robert Ryan and Harry Belafonte, was *The Odds Against Tomorrow.* If he believed in omens, Medina thought, he'd be running for the exit.

Medina did not believe in omens. He believed in Swiss francs; he believed that the element of surprise might work very well for a dead man who placed himself properly while other men watched an airplane crash in the ocean; and he was starting to believe it could be wonderfully profitable to meet Kyle Corbett at Regocijo.

NINE

ONCE A MONTH, THOUGH ON NO SET SCHEDULE, Sasha spent an evening isolated in his basement workshop and quietly briefed the cat. Like most men in the intelligence community, he had heard rumors of his own existence—had even known when believers first dubbed him "Sasha"—for years. Before Ivan the Terrible distinguished himself by getting noisily trapped in Sasha's garbage can one night in 1982, the solitary self-briefings had always heightened Sasha's sense of alienation. An agent run by any government could at least depend on a case officer to hear his troubles. In this sense, Sasha was not an agent at all, but very much an operative.

He had long ago given up the notion of sharing his secret with any human, but Ivan the Terrible, grown from a scrawny young delinquent into a sleek gray tiger-stripe tom, was a cat who knew how to listen without making value judgments. Sasha had found himself whispering to the cat one night across a pair of ruled yellow pads and an open tin of Chicken of the Sea, and his self-briefing went uncommonly well, and Ivan seemed to enjoy the attention even after the tuna was gone. While stirring the ashes of his notes that night, Sasha had resolved to pick up one of the latest CCI bug-finders. It seemed vanishingly unlikely that his basement would be bugged, but a commercially available Mantis unit would remove all doubt about audio bugging. To be exposed while talking with a house cat, after years of flawless espionage, was the kind of cosmic joke that inevitably would be retold throughout spookdom. Sasha went to considerable trouble so that he could talk espionage to that cat because, by God, it worked.

On this evening, Sasha finished his old business and then, after scribbling on the left-hand pad, proposed his next move. "Scenario: I tell them about the swap and give them the Regocijo site, too," he murmured to Ivan, who merely flexed a forepaw and watched the pencil intently. Perhaps it reminded him of a mousetail. "That gives them one intact aircraft, if they're competent. But"—he moved the pencil to the other pad—"that eventually could narrow the search pattern for me."

That second pad contained only a list of names, a list that had narrowed by necessity over the years. The list included all, and only, the men who *could* have passed all of those messages over embassy walls. The length, and the complications, of that list had been Sasha's initial reason for these monthly self-briefings; with a memory that was

□□□

less than absolutely perfect, he knew he must refresh it by writing and updating that list periodically, with careful rethinking on the validity of each name, then destroying his notes. The idea of keeping such files in the house on paper or hard disk was more than horrifying: it was obscene. Sasha felt no comfort knowing that the list of names, once over a page long, had become easier to remember. For the list could not grow longer, only shorter, as men died or left the field on which this global game was played.

The fundamental problem for Sasha, as a player, was that CIA had two moles in Dzerzhinsky Square. Only their case officers knew their identities. Neither was aware of the other's existence in the KGB, but either of them might one day gain access to the KGB file on Sasha. In which case, CIA and NSA would soon know everything in that file. Therefore, with the list now truncated to less than a dozen, it was absolutely crucial that every morsel of Sasha's revelations be known to a select list—each of whom might be taken for Sasha.

Some of those names made him smile. Helms, who'd been hounded out of the top slot: no longer on the list, but he'd been on the early ones. No matter that it was ridiculous to even consider it; for a time, Helms *could* have done what Sasha was doing.

Charles Foy, whose entry into the middle echelons of NSA had been thought political, years before. But Foy had risen by shrewdness and tenacity—and he'd known every secret Sasha had exposed. Definitely still on the list. And Foy's deputy, Sheppard? Impossible to know with certainty, but Sheppard might have had access to every datum over the years. He belonged on the list. Aldrich, however, had come into NSA too late to have access to the early stuff. Sasha mildly regretted keeping that name off the list.

Colby, up through the ranks and stepping on toes as he climbed, first a protégé of Helms but finally his nemesis. No longer on the list. Too bad; some people on both sides might once have bought that one.

Randolph: a long and checkered career in CIA, one of the few who'd gone through the ranks to the very top. It could be Abraham Randolph still. Weston, next down the line, had been around the Company almost as long as Randolph and might be slightly more believable. Weston could have divulged thousands of critical items. What a useful irony that the man who had made a pastime of searching for Soviet moles in the CIA could still be Sasha himself! Unruh, privy to most of Weston's operations, was as unlikely as Sheppard but still a possibility.

And Maule and McEachern in CIA, as well as Elerath and Vasilik in NSA: two now near retirement, the other two still candidates for a few more years. And who could tell when an embolism or a drunk driver might shorten the list at random?

"Can't do it, Ivan; at least four candidates who don't yet have the need to know. And in three cases there's no compelling reason why they ever will." The cat yawned and tucked its forepaws under its breast. "Play it close to the vest, hm? You're right, I can't let them narrow the search any further. The Blue Sky craft is better than nothing."

He continued to stare at the cat, which closed its eyes and began to purr. It did not show interest when he began to scribble again, lining out, rewriting, speaking disjointed phrases now and then.

It bestowed only a bored glance when Sasha, tapping on the pad, said, "Scenario: I report Black Stealth One as described by witnesses to be a flying wing, a vertol at that, with some means of becoming literally invisible. No more, no less. I tell them it must meet those criteria to be the real thing. Everybody on the list has the need to know those details, even those of us who haven't actually seen it."

Ivan and Sasha traded a long glance, and Ivan blinked first. "So the welcoming committee will know it's paying for a gold brick. As for the poor bastard who's doing all the flying: at the least, he won't get the ransom money. Without the devil's own luck, he won't get back at all.

"Well, it can't be helped, Ivan. I can't divulge any more because if I burn *myself* over this, I can't be in place later. You understand that by now, surely."

It may have been some faint noise; or perhaps the unusual note of supplication in the man's voice. For whatever reason, the cat flowed up and across the table, springing unhurriedly from table to workbench to shelving, where he sat peering at a mousehole with iron-clad patience.

"All right, you don't understand. I can accept that," Sasha said, tiring of this parodied conversation, yet unwilling to abandon it. He studied Scenario Two briefly, then sighed and gathered the paper pieces of his alter ego for ritual cremation.

□□□

He turned before kneeling at the furnace. "Let me tell you something, Ivan," he said to the back of the cat's head. "There are times, these days, when I'm not sure I understand either."

TEN

ON A WEDNESDAY AFTERNOON, PETRA WHIRLED out of Brown University's failure analysis lab in a foul mood, sockless in her Reeboks, shoving her zippered nylon bag down into the bike's basket as if the nylon carried the image of her prof's inscrutable face. Hsia had dinged her seven points for ignoring conventional approaches on her term project—but she could regain those points before end of term by pulling an all-nighter, doing it by the book this time.

She fitted her helmet on, thrusting stray tufts of honey-tinted hair under the helmet's plastic rim so they wouldn't whip into her eyes, then donned her bike chain like a necklace and swung a slender jeans-clad leg over the old American-made Schwinn. A man's bike, not even one of the trendy foreign jobs, but the thing was sturdy as a brick with that extra bar on its frame and mounting it was no problem for someone who never wore skirts on campus. For Petra Leigh, the Schwinn made a statement as clear as Uncle Dar's old musclecar.

She saw that the traffic on Waterman wasn't heavy yet, and calculated she could make good time heading north along Elmgrove. To pull that all-nighter, or to snack from her apartment fridge and then meet Randy and Jason and Bev to parboil Hsia over pitchers of beer: that was what Petra thought about as she pedaled hard, giving a workout to thighs she imagined were too chunky. Jason might come on like the Western world's most dedicated grad student, but she knew his interest in curves went beyond bridge catenaries. If she expected to pick his formidable brains next term, it was time she got him thinking about her as worthy of picking, too. *What's the reciprocal for Petra? One over Petra,* she recited the engineering joke to herself. She probably wouldn't let that happen. Jason was sweet, though still a boy in some ways . . .

She noticed the black Ford Tempo only as one of several cars that jiggled in her helmet's tiny rearview. The Ford fell back, but never more than a hundred yards behind her during the twenty-minute ride to her place.

She locked helmet and bike together, noting that only one other bike leaned against the porch rail of the fine old clapboard house which was, in Petra's opinion, going to simply collapse one of these days from the sheer weight of students and books. Her room with its shared bath was on the first floor, and Petra knocked a quick tattoo on

□□□

Bev's door as she passed it, getting no response, expecting none. She was visible from the street as she continued past the stairs and unlocked the door to her room.

That decision over the all-nighter was still to be made, or so she thought, as Petra popped a cassette into her player. The new-age synthesizer music of Kitaro, otherworldly and abstract, often helped her concentrate. She dunked a sprig of broccoli into Cheez-Whiz, began to nibble, and flopped her project notes open to Hsia's marginal comments. Their gist was that she must walk flawlessly before she could fly over conventional stuff. But God, traditional engineering practice could be dull, dull, *dull!* Two stodgy approaches occurred to her immediately; she grabbed a pencil and jotted them down, with tiny draftsman's numerals below, 0:45′ and 0:30′. It should take her no more than an hour and a quarter to dispose of both those silly exercises.

She heard the knock at the front door as it echoed down the hall, and ignored it. The knock at her own door, a minute later, made her jump. Bev never knocked like that. "Randy? Come on in, I don't think I can—" The door swung open, but it wasn't Randy.

"Miss Leigh?" The man was tanned, windburned, and middle-aged, reminding her of a slightly overweight Marlboro man, with graying hair that could use a trim, dressed casually in tan gabardine pants with an Indiana Jones leather jacket over a plain sportshirt. Petra's first impression was that she had seen him somewhere before, but he did not come in. He held a flat plain-wrapped package in his free hand. "Miss Petra Leigh." His tone said he was certain.

"That's me," she said, pushing away from the rickety table, faintly embarrassed to be caught with a mouthful of Cheez-Whiz.

"For you," the man said in a gravelly voice that registered from somewhere, sometime. His smile seemed diffident but businesslike.

Petra walked to the door, knowing it was not smart to allow strange men into her room, seeing that this one did not seem anxious to enter anyway. She took the slender package, smiling her question instead of voicing it.

"I'm supposed to wait," was all he said, nodding at the package as he handed it over. "If there's not a note in there, somebody goofed." Then he stepped back into the hall and pulled the door shut.

Petra tore the wrapping off to find a pound of See's candy, the soft centers she'd loved since she was old enough to ransack a dresser drawer. For every special occasion in her life, Uncle Dar had given her a pound of See's. She smiled and opened the note, typewritten on plain paper, and then the smile began to fade.

Pets: everyone in the family is fine, and John Smith will see to your safety. He will bring you to us in an unmarked black Ford (sorry, no spare Javelins) but don't expect him to tell you why. Phil and I will explain later, and there is nothing to worry about if you hurry. Pack for a weekend outing. If you have any problem with this, call my secretary, but for your own safety, waste no time. Smith knows his business. He has watched over you before this!

□□□

Somehow, those mentions of "fine" and "safety" made her feel less than fine and not awfully safe even with a man who was obviously a bodyguard standing right on the other side of that door. Then she *had* seen Mr. Smith before. Never until this instant had James Darlington Weston's occupation seemed entirely real to Petra, and images from the "Spy v. Spy" cartoons in *Mad* magazine fled ludicrously through her mind. The candy was right, the nickname strictly family, and she could see a black Ford parked outside, but Uncle Dar's initial had been scrawled in a hurry. She opened the door again. "I'll need a few minutes," she said to the man's back. "You'd better come in. Have some candy," she added as she tossed the box on the table.

He closed the door softly, then strode to the window as Petra began to stuff extra clothing into a TWA bag. "Want me to put the food into your refrigerator?" His attention to such a homey detail lessened Petra's attack of nerves.

"If you would," she said, folding a fresh bra, selecting a pair of medium-heeled wedgies, remembering her hand calculator almost too late. T-shirt, two pairs of L'Eggs, a skirt that didn't show wrinkles, and a blouse that did, but whatthehell . . . "Do you know how long I'll be gone? This is going to play absolute havoc with my schedule, Mr. Smith."

"Just a day or two, I think," said Smith, closing the refrigerator door. "It's only a precaution, Miss Leigh. I'm sure you'll be laughing about it by Monday. You might bring a book. I'm not the world's greatest conversationalist."

"I suppose you do this all the time," she said, trying to keep the tremor from her voice.

□□□

"Not often," he admitted, watching her zip the bag over Roark's book on stress and strain, checking the expensive watch on his wrist. "Ready?"

"I hope so." She hefted the little bag.

"Where's your phone?" His smile was easy. "I need to set someone at ease about you."

Blushing, she hauled a small pile of dirty laundry off the windowseat to reveal the Princess phone with its long curl of cord. "You never would've found it," she said.

He grinned back, lifted the receiver, began to punch at buttons. But when he put the receiver to his ear, something shifted in his expression. He held the receiver out. "Is your phone bill current?"

"Of course," she said in irritation.

He tried the operator, but had no joy. "Then we could have a problem," he muttered. "There's a back entrance from here, I believe." He reached out toward her stereo, and Kitaro faded with the set's power light.

Petra snatched the receiver, heard nothing, not even a dial tone, and felt the blood draining from her face. "What does it mean?"

"Probably nothing," he shrugged, not very convincingly, and now a little charcoal-black automatic was in his right hand as he stood near the window. He spoke slowly and distinctly. "See that black Ford? Wait until I drive it away from the curb and to the alley. Then you go out the back way to the car, and don't stop for anything or anybody. Is that clear?"

The gravel in that voice was now sharpened flint. It prodded, and you obeyed. She nodded, her mouth suddenly dry.

He copied her nod, reseated the handgun in his

left armpit, and headed for the front entrance. Petra heard the door slam and punched nine-one-one, the first number that came to mind, into the phone. She might as well have been holding a hunk of broccoli to her ear.

Petra checked the inside lock, wishing she had time for a note to Bev, seeing John Smith through the window as he sauntered to the black Tempo. *Like he hadn't a care in the world,* she thought, *but that just means he's good at what he does. I wonder if he checked the upstairs hall.* She looked quickly into the hall, then saw the black sedan pull away outside and, with what she hoped was perfect timing, felt the deadbolt snap as she backed into the hall. An instant later she was pelting out the back, down wooden steps, and through a back lawn that had once known tender care, leaping over someone's rusted hibachi, the TWA bag overbalancing her so that she almost fell before reaching the back gate.

The Ford was waiting in the alley. The man's only comment as she dropped her rump into the seat was, "Buckle up," and she did, letting her head fall back against the headrest, trying to take long breaths because that was supposed to help when you felt like fainting or, worse, blowing chunks of Cheez-Whiz and broccoli into your lap in a back alley in Providence, Rhode Island.

He said nothing more until they were on the turnpike, attending to his rearviews, driving wonderfully well with a fine sense of what traffic ahead was doing, or about to do. Then, "It's a no-sweat run now, Miss Leigh. We'll pick up Route Ninety at Worcester. Relax. Listen to the radio; read a book."

□□□

She shook her head, aware that his peripheral vision was so practiced he could study her while looking straight down the turnpike. "I'm too wired, Mr. Smith. You *are* Mr. John Smith," she said with exaggerated coolness.

"Yes and no; why kid you? Call me John. Johnny if you like it better."

"Then you'll have to call me Petra, if that's allowed."

For the first time he laughed, and that was unsettling because, dammit, now she *knew* the man was familiar. "Sure," he said, "so long as we remember you're my boss's boss's boss, once removed."

It began to seem as if the Cheez-Whiz would stay down, after all. "Is there anything about this that you can tell me?"

"Not a lot, M—Petra. There are several ways to zap a phone line. I'm surprised they didn't just monitor it; that's what I would've done."

Unable to keep the edge from her voice: "How many times have you tapped my telephone, John Smith?"

"I never have—but if I had, I'd have to lie about it."

"That's no answer."

"Bingo," he said, and pointed to a sign: WORCESTER 12 MI.

Petra rummaged in her bag, but left the Roark book where it was. There was simply no chance that she could concentrate on engineering stress when her own internal stresses remained so high. *You've always thought intelligence work must be wonderful and exciting, idiot. Nobody ever told you a simple ride in a car could turn your knees to silly putty and your stomach into a butterchurn.* But the ride couldn't be all that simple. She had been in danger—might yet be in danger. Petra sighed and closed her eyes, reclining in the seat a bit, willing herself to breathe regularly, think and act regularly.

After ten minutes or so, her eyes snapped open. "Why don't you just call on your radio and tell someone about my telephone? Don't you guys carry some scrambler gadget?"

"When we have a transmitter," Smith agreed. "I'm not carrying one. Nobody backing me up, so it'd be pointless."

"We could stop and phone."

"Affirmative, we could phone, if we could stop, but negative, we can't stop. Orders," he shrugged.

"Stopping must be a high-stress point," she guessed.

"You could put it that way. It's a window of very high vulnerability, is how we'd put it."

Petra chuckled. "That must make life interesting when you have to go to the bathroom."

"Life is always interesting. And yes, we'll make a rest stop in Albany."

"And after that?"

"I'll call from there and find out," he said, and saw her head jerk in surprise. "Hey, they don't tell *me* everything either." He yawned, a deep inhalation that pushed his chest and belly against the restraint belts. "Can't afford much of that," he said, and fumbled into the footwell behind her seat for a moment, bringing out a cheap plastic thermos canister which he thrust between his knees to unscrew its cap one-handed. "You a coffee drinker?"

"Show me an engineer who isn't," she snorted.

□□□

"I've got this down to a science," he said, "but you might hold the cup for me."

She did, watching him pour a half cupful. Then he put the thermos between his knees again. "Some of those packets of sweetener in the glove box, I think," he said. Holding the cup of hot coffee in one hand, Petra began to poke with the other into the little storage compartment.

She did not see what he was doing with his left hand at the lip of the thermos, but when she turned back to him, he was turning onto Route Ninety. "You must've used it all," she said.

"Oh, well." He took the cup from her and sipped, squinting into the late afternoon sun as the Ford's nose turned westward. "Gaah. I've tasted better," he said, but went on sipping.

With the last sip, he stifled another yawn in his teeth and handed her the cup. "You'd best have some too," he said, "in case you have to drive awhile. I haven't had much sleep," he added.

Without apology, Petra pulled a Kleenex from the packet in her bag and swabbed the cup clean as she'd been taught by her mother when drinking after strangers. It did not occur to her, when pouring from that thermos, that she was trusting this stranger in ways far more intimate than a shared cup.

Her face a parody of itself, Petra stuck her tongue out after her first sip. "Gaah is right, John."

"Call it insurance and drink the lousy stuff. We can get a refill in Albany," he said. She sipped slowly and obediently, and all too trustingly. And somewhere between Worcester and Springfield, she began to nod, only faintly aware when he lifted the cup from her indolent fingers, and the

□□□

sun was in her eyes and the muted thrumm of the Ford lulled her into complete lassitude.

Petra was snoring lightly when the Ford stopped for fuel in Rotterdam, west of Albany. She did not wake when it turned southwest in the dusk on Route Eighty-eight, nor when the headlights first began to reflect from signs mentioning Elmira. She did not even open her eyes when, sometime later, the adhesive tape began to encircle her wrists and ankles.

ELEVEN

GARY MACALLISTER DIDN'T MIND THE SNAKE PIT graveyard shift, not even when he drew gate duty. There was so little to do, he could pull a paperback from his lunchbox and read maybe six chapters of Stephen King before first light. When a car did come through after midnight it was usually Ullmer's old Volvo. Not this time, though.

Gary laid the book facedown under the counter as he spotted lights heading his way, and stepped outside standing tall, tugging at his guard uniform coat. Wickham, the shift captain, had long ago pointed out that when anybody came onto the grounds this late, it was most likely NSA brass on some level. Not this time, though.

The black Ford flicked its lights as if waving for attention, turning aside instead of stopping with its nose at the gate so that Gary had to walk around

□□□

the corner of the guard shack. Wickham had also said, though it did not yet occur to Gary, that this maneuver kept the video monitor, steadily swiveling to scan the gate area, from seeing past the shack. Gary sighed; probably the driver was lost. It had happened before. Not this time . . .

Gary saw a girl asleep in the front seat but, as he strode around the front of the car, did not see the driver clearly until he emerged, and thanks to the lingering spell of Stephen King, Gary nearly fainted. Above a worn, zippered leather jacket the driver's face was the face of a monster, puffed and grotesquely flat, and then Gary realized the man was wearing pantyhose stretched over his head. Gary would have pulled his sidearm but the man had beaten him to it, pointing what might have been a Glock automatic pistol at belt-buckle height.

"Hands on your hips," said the gravelly voice, not a voice he recalled and not one he enjoyed hearing. Gary complied and swallowed hard. The man glanced quickly at the shack, perhaps judging the location of the video camera. Then he gestured with the pistol. "Turn around and sit down. Give me your coat and hat."

Gary did it, knowing he had to stay calm enough to memorize the car's license number and a hell of a lot of other things, having trouble because he was trembling with a rage that was tempered by fear. He felt the muzzle of the handgun behind his ear as he dropped his coat on macadam. "Behave and you'll be okay. Get cute and I blow your head off. Understood?"

Gary managed to say, "Yeah," on his second try. He felt his sidearm slide from its holster, heard the rattle and click of its ammunition falling into the man's hand, knew the weapon was useless as it was thrust back into place. He clasped his hands behind him on command and heard a zipper whine, then felt wide tape binding his hands tighter. At another command he lay prone, wondering if he should try kicking as the tape circled his ankles, knowing damned well he wouldn't, realizing as his legs were forced back with tape connecting his belt to his ankles that he couldn't even crawl, now.

"You're doing fine," said the voice he couldn't see, but he doubted it because the last silver strip of duct tape went across his mouth. Gary figured then that the man intended to kill him.

But maybe not yet. From the tail of his eye, Gary saw the man drop the old leather jacket, then don the uniform coat and hat, backing around the edge of the shack now, facing Gary and waving cheerfully as he disappeared toward the shack's door. And Christ, but it was cold lying there at one o'clock in the morning! A moment later, just as Gary began to test his bonds, the man was back, hatless, cutting the tape from Gary's belt and ankles with a clasp knife that could have been used for shaving.

The man's arms were short and thick, and hauled Gary upright as if he weighed nothing. "Open the gate," he demanded, and Gary had a flash of hope as he rounded the shack with his captor on his heels until he saw his own hat hanging from the video monitor. Wickham might still get curious about that, if he was watching the monitors. Or he might not.

That pantyhosed son of a bitch was sure good

with tape, Gary thought, feeling fresh tape link his left wrist to the back of his belt before the clasp knife freed his right hand. Another flash of desire, this time to use the alarm signal, until the man said, "By the way, the woman is a hostage. I want to see something in there, that's all; then I leave. Punch the wrong access code or get me into a gunfight and she dies. But not before you do."

Gary flexed his hand carefully, and then punched the code in, and the gate began to slide open. He felt himself propelled outside; watched the man toss his old jacket into the car; then he was made to lie across the Ford's sloping hood, holding on with one hand, as the man drove the car slowly around and through the opening. He almost fell off as the car stopped, the driver still armed and watching as he stepped back to the shack to retrieve the hat with a flick of his hand. Gary knew the monitor at Wickham's station would not show the edge of the open gate; its field of view was limited to things outside the gate. You weren't supposed to have to worry much about what went on inside.

The man parked near the lowered doors of Blue Hangar, which had been partitioned off a week before so that even the guards could not see what was in half of it. The Ford stood where perimeter arc lights permitted a slice of shadow, before the guy got out and whipped the tape from Gary's mouth. Gary began to wonder how much the bastard already knew about the place. Evidently quite a bit: "Who's your shift captain, and how many others on this shift?"

Gary swallowed. "Too many. Look, face it, buddy, you better quit while—"

□□□

That was as far as he got before the man back-handed him, grabbing him by the collar, leading him to the passenger's side of the Ford where the woman still slept. "You face this," said the man. "I succeed: I leave the woman with you and we all live. I fail: we all die, no ifs, ands, or buts. That's a promise. It means you and I are on the same side. Which do we do, live or die?"

"Shit," Gary muttered. "Shift captain is Cully Wickham, he's probably at the comm center. Gabe Trotti's the other man. Makes his rounds on a weird schedule the comm center gives us."

"Stays with the shift captain between rounds?"

"How'd you know?" asked Gary, but got no answer.

His captor was silent for a moment, then said, "You know where the monitors are, so you know the best way for us to get to the comm center. We wait for Trotti to make his rounds and follow him back, and we all get to live. Or you screw up," he added grimly, "and we don't."

Gary nodded. "I better have my hat and coat if this is going to work," he said, wondering again if the guy was going to slip up because if he did for even an instant, by God, Gary would be on him like a coat of paint.

But the man was very careful, shifting hands as he shrugged out of the coat, keeping that evil little weapon pointed where it would give a man a new navel, roughly thirty-eight caliber. He tossed the coat, then the hat, to Gary and followed as Gary moved off toward the hangar's air-conditioning plant. Gary pulled his ID card and slipped it into the slot, then moved inside the welcoming blackness and waited, crouching. This was it, the moment when he had an advantage because he could see out but no one could see in.

A beam of light speared him, narrowing quickly; one of those little pocket Maglites, naturally, and he was caught crouching with his hands open. "I can just kill you now if this is how it's going to be," said the gunman. Gary tried to grin but failed, and flicked on the room lights knowing he'd used up all the hero in him.

Gary led the way to the stairs, hearing the tiny creaks of the metal as he moved upward to the upstairs door, the one that unlocked automatically with the fire alarm circuit but, as only the guards and Ben Ullmer knew, would also open with a guard's ID card. It had been installed as an internal fire escape for personnel in the Snake Pit library. "I'm gonna turn the lights off now," Gary said.

"Not 'til you tell me why."

"You can see light through a little crack under this door," Gary explained. "The library night lights aren't bright, but when we make our rounds we snap on the overheads for a looksee. We'll know when Trotti goes by."

"And wait a half hour or more?"

"Sometimes," Gary agreed.

"I'm double-parked," the gunman said wryly. "We go in now and take our chances."

"Yeah, what's it to you if I get killed," Gary muttered, but he inserted his card, took a deep breath, and pushed through into the big, dimly-lit room with its steel shelves, holding the very apex of a century's flight technology, that towered to the ceiling. They moved quickly to the main door with its wire-embedded window, and only a blind man

□□□

would have missed the sudden flare of light from the hallway outside. Footsteps. A door open down the hall.

"Does he come in here?"

"Always, to hit the lights. He's *supposed* to," Gary said, as if justifying what was about to happen.

The man stepped back, hauling the roll of tape from his jacket fast enough to make Gary flinch again, and Gary might have just possibly had time for his move as the tape ripped, but then that instant was gone forever and the tape went across his mouth. It smelled like chewing gum.

"Lie flat against the wall here," the man ordered, barely above a whisper, and Gary followed orders again, now more frightened for Trotti than for himself. They weren't close friends, didn't even have the same politics; but it was almost worse watching this happen to a colleague you trusted, and who trusted you, than to get it yourself. Almost. Should he kick against the wall? *Don't even think about it . . .*

Another door opened nearer, and soon closed, and then Gary heard the distinct click-step, click-step of Trotti's shoes with those damned taps he wore to keep his heels from wearing.

Then the swish of an ID card, a faint clack, and the nearside door opened because as always Trotti walked two paces to the main light switch, and with his chin on the tiles, Gary saw the door swing shut but Trotti did not look around at the gunman standing fully in the open behind him, the automatic now in his left hand.

When Trotti did turn, the man hit him a terrible blow just below the sternum, his right fist coming from thigh height and plunging deep into poor Gabe Trotti's soft gut, and if the gunman hadn't snatched at Trotti's coat lapel, Gabe would have sprawled across a row of chairs. Gabe's feet turned inward, almost dancing really, as he bent double with both hands clutching his belly, hat falling to the floor, Gabe's bald spot comically and pathetically revealed.

"Down," said the gunman, and kicked Trotti's ankle, keeping him from a loud fall by that pitiless lapel grip. Trotti went down on one side in a fetal position, trying to breathe with a diaphragm that was almost totally paralyzed. Gary, who had two older brothers, knew that you didn't die from a hard right to the gizzard. You just felt like you were going to, and you could no more call for help than you could fart Beethoven's Moonlight Sonata.

With a quick, hard look toward Gary, the gunman stood over his new victim and tore off strips of tape while Trotti began to gasp a little air, sticking one edge of each strip neatly to the edge of the nearest reading table. That little detail was the thing that made Gary Macallister hate him the most, the way he did everything as if he'd thought it out coldly, maybe done it a thousand times before.

Then he knelt, shifting his gaze to Gary now and then, but talking to Gabe Trotti. "Make one noise and you'll never make another," he said, the pistol aligned along Trotti's big Italian beak. "Breathe through your nose, now," he added, and fitted the tape cruelly over Trotti's little mustache.

Trotti's hands came up, but weakly, and though it was a struggle for a moment with that tape flicking and sticking while Trotti tried to ward it off, it was never much of a contest and soon his wrists were bound behind him. The ankles went even faster but at least, Gary thought, poor old Gabe was breathing well enough to get his color back. His face was a deep red, in fact, as the gunman trussed his ankles to his belt.

By now, the big roll of silver tape was smaller than it had been, and as the gunman looked at the roll, Gary thought that monstrous face would be smiling without the pantyhose. After a practiced glance at the table legs, the man eased two chairs away, dragging Trotti on his belly so that the table legs exactly flanked Trotti's bent elbows.

It took a moment for Gary to see the logic of it, but when tape linked each elbow to a table leg, and with his knees bent back, there was no way Gabe Trotti could go anywhere, not even bang his feet. Of course a man could bang his nose against the tile, if he were so inclined.

"Now you," said the man, gesturing with the automatic toward Gary. "But first give me your ID card. And remember if I have to kill any of you, every one of you gets it."

At least Gary didn't have to lie facing Gabe's furious gaze. With his elbows taped to the legs of another table, he wondered what the rustling signified until he managed to turn his head as the gunman stepped into the hall. His shoes stuck out of his hip pockets and he wore Gabe Trotti's brogans, unlaced, their heels tapping a false message as they moved off.

Gary kept expecting gunfire, hearing only his and Trotti's breathing, until two sets of footsteps echoed in the corridor a few minutes later. The gunman knew how to use an ID card, shoving an enraged Cully Wickham through the door ahead of him. Gary saw, as the gunman forced Cully to lie prone beside a third table, that the shift captain's wrists and mouth were already taped.

Wickham's mistake was trying to kick as the tape circled his ankles. The man knelt on Wickham's back, bouncing his forehead off the floor with his free hand. "Suit yourself, if you want more of this," he said, ignoring Cully's groans. Gary had often wished he could give Wickham a whack like that. Now that somebody had, Gary could only feel helpless rage over it.

Moments later, Cully Wickham lay secured under the heavy table, facing away from the others. Gary could not see the gunman now, but watched as Trotti's shoes dropped to the floor. He did see the man as he stopped in the corridor doorway.

The guy must've been on a tight schedule because he was checking his wristwatch as he spoke. "I'll be back now and then to check. The man who has managed to get even one arm loose will get a slug through his kneecap. Think about it," he added darkly, and Gary heard his pace quicken in the corridor.

It was so quiet after that, Gary knew when the phone rang downstairs fifteen minutes later. It stopped, then began again and went on ringing for a long time, the loneliest sound Gary Macallister had ever heard. Shortly afterward, the gunman ducked into the library again, said, "You three just may make it," and left on the run.

It must have been another ten minutes before Gary heard the soft thrumm of a big motor and

□□□

creakings of metal. It sounded like hangar doors opening but that didn't figure, unless the guy was driving his Ford inside Blue Hangar to hide it. For sure, he couldn't tow those long-winged aircraft away through the gate, and rumor had it that nobody on earth really knew how to fly them.

The two-tone hoots of sirens were so faint at first that Gary thought he was imagining them. But the sounds grew fast, so fast that the chuffing that abruptly started to reverberate from the hangar was soon drowned out, and when he heard tires squalling outside Gary expected to see the gunman burst into the library, back to his hostages. Maybe, Gary thought as feet pounded up the corridor stairs, the guy would be content with the girl in the black Ford.

In the ferocious tumult of the next two hours, Gary Macallister kept asking if the gunman had gone over the fence. It was two hours before someone told him exactly *how* the guy had gone over it.

TWELVE

"THEY WOULD'VE HAD HIM IF IT WASN'T FOR those goddamn sirens," said Ben Ullmer, stepping aside for a shirtsleeved forensics tech. The black Nikes and jeans were the last things Ben had expected on a fed, but the forensics man's blue windbreaker left no doubt with its huge white FBI lettering across the back. They were all over the hangar by first light, stretching yellow bands of tape to cordon off areas of interest, leaving only a corridor for foot traffic through most of Blue Hangar. "Did you know a guy in the lead car said he saw something big lift off the runway as they were driving past the main gate?"

Dar Weston nodded, blinking away the sensation of hot dust under his eyelids. He had taken the Lear to Elmira after Ben's call without waiting for details, taking only Terry Unruh because Terry was the one man under him who already knew about Black Stealth One. *And how many will know by noon? A thousand? A million?* "If he didn't finish fueling up, he might be safely on the ground by now," Dar said.

"Count on it," said Ben, "if he hasn't augured it in. Since he doesn't have wet wings, the tank holds only twenty gallons and the hellbug cruises at six gallons an hour. 'Course, he could stretch his range by loafing along; but I don't much think this guy's a loafer."

For the first time since he stepped from the Lear, the CIA man found a trace of hope. "Without long-range tanks, we still might have a crack at him. With a hostage along, what does that do to his range?"

"Not much," Ben admitted. "Let me show you on the wall map," he added, pointing to a section of hangar wall which abutted the offices. A set of air navigation charts had been pasted together, yielding a map big enough to require the ladder that leaned against it.

"Be there in a minute," Dar said, looked for Terry Unruh's blond mop of hair and black down-filled jacket, waving as Unruh saw him. The lank Unruh broke off his discussion with a man whose three-piece suit said FBI more clearly than any lettering, and walked quickly to meet Dar. One thing about Unruh, those pale blue eyes could watch a dozen things at once. Damned good man, Terry Unruh, with a Master's in chem engineering and twenty years in the Company but with two strikes against his rising higher.

Strike one: his involvement with drugs many years before, as an undergrad toying with the kinds of chemicals that could alter your metabolism in funny ways.

Strike two: his lying about it. They'd found out during an annual "flutter," the polygraph tests given to Company men in the ranks. In the old days, Terry might've been fired, especially since he'd passed the flutter on those same questions before. But then the Company had fired Ed Howard, who had gone straight to the Sovs in revenge. These days, a man with Terry Unruh's old sins might be kept—but not promoted too far.

"How are you getting along?" Dar asked, not loud enough to carry.

"You'd think we were on the Other Side," Unruh said, with a baleful glance toward the FBI techs who were working the hangar floor over with cordless Dust Busters, changing bags often, inscribing each bag.

"We are, in a trivial sense," Dar replied. "I don't have to tell you how long the Feebs have been waiting for a chance to show us up. This is domestic federal crime, so I can't fault Ullmer for calling them in. Just keep smiling, and bring me any salient detail that turns up."

"Not to step on any toes, Dar, but the plumbing for this operation has got to change radically, and fast. Won't we need an ops center for this? It's going to get big," Unruh said a bit defensively.

"I know; and don't be so afraid to tell me when my fly is open," Dar said, patting the man's shoulder lightly. "As it happens, we've got a good location below that big wall map and we've got to share control with NSA. Ben Ullmer won't complain if you set it up, he's got more important worries and so do I. Get someone to rig partitions and scrambled extension phones; coffee, tables and chairs, the usual. I'll trust you to do it right. Just remember I'm going to be mobile as hell."

That was the way to keep your man happy without promoting him, Dar reflected while walking to the map. Give him his head, let him enjoy the job, and praise him when he does it right. Of course, that presupposed an employee who was both smart and dedicated. Unruh fitted those specs so well it was almost frightening.

Dar could see from reflected glare that the sprawling map, which Ullmer had begun to attack with a felt-tip pen, was overlaid by a thin layer of transparent plastic. Ullmer, his half glasses perched far down on his nose, leaned back on the ladder for a better look and nearly fell.

"Careful," Dar said, one hand reaching up to push against the NSA man's buttocks. "This country has never needed you so healthy as it needs you now, Ben."

Ullmer only grunted and finished drawing an arc, using a hand-lettered tape to define a radius outward from Elmira. "This line is the hellbug's range from two A.M. to maybe dawn. Four hundred miles," he said. "Maybe five hundred if he throttled back for minimum fuel consumption. Top speed's about a hundred and fifty knots, but you save a lot of fuel by throttling back."

Dar watched the longer arc take shape. "So he could already be in the edge of Ontario, or near the North Carolina border, if he's really good."

Ullmer stepped down and folded his arms as both men stared at the map. "He's the best. He'd have to be, just to get the hellbug out of the hangar and into the air, first time he ever saw it. I would've said it couldn't be done by anybody who didn't know the hellbug inside out."

"Are all your people accounted for?"

"We're tracing a pair on vacation; neither of 'em flies, so far as we know. If you mean Raoul Medina, shit, he's in my office getting sweated by our people. He was home in bed—and not alone, either. Mad as hell; can't much blame the guy. They say he drove like a maniac getting here."

"We've got to blame somebody," Dar muttered, "starting with me in the Company and Sheppard in NSA."

Ullmer unwrapped a cigar, turning his head slowly, his voice gruff: "This wasn't the plan. Or was it?"

"Christ, no! But the Other Side *is* primed and ready to take what we offered as Black Stealth One. This"—Dar waved toward the forensics men—"may mean they were readier than we thought. Who's to say the pilot hasn't already landed in Quebec or on some Russian trawler?"

"Quebec, maybe. Not a trawler; the hellbug's wings are too long and they're bonded on. Have to saw 'em off to get it into a cargo hold, even if the son of a bitch could land it vertically, which I doubt. Even Medina admits she's a handful to hover. And I tell you for flat-ass certain, *Medina hasn't checked out anybody else.* Hasn't even been here past his usual shift; too busy chasing nookie."

"Well, we're all going to be damned busy chasing Black Stealth One, Ben. God knows where I'll be by this time tomorrow."

"I'll be with you. Wife's already packed my bag." Ullmer saw doubt in the CIA man's face and flushed. "I'm no older than you are, Weston, and nobody knows what that airplane can do better than me. Who the fuck else is better qualified to hunt it down?"

Dar held his palms up and out as if warming them with the heat of Ullmer's objection. "Point taken, Ben. But pretty soon, your runway is going to look like Dulles International and we're going to have to start looking like a team with a plan. I'm open for ideas."

"Hell, that's easy. First thing we do is put the Air Force and ever'body else with a clearance in the air flying tight grid patterns. Also, keep light civilian air traffic on the ground, however we do it. Searchers will need a three-view of the hellbug, something that doesn't give too much away." Ben allowed some glum satisfaction to creep into his voice: "Marie's already putting it together upstairs. Next thing is, we send Raoul Medina by fastest possible means to fly Blue Sky Three to Llano Majado. If the Sovs are busy stealing the fake, they may not be looking for the real one. Of course, if this is a big Sov operation, they may already have both of 'em. That's something we need to know, and Medina will have to be ready for an ambush."

Dar Weston rubbed bristles on his chin, gazing at the wall map. "If it's a big operation, they may have fuel dumps waiting for a long flight in stages. Make sense?" He saw the NSA man nod and continued: "That's something we could release under a cover story to state police. Give the Feebs something to do, too. But what if it isn't? What if this is a singleton, some American or Canadian? Don't ask me how, I don't know! We know the man speaks unaccented American English, and the guards seem to think he's not a young man. It wouldn't be the first time a freelance thief played for big stakes."

"I can't believe a singleton, out there by himself without a support organization," Ben said, and paused. "Only guy I can imagine who'd have a prayer of flying it like this has been dead for years." He shrugged as if slipping from under a cloak of memory and turned to face the taller man. "But one thing I do know: anybody who spots the hellbug must take it out right then and there. The longer that fucker flies it, the more likely he is to learn all its stealth systems. No simple close passes, no fuckin' around. Fly through a wingtip or something, shit, it isn't armed and it'll only do a hundred and fifty knots flat-out. You could take it out with a fast chopper."

Dar Weston was nodding, thinking it over, as he saw Terry Unruh pacing toward them. "There's the hostage to think about," Dar said. "But here's a scenario you might like: it's not a woman, it's a copilot in drag. Or in any case, the hostage is on the other side; a fake." He watched Ullmer chew that cigar, trading gazes with him. "If we take that tack, it might play better when the press gets hold of this—and they will, sooner or later. If we destroy the plane in flight and the hostage turns out to be genuine, we don't look like uncaring butchers."

"But that's what we will be," Ben Ullmer muttered, shaking his head. "I forgot about the hostage and I'm having second thoughts about this. I know, Job One is to make the bird unflyable. Maybe it can be done without dicing it up in midair. What d'you think, Dar? Fuck the press, I'm not into ordering an innocent woman killed." He turned, hearing footsteps.

□□□

Unruh carried a large sealed bag in one hand, holding it up for inspection. Through the plastic film they could see a slender hardbound book, the color of dried blood, and a stiff card that might have been a credit card. "Had to promise to hold it this way, and give it right back," he apologized. "They've already dusted the stuff and checked the prints by digital link. These were left in the passenger seat of the Ford," he added, "evidently genuine; they tally with the woman's ID here. An FBI forensics tech tells me they get faint traces of model airplane cement from the car and other stuff the guy touched. He probably left these to prove he had the woman. Hardly more than a girl, actually. Driver's license says she's twenty-two."

Ben Ullmer stared at the bag, then snorted. *"Formulas for Stress and Strain,"* he remarked. "Funny kind of book for a girl to be carrying."

Dar squinted, remembering. "Model cement; we used to rub it into our fingers to fill fingerprint whorls. This guy is using old-fashioned tradecraft but I'll bet they didn't get any usable prints from him."

"Just the woman," Unruh agreed. "The book has her name in it and an address in Providence, Rhode Island."

Dar Weston felt a sudden jolt, as if his stomach had been pierced by a meteorite as cold as deep space. Taking his work seriously, he never discussed his family with colleagues except, of course, those few he had known for most of his lifetime. What's in a name? Terry Unruh had no way of knowing. With unwilling fingers, Dar grasped the bag and stared at the card inside, a Rhode Island driver's license, and his world narrowed suddenly to a single image, an image of Petra Leigh falling forever in a cloud of debris.

THIRTEEN

SUGAR GROVE, WEST VIRGINIA, POPULATION 56, lies sequestered between steep, heavily wooded ridges that loom like eyebrows over the townsfolk. The village harbors a fine old Appalachian dialect and a postal drop. It is possible to get kerosene there in the shadows of those steep mountain ridges, or an illegal, equally flammable product sold in Mason jars to fuel the lamps of the inner man; but not much in the way of FM broadcasting. Locals do not bother twiddling knobs on FM portables because line-of-sight transmissions do not penetrate there through rocky ridges. This natural shielding runs for some distance beyond the town, and a few miles north of Sugar Grove the casual hiker must retrace or climb a mountain because the signs make very clear that trespassing beyond that chain-link fence is a federal crime.

□□□

This isolation from stray radio frequencies is precisely why the NSA, and later the U.S. Navy, chose to build secret listening posts including a huge dish antenna fifty yards across and a submerged communications center. Now and then, NSA officials pass through Sugar Grove. Occasionally, special maintenance teams drive out to the remote antennas in a flatbed or a pickup truck to work on the Big Ear or the twin Wullenwebers which form essential parts of what is probably the world's most sophisticated communication network. Rarely, the chop of helicopter blades echoes through the long hollow. Fuel drums of three kinds are stocked on-site by the U.S. Navy for those rare occasions, choppers being such sots for fuel.

The simplest way to appreciate all that technology hidden in a West Virginia hollow is to look straight down on it and, thanks to Soviet satellites, Sugar Grove is a popular subject for photography from orbit. The main operations building, of white cinder block, has no windows because its occupants are not supposed to be thinking about all that splendid mountainous isolation. Nor would they be likely to suspect the damnedest-looking airplane on earth touching down on grassy stubble shortly after dawn, a mile from that windowless building.

Petra's first impression, on waking, was of the dull ache at the base of her neck. She started to reach out, and to yawn, and found that she could do neither because her wrists were tied to an immovable post—her ankles as well—and something that smelled like Wrigley's Spearmint was pasted over her mouth. She could even hear the hiss of air through small holes that someone had cut in the tape so that she could breathe through her mouth. For an instant, as long as it took for her to whimper while her vision made sense of her surroundings, she was terrified with the nameless dread of a child. And then she remembered; not everything, but too much, enough so that she kept from wetting herself only through great effort. And that made her mad enough to quell panic.

Puffing, wrenching furiously at her bonds, she realized that she sat in the right-hand seat of some kind of grounded aircraft, perhaps a helicopter, in a narrow valley flanked by wooded heights. The left-hand hatch, functioning both as a door and a window and formed mostly of clear plastic, was raised, gleaming in the early sun like some enormous contact lens. Her hands and feet were taped to a control stick which was evidently locked, yet she could feel something give. She fought harder.

"That's enough!" Petra swiveled her head and stopped. There were voices that had to shout to be taken seriously. This was not one of them. Its owner, Mr. John Smith, peered around the door opening. He looked like bloody hell, the crow's-feet at his temples almost meeting the puffiness under his eyes. A middle-aged man who has missed a night's sleep does not bubble over with pleasantries. John Smith proved it, squinting at her: "You break anything and you get broken."

"I've got to go," she said. Amazingly, the little holes in the tape let her say it, though not very loudly.

"You go where I go," he grunted, and now she saw that he held a big floppy bag on his shoulder.

□□□

He was trying to fit its mouth into something behind the open hatch.

"I mean, I have to *go,"* she said louder. "To the bathroom." It sounded like "wathroom" through the tape but she saw sudden comprehension in his gaze.

"In a minute," he said. Petra realized that Smith was using a camper's plastic waterbag, a squarish thing that might hold five or six gallons, to fuel the vehicle. He cursed softly, shifted the bag, then seemed satisfied. The sound of liquid splashing into some cavity behind her did not make Petra's self-control any easier. To take her mind off her full bladder, she used a trick she had learned when facing a final exam with a mind suddenly gone blank: she thought of something worse.

This man knows about Uncle Dar, she thought, *but he is no friend of ours. Or of my country. He hasn't taken me away for the usual reason men take women. I'm just a piece of some game to him, a pawn, and since my uncle is involved somehow, it is a huge game. Very few big games end with all the pawns alive.* Abruptly, she decided to think about her bladder again, but she would not cry; damned if she would cry.

At last he lowered the empty bag, locked the tank's cap, and moved around to lift the hatch on Petra's side. For a moment they traded glances; hers angry, his devoid of expression. Then he said, "You can go behind those bushes, but the place is alive with rattlers so be careful. A gentleman would turn his back, but I won't. We're miles from water or people. If you run, I shoot you; it's that simple."

Seeing her nod, he unwound tape from her an-

□ □ □

kles, then her wrists, sticking one end of each tape to the smooth leather of a toolkit on his belt so that the tape hung down, ready for reuse. He made no comment as she ripped the patch from her mouth and tossed it away. He showed her how to position her feet as she exited backward, and steadied her when the entire aircraft rocked alarmingly in the process. She went where he pointed, dismayed that those bushes were hardly more than knee high, scanning the stubble for snakes.

This was not the first time Petra had shucked her jeans behind a bush, and she took a perverse pleasure in the sounds her body made, hoping it would embarrass John Smith. Leaves made a poor excuse for toilet paper but they were better than nothing. She slipped a jagged piece of stone into a hip pocket, turned away, and stood up to arrange her clothing because, as promised, he stood facing her ten yards away, arms folded, with that automatic pistol in his right hand. She had never seen a handgun quite like it. It looked like a plastic gizmo from *Star Trek*.

And then, for the first time, she saw the vast wingsweep of the aircraft, with no identifying marks of any kind, and realized that her mouth was hanging open. "Get back in," he said, gesturing with the sidearm, "I'm not through fueling this thing and I won't have you running loose."

It was not the chill breeze that lifted gooseflesh on Petra's arms. She had studied the human-powered aircraft of MacCready and MIT, and the pioneering Bowlus designs, in Applied Structures. This thing seemed generations beyond them all with that gaping mouth that surrounded the cockpit, and the multibladed fan half hidden inside.

And in a way, it looked frighteningly alive. She paused beside the cockpit, gripping a handhold. "Why don't I just stay with you? I won't run."

"You sure won't." His hand on her backside was not gentle, boosting her upward. "Hold on, what the hell is that?" He dug two fingers into her hip pocket and produced the fragment of stone, then tossed it away, his hand returning in a slap that stung her rump. She lay facedown in the seat now, her right breast mashed painfully by the seat's thigh support, and these multiple insults proved too much for the daughter of Philip and Andrea Leigh of Old Lyme, Connecticut. Petra kicked hard, felt her heel connect, and began to scream as she kicked harder.

Abruptly she felt herself lifted by the back of her belt and shirt collar, snatched upward and back as if she were some hollow store window dummy. He dropped her flat, full length, in the dust, cutting her off in mid-yell, then sat on her lower legs until he had taped her ankles again.

He then proceeded to spank her as she had not been spanked since she was six years old for using only one of the words she was using now. When she managed to grab the edge of his jacket, he merely spun her over and forced her hands together, holding them with only one of his own hands while he taped her wrists with the other.

In common with many women of gentle breeding, Petra had never fully understood the disparity of male and female upper body strength, especially when accompanied by an extra seventy pounds, until now. Humiliated, terrified, and with buttocks that burned, Petra clamped her eyes shut as if that would stop her tears. She felt herself

□□□

hoisted over his shoulder, then lifted bodily into the aircraft, offering no resistance until she felt the wire circle her throat.

"Hold still unless you want to strangle," he said, fumbling behind her head, his face so near she could feel his heat on her cheeks. "You asked for this, kid." When he stepped back, she saw the blood at the corner of his mouth before he spat more of it onto the ground. He took a small pair of cutters from the kit clipped at his belt, snipped behind her head, and drew a coil of black anodized wire out. He cut two pieces, each a yard long, and secured her to the control stick again. "I told you before not to break anything. If you do, this whole rig can fall right out of the air—and so will you. Now behave yourself, I'll be back soon." And with that, he circled the cockpit to retrieve that plastic fuel bag before trudging off, parallel to a dry gully.

Petra could open her hands enough to grasp the control stick, but stretching her fingers toward that cruel wire only tightened the loop around her throat. She wanted to sob, but that hurt too. It was hell when she could not even abandon herself to justified self-pity.

Well, what could she do? *Think, dammit; that's what,* she decided. One thing sure, she had heard Smith's voice before all this began and he or one of his cronies knew Uncle Dar well enough to fake that note. Somehow, her kidnap and the CIA were connected. Those damned spooks had lots of ways to knock you out for hours and, in fact, the sun said it was nearing midmorning. She could see the pilot's console, with only a few small instruments instead of the massive array in most aircraft she had seen. Not even a clock, though it had a swiveling video screen with a keyboard. All the lettering was in English, but that didn't mean much; she'd heard a prof say that the international language of flight was English too, though the language of spaceflight would probably be Russian.

Everything around her was stripped to bare essentials, the few interior panels not even painted, and she guessed correctly that they were made of filament and polymers, exotic stuff with an unfinished look. She had seen no sign of a hangar, so Smith had already flown here to refuel. Where from, and where to? Perhaps he would tell her, but not if she continued to fight him. She would escape this brute, no question about that; and the best way to do it was first to convince him of her obedience.

She thought about Smith for a while. Medium height, hard face, not young; old enough to be her father, with a gut that protruded a bit over his belt buckle and heavy sloping shoulders beneath that old leather jacket. His hand and arm strength were incredible, and he made every move with the coordination of a card-sharp. *And I know him from somewhere,* she thought with increasing certainty.

She heard him before she saw him, shuffling in a slow trot with that bag over his shoulder, head down like a coolie as he approached through the scrub. She lay back, eyes closed as if asleep, and felt great satisfaction at his heavy breathing as he began topping off the tank. Presently she heard the cap snap into place, and a moment later he stuffed that plastic bag, still sloshing with fuel, behind her own seat. Petra did not enjoy the aromatic odor, though it reminded her of the blends she used to smell in the pits with her father. Gasoline, then, not jet fuel.

She eyed him silently as he sealed her hatch, and noted the care he took when climbing in, seeing her horizon dip and sway as this unbelievably flimsy vehicle flexed with his entry. Then he reached down and retrieved the wire from her ankles, then her wrists. They were still taped, but no longer to the control stick between her knees. Grunting, he managed to reach behind her headrest to untwist the last wire, and she felt the tension across her throat release as he spoke, coiling the wire neatly without looking at it. "There might be some buffeting at takeoff, kid, so you'll want to harness up. If you force me to, I can always wire your neck up again. I won't like it if you make me do that, and you'll like it a damn sight less."

She might have handled it differently if she had read any sign of pity or friendliness in his face, but all she saw there were determination and maybe a touch of anxiety. She nodded and watched him thrust a metal link through the loops of his own shoulder harness, so that all harness ends terminated with a fitting across his lap. She tried to link her harness the same way as he brought the strange craft alive, but when the engine's soft whisper steadied and he tested the controls, she was still fumbling hopelessly.

"Ah, shit," he muttered, "I liked you better asleep," but he reached across to help. Not to do it all, only to give minimal assistance. A vagrant shred of memory, of a man who had treated her that way many years before, tugged at Petra but she would deal with it later. Right now, she wanted to be strapped in tight because if the motions she felt through the seat were any indication, this gigantic paper airplane was going to start flapping its wings any second.

Before the pilot moved the throttle beyond idle, he did a curious thing with his feet, pressing on two pedals that she took at first to be brake and steering pedals. But the exhaust rush, hardly noticeable until now, suddenly took on a different note with muted whistles in it. The pilot throttled up, watching his instruments carefully, and then something began to tremble under Petra's backside. She looked over her right shoulder, seeing the sudden dust storm below the wing. The wing's backward sweep was such that she could barely see it, but it was no longer sagging downward. It was sloping up, flexing as it tilted, but by the time Petra decided the wings *did* flap, she saw the brown earth dropping away.

No, the wings did not flap, but they seemed to be filled with helium. Without helicopter blades or rockets, the vehicle was rising straight up, then nosing forward, dipping a little, almost skimming the brush as it began to pick up forward speed in a whispering rush that changed as the pilot moved those pedals. Only one American military airplane did that, and no light planes at all. *But I don't know what the Soviets have,* she thought.

Petra knew an airspeed indicator when she saw one. Before it registered thirty knots, a little over thirty miles an hour, Smith had the control stick tilted to the left. The great bird responded sluggishly, and the gust of breeze that struck them before they had risen a hundred feet became a near disaster. The pilot's hand slapped the throttle hard, his feet mashing those pedals, and Petra saw scrubby trees rushing up at them as the aircraft heeled over, pivoting so that the nearside wing missed the upsloping terrain by a foot or so. Then the craft was rising again with a sickening lurch, headed toward the narrow end of the little valley. And even when the tachometer needle strayed toward the red, the engine sounds were muffled.

They circled twice in a tight climbing spiral before rising above the ridgeline, at a pace so lazy as to seem in slow motion, and only then did Petra see the great electronic ears spread out in the distance below. Not far from their takeoff point lay a concrete pad with painted legends and a low shed nearby. "Where are we, Canada?"

"West Virginia," he said, throttling back now, the aircraft still climbing although the antenna complex now slid from sight behind a ridge. "It's a spook listening post, one of the biggest. And this is a spook airplane. Appropriate, huh?"

She ignored the grin that went with his last comment, swallowing to keep her stomach where it belonged. "You're not one of my uncle's people," she said.

"Nope." He tilted the video screen so that it faced him, and began to finger its keyboard. "I'm not anybody's people, Petra Leigh. For that you can thank your uncle's people, the whole miserable lot of them." He swore at the screen, scanned the horizon, then tried the keyboard again. And swore again. "If only that dumb schmuck weren't so cute with passwords," he added.

Petra made it light, airy. "What schmuck?"

"No you don't, kid. Get this through your head: if we don't get shot down or forced down or just plain *fall* down, sooner or later you'll have a lot of people asking questions. I've spent a long time working this out alone, but some of my enemies used to act like my friends. I know how they think—or at least you'd better pray that I do," he added, punching at the keyboard again. His disgusted grimace suggested another failure.

"When do we get to eat, Mr. Smith?"

"I've got water, cheese, sausage, raisins. Sorry, no eggs Benedict," he said, rummaging with his left hand behind his seat.

That was the instant when she knew him; not the whole picture, but the essential bits. A friend of Uncle Dar's from long ago, one who had learned her breakfast favorite at Old Lyme, but a friend no longer. If she kept cudgeling her memory, she might remember his name. She tried to keep the light of this small triumph from her eyes, accepting the old suede bag as he swung it toward her. He'd put his repair kit back in the bag, which seemed to be full of duct tape, tools, and bottles. She held a bottle up and looked at him.

"Don't drink that, it's full of tetraethyl lead," he said quickly. "Food's at the bottom. And be careful with those cardboard tubes. They're dangerous."

She took inventory, trying to remember it all, even the flimsy bag, model cement, and the tubes of epoxy. The water was in a pair of two-liter plastic Seven-Up bottles. She opened the pound box of Sun Maid raisins as well, and took a handful, pretending not to study the instrument panel. The magnetic compass and the sun agreed that they were climbing almost due south.

While she was chewing, he loosened his shoulder straps for more comfort. "The Cherry Seven-Up bottle is yours," he said. "The diet bottle's mine.

□□□

Can't fill 'em again 'til we land, and you keep your hands off mine."

"Oh boy, but you are one tough guy," she said acidly.

A shrug. "Those are the rules. They could get tougher," he reminded her, dividing his attention between the keyboard and the mottled terrain that stretched away below, a rumpled coverlet with long parallel ridges made more flat and featureless as the aircraft continued to climb. He smiled to himself, tilting the control stick to the right, her own stick following suit.

The great bird banked obediently, almost silently, to the right, sliding down invisible corridors of air. Petra took a swallow of water and recapped the bottle. "Changed your mind already, Mr. Smith?"

"A piece of it," he said, and pointed to the right, far ahead. "See that high ridge? Should be some nice thermal air above it, and we can throttle back. If I trusted this sucker for an in-flight restart, I could shut 'er off for hours and let the ridge take us where we're going."

"And where would that be?" It did not occur to Petra until too late that her purring tone was one she generally employed on much younger men.

"You're about as subtle as a tire-iron, kid. South, actually southwest for the moment, as any freshman engineering student should know by now. And you're almost a senior. If I were fool enough, I could show you Roanoke or Asheville on the way but until I get chummier with the brains of this thing I intend to stay well clear of big towns.

"It's been a long time since I was bewitched, bothered, and bewildered by a kid with a cute ass, so save it. We're going to be together for a few days; don't make me hurt you and don't act empty-headed because that would piss me off. When I'm pissed off, I don't care how bad you hurt. For that matter, you could just step out that side right now and things would be easier for me. All that matters is that people *think* you're in here."

Petra watched distant clouds drag shadows over ridgelines below, her ears popping as the aircraft began to descend with the tachometer needle at idle, and she swallowed hard. "What people? I've been kidnapped, I'm scared, and I don't know what this is all about. Surely you can tell me something. You owe me that much."

His glance held cynical amusement. "I owe you zip. All the same, when you're scared enough you can do something stupid that'll get us both killed." Their descent, now, was carrying them parallel to a series of ridges that seemed to stretch toward the southwest like a single mountain as far as she could see, with vast popcorn bulges of cloud-hugging ridges here and there.

A thin, silver line scrawled a curving "Z" into the nearest ridge and a tiny, squarish black dot traversed it faithfully on tinier wheels. Petra could see the boundaries of farms as geometric shapes, the farm buildings as tiny rectangles, some with sheet metal roofs that glimmered in the sun. In the far distance lay two small towns. She realized now that the pilot was, as he had promised, keeping his distance from population centers.

A series of faint, buffeting pressures shook the craft lightly, and the pilot seemed to be hunting in the clear air for something elusive. As he searched, he said, "You'll learn some things anyhow. I stole this thing from a spook hangar near Elmira, New York. I took you along and left your ID in the Ford so they'll think twice before they shoot us down, assuming they find us. You can pray that they don't find us. And heeere we go," he said, nodding. "We've got some thermal air under us now. I've never flown this thing before last night, so I've still got my training wheels on."

Petra loosened her harness as she had seen him do, sitting up straighter, beginning now to almost enjoy a ride she could tell her grandchildren about—if she survived it. "It looks easy enough," she said.

"It's a tipsy bitch, but it's got no power assists outside of tabs the autopilot can operate for straight-and-level flight. Even have to operate the waste-gate ducts by leg power. It's a lot tougher than it looked on the prints, but your legs are your strongest muscles."

"I'm a cyclist," Petra said.

"I know. I followed you from the campus yesterday."

"How long have you people been planning this, Smith?"

A faint smile as he shook his head. "One people. Me. I figure they owe it to me—*shit,*" he finished, slamming the stick hard to the left.

Without warning, some invisible demon of clear air had thrust the craft upward, but not on an even keel. The left wing flexed in an impossible bow, not folding but tilting the entire aircraft so that Petra's right-hand horizon lofted until it seemed that the wings must be as vertical as a telephone pole and Petra was staring straight down through her hatch window. Caught by surprise without snug restraints, her shoulders sliding past the straps, she slammed her right arm outward for support, striking the flimsy plastic hatch hard near its lower latch. An instant later the hatch lay ajar, Petra falling out as far as her torso, the sudden battering of wind on her face forcing her eyes shut, her taped wrists preventing her from helping herself. She could scream, though, as she felt her hips sliding from the loosened lap belt.

The rough hand at her belt jerked her inside so hard she yelped as the hatch edge scraped past her ear, and then she was holding tight to the seat with her bound hands between her thighs. Instead of sobbing, Petra lay back and gasped, shaky inhalations that continued long after the aircraft had returned to normal flight. Only when she looked at him, her teeth bared ferociously, did he let go of her belt.

"Secure that hatch, it's not broken. And don't ever do that again," he said, as if someone were shaking him while he spoke.

She had already levered the latch tight again, needing to turn sideways because her wrists were bound, when she realized all of what he'd said. "*Me?* You're flying this goddamn thing, you crazy old bastard!" She began to tighten her harness again as well as she could, now almost crying in a reaction her close friends could have predicted: rage. "Tie my hands and feet," she snarled, and, "let me loosen these things," she accused with a sob, and, "turn this rinkydink cardboard contraption on end, and—and *blame it on me,*" she howled, watching him through slitted eyes as she regained her self-control. More quietly, and with the sweetness of ant paste: "But I promise to do better, Mr. Smith, really I do."

He looked away, and when a sudden nudge of turbulence made him look ahead, Petra saw a blush fading under the tan on his craggy features. "Okay. You're right, kid. I was just—fuck it, you're right." He stared off, clearing his throat, and Petra realized that he was trying to keep his voice steady. Then he turned back toward her, gesturing with his free hand. "I'll pull that tape off your wrists. You couldn't be dumb enough to try anything up here." She watched his hand unwind the tape, seeing the black hairs still standing erect, realizing that he, too, had been badly frightened.

If there was truth in wine, there was more of it in fear. The first question that occurred to her was, "If you didn't care, why didn't you just let me fall?"

"I don't know. Probably should've, thanks for bringing it up. Maybe next time I will."

"You need me alive for something, don't you?"

"Not in any way you'd believe," he said, "and I don't want to talk about it. You got lucky. We're both lucky, in fact. See that?" He pointed to the altimeter, recording their rise although the engine was idling. "I'm going to try something."

With that, he thumbed a detent on the throttle and flicked off a switch. The whisper of the engine ceased, but before Petra could speak, he released a grin that was utterly and innocently boyish. "We're still climbing. There's a lot of skin and a lot of drag on the hellbug, but she's soaring. Hot damn!"

"Is that what it's called?"

"Sure, why not," he mused aloud. "Its name is Black Stealth One, Petra. Some guys on the project called it the hellbug." He compensated for a gust, looking far off; perhaps, she thought, far into the past. "Some people who make policy in this country decided they needed this thing because they didn't trust other guys who make policy. Then some other squeaky clean policy maker decided they didn't trust me, either."

"When did this happen?"

"Long time back; doesn't matter. I got burned like you'd burn a match, used and tossed out. They thought I was dead." As if to himself, softly: "They tried, God damn them, they gave it a real good shot." His sudden glance at her was quietly fierce. "I was straight, you understand, this wasn't punishment. Just policy on somebody's part. Happens all the time. I've been dead for years, kid." Into her questioning frown he grinned again. "But now I'm burning 'em back, the whole bloody-minded bunch of 'em. And you know what? By God, I feel alive again."

"You're a phoenix," she said. "You know, flying up from—"

"You don't have to explain it," he cut in. "Jesus! College kids think they know it all . . ."

"I know more than you think," she said softly.

"If you don't, I fear for the future of engineering."

"You helped build this airplane, maybe even designed it. That's the only way you would've seen blueprints a long time back, or worried about control forces. And that's not all I know."

His reaction was an exaggeratedly slow movement of his head until he was staring directly at her. "Well, I'm a dirty bastard," he said.

"At least we can agree on something, Mr. Corbett," she nodded.

FOURTEEN

KAROTKIN, WITH DEEP-BREATHING EXERCISES, managed to regain his calm before the others reached his office. It was important that he appear unflustered, even bored, in the face of an operation that seemed not so much blossoming as exploding. At the moment, no one could say whether that explosion was showering them with shit or pure gold. Nor, for that matter, whether it would be the KGB that got showered or the GRU, its archrival for Moscow's favors. Suslov walked in first, trailing the journalist, Yevgeni Melnik.

Suslov sat down with only a dry smile and a gesture as if presenting Melnik. "I need time to finish reading the file, comrade Karotkin," said Melnik, who had learned of his own involvement in the past half hour. Karotkin agreed, though he was not happy to see the bulk of that file. It was always an error to tell a man more than he needed to know, even a man with a wife and three children in Smolensk.

An excellent interviewer with a decent command of idiomatic English, Melnik knew how to follow a fast-breaking story in the West. His costume provoked an occasional suspicious glance in the embassy because the tanned little fellow with the loafers, wrinkled trousers, quick smile, loose tie, and ever-present Pall Mall looked so much like an American. Melnik usually needed rewriting because having noticed everything, he tended to mention everything; but his debriefings were things of beauty. A genuine print journalist as well as a spy, he was suspected by some Westerners as KGB because his loafers were by Florsheim whereas most Soviet scribblers shopped, if appearances counted, at Goodwill. In short, Yevgeni Melnik was exactly the sort of man who would already be on a CIA list, ready to be branded "undesirable" by the Americans the next time they decided to demonstrate their displeasure in a highly public way. Meanwhile, Melnik was acceptable so long as he did not get in the way more than any other journalist.

Melnik was still speed-reading when Karotkin responded to the buzzer. "You are here only for background, Melnik," Karotkin said quickly. "Save any questions for later."

Gennadi Maksimov made his usual entrance, sweeping the room with eyes like gray ball bearings, seeming to invest the room with a military presence as he smiled and nodded. They all knew comrade Colonel Maksimov and the figure he cut even in a three-piece suit. They had known him sober and correct, and they had known him drunk as a *muzhik,* always joking then. He would not be joking now because the man who entered behind him was Karel Vins.

At the level of colonel and above, a man like Maksimov could be both old soldier and diplomat, no longer required to maintain the physical fighting trim of a commando. But the man they knew as Karel Vins was on the rolls as a major. And majors in the *Glavnoe Razvedyvatelnoe Upravlenie,* the GRU, were the Soviet elite in military intelligence. An erect, pale-eyed, straight-haired blond of medium height and on the muscular side of forty, Vins might pass as a Finn. He would be good at languages, better at surveillance—and superb at killing.

Maksimov had not said he was bringing his man. To do so without prior agreement was the kind of gesture the GRU could afford, a way of underlining the fact that Soviet military intelligence and its trained killers were above KGB control. Karotkin noticed the comical movement of Melnik's scalp as the little journalist recognized Vins. That meant Melnik knew his way around.

But still a journalist, as he proved when Karotkin made the introductions. "Vawlk," Melnik murmured as he was identified to Vins. Without the slightest change of his pleasant expression, Karel Vins made a faint inclination of his chin and then passed his gaze on to Suslov. A very few men in the GRU elite were known by nicknames in Soviet circles. Sretsvah, the remedy, perhaps in London to remedy some imbalance; Grichanka, the Greek, rumored a casualty at last, at the hands of an Albanian; Vawlk, the wolf, whose street name was

□□□

Karel Vins. Maksimov might know the name Vins was born with; more probably not. What mattered, and what Vins chose to pretend did not matter, was that the *vawlk* was already a legend even among his KGB compatriots who admired, envied, and feared him.

The trainees of Cuba's Dirección General de Inteligencia, or DGI, had translated his nickname easily as Lobo during his Cuban tour as an "advisor." Few Soviet field operatives were as well qualified to bring a big operation home in a Latin American country, and the presence of Karel Vins automatically raised the status of the operation. It did not necessarily mean that deadly violence would follow. It meant that a lethal instrument was at hand.

Vins waited for Maksimov to sit, and then sat at his back without comment. Maksimov adjusted his creases and then, in his familiar strong baritone, said, "I must hear it from your mouth, comrade Karotkin: have we really stolen the Black Stealth craft?"

"It would seem that we have," said Karotkin, "judging from the communication traffic we are monitoring. True, it happened sooner than we thought. Since your own people ran the Bulgarian connection, you would be the best judge of that."

"Comrade Major Vins, under Bulgarian cover, had a face-to-face with the American," said Maksimov, and turned to the man behind him. "Your assessment?"

"Latino, American citizen, former military pilot; real name Raoul Medina," said Vins softly, as though reading from some dull text. "He is probably what he claims, the test pilot for the stealth craft. Courage of the kind they call machismo, which is the kind that can demand more of a man than he can give. Such a man might commit a great crime ahead of schedule because he feels his nerve running out, or simply because of some unforeseen factor that tells him, 'now or never.' His car is parked at the facility in Elmira. I would say he is an unlikely decoy," Vins ended with the merest trace of humor.

Suslov, who had been thinking exactly that: "Why not?"

"The Americans avoid putting nonprofessionals at risk," said Vins, to whom there was only one profession. "And American professionals have *some* tradecraft. This man Medina is clever and determined, but as to professional tradecraft? Aaah," he said, now smiling as he waved a hand lazily. The smile faded with, "But could Medina be some decoy, a superb actor? We proceed with that possibility in mind."

Karotkin caught the implication and knew that the GRU had received sanction for the job while the KGB was still wondering. But damned if he would show irritation. "Then we do proceed as planned. You have little time to spare if you intend to meet the American in Mexico, comrade Major."

"Or," Suslov put in smoothly, "he may have more time than we thought." He glanced down at the notebook on his knee, placing the point of his pen on the left-hand margins of three lines as if completing a ritual. "Since dawn this morning, my people have had more traffic intercepts on data collection channels than we can handle. As you know, we can draw many conclusions even when we cannot decrypt a given message."

□□□

Karotkin was annotating and stacking cards, expressionless, probably angry because Suslov had not briefed him in advance. He would have to smooth Karotkin's ruffled feathers later by proving that there had been no time for it. The others waited politely until Suslov went on. "That Elmira facility is crawling with American operatives. They have a jet-fuel truck on that little runway to handle all the executive jets shuttling in there. Every military aircraft within five hundred miles of Elmira seems to be on alert status—including Canadians, who evidently have been alerted as well.

"Some air national guard personnel have been placed on standby. Each state governor is the commander-in-chief of that state's national guard, and usually honors requests by the White House. If you can believe this, comrades, some of the traffic from a state governor is by telephone, unencrypted and clear. We intercepted two interesting bits, clear unscrambled English, in Virginia and Kentucky: their Civil Air Patrols were asked to stand by for a search for a stolen aircraft. Believe it or not, they refused."

"Refused?" It was possible to surprise Vins, after all.

Suslov chuckled. "Their Civil Air Patrol does not take part in law enforcement, nor does it search for a downed aircraft with no flight plan or other known flight corridor. But a governor also alerts the state police, which operates some small aircraft and rotary-wing craft. From what we can determine, *everything that flies under military control in that region is on alert status.*"

Maksimov snapped, "What region? Black

□□□

Stealth One is supposed to have transcontinental range."

"A five-hundred-mile radius from Elmira. Comrade Colonel, they seem to know it will be in that area," said Suslov. "So far, they have made no statement to the press but as soon as they do, our man Melnik will be in on the chase."

Maksimov, perhaps the slightest bit amused: "You are waiting for a statement from the NSA? American presidents have grown old waiting for that."

"We have already telephoned anonymous tips to *The Washington Post* and *Aviation Week,* comrade Colonel. The American press will not long be denied," Suslov joked.

Maksimov stroked his chin. "Why would we want this in their press?"

"Because"—Suslov smiled—"it will create more confusion, while ruining the careers of their most experienced men."

Maksimov shrugged away this news as if such matters were for bureaucrats, below the notice of a warrior. "I am thinking that the aircraft's range may be a factor if Medina was forced to liberate Black Stealth One before its long-range tanks were fitted."

"Or perhaps the aircraft will not take off with those tanks full," Vins said. "It would not be the first time a military design in the field failed to meet the designer's hopes." His tone suggested that he had faced the same problem more than once.

Karotkin had kept his silence until he had something to add. Now he said, "If that search area expands geometrically before the day ends, we can guess that Black Stealth One does not have long-range ranks, and is being refueled on the ground."

"The one thing that bothers me is that our thief expects to refuel it while the country's entire body of law enforcement is chasing him." The notion offended Suslov's sense of order, of propriety. "The man is insane."

"Not chasing him, but searching for him. I am not sure you fully appreciate the difference, comrade," said Vins in that deceptive soft murmur. To the KGB men this was a goad because, as was well known, GRU field operatives trained for years to elude pursuers and, more important still, to avoid being spotted in the first place.

"In any case, comrade Major Vins will be on a commercial flight to Mexico City in two hours," said Maksimov quickly, with a glance at Vins which might have been a warning about manners. "He will need time to brief the team we are bringing in from Cuba. Unless Black Stealth One is much faster than the American search pattern indicates, they will be in place in western Mexico with time to spare. The rendezvous with the American is an old airstrip bordering a coastal swamp down the coast from Mazatlan, near a village called, ah, Llano Mojado. An ideal spot to load an aircraft onto an ocean-going cargo craft."

Karotkin's fingers scuttled for fresh cards as he said, "I should think we could simply fly it to a safer place."

"Several problems there," the colonel sighed. "We dare not risk crashing it before we have thoroughly examined it, and that cannot be done in a Mexican swamp. Besides, the Llano Mojado rendezvous is politically more expedient if the operation becomes a *proval,* a calamity. Let us say the American has worked out some way to hold on to his ransom money. We do not want him to know how or where we propose to move the aircraft."

Karotkin: "And how does a naval vessel move through a swamp?"

"An air-cushion cargo vessel," Maksimov smiled. "The team is all plausibly deniable except for two naval officers. If faced with capture, they know what is expected of them. And from there to a Nicaraguan hangar"—he shrugged—"is a matter we need not burden you with."

"Of course," Karotkin said curtly. "You seem to have accounted for all eventualities, comrade Colonel. My compliments; but as long as you have the sanction, I hope you are not counting on KGB for five million dollars' worth of Swiss francs in ransom money," he finished with some smugness.

"That small detail is already in flight by diplomatic courier," Maksimov replied, "to avoid any possible questions." Every man in the room knew that it was no small detail. The sum was wildly in excess of the usual payments made by the Soviet government to thieves. "Comrade Major Vins will sign for it in Mexico. That and certain other implements of his own choosing," he added with a heavy attempt to be droll.

Suslov: "You speak as though the payment were real. Surely—"

"Surely the GRU would not risk losing such a monster fish by using an artificial lure," Maksimov said easily. "We do not know what clever tricks this man Medina may have to satisfy himself before he makes the trade. We do know that our bait is real. Traceable by transmitters in the banding

□□□

seals, but real." Maksimov saw only disbelieving stares from the KGB men, and now he spoke bluntly as if to children. "Do we want Black Stealth One more than we want the money? Yes? Then we pay its ransom!" More gently, then: "Of course, many things may happen to a thief after he runs with his ill-gotten money, comrades. Mexico is still a wild country, where a running man might be overtaken and eaten by wolves."

"Those, ah, other implements," Suslov said, the barrel of his pen raised. "Will they include two-way communication links?"

"The equipment would be too heavy," Karel Vins replied, "but I will carry a flashlight adaptable as a burst transmitter. What I need from you is a schedule of uplink windows."

Suslov nodded and stood up. He would have no difficulty providing a schedule listing the times, or "windows," when atmosphere-grazing Soviet satellites would be staring down at Western Mexico. And certainly Suslov was not about to comment on the fact that the *vawlk* could choose to transmit progress reports during this operation, but not to receive instructions. If Colonel Maksimov trusted him with millions in cash, surely Vins was on an inside track to the top. And one did not question the loyalty of such a man in his own presence.

FIFTEEN

"COBBETT? DOESN'T RING A BELL," SAID CORBETT, certain that his denial was pointless but trying it for luck. He frowned at his video display, pretending that it held most of his attention as he continued to try access codes. He wore a tiny earpiece in his left ear with a microphone boom and a slender cable that snaked across to a radio unit on the console. A similar unit protruded from the console on the girl's side. From time to time, he punched a different channel.

"Kyle Corbett," said the girl, enunciating the "r" in a way her down-east accent normally did not. "I remember the alliteration, Corbett. If you don't know your own name we're really in trouble. Oh, you're a lot older now—God, you must be a fossil, I couldn't have been more than five or six at the time, but I remember you. Two helpings of eggs

Benedict, heavy on the sauce; I resented you for that. Wouldn't shoot off a bottle rocket for me, but you showed me how to do it. Did you know I got grounded for a week for setting a handful of those things off by myself after you left?"

He chewed his upper lip to stop the corner of his mouth from lifting as he recalled that carefree weekend. She'd been a tomboyish little fart, curious about everything. "Served you right. Whoever said a little learning is a dangerous thing was talking about kids," he said, glancing back at the video. "Damn," he whispered, clearing the keyboard again.

"You cut the phone wires to my apartment, Corbett," she said matter-of-factly.

"To the whole house. Sue me." He was now punching in new codes and booting the computer rapidly.

"The waiting line to sue you must stretch over the horizon by now," she said, and paused. "The See's candy, my nickname—you don't forget much, do you?"

"Not where double-crossing is concerned. You're proof of that."

"But you don't really want me hurt."

Her voice held its cadence, but something was missing in its timbre: the aggressiveness, he decided. She wasn't entirely certain, bluffing her way. He called it. "You're not a little kid anymore," he said, giving her the kind of look that earned him breathing room in a cantina.

She took her time responding, thinking it over, in a way that reminded him of Dar Weston. "Oh, I think you could kill *some*body, Corbett. But you're the only person Uncle Dar ever brought to

□□□

Lyme. And he's a great judge of character. He would never have chosen a friend who could kill an innocent hostage."

"Thank you, Dr. Freud," Corbett said, scanning the skies and fighting off a yawn. "Try this one: if it came to a choice between his country and his family, which one would he choose?"

No hesitation this time. "Country first, family second," she said. "That's been a sore point between him and my dad."

Corbett's glance was sudden, only long enough to assess that open, freckled face. She seemed to be holding nothing back, taking her world as her elders had described it. "Tell you what, Petra: hope and pray that you're wrong. The only reason you're here is that the feds just might not try to knock this thing down if Dar Weston's niece is in it." He tried to bite off a yawn but failed, checking his wristwatch, then selecting a map from the sheaf that fanned from a cloth pocket near his left thigh. "It was just your bad luck that Weston doesn't have a daughter of his own." He could see her face without a direct glance. It reflected no sudden concern or suspicion.

"Nothing lucky about it," she said, surprising him as she grasped an edge of the nav chart to help unfold it. "He couldn't do justice to kids and his career."

"He told you that?"

"He's said it to my mother often enough. I hear them, sometimes. I—that's none of your business," she ended brusquely.

Now he was studying the terrain, matching its features to the chart. As if to himself he said, "It was my business, once upon a time."

"That's a hoot," she said.

"When he's half a world away from his family, Petra, even a man like Dar might need to talk to somebody. I knew everything about you long before I met you. And if Dar really thinks he'd sacrifice you to get this airplane back in pieces, I'm betting I know him better than he knows himself. Stuff like that is easy to say when your back's not against the wall."

"Paper empiricism," she nodded sagely.

"Say what?"

"That's why psychology isn't a real science," she recited briskly, as if removed somehow to a classroom in Providence. "A lot of researchers ask people what they'd do *if,* and take the paper answers as gospel. Paper empiricism; but Uncle Dar has always put his country first. That's as close to a sure thing as you could hope for."

He pointed toward the western horizon, where a contrail was slowly dissipating high in the stratosphere. Parallel to it, farther to the south, a steely glint no larger than a pinpoint steadily drew a hard white line across a turquoise background. They were obviously on a heading that would cross beneath it, but several minutes and many miles ahead. "There's your lab hardware, Petra," he said. "They just may be setting up a graph and hoping we're a point on it. Not likely those guys will see us, and they damned sure can't pick us up on ordinary radar or IR sensors. But if they do spot us, we'll sure find out which of us is right about Dar. Assuming the decision isn't out of his hands, which it may well be."

"Intervening variables," Petra said, still following the progress of the turbojet across the heavens.

□□□

Corbett, exasperated, burst out, "Jesus Christ! Are you taking this seriously, kid? Your own life's on the line; those jets up there could slice and dice us with an easy pass like a machete through a dandelion; and here you sit, lecturing me on scientific method. *Jesus,*" he said again, trying to regain his concentration on the chart.

The girl held her palms up, eyebrows elevated. "What the hell d'you want me to do, get out and push? I'm trying to *keep* from thinking about what happens if I'm right, and they catch us up here. There's nothing I can do to save my own life, you old fossil! I would if I could."

"Quit shouting in this fishbowl," he commanded, all the more irritated because the girl was perfectly right. Better to have her chattering like a cageful of magpies about anything, hell, Paris fashions or rock music, than out of her mind with fear. And why hadn't he thought of that himself? A night without sleep was one reason.

There'd been a time when he could party all night and then strap into an aircraft at dawn and, with a few minutes on 100 percent oxygen to blow out the cobwebs, do a morning of precision aerobatics without an instant of brain-fade. But on Black Stealth One, they'd never accepted the weight penalty of an OBOG, an on-board oxygen generator, so he could not even fly the hellbug at its own design ceiling. *She's right, I'm a fossil right out of a fucking museum,* he admitted silently, *and I'm not operating at a hundred percent.* "One thing you can do is hold the chart steady, kid. Your fossil pilot needs to figure out where to park this thing for some fossil fuel."

She steadied her wrist on the video cabinet.

□□□

"One thing you can do, too: stop calling me 'kid.' You know my name."

He nodded, noting the slow unwinding of the altimeter that told him his thermal current had played out, wondering if the girl was beginning to exhibit the classic behavior patterns of many hostages. Sooner or later, with no power to affect the course of their lives, many would turn to their own captors for closeness, cooperating, even imagining for the moment that captor and captive were colleagues. Some more than others; some sooner, some later. And some, never. Petra Leigh did not seem like the kind of young woman who would succumb quickly to such a malady. *Could be sandbagging me,* he reminded himself.

But it might not matter if she were sandbagging, if she were also cooperating in the meantime. A little friendlier interaction on his part might pay off in the long run. He tapped the chart and, thinking about cooperation, said, "Here's where we are, Petra, over North Carolina. Asheville is off to our right, near the horizon, and I don't see any signs of more thermals. Now let's hope I can get a restart." With that, he refolded the chart and attended to his instruments.

"I hope you can't," she said. "Whoever you're doing this for, I don't want to meet them."

The faint whisper of huge impeller blades windmilling behind them became lost now in a sputtering hiss that reverberated in the cockpit, then steadied. He grinned, watching the tachometer, moving the throttle gently. "Saved us a bucket of avgas. That means we might really make it across the Gulf."

"We're going to Cuba," she said accusingly.

□□□

"Well—my route depends on whether I can find the right access code in there," he nodded at the video terminal. "Those guys in Cuba would nail us faster than our own people, if they spotted us."

"*Our* own?"

"Shit; *your* own. One point for you, Petra; I'm too old for flags, and you may as well know it. Here, hand me that mini-tel," he went on, pointing toward the tiny headset that hung from its Velcro loop near her radio.

She handed him the twin of the one he wore, different only in that the earpieces fitted opposite ears, and saw that he could operate two radio units simultaneously. "I don't suppose you could find us some new-age music," she said.

"Why, sure. Who gives a damn about checking the weather that could shred this thing like Kleenex? Or the guard channel that might be full of our descriptions." His glance was jaundiced. "I told you to bring a book."

"I did. You borrowed it." No recriminations, just the facts.

Attending to the keyboard once again, he opened his mouth to swear, then glanced her way. "I don't suppose you're a computer whiz. I never was much good with 'em," he sighed.

"I'm not a real hacker, but I can find my way around a menu," she admitted. "You sure aren't breaking into anything that way. You *are* trying to break in." It was not a question.

"A while back, you said you'd try to save your hide if you could. Well, maybe you can. I'm looking for a password, Petra. If I can find it, I should be able to paint this bird so that it can't be seen—or recognized, at any rate." He saw the look that passed across her face and showed his teeth in a broad grin. "Forget paint brushes or gallon cans of lacquer. You know who I am, it can't hurt. Yeah, I helped design the hellbug and believe it or not, you can paint an airplane's skin electronically. Can't do that on something that flies at Mach two, but this slow bird has a plastic skin. The paint program is in that black box somewhere," he added, flicking a finger against the monitor.

Her first response was to fold her arms, hunch her shoulders, and stare out of the canopy. Her lower lip, he decided, was fetchingly prominent though she probably had no idea how like a pouting child she looked with the sun highlighting the freckles that bridged her nose. *Right; a hell of a cute little number who's not through blossoming. And she'd wield the hammer at your crucifixion,* he told himself. He gave her time, switching channels on the radios which only he could hear. He was picking up some commercial air and, of course, the vortac signals from navigation beacons which made his charts work so nicely.

What he was *not* picking up was any suggestion that the search had begun. It was downright eerie, until a suspicion struck him so hard he grunted. What if they'd known all along that he was still alive? Just what if this entire scam had been mounted, yes, with Medina in it too, so that good ol' capable, dead Kyle Corbett would surface after all this time and fly Black Stealth One to Mexico, taking all the risks and maybe finding a shallow grave near Regocijo?

He knew the girl was speaking, but did not really hear her, so intent was he on this stunning surmise. He only shook his head, tapping the mini-tel at his right ear as if listening to some message. *But they couldn't have known I'd steal the hellbug and take the girl with me, Medina didn't know that either. So the operation would already be balls-up and they'd be mounting a search anyway. They would have put in those long-distance fuel tanks before letting Medina contact me. And ol' Speedy must be wondering, about now, if I'm really going to show at Regocijo, now that I have the hellbug instead of a rented car. He'll be pissed that I didn't warn him I'd take the hellbug, but he can't admit to anyone that we've got plans of our own—if those anti-theft riot gas cartridges are really in the Regocijo hangar.*

Medina had claimed those cartridges could fill an entire hangar with malonitrile gas, nasty stuff that could flatten a man for a half-hour. If so, the stuff should be able to zap a few guys who were too busy watching Medina crash to see a cloud of gas moving in on them from upwind. Corbett just hadn't bothered mentioning that he would do it from the air. The hellbug made it perfect because one good man with a sidearm could take on the bad guys while they were down; and if the money were really there it should make a sizable bundle, easy to find and just as easy to fly off with.

The plan he'd worked out with Medina was, moreover, exactly the kind CIA would run from, no matter how much they wanted Corbett. That meant, in all probability, Medina was trustworthy. And besides, there was that final factor, the gut feeling. Speedy? Sell him out like that? He said aloud, "Naah. Crazy."

Without looking at him she shot back, "Not from where I sit."

□□□

"Not *what* from where you sit?"

"What I said."

"I was busy."

"You were talking to yourself," she said, making a shallow vee with her mouth, the sort of deliberately false, prim smile that Andrea Leigh might have made. "I said, I want us to be seen, I just don't want to get killed."

He lifted his gaze and moved his head as if searching for a fly in the cockpit, and spoke as if to that fly. "Well isn't that swell, isn't that just cute as pie? She wants the candy, but not the zits." Then, gazing full at the girl, he said, "Read my lips: if they see us, they'll try to take us down."

He saw her swallow hard, heard the uncertainty in her, "You don't really think so."

"I don't think they'll *shoot* us down, until they find out I can make this thing dance. I think they'll try to force us down first; that's what I'm counting on, it gives us more of a chance than if they just see us and jump our ass. You know how much this airchine weighs?" She was shaking her head as he bored in with, "Half a ton loaded—we're sitting in cotton candy. You know how much a jet interceptor weighs? Twenty or thirty tons, and those titanium wings wouldn't even know it if they snipped off a few feet of us. And they'll fly ten times our top speed. Force equals mass times velocity squared, you're a goddamn engineer, you figure it out."

There were other ways they might use to force him down, ways more likely than the one he had shown her, but to guess them herself, Petra Leigh would have to know the flight envelopes of everything that flew. He saw her blinking and waited.

□□□

"On first approximation, I'd say we need five thousand times more inertia before we tangle ass with 'em," she said, trying her best to smile.

And when he began to laugh, great bellows that made his gut surge against the restraint strap, she laughed too. "Okay," he said at last, wiping his eyes. "You'll probably graduate. But barring all that magical inertia, if we get bounced, first of all you realize you're going through the wildest carnival ride you *ever* saw or heard of, and if I'm as good as I used to be, you'll be doing it for a long time because they aren't gonna quit and I sure won't. No king's X, no time out to wipe your barf off your back. Second, Petra, I am not going to be taken alive; accept that as an axiom. They don't want it much, and neither do I."

She seemed to be puzzling over something and finally said, with a grimace, "Barf off my *back?*"

"Negative g forces can slosh it around. Trust me."

"Trust you," she said, eyes half closed with comical mistrust. "And what else will this paint job do for you?"

"Uh—hell, what else you want? All it does is make it hard to spot us, ki—Petra. It's not an offensive weapon, if that's what you mean. This thing doesn't have a popgun on it."

"But you do."

"That's exactly what I do have. Lot of help that's gonna be in aerial combat, I can tell you."

"All right," she said at last, "I'll try. And if I try, I want a promise from you. Not if I succeed; if I try." He was careful to avoid showing any response until she shrugged and went on: "You let me go before you land this thing at wherever you're taking it."

He turned the video monitor's swivel so that monitor and keyboard were accessible to them both. "Fair enough. You won't believe this, but I never intended to hand you over to anybody. That wasn't part of the plan," he said. "But of course you don't believe that, I'm just a, a—" His hand churned the air for inspiration.

"Terrorist," she supplied.

"What?"

"Well—kidnapper. Scuzzball, spy, traitor, crotchsniff, thief, asshole, con man—"

"Enough, already!"

"Cradle-robber, dirty old man." She uttered the last without evident malice, merely two more phrases that she was donating as she became interested in the keyboard.

"I think I may have enough to hold me awhile," he said, faintly outraged. "Crotchsniff? Asshole? You're an engineer, all right. You talk like a grad student."

"I haven't neglected the liberal arts," she made her false, shallow-vee smile for him again. "Look, I understand you're free to break a promise. But I'm not. Whatever you do with me, you'll have to live with that."

" 'Guilt is the mother of insomnia,' is how Dar used to put it," he said. "I sleep like a log; trust me."

"Yeah, you said that before. Just don't imagine for a minute that I won't love it when Uncle Dar gets his hands on you, Corbett. Because I think he will, one way or another, and if there's anything left afterward maybe he'll turn the pieces over to my dad."

□□□

Corbett saw the flash in those eyes, and knew that every word had been plain truth as she knew it. Which meant that she was still living someone else's lie; perhaps would continue to live it forever. It was not Kyle Corbett's place to tell her, now or ever, that she was not the niece of Dar Weston.

She was Weston's only child.

SIXTEEN

BRIEFING THE DIRECTOR OF CENTRAL INTELLIgence on the scrambler line, Dar had a channel as secure as NSA could make it. He retained enough awareness of his surroundings to circle a thumb and forefinger for Terry Unruh, who was manhandling a color copier into their jury-rigged ops center. "Just myself and Terry. Yes, he and Ullmer both know she's my niece, I wouldn't have been smart to hide it. . . . No, FBI is treading very gently; I'm a little surprised. I suppose we have you to thank for that, Abe. . . . I see. Well, a foreign perpetrator is still plausible, but I don't think it's true. Witnesses all claim he sounded beer-and-Rambo American."

Although domestic cases of this sort would ordinarily be covered by the Federal Bureau of Investigation, Randolph obviously had his own reasons for wanting CIA to handle it. In a sense it was fortunate that the operation had involved a deal by foreign nationals, and was expected to cross national borders, because now it was not entirely a domestic matter for the FBI. Using that as his wedge, Randolph had obtained White House approval for his agency's involvement. Foy's NSA was deeply involved because Black Stealth One was, after all, their bird. Now all three of the nation's biggest intelligence agencies would be working "together," though always, always in competition. And Abraham Randolph's neck was out a mile, Dar thought, and Abe knew it. If CIA could not get that airplane back, someone very senior would be in for a long fall.

Dar moved aside as Unruh, doing scutwork ordinarily handled by lesser people, patched in two more telephone lines near him, and turned away to speak. It was rare that a top-level conversation proceeded in such chaos. But then, it was equally rare for top-level men to take such an active role as Dar's. That role was permitted to him only because he *was* playing it inside CONUS, the national borders.

"There's Ullmer, of course, and his man Medina; and I expect Sheppard will be landing here any minute. Ullmer insists on being in on the chase with me. . . . How can I, Abe? Besides, the man knows what Black Stealth One can do. I'll be glad to have him. . . . Negative, the less Medina knows, the better, since he'll be running pretty much in the open and he's in a very burnable position. Medina would never get it into his head that—well, Ben Ullmer himself says the Blue Sky craft is obsolete. If the Sovs already have Black Stealth One, the older aircraft is beside the point and no great loss to us. But if they *don't* have Black Stealth One, then maybe they'll grab Medina's crashed offering and run off with the pieces, and that at least buys us more time.

"But we're not talking policy with Medina. Besides, he's scheduled out on a McDonnell almost anytime now. I think they'll get in-flight refueling between here and San Diego, then Marine Harriers will set the team down in Mexico before dark. . . . Only Medina plus two deniables, Mexican nationals he'll pick up in San Diego."

This time, Dar waited patiently for a long minute. Then, "I thought we'd settled that, Abe. Just one little push right now, with relations as touchy as they are, and Mexico could be another Iran. If their Federal Bureau of Security gets wind of this and sends plainclothes *Federales* into Regocijo, the main thing that'll matter is whether our people can evade. Our Mexicans are plausible and Medina claims he could pass and make it out alone. More people just might tempt a firefight on Mexican soil. . . . No, actually it was Unruh's argument, but I'm backing him."

Dar looked up as Unruh ushered in a newcomer. "Wup; Bill Sheppard just walked in. I'm sure he'll know what Foy wants to do about the—the hostage situation." He could not say, "my niece"; he wanted to say, "the daughter I have plausibly denied for twenty-two years," but that would have reversed Abe Randolph's decision instantly, to say nothing of the repercussions later. "I simply don't know how, Abe. Somebody on the other side did his homework, that's all. . . . I'll call her parents myself later, when I know what spin to put on the news."

"Spin" was a grotesque way to put it, he realized. The decision was not yet firm whether the United States Government would decide to send Petra spinning to her death as an expendable casualty the moment it got the chance. Abe Randolph had made his choice clear the instant he got Dar on the phone: regardless of the hostage's identity, he'd said, she was not *a* prime consideration. Thanks to the predictable reaction of the popular media, she was *the* prime consideration. CIA had taken its lumps for a certain callousness in the past—"its formerly sanguinary views," in Abe's dry parlance.

In one compartment of his mind, Dar was wondering whether the Director of Central Intelligence would have made the same decision had he not been flashed the news of Petra's identity. That was the kind of question he must never ask; it was prying at the teeth of a gift horse. Randolph had given him the option of continuing to ramrod this thing, and Dar had chosen to stay. Though Dar had always felt the highest respect for Abraham Randolph, never before had he felt like hugging the man.

Dar put the phone down, sighed, and shook hands with the wiry little scholar, Bill Sheppard. "You've met Unruh," he said, trying to maintain a pose of briskness when he felt like bursting into tears.

Sheppard, looking a bit rumpled in shirtsleeves with his tie askew, was trying not to stare. "You're handling this directly? Under the circumstances I'm, ah, sure it can't be easy for you." Of course

□ □ □

Sheppard would know about Petra already. It had been foolish to hope otherwise.

"I'm just following policy on this, Bill, not making it." He realized how edgy that had sounded, when he needed all the diplomacy at his command. He forced a smile and indicated the coffee bar with its pile of doughnuts nearby. "You and I get to chew over the tactics, and you can start by chewing on a glazed old-fashioned if you like. Oh, and an APB you may want to edit. We've just finished it," he said, handing over the printout. Some version of that all-points bulletin would soon be issuing from laser printers in several states. That APB would have been out already were it not for the need to coordinate everything this way, face-to-face, with a sister agency. All this complication was buying time for the other side.

Dar noted that Bill Sheppard continued to eye him quietly as the NSA deputy strayed toward the doughnuts and coffee, studying Dar over the top of the APB. Certainly it wasn't going to be easy, but perhaps easier than going back to his office in Langley and ramming his head against the wall. The hardest part might be having to tell Phil and Andrea to be ready for the worst. He would say that in any case, but there were ways to imply good reason to hope, and ways to deny much hope. It occurred to him suddenly that he had no real choice on that call; whatever the decision here in Blue Hangar, he would have to shore up Andrea's courage until the last shred of his own hope was gone. Until, in fact, he had seen Petra's body, so near an exact copy of her mother's . . .

Moments later, the door from the offices flew open as Medina entered with Ben Ullmer in tow.

□□□

". . . unless you have to. Listen to me, Medina: *we don't give a shit about the fuckin' airchine.* It's a gift; bust it up, but not so much that you lose your hide for it. Oh hi, Bill, with you in a minute." Medina carried a leather one-suiter over one shoulder and a bulky sport equipment bag at his side, saying nothing, nodding frequently as he swivel-hipped his flamenco dancer's rump between folding chairs and into the hangar proper, merely using the place as a shortcut toward the runway with Ullmer hurrying after. Ullmer continued until they were out of earshot: "Recheck the pressure in those scuba tanks. If we had a KH-12 available, I could get us a steady satellite link but that's out. . . ."

Dar met Sheppard's gaze, and both men smiled sadly. "Ben wants to go himself," Dar said.

"Wouldn't that be a picture? High blood pressure, corns the size of manhole covers, and a Georgia accent thick as candlewax. But that's not why he's so anxious," Sheppard replied slowly, making a scientific experiment of dunking his doughnut. "Ben loves his people. He wants to empty his entire brain into Medina's, give his man the benefit of every scintilla of knowledge he's accumulated in over sixty years."

"But he can't."

"Of course he can't. But he can't stop himself from rattling on, thinking out loud, hoping some drop of that"—he was chuckling now—"that tsunami of words will help Medina. Whereas you and I know better."

Dar tried to make it light. "Refresh me."

Sheppard took a sopping bite, shrugged, and wiped his chin. "Nothing can help Medina but what he's already internalized over the years, plus whatever his adrenal medulla can pump out for him in the very millisecond he needs it." Sheppard's owlish gaze was mild, his stand unassailable. Almost.

"Plus luck," said Dar Weston in a choked voice, turning away so that the NSA deputy would not see the sudden upwelling of tears. He might have tried to prepare Petra for such barbarous possibilities as this, urged martial arts training, everything it took to make his daughter more than the equal of a kidnapper. Because he had not done any such thing, he had nothing left to hope for except her luck. *If Sheppard tries to lecture me on the statistical foolishness of luck I will throttle him with my bare hands.*

"Oh yes, that's a given," said Sheppard around another soggy mouthful. "Problem is, it's given randomly on all sides."

A distant surge of white noise, accompanied by keening whistles, suggested something very much more potent than a Learjet taxiing into the distance. Ben Ullmer hurried in with that sore-footed stride moments later, scratching his bald pate and muttering.

Sheppard: "How is Medina taking it, Ben?"

Ullmer: "The dumb shit, he's just happy to be in a Phantom Two. He'll be in Dago in less'n three hours, meeting those Company mercenaries for the last leg. I expect that's when he'll start taking it all seriously." His sigh would have been appropriate for a wayward son. "I wonder where the hellbug is now," he added.

"It has to be down," said Sheppard, "unless the pilot expects to glide it to Moscow." Scanning the big wall map, he went on, "He's got to have fuel dumps along the way, and some help. It just won't play any other way unless the man is crazy."

"The hellbug will soar," Ullmer replied, "especially without much of a fuel load." He pulled up a folding chair, reached for a doughnut, thought better of it. Seated at a worktable with Dar and Sheppard, he studied the deletions Sheppard had made in the APB while Terry Unruh, lost in his own thoughts, paced behind them.

"Looks good, I guess I was saying too much," Ullmer said, dropping the page with the neat lines Sheppard had drawn through a few phrases. "Except one place. You cut out the caution against destroying the hellbug."

Dar took a deep breath, but held his silence. "You can build another one, Ben. The Sovs will be monitoring radio traffic and chances are overwhelming they'll realize the airplane can become visually low-observable on demand. That's okay, so long as they don't find out how. We're giving them a chameleon paint job as it is. But the real pixel skin must not be seen by the other side, not even a piece of it," said Sheppard.

"I'm thinking about the girl," Ullmer said, "and you know it. She's not a ringer or a copilot. She's a goddamn hostage. Must be twenty people who know that already. You want the Feebs holding that over you?"

Very softly, pulling at his tie and with a glance toward Dar that might have contained guilt, Sheppard said, "That decision is over my head, Ben. Like Dar, I'm not making policy, I'm just implementing it."

Ullmer licked his lips and nodded, glancing to

□□□

Dar, then to Sheppard. "Say we find the hellbug well inside the continental U.S., where we can try to force it down. What does policy say about that?"

"Judgment call," Sheppard said. "But it may be in Canada already, or near the border." He shifted position to peer at Dar. "Do you know how much I hate this, Weston?"

One of the telephones rang. Before Dar could reach it, Terry Unruh had snaked an arm out. "Ops center; Bumblebee here."

He's already given us code names for this, thought Dar. *And I don't even know mine yet.* "For the record, the DCI has made the hostage's welfare the prime factor. I won't pretend I'm not relieved."

Unruh, holding the phone against his chest, said, "Mr. Ullmer: Black Stealth One runs on aviation gas?"

"One hundred, one-thirty," Ullmer nodded. Dar thought he saw something in Unruh's face: fear, or excitement.

Unruh persisted, "Could it fly from here to Sugar Grove, West Virginia, without refueling?"

Dar's "Christ! Have they found her?" was lost among two other voices.

Ben Ullmer knocked his chair over getting to the ladder, where he stretched the tape. "It's an easy reach," he said over his shoulder.

"Fifteen gallons of avgas were stolen early this morning from the chopper pad up the valley from your own facility in Sugar Grove," Unruh said. "With your permission, I'm going to call for a microsearch of the area," he said, looking at Dar.

"Do it," said Dar and Sheppard simultaneously.

While Unruh spoke earnestly into the phone, Dar strode to the map. He watched Ullmer swing

□□□

an arc from Sugar Grove to St. Louis, past Memphis, then southeast to Jacksonville, Florida. Then the grease pencil dashed a straight line starting at Elmira, passing through Sugar Grove. The line continued through Tallahassee and, with Ullmer squatting to complete the line, into the Gulf of Mexico.

Dar's smile was not very convincing as he turned to Sheppard. "Not much to go on, is it?"

"No. Not enough to send us chasing down a grease-pencil line in a Lear," Sheppard agreed.

Unruh cradled the phone and looked up from his notes as Dar patted his shoulder. "You sent out a query for thefts of avgas, I take it," said Dar.

"By way of the Feebs," said Unruh, "I mean the Bureau."

"Quick thinking," said Sheppard.

"Very," Unruh assented, "an hour ago. But not mine. Mr. Ullmer's assistant, Marie. Said if I didn't, she'd ask them herself."

Ben Ullmer had a laugh like a farm pump, and did not use it often. "She would," he said, subsiding. "Any other suspicious stuff like that?"

"Since early today, only two more reported," Unruh said. "A holdup for five gallons of unleaded in Queens, and a hot-wired station pump in Algona, Iowa."

"Hey, wait a minute. That Iowa thing just might be possible," said Ullmer, glaring at the map.

Unruh: "For diesel fuel?"

Ullmer's baleful look said he'd been swindled. "Another good call. How'd you know it couldn't be diesel?"

Unruh blinked. "Well, I didn't think airplanes used it."

□□□

"Not many do," Ullmer said grudgingly. "Bill, if it comes to a vote on the hostage—"

"Only two votes count here," Sheppard cut in, checking his wristwatch. His meaning was clear: CIA and NSA. And every second of delay counted against them. Sheppard threw his pencil down and leaned forward, elbows on the table. "Weston, I'll compromise if you will. I'll reinstate the phrase that prohibits forcing it down."

"If?"

"If you'll agree to taking it down, any way possible, the moment we have solid evidence that it's within a hundred miles of our borders."

"The shoreline is a border. Fifty miles," Dar countered. "Solid evidence means visual contact."

"Would you compromise on seventy-five?"

An agonized pause. "If I must," Dar sighed.

With a single abrupt nod, Sheppard committed himself. "Agreed. Here, get this thing into the computer," he said, handing the printout to Ullmer.

"I'll take it to the Bureau," Unruh said, waiting for Ben to make erasures. "It goes to everybody with dedicated aircraft, right? Army, Navy, Marines, Air Force, Coast Guard, Air National Guard units, and state highway patrols."

Dar nodded and felt a massive weight lift from his shoulders as Unruh darted out. At least he'd bought Petra a little time.

Dar, studying the map, mused, "We may be able to limit the individual states' involvement to those along the Eastern seaboard. The governors have the power to refuse, you know."

"That's what martial law is for," Sheppard snapped. "It would also let us ground all private aircraft. Make the job a lot easier."

□□□

Dar almost laughed. "You can't."

"The hell you say," Sheppard said, perplexed.

"*Ex parte Milligan,* Supreme Court decision," Dar explained quickly. "Martial law can't be applied where the civil courts are functioning. I hear they're still in business, Bill."

"I didn't know you were a lawyer."

"I'm not. I've just heard the argument in Security Council meetings. Personally I'd declare martial law myself if I could. I guess that's why the court said 'no.' "

The telephone buzzed. "What's my code name on this?" Sheppard asked.

"Christ, I don't know," Dar said, and grabbed the receiver. "Ops center, Bumblebee here," he lied.

Ullmer and Sheppard watched in silence. "My God, that's wonderful," he said, closing his eyes as if in prayer. "Certainly didn't take you long. Any other tidbits? . . . It's enough. Well done; you've earned a commendation." He simply could not remain seated, but stood up, stretching, wiping his face to remove the moisture at the corners of his eyes.

"Well?" Sheppard was a patient man, but within limits.

"They're analyzing fresh human excrement and scuff marks less than a mile from the chopper pad. And they've found a piece of duct tape. With right thumb and forefinger prints of the hostage, clear and unequivocal."

Ullmer was up instantly. "Let's fire up that Lear and fly down the line," he said, pointing to the wall map.

"This is my post for the duration," Sheppard said to Dar. "Weston, this isn't an official objection but—what can you do in a Learjet that a squadron of naval aviators can't do better?"

Dar, without hesitation: "Make decisions about what that squadron does."

"Well, this *is* official, from Dernza: we doubt you're the right man to make those decisions in a midair confrontation. I just wanted you to know."

"Let's leave the second-guessing for debriefing, shall we?" Dar's voice was tight, but steady.

Sheppard, softly: "No offense intended. You're leaving Unruh here?"

"As my deputy," Dar nodded, feeling the surge of adrenaline course down his arms and legs.

"And, Ben," Sheppard continued as the others reached for luggage, "don't make me ask for frequent bulletins."

"We'll keep you in the loop," Dar said, pausing at the edge of a partition. "I still don't even know our code names yet. You'll find Unruh is so efficient it'll scare you."

SEVENTEEN

"WE'RE TURNING," THE GIRL SAID, LOOKING UP from the video monitor.

"Can't fool you for a minute," he said laconically, easing the stick upright again. With no power-assist for the controls, the craft needed severe steering and more muscle power than Corbett liked. *Have to bitch at Medina about that,* he thought idly. *And he'll tell me I'm just getting old, and we'll both be right.* He kept an eye on the contrails on his western horizon, four fast jets streaking north at medium altitude.

"Your repartee stinks, Corbett."

"You're just browned because you can't find the paint program either," he said, and saw her jaw tighten. "Look, I'm sorry; I know it's frustrating. And we're turning a few points southeast because there's usually choppy air over Atlanta."

"Uh-huh. Not to mention a few million people," she said dryly. "I think I see it under the haze to the southwest."

"That's it. Plus Dobbins Air Force Base, which doesn't thrill me. We've got to thread our way around a lot of military bases in these parts. I've spotted more contrails than I like in the past half hour or so, and they're radioing a lot of negatives on several channels. They could be searching."

"Then why come this way?"

"Because," he said patiently, "Okefenokee is about two and a half hours from here."

She gritted her teeth and swore at the video terminal, cleared the display and sat back, rubbing her forehead. Then she snapped her head around. "Is that where you're delivering this? A Florida *swamp?*"

"Not delivering, just parking; and Okefenokee's mostly in Georgia. I don't think anybody will realize how far we can stretch a tank of avgas. We've saved an hour's fuel riding Blue Ridge thermals and—let's just say I need to get to Florida. But first I'll need to refuel, and if I were flying search grids, the last place I'd look for this airplane is in a cypress swamp." He delivered a solemn wink and then put his forefinger to his right ear, turning up the gain on the radio. "Oh shit," he said softly.

He had set the second radio on a police frequency scan pattern only as an afterthought, because highway patrol aircraft flew at heights and speeds similar to his own. The good news: it had paid off. The bad: some Georgia bear in the air had spotted them.

Unlike military pilots, airborne highway patrolmen used little jargon to their home bases. "You betcha," an educated Georgia cracker was saying, "looks just lahk your description. No insignia; scary-lookin' thang. If it had a tail it'd look lahk a dragonfly, but it doesn't have one. I'm patrollin' Route Eighty-five north of Athens and he's maybe fahv miles west of me. 'Bout eight thousand feet headin' south, maybe southeast, a hunderd knots or so. Over to you, Thirty-one."

Crackle. A female dispatcher's voice: "Wait one." Crackle. Corbett felt centipedes of tension crawling up the back of his neck as he waited. Then the same voice: "Remain in visual contact, Eighty-three fifty-three, but do not approach. Give me exact coordinates and expect a flight of Air Force jets to take over surveillance."

Black Stealth One was at seventy-five hundred feet, and had passed a highway arterial moments before. The little city of Athens, Georgia, lay on the southeast horizon. No question about it, the search was on and now it was becoming a chase.

"Sorry, I need the video," he said to the girl, and swung it toward him. A yellow key labeled "AFT SCAN" lay apart from the computer keys. His first discovery on the keyboard was that one press gave him a rearview, the second press returned him to the computer—a feature he had not expected. Thanks to video scanners linked to the computer, Corbett could see around the gaping mouth of the fuselage. As he moved a tiny joystick next to that yellow key, the video scanned the skies behind. In his right ear he could hear coordinates that sounded right, and this was no time to check the chart to be sure.

"What's happening?" The girl's sharp glances took in every motion he made: the toylike rearview adjustment, his quick movement on the throttle, his own glances into the vast volume of air ahead with clots of gleaming cloud.

Above all, thought Corbett, *I can't have her panicky.* "Change of pace. We're going to hide out awhile in cloud cover." The hellbug's acceleration was gentle but firm while it climbed as if to divert around a huge, flat-bottomed cottony cumulus to the south. *If I make any sudden correction right now he'll know I'm monitoring him.* Corbett switched the left-hand radio to the "guard" frequency, but heard nothing.

"Something spooked you, Corbett, I want to know what to expect," said the girl.

"Ah, there he is," Corbett muttered, nodding toward the video. As he twisted the tiny stick on the keyboard, a silvery spot became magnified until it became a small airplane, seen almost head-on from slightly above as it followed them. "God damn, a bird dog! Petra, there's a Georgia state cop in an old Cessna One-seventy hanging back there. In the Air Force we called it an 'L-Nineteen bird dog.' I can probably outrun and outclimb him, but he's called for help and I expect he'll get it."

"What do you want me to do?" Her voice was very small.

"I need the video to watch for something a hell of a lot faster," he shrugged. "Just snug your harness up." They passed fleeting wisps of cloud that lurked like pilotfish near the huge white mass to their left, and Corbett waited until one of the larger wisps hid their view to the rear.

Then, at full throttle, he flicked the control stick hard to the left and pulled it back. The craft responded in a hard bank to the left, sweeping directly into the solid mass of cloud. The effect was exactly the same as driving very fast into a fogbank, with the added charm of sudden bumps that alternately lifted them from their seats and pressed them downward.

As the girl gasped in terror at porpoising headlong through fog at a hundred and fifty miles an hour, Corbett throttled back and watched the altimeter, continuing to bank the gossamer craft in a turbulent upward spiral. After a long thirty seconds, they broke out of the cloud top with dramatic suddenness. Corbett applied more throttle but pressed his feet on the pedals, feeling the bite of harness as his body tried to lunge toward the windscreen.

"Nice thing about the waste gates," he said to the girl, "is that you can put on the brakes like nobody would believe." He began to rotate the craft without banking, one eye on the compass, and then cautiously eased downward into cloud again. At that moment, in an aircraft expressly designed for utter quiet, they heard the rasp of an air-cooled engine pass very near and diminish ahead of them. They nosed out from the southern end of the cloud then, moving very slowly on jets of diverted wastegate air that supported them like a three-legged stool. Corbett adjusted the waste gates, seeing a flash of aluminum as the Cessna disappeared around the cloud in a gentle bank.

"We're going sideways," the girl exclaimed.

"I wasn't sure it would," Corbett admitted, and pressed a finger against his right ear.

"Must have gone into a cloud," he heard the state trooper say. "This is bumpy stuff, Thirty-one, I'm gonna hang around and see where he comes out."

□□□

"We copy," said the dispatcher. "Uh, the Air Force needs your exact coordinates. Any maps in there?"

"Somewhere," said the Cessna pilot. "Stand by."

Inside Black Stealth One, Corbett listened and fumed. He could not loiter here forever, but the next cloud in a southerly direction lay several minutes away, and it showed signs of developing the towering hammerhead shape that warned of severe turbulence. A cloud like that could literally twist the wings from a light aircraft. He throttled back until the great swept wing barely crawled across the underbelly of the cloud, circling lazily, the right wingtip grazing vagrant wisps of white, flexing in pockets of clear turbulence.

He punched the yellow key and swung the video toward the girl. "You may as well take this, it's not much use to me right now."

She addressed the keyboard reluctantly, with repeated nervous glances outside. "Would you mind telling me what we're doing now, Corbett?"

"We're parked with the motor running," he grunted. "They've got to come down under the clouds to see us, and Air Force jets gobble fuel at low altitude. Find the damned paint program, I'm busy."

The Cessna pilot had radioed his position at eighty-three degrees, forty minutes longitude, thirty-three degrees, fifty-five minutes latitude. Directly ahead, Corbett could see a small paved runway flanked on one side by neatly aligned aircraft, two of them with the sticklike, incredibly elongated wings of sailplanes. The chart on his knee said it should be the sailplane base outside of Monroe, Georgia.

□□□

The rising, then falling rasp of a nearby engine signaled another pass by the Cessna. Corbett did not see its aluminum hide until the patrol pilot, banking abruptly to the right, dropped the nose of the bird dog and began a shallow dive toward the south. Corbett eased his own craft up into the fleecy belly of his cloud, perplexed. Why would the Cessna break off its pursuit?

The patrol pilot's next transmission explained a lot. "Thirty-one, this is Eighty-three fifty-three, fugitive sighted southwest of me near the Monroe strip, no more'n a thousand feet off the deck. Could be in the landing pattern. Don't see him raght now but I got a glimpse. He sure got there in a hurry. Hold your horses."

"Your help should be on-station soon," the dispatcher replied. "I'm dispatching units from Route Twenty to that airstrip. Standing by," she added calmly.

Corbett eased downward into the clear, still in the shadow of the cumulus, and at that instant he saw the achingly clean lines of an Air Force F-16 as it streaked overhead in the distance, a deadly silver dart with a rakishly underslung intake duct. Before Black Stealth One nosed into its foggy haven again, Corbett had spied the second interceptor plummeting in a long arc toward the Monroe strip, its drag brakes already extended to slow its ferocious plunge.

The turbulence in his cloud, Corbett knew, could grow from gentle to lethal at any time. Merely to kiss its edges was inviting catastrophe, but he could see no better choice. He steered north by compass for what seemed an age, breaking out of the cloud again and throttling up to rise near its bulbous tops.

Presently, though he did not manage to intercept the military frequency, Corbett heard the disgust of the Cessna pilot. "It was a sailplane, Thirty-one. He's so slow he's still on final approach. I tell you flat out, that looks different from the airplane I was followin'."

Black Stealth One, meanwhile, slid into the open toward another cloud to the east. Because a cloud constantly changes shape, Corbett could see through occasional rifts that the Cessna was now bird-dogging another cloud somewhat above and westward a few miles, sniffing around the wispy perimeter, its pilot too cagy to risk plunging into that ugly gray mass.

Presently the girl looked up. "I can't concentrate. It feels like we're bouncing around."

"We are," Corbett nodded, and tapped his right ear, grinning. "The highway cop lost track of which cloud we ducked into. Maybe because prevailing winds are taking the clouds northeast, or maybe because their shapes have changed so much. Damn, I wish I could find the frequency those blue-suiters are using."

"Talk sense, Corbett."

"Air Force jocks, a pair of General Dynamics F-16's—*there,*" he pointed suddenly toward the heavens to his right. "Look ahead of that faint contrail for the silver speck." But almost as soon as she looked up, the nearby edges of cloud cover sealed off the view. "Those guys are practically falling out of the sky, Petra; they can't fly as slow as the Cessna so they're circling the cloud at a steep angle. Pull out five thousand feet off the deck, zoom up to twenty-five thou or so, around and around the wrong cloud, waiting for us to pop out. I don't think the bird dog has much credibility left," he chuckled.

Petra merely "hmphed" and studied the video monitor again. Corbett did not add that, to use his best cloud cover, he was moving east of his course. At this rate he'd be over the Atlantic when his fuel ran out, but Corbett did not abandon his tactic until the twin-jet Thunderbolt sizzled across the sky some distance ahead, into the region circled by interceptors. Meant for close support of troops on a battlefield, the craft had the lines of an airborne tow truck. Its pilot gave no sign he had seen them.

As it happened, Petra was looking up at the time. "Boy, now that's *ugly,*" she said.

"Good God," Corbett muttered. "This place is going to be wall-to-wall airplanes." There was nothing to be gained by telling the girl that an A-10, a Fairchild Thunderbolt, was built around a rapid-fire cannon that could obliterate a tank. *Oh yes, it's an ugly bastard. And it can loiter a lot slower than a Mach two interceptor.*

Black Stealth One surged on toward a series of puffy cloudlets that seemed deceptively near. Corbett chafed at his slow pace, expecting to be jumped at any moment, sliding down an imaginary line that might keep him hidden a few moments longer. He dared not approach the ground too closely because from miles above, a young pilot's sharp eye could spot a hedge-hopping aircraft more easily than the same aircraft flying somewhat higher.

"Corbett"—the girl sighed—"I just can't break in

any further than the second menu in this thing. Are you sure there's a 'paint' program in here?"

He could not say, "Speedy swore that it was there," nor any similar assurance, else she might recall it later; and Medina would suffer for it. "I know it's what this airchine is all about. It had better be in there," he grumbled.

"All I've found is the main menu, and the secondary."

"Secondary?" He was damned if he'd admit, again, just how little he knew about computers. Some fine airplanes had been designed with slide rules, and Kyle Corbett had rarely used anything more sophisticated than a hand calculator. "Show me," he demanded.

"Here it is." Her fingers flew over the keys, and the screen passed from the main menu after she keyed "Subrout."

He watched the saffron text scroll down the screen, thinking idiotically that if he had a quirt he could lean out and whip the damned airplane a little faster. "'Protect Xmit,' no; 'Flir,' no; 'Fueldump,' 'Xsec,' 'Pixel,' whatever that is; 'Submun'—"

"What's a flir?"

Pronouncing it correctly as she had, to rhyme with "cheer," made him smile. He enunciated each letter for her. "Forward-looking infrared," he explained. "Good to have it but that's not what we're looking for. Or are we?" He'd used FLIR in its primitive days and, if he knew Ben Ullmer, this version would be state-of-the-art stuff. Maybe good enough to spot a distant aircraft before it could spot the hellbug. "Try it, Petra."

□□□

She did, watching the golden scroll, lifting her brows in unspoken question.

He read the basic instructions, ignoring the thin scrawl of a fresh contrail that arrowed far above them, concentrating on the illustration which depicted the screen and keyboard. Evidently, once he pressed the "execute" key, the tiny keyboard stick could be twisted to adjust the FLIR gain. By moving the stick he could scan in all directions, including rearward.

Corbett hit the key. "Now you're talkin'," he breathed. The image had false color, painting a pink tinge to the image of the cloud ahead where it reflected bright sunlight. He twisted the stick; the cloud grew red, even better defined than with the naked eye. He diminished the gain and saw the cloud fade to a faint pink. A hard pinpoint of scarlet inched slowly across the bottom of the screen.

Petra pointed at the scarlet dot. "What's moving?"

"It's not, we are. Somebody burning trash, I guess; see the smoke?"

He reduced the hellbug's power as they neared their target, a somewhat smaller cloud with fuzzily defined edges. Skirting the thing, Corbett moved the tiny stick for a rearview, which caused a dizzying shift on the screen. "This is more like it," he said. A full half-dozen crimson dots moved across the screen, growing larger and smaller, winking off and on, in a mesmerizing dance. "Those guys are thirty miles away," he said. "Infrared won't penetrate clouds much, that's why their emissions keep disappearing in the center of our screen."

Petra's engineering curiosity seemed to be growing stronger than her fears. "Those are jet exhausts, aren't they? I count eight—nine," she said as he aimed their canopy toward another cloud to the northeast. "That patrol guy sure has a swarm of help for somebody who lacks credibility."

"I hope they have a nine-way pileup—ah, no I don't really," he admitted. "I just want to see 'em dwindle to nothing."

"Some of 'em are just a single pixel already," she observed. "Fading to pink."

"Okay," he said, adjusting the screen to show the view ahead, "I'll bite. What's a pixel?"

She stared at him with disbelief that infuriated him because it held amusement. "A pixel," she said, "is the basic dot that makes up everything on a video screen. You really didn't know?"

"Screw you, kid." He took a deep breath, let it out slowly, then said with less asperity, "You mean, whatever you see on that screen, words or pictures, it all comes down to a pattern of pixels."

"Sure," she said.

Each staring into the other's face, they said it simultaneously: "PIXEL!"

Corbett tapped gentle fingers against her wrist as she reached for the keyboard. "Not yet, Petra. For all we know, it'll start out by turning us into a goddamn billboard. First let's snug up under that next pile of cumulus and let the IR do its thing."

She smiled and nodded, settling back, the pleasure still evident in her face even though he was not yet certain they had located the paint program. *Lordy but that's a great smile,* he thought. *I wish she wouldn't do it. What kind of man does it take to drag a kid with a smile like that into a sky full of young bucks trying to whack us out of it?* He knew what kind of man it took, no matter what the stakes. He could take no comfort in knowing that only the ultimate betrayal could have made him into such a man.

Lurking beneath the flat gray bottom of the cloud, using his waste gates at half throttle, Corbett slowed the hellbug to scarcely over thirty knots. Far to the south, the screen revealed a dozen tiny reddish dots that waxed and waned like fireflies on some distant planet. From due north, a faint pink dot grew into a tiny, short-tailed comet, but its color did not intensify.

Corbett found it easy to translate the screen's coordinates into the real world; he saw the silvery gleam of the little executive jet when it was still fifteen miles away, banking toward them. Easing the throttle forward, he adjusted the waste gates and let the hellbug levitate straight up until it penetrated a few yards into the murk of the cloud. Hovering in the gloom, with virtually no forward speed, Corbett could still feel soft bumps and hear subtle creaks in the structure of Black Stealth One.

"Thanks to my computer expert," he said, "I knew this guy was heading our way before I could see him. You've got to understand, I'm a few years behind the times. Not by choice."

She shrugged and said nothing, watching the screen. Because of the cloud's absorption of infrared light, the screen was now featureless. Then a keening whistle dopplered up, became lost in a white-noise roar, and faded into the distance. "I guess the good guys don't like to go through clouds," Petra said wryly.

"Good practice to avoid 'em," Corbett replied, letting the hellbug drop slowly out of the cloud,

□□□

using his waste gates to pivot the entire ship. "Even for a Citation."

"Doesn't sound macho enough to be military," she said.

"Nope, an executive jet," he said, adjusting the screen to locate the aircraft again. He saw it then, racing away to the south, and noted the distinctive high horizontal tail. "Only it's not a Citation, it's a Learjet."

"Okay to try the pixel program?"

He could have kissed her for that. In spite of everything she seemed anxious only to solve a high-tech riddle, even though the solution would shorten the odds against her captor. "Have at it. Just don't let me catch you printing your name across the wings."

"Could it really do that?" She was already keying into the secondary menu.

"I don't know. I'm the guy who didn't know what a pixel was, remember?"

She giggled, perhaps at the self-disgust in his tone, and then she found the paint program. Corbett thought it fitting that the program would be camouflaged under a word he could not recognize without the help of a college girl.

And every passing minute took them farther to the south, but used up more precious fuel. Corbett found enough thermals to stretch his time aloft, but that fuel gage inexorably counted down the pounds of fuel left in his single tank. By the time the girl executed their first chameleon attempt with the pixel skin, less than four gallons of fuel remained in the tank of Black Stealth One.

EIGHTEEN

"IF YOU'RE GONNA KEEP MOVING AROUND," SAID Ullmer, "better put on your helmet. Could get bumpy up ahead."

Dar had been peering from portholes of the Learjet's cabin, an upholstered tube scarcely wider than a man's reach, shifting sides every time his anxiety demanded it. The Lear banked gracefully, giving wide berth to a lump of cumulus, and turned west at over five hundred miles an hour. Dar squinted at the brilliant multiple halo surrounding the cloud, let his gaze roam ahead toward the region where their first definite sighting had been reported. For an instant, something in the north face of the nearby cloud brushed the edge of his vision, a glimpse so fleeting that it did not register as anything more than a faint dark line. To Dar Weston, it registered as a tiny portion of the horizon seen through cloud. It was the wingtip of Black Stealth One, protruding from cloud-wisp forty miles from its reported position. "Pretty smooth so far," Dar said, but buckled himself into the seat across from Ullmer.

"Some cloud cover building to the south." Ullmer nodded out his porthole. "Not much for us, but it might be rough on the hellbug." He had patched in his headset to the NSA console that took up most of the partition separating the cabin from the Lear's pilot. Long ago, Ben Ullmer had found that he could listen to three designers argue simultaneously. It was even easier to monitor three channels, a feat he found possible on the NSA console. Its video display, similar to Corbett's, began to show moving pink pixels that brightened as he watched. The exhaust of Black Stealth One had not registered because Ben himself had supervised the routing of its exhaust for maximum cooling inside the central duct.

Dar, plugging his headset in, heard his own pilot say, "Blue leader, Lear three-two-eight entering your airspace, speed five-zero-zero knots at one-zero thousand five hundred, bearing two-seven-five magnetic, with Wasp and Hornet, over."

With frequent scrambled voice communication to Elmira, Dar had known for two hours that Terry Unruh had coded him as "Hornet," Ullmer as "Wasp." Mindful that the pilot of Black Stealth One might be monitoring any available frequency, Unruh had also passed certain instructions to military air commands by land line—a channel not available to the hellbug. The men combing the enormous volume of space near Athens, Georgia, knew far more than they were supposed to say on

□□□

any radio channel. They knew, for example, that they could engage that tailless wraith only as directed by Hornet or Wasp.

A young, hard voice responded, "Roger, Lear three-two-eight, I have you on scope but no bandit to report on radar, IR, or visual. That initial sighting may have been in error unless bandit can hover in a cloud indefinitely."

"Wasp here, Blue leader," Ullmer cut in. "That's a possible affirmative depending on how good he is, over."

"You've got us curious to see him, Wasp. Want someone to try flushing him out? We have an A-ten on the deck, and Navy at three-zero thousand. A pair of Broncos stationed at five thousand, they claim they can loiter in pea soup."

"Don't do that," Dar exclaimed, forgetting what radio protocols he knew. Ullmer's glance was surprised but not hostile. Flushing slightly, Dar went on, "Uh, Hornet here, Blue leader. Be advised the pilot is not alone, over." *You could kill my daughter, you callous idiot,* he raged inwardly.

"Wilco, Hornet," said the F-16 pilot, in the bored, "no-sweat" tones cultivated by fighter pilots. "We can widen our pattern. I've got four-zero minutes fuel left. Red flight is on alert and can take up our station, over."

Ullmer saw Dar's hopeful nod. F-16's were less than ideal for this work, and Ben had offered little hope that they would succeed. Still, "Wasp to Blue leader," he said. "Understand your offer. If the Broncos hold the tight pattern, we'll circle higher while you widen your pattern. We'd appreciate your replacements."

"Wilco, Wasp. Blue leader out."

□□□

Dar leaned back, pinching the bridge of his nose as if to squash the pain building between his eyes. *A hell of a time for eye strain when I'm so near recovering my only child,* he thought. Dar was not what others would call a believer in fate, but as he pressed his face to the porthole again he wondered if this might be some kind of retribution for choosing to place his country ahead of his family.

He had recognized the choice in 'fifty-three, while engaged to the willowy, elegant Helen Longworth. Her father, CIA deputy Creighton Longworth, had made his approval plain and the match had seemed natural, even inevitable. The whole arrangement had toppled when Helen made her demand. She had grown up without her absentee father, she said, and did not intend to marry a man who spent years at overseas posts where wives were not permitted.

Helen had assumed that her father could simply adjust Dar's work, as a marketing executive might adjust the travels of a salesman. She met their explanations head-on, and eventually returned Dar's ring. Creighton Longworth observed to Dar that every parent is a Frankenstein who creates his own monsters, and continued to champion Dar in the Company. It took Dar over a year to realize that the failure had been his own: he would never consider marrying unless the woman needed him. Yet she might not see him for years at a stretch. Helen had been wise.

After that, Dar settled for alliances with women who needed him for the short term, and honorably admitted to each that he would never marry. He made certain that Creighton Longworth knew their names. He took pains to avoid any entanglement that might jeopardize his work. Until Dani Klein.

Stationed at Langley after his Near East posting, Dar made long trips to the Philippines but met Dani at a Washington soirée during a three-month stateside respite in 1964. Small and blond, Dani Klein had been born to German Jewish refugees in wartime Baltimore. The girl had gone to Europe when her parents repatriated but remained an American citizen, returning to America at age twenty-four, fluent in four languages and lively as a sparrow. A blue-eyed, freckled blonde, Dani Klein shattered Dar's stereotype of the German Jew.

He was surprised to find she thought him endearingly awkward. She was amazed to learn he thought her sexy. Perhaps, he said, it was that hint of an exotic accent in her voice. Old Longworth saw no reason why Dar should avoid a young State Department translator, leaving her Jewish background undiscussed in the Old Boy network because, of course, Dar Weston never intended to marry.

In 1966, while sharing a weekend suite at a Vermont country inn with Dani, Dar told her he would soon be leaving again. He said nothing about the Philippines or spy aircraft; only that he understood why she could not wait for him.

Dani, sitting nude and cross-legged in artless glory on sheets damp from their lovemaking, stopped him with a forefinger over his lips. "You understand nothing, my love. Why should I not wait, so long as you will come back?"

"Time moves slowly when you're young," he

□□□

said. "I could be gone six months, maybe more. It's not fair to ask that."

"Find me a fair world; I will emigrate," she replied, her gray eyes serious. "In the meantime, like you, I have my work. Even if you left me, I would have that."

He drew her into his arms, kissing her closed eyes, feeling her small perfect breasts against his body, and swore that he would never leave her by choice. They made love more frequently and more tenderly that weekend than ever before, or ever after.

To his immense surprise, Dar was brought back from the Philippines only three months later. Dani welcomed him with solemn joy and with a few more pounds that, he said, bordered on the voluptuous. On their second night together, she made one confession while hiding another.

Dani said she had originally returned to America with a secret agenda, a promise she had made to an Israeli friend after protracted talks and one very strange interview. Other Israelis had contacted her on occasion, needing small favors, nothing that even faintly smacked of espionage; she had told them she would never do that, but still—

In short, Dar Weston's lover was an agent in place, a mole for the Mossad, very likely one who would never be used in any important way. Dar, quietly furious, commanded her never to speak of it again. It was the one facet of her that he would not, could not share. "You've broken their most basic rule, Dani," he said in tones that must have frightened her. "You've told someone. Only you haven't, because I didn't hear it. If you love me,

I must never hear it again. Good Christ, I'm attached to the State Department myself! What if they decided to give me a polygraph?" Angry as he was, he did not call it a "flutter." That was spook jargon, and Dani did not know his true employment.

She promised, crossing her heart, drawing a scarlet fingernail across breasts that had grown larger in the three months of his absence, and delighting in them, he did not suspect. Perhaps, he realized later, she told him one secret to lessen the internal pressures of the greater secret she carried inside her.

His next mission involved SR-71 overflights based in Japan. The peripheral work demanded savagely long hours and took longer than it might because, so far away from Dani, Dar himself did not handle it well. Dani's letters were full of her love and joy but also, increasingly, with a shadow of something opaque which he could not identify. Her final letter to Japan, after six months, mentioned a "necessary" vacation in Canada. Dar continued to write as always, and finally returned in the summer of 1967. Dani had disappeared.

Her last letter, posted to him through State cutouts, had been held in accord with the envelope's instruction. He still had it, could recite it verbatim.

My love:

You have made your position clear on marriage. Please believe that I do not complain. My choices, all of them, were and are my responsibility. Yet I am not so strong as I thought, and for reasons sufficient for me I can no longer live for you alone in this way.

□□□

I am sure that you could find me eventually, but think hard. I beg you, do not seek me out unless you are ready for the dread rigors of the family man.

I kiss your eyes. Dani.

Dar spent one sleepless night before making the only decision he could live with, and immediately found an elation he had never known before. He called in some IOUs for aid in Canadian records and took emergency leave. It no longer mattered what cool disdain his family might show toward a Jewess. He could indeed balance a career and a marriage, if that marriage was with Dani.

He traced her through her work permit and found the address in Montreal, a three-story brick apartment house. The owner, a hefty middle-aged widow with the sad eyes of a beagle, had been an old friend of the Kleins in Germany.

She recognized Dar's name, but said that Fraulein Klein no longer lived there. She sat him down in a parlor full of knickknacks and shuffled away to make tea, which she served in ornate Austrian china.

Dar realized immediately that the woman was testing him as she sipped and probed in her solid, direct hausfrau's way. "I think I can set you at ease about my intentions," he smiled. "I intend to marry Dani, if she'll still have me." And then he showed her the letter.

The woman's reaction was unexpected. As silent tears began to slide down her cheeks, she said haltingly, "I show you this not because I choose. Because *she* chose. I hope you will walk away and leave me with—what I have of her. But kommensie," she said, and led him to a small room.

It was a pleasant room, its windows overlooking a tiny formal garden. He recognized a scarf of Dani's, hanging from a cotton string, its gay paisley print an ever-changing mobile over the crib. In the crib, an infant of perhaps three months slept.

"This is all we will have of Dani," said the woman, barely above a whisper. "She survived the birth only three days."

When he could think coherently again, Dar asked for details and got them with cheap brandy in that oppressive little parlor. The one detail of which he was certain was that he intended to keep his tiny daughter, now that he had found her. Had he not chosen to seek Dani, to marry her after all his simpleminded philosophizing, he would never have known why she had been so plump in their last times together. Nor why she had warned him that his choice involved ". . . the dread rigors of a family man."

Had Dani suspected that she might die in childbirth? He would never know. He knew only that she had chosen to bear his child, and to raise it alone if necessary. And when the tiny child awoke, crying for her bottle, it was Dar who fed her, the good hausfrau seemingly resigned to her loss already.

Dar took no chances on that. He called in one more favor and boarded a Company proprietary turboprop, flying straight to New Haven with Dani's daughter in his arms. Phil and Andrea Leigh met him at the airport, and Dar talked all the way to Old Lyme.

Andrea, for once, remained speechless for an

□□□

hour. She had chosen to remain childless for years and then, ironically, found that she was barren. To Phil's suggestion that they adopt a child, Andrea had always refused. She would raise a Weston and a Leigh, or she would remain childless. Now, with an abruptness that staggered her, Andrea faced a possibility she had never imagined. Dar Weston was prepared to raise the girl himself, but there was an alternative, one that would give Dani's child both a mother and a father who was no absentee.

To her credit, Andrea Weston Leigh was indecisive on only one point: should she obtain adoption papers, or spend a year in Vermont? Phil, with a deep understanding of social nuance among Connecticut families, made that decision, determined to raise the girl as his own.

They made only one mistake. While Andrea was dropping subtle hints about pregnancy in Old Lyme, Dar spent two weeks near Bennington, Vermont, with the tiny girl, whom Andrea had named "Petra." In that time, Dar learned how to rinse a diaper in a commode and how to test the temperature of a bottle of formula. And he learned that a man's deepest, most passionate tenderness for a woman cannot plumb the depths of his commitment as profoundly as the heartbeat of his child in his arms. By the time Andrea arrived in Vermont, Dar knew that he must somehow overcome his emotional links, become an uncle and not a father. He had sworn it, and he would do it.

For twenty-two years he thought that he had succeeded.

As Dar gazed blindly out of the Lear's porthole, he was roused from his reverie by Ben Ullmer,

□□□

who was speaking into his headset. "Go ahead, Bumblebee, Hornet's on the circuit."

Terry Unruh, in Elmira, sounded upbeat and crisp. "Forensics crew at Sugar Grove has identified your bandit, Hornet. Seems that high-octane fuel stripped away a little of the cement on his fingers. They got two partials and a thumb, no question about it."

"Don't make me wait," Dar said ominously.

"Former Snake Pit designer, reported killed in a boating accident years ago. Ex-Company too, fellow named Kyle Corbett."

"Sonofa *bitch,*" said Ullmer.

Dar could only nod, his mouth suddenly dry, his breathing shallow as a wave of heat climbed the back of his neck. How could Corbett still be alive after all the evidence to the contrary? Well, he had obviously survived and if anyone could steal that God-damned airplane, it would be Corbett. It all added up; in the intimacy of their friendship while thousands of miles from home, Dar had told Corbett things he had sworn to withhold. Kyle Corbett knew about Petra, and obviously he knew a great deal about revenge.

NINETEEN

"YEAH, THAT'S IT," SAID CORBETT, TALKING THE girl through her motions, the graceful swept wings responding to her hand on the copilot's control stick. "She's going to want to bank to the left when I'm hanging out there; drag and weight both. You've got to keep 'er on an even keel."

Petra's voice was tight, and held a quaver. "Just don't fall. You know I can't land this thing." She had seemed willing to wrestle that plastic fuel bag from its niche, but as Corbett explained his desperate move her eyes had grown round with fear.

"We're only doing forty miles an hour, Petra," he grunted, turning around so that his rump nudged the instrument console, loosening his restraint harness as far as it would go. "It ought to be easy," he said, hoping.

And it had better be damned quick, he reminded

himself. Ten pounds of fuel remained in the tank; call it a gallon and a half. They were a mile high over the swampy plains of southeastern Georgia, with twenty pounds of avgas in that bag, stinking up the cockpit with fumes. Who had decided the fuel filler cap should be mounted flush in the hellbug's skin directly behind the pilot? He couldn't recall. All that mattered now was whether he could fight the airstream, hanging halfway out of his hatch facing aft, and feed that fuel in while trusting his own hostage to keep the aircraft steady. Too many ironies to count. *Focus on hooking those straps so they loop around a thigh and an arm,* he commanded himself. *And don't think about what happens if you get hung up outside and she has to ride the hellbug down with a dead engine. Time to think about that when it happens. Meanwhile, see that it doesn't.*

Corbett forced himself to grin and wink as he opened his hatch. The girl reacted silently, as if he had just made a repulsive joke, then stared ahead. Good. Now if he could just force the hatch halfway up with his right arm and shoulder—to reach out and find—that—big—filler cap. *Got it. Few inches farther back than I thought, almost in the duct. Wind blast isn't so bad but suction toward the duct gets hairy here. Snap the cap's lever and twist. Careful; pull the cap in and drop it in the seat.* He had feared that the airstream would siphon the remaining fuel out, so he had throttled back until Black Stealth One was barely controllable by a novice. "So far, so good," he said, his head halfway out, hauling the fuel bag to the lip of the hatch. The girl did not reply.

Eighteen inches below the hatch lip lay a tiny

□□□

trapdoor, a spring-loaded fairing. It had been designed as a flush-mounted step, so that a pilot could shove inward with his toes and plant his foot during entry or exit. It remained to be seen whether he could stick his heel into that niche, while facing backward toward the hellbug's great inlet scoop. The inward curve of the skin made it fiendishly tough for a man with short, thick legs.

Facing backward, sliding his right leg over the hatch sill, Corbett found that he could not reach that foothold unless he slipped more of his other leg free of the harness; and this was not a good time for a man without a parachute to look down. Inching out, he felt his heel connect with something that yielded. He began to push down with that heel, trying to straighten his leg. Slowly, using all his strength, he began to rise, the hatch heavy across his right shoulder because of the wind load.

Corbett's sense of balance was finely honed, and he knew that the hellbug was starting a shallow bank, just as he'd said it must. He was already fumbling the fuel bag into his arms when the girl made her correction, but she made it too fast.

The drooping left wing came up swiftly, inertia forcing his face against the fuel bag, and his heel slipped from its purchase. Instantly Corbett was hanging halfway out, his right-hand trouser leg flapping as the hellbug tried to inhale him, the harness biting into the calf muscle of his left leg, the stench of avgas thick in his lungs. Corbett could hear tiny moans of anguish from the girl, almost the same sounds some women made during sexual climax. His left arm and leg strained convulsively, dragging his gonads across the sill so hard it took his breath away.

□□□

Fighting a wave of nausea from the pain, he turned his head and saw her, glancing quickly from him to the instruments and back to him, and he tried to make it seem less than the near thing it had been. "Nice try," he gasped.

"Don't say that, oh God, I'm trying," she moaned.

"Shut up. Steady as she goes," he grated, and found the step with his heel again. Still weak with the ache that radiated from between his legs, he tried three times before he could straighten his trembling right leg. He could feel the craft trying to bank, saw control surfaces move as the girl responded. Now he had the fuel bag in both hands, the hatch lip biting into his left forearm as he fumbled with his free right hand to introduce the bag's flaccid neck into the filler opening.

He took a deep breath and forced upward against the bag, tilting it, partly flattening it against the cabin skin. Fuel began to pour out. Most of it went into the filler neck, but a filmy mist of high-octane fuel began to stream backward, sucked directly into the hellbug's gaping mouth. He glanced back, focusing into the huge opening, and that was a mistake because it made him think about things he did not want to consider at this moment.

Inside the duct was a whirling blur of motion, the big impeller blades of Black Stealth One, sucking an explosive mixture of air and fuel through, hurling it out behind. The inlet's screen mesh, solid enough to deflect a bird, might keep him from being swallowed if he lost his purchase. But if that fine mist of avgas hit anything hot on its way

□□□

through, the sudden firebloom would scatter their fragments over half of Georgia.

Corbett concentrated on flattening the bag, grateful for the wide filler neck, feeling the almost imperceptible slip of his heel from its purchase in the shallow step. A half cupful of fuel sloshed out and was swallowed in an instant by whirling impeller blades. *Never again! Didn't have to risk the kid with this prehistoric in-flight refueling, could've landed and taken my chances.*

He was tiring; could actually feel the energy leaking from arms and legs as he hugged the hatch sill. A half gallon of fuel was visible, caught in a fold of the translucent plastic, and when his heel slipped from its tiny ledge this time, he was ready. His fitful lunge inward against the harness pulled his crotch across the sill, and he was able to maintain his grip on the bag only because it was nearly empty.

He dragged the bag inside, found the filler cap without looking, managed to reach outside and twist it into place without dropping it. And then he was inside again, struggling weakly from the harness loops that had saved him twice. He twisted in the seat, so drained that he could barely sit erect, and somehow managed to drag himself into his harness properly.

He reached for the control stick. "Good work," he said. "I'll take it now."

"Your face is red as a beet," she said in wonder, relinquishing her stick.

"Embarrassment," he said, and gave her a sick smile.

She raised her hands aloft, making claws of her fingers. "Aaagggh, how I hate that macho man stuff! Why don't you just admit it, Corbett? It's okay to be scared; I was scared too."

He nodded at the fuel gauge, then said, "You handle fear your way, I'll handle it my way. Sure I was scared; I've got nicotine stains in my shorts. I've also got a beer gut, which is why my face is red from huffing and puffing, okay?"

"That's honest," she said. "And speaking of stains, I, uh, I've got to go again. I really do, in the worst way."

"Go ahead. Jesus," he exclaimed suddenly, "you didn't know! There's a relief slot built into each seat, Petra. This thing was designed to fly two days without landing." He snugged back into the seat, tapped the printed legend set into the forward lip of the seat. "It's kind of self-explanatory; works for both sexes, they tell me."

He made a show of putting on his mini-tel, attending to his instruments, ignoring her as she studied the mysteries of a seat with its own small trapdoor.

After a minute or so he heard her cycling the little actuator experimentally. She muttered, "It sure isn't the Ritz. I'll have to shuck my jeans."

"Or stain 'em. Suit yourself, we'll be up here another hour if I can stretch it that far."

Another long moment while he consulted his charts again, making himself conspicuously busy. Then he heard her say, "Good lord, it even has tissue. Am I doing my doo-dahs on some poor farmer's head?"

"Fluids go through. Solid waste is retained," he said, as impersonal as he could make it while a young woman prepared to use a toilet beside him. At the moment, he was slowly gliding down from

□□□

twelve thousand feet with the engine off. At five thousand he would restart and begin a gradual climb again. It was slow, and it was chancy; but it could greatly increase their range.

Because he could hear her progress he began to hum a tune, attending to the intricacies of the "pixel" program on the video monitor.

From the girl, in strained sarcasm: "Louder music."

If she could joke about it, he could. "What would you like, Handel's Water Music?"

A chuckle, deep as a man's. "Better try the twenty-one-gun salute from the 1812 Overture."

Presently she sighed in relief. Corbett paid her little attention because he had just found the "buzzard" subroutine, and punched it in while craning his neck to see the upper surface of the wing. "It works," he breathed. "My God, how it works!"

The girl, zipping her jeans, studied the monitor. "What did you do?"

"Check the wing on your side," he suggested.

She did, and gasped. "It's—oh wow, we've got feathers, Corbett!" She laughed in sheer delight, then swapped grins with him. "Are vultures really dark brown?"

"This one is," he said. "You notice, out near the tips, the spaces between the big pinion feather patterns are tan and olive green. That probably works for anyone looking down. Can't see the underside, but—"

"Probably blue to fool people looking up," she finished for him. "It's not really perfect, from close up like this."

"Give 'em another five years," Corbett replied. "Meanwhile, when they debrief you, somebody's going to shit a brick. This is 'eyes only' stuff, Petra. For God's sake, don't even hint about it to outsiders."

She nodded and fell silent while he rechecked their position. Their path had taken them past Athens, then southward over coils of sluggish river and marshland. He saw her studying the terrain. "The town to our left is Vidalia; river's the Oconee," he said.

But she was thinking along different lines. "The longer I'm with you, the less sense you make," she mused. "Once you turn this airplane over to whoever gets it, why should—well—my uncle, for example, think it's still a secret?"

"Who said I was turning it over?"

"All right, for the sake of argument I'll pretend you won't. You give me this stuff about being a man without a country, but you don't want me to give away my country's secrets. I mean, what do you care?"

Corbett took his time, switching the monitor to FLIR mode, seeing no strong aircraft emissions. Then, savagely, "Screw 'em all. The Sov spooks, everybody else's, and especially, oh yes, *especially* Uncle Sam's alphabet soup of agencies who have no compunctions about burning a loyal employee. They've always got their reasons; screw their reasons, it's my personal ass they tried to burn." A short, unpleasant bark of a laugh. "In my case, literally burn. God damned near did it. Just pure luck they didn't."

"In some ways you can be—halfway decent, actually," she said. "I envy the education you must have had to help design this plane. But what really gets me is that you were Uncle Dar's friend. Not

□□□

one of the Old Boy net, as he calls it, but he didn't care. He doesn't make friends with bad people, Corbett."

A long sigh, as he considered telling her to shut the fuck up, maybe slapping her to drive the point home. And for some reason he found himself incapable of that. There was much that he must not tell her, but some of it? Maybe. Why the hell not? It might leak through enough offices to redden some faces, might even force one into sudden, unsought retirement. "Let me tell you a story, Petra. About two guys fishing on the Potomac."

He'd left the Company for the Snake Pit; spent years under Ben Ullmer on several special projects, he said, careful to avoid telling her things she did not need to know. He did not even hint to her of his work on new versions of the false shrubs that oriented themselves aerodynamically, falling from a Lockheed Quietship over East Germany, impaling their stems so that they would stand in plain sight within the landing pattern of a MiG and record the emissions of Soviet top-line electronic gear.

Instead, Corbett talked about his work on Black Stealth One, remembering to maintain Medina's cover. "So our retreaded ex-spook got a lot of flack from a colleague, little tinplate hotshot named Medina. Just a personality conflict, I suppose, but it sure made our man value his time off.

"So he gets a chance to spend a weekend in a flat-bottom boat with an old friend. They don't even share much shoptalk, maybe a hint that some project's becoming a real bastard, something the other guy already knows." He turned to her, his eyes smouldering. "At the very worst, a thing to get you a royal ass-chew if your best friend cops on you. Not worth blacklisting you for, much less fixing you up with a fatal accident. The truth is to this day I don't know why."

"You're certain someone did that on purpose?"

His laugh was almost a snort of derision. "You be the judge. Second morning with the boat on the Maryland side, a cooler full of Heineken, just a touch of mist on the river. Little Evinrude was cranky to start but our poor boob thinks he's a mechanic so he fiddles with it while his good buddy lugs the other stuff into the boat. Including the spare fuel can, one of those steel jobs with a screw-on cap you can get your fist into."

He saw her gaze steady on him, both of them fully aware that Corbett was the boob and Dar Weston the buddy, and she seemed scarcely to be breathing as he went on: "They'd fished this way a few times before, but this time the best buddy has a beeper on his belt. Never before, just this time. And of course ol' buddy-buddy has a 'phone in his tow car, one of those belchfire ponycars that I am *sure* you've seen. And the good buddy is back at his car a couple of hundred yards off, and comes back to the boat with a face a mile long. He tells our fool the bad news while snugging the fuel can down where you can reach it while you steer the boat. Very thoughtful.

"The bad news is, his beeper went off—and maybe it did, who knows? So the buddy says he called in, and maybe he did. There's some little brushfire back at Langley that requires him personally, but it won't take long. Well, hell, that's no problem. The buddy will make a quick run to

□□□

Langley. Back in a couple of hours. No sweat, right?"

"No sweat," she said, prodding him on.

"The boob says sure, he'll mooch along in the boat and find where they're biting and watch for the car, but—I remember this very well—as he putters away from the landing he says don't expect all that Heineken to wait. And the buddy shouts back, 'I trust you.' Wasn't that sweet? Then he drives off.

"Ten minutes later, just noodling along against the current, the goddamn old Evinrude packs up; something I don't think was in the plan, somehow. Our boob manages to steer into shallows with cattails higher than Iowa corn. Drops anchor. The way the engine stopped, sounded like it was just starving for gas. Our guy starts to haul the gas can a little closer so he can reach the pump.

"And something thunks inside. Not loud, but when you've fiddled with mechanical stuff all your life you get attuned to certain noises. This wasn't a fuel pickup sound, or—"

"All right," she said breathlessly. "I don't want a list of what it wasn't!"

He shrugged and continued. "The cap unscrews. The can is half full of gas, but there's enough sun to shine on the bottom where there's a flat brick of something like, oh, jack cheese. It's wrapped inside a bag. It comes out nice and easy. It's got something like a ballpoint pen jabbed into it, with a screw-type plunger on top."

"Now you've lost me," she said.

"It's a pound of plastique, Petra, the most concentrated chemical explosive on earth. The chemical detonator can be set for various times with that screw adjustment. Do you have any idea of its radius of destruction with a few gallons of gasoline on a small boat?"

She gazed at him slack-jawed, as outrage grew in her face. "My uncle would never, never do such a thing! Maybe that bomb was intended for him."

"It was his boat, and his gas can, and that chemical fuse is a one-hour item at most. I sure didn't do it myself. Maybe he didn't build that booby trap, but he put it in there, all right." Corbett punched an instruction into the keyboard and added, as if to himself, "You bet he did."

"He's not a killer," she said, choking it out. "You're lying, Corbett."

"Uh-huh; yeah. Listen, it was misplaced loyalty that put me where I am. I realized that while I was staring down at a brick of C-4. Dar Weston, not a killer? He set booby traps in Greece in 1944, or so he told me. I believe it."

"God. That's true—at least my dad told me it was true." She was almost whispering, half submerged in old memories. "So what did you do?"

"I was a dead man. There was no way I could go back to the Snake Pit, for all I knew my own people had made the decision to burn me. I dumped the brick back, jumped down into chest-deep water, and flailed like hell through cattails to the shore. The highway wasn't far off, but I didn't want to get picked up all muddy and sopping wet. I skirted the shore feeling like the whole world was watching, heading upstream. Might've been another ten minutes, less than a mile from the boat, when that C-4 went up. Jesus, it made a fireball you could've seen for miles."

□□□

Petra said nothing for perhaps a minute. Then, "Why didn't I ever hear about it?"

"Why would you? Hell, it probably wasn't even in the papers. I'll bet Dar had a good story worked out, though. And I'll give you odds he was parked in that Javelin somewhere along the river, listening. Petra, when people in my line of work go belly up, sometimes it doesn't make the obituary column."

"I suppose," she said softly. "What did you do after that?"

"Doesn't matter," he said, punching again at the keyboard, looking back at the swept wing. He had told her all he could without placing Petra herself in possible jeopardy. No point in describing his pilgrimage with thumbed rides to Depew, a suburb of Buffalo; withdrawing his spooker from the post office box in Depew; outfitting himself at St. Vincent De Paul; buying a '72 Datsun in Buffalo using his spooker ID; crossing the toll bridge into Canada; then returning a week later through Duluth on the next leg of his trip to Mexico.

Those Thai rubies, something he hadn't mentioned even to Dar, had made the difference. The interest on eighty-seven thousand dollars, added to the salary of a Mexican crop duster's mechanic, might have kept him safely dead and tinkering with airplanes for the rest of his life. He had even given up all plans for revenge—until he saw Medina's ad in *Sport Aviation. A shame I can't talk about those bits,* he thought. *But I'd be sorry later.*

"Corbett," she said earnestly, "I don't know what to believe. I suppose it *might* be possible that Uncle Dar *might* be capable of such a thing, if he thought you—look. What if, don't ask me how, but somehow, they got what they thought was absolute proof that you were a Russian spy or something?"

He saw the agonized hope in her gaze, and smiled sadly. "Or what if I really was, and they found out? Same thing. I spent sleepless nights for two years afterward, trying to explain it in a way that would take Dar off the hook. I never found a scenario that would justify it, Petra. And who better than Dar to catch me napping?"

"I never thought a reason like that would justify murder in my own country," she said.

"Me, neither," he replied, refolding a nav chart, watching the altimeter as Black Stealth One descended to a few thousand feet above a broken, creek-veined plain. "But it won't hurt my feelings if you report every damn word of this to your favorite uncle, next time you see him. You can tell him I kept the secrets, all of 'em. The son of a bitch," he finished under his breath.

She turned her puzzled frown from him to the terrain below. "Are we out of fuel?"

"Not yet. But jet interceptors don't fool around much, this low, and now I don't think they'll spot us from above. See the wing?"

She twisted, studying the wing surface. He had finally learned the trick of using the video monitor to give the computer a viewpoint, a point from which a viewer must be fooled. If that viewpoint were infinitely far away above, the computer would look below and "paint" the skin with a replica of the terrain as they passed over it, perfect camouflage against a viewer high above. As they passed the fenceline from a fallow field of rich dark soil to a field green with cotton, a shadow of

□□□

green swept across the upper wing skin to replace the rich brown of a moment before.

She saw a man standing next to a pickup truck on a dirt access road. The man did not look up but, "Could people on the ground see us now?" she asked.

"I don't know. Most likely our belly's blue. I could go outside and see."

"You go to hell, is where you go."

"Not far off the truth," he said, restarting the engine. "The middle of the Okefenokee might be hell at night, so we're going to see if I can stretch a glide to its southern edge. And that's over the line into Florida."

TWENTY

YEVGENI MELNIK, WHOSE TASTE FOR VODKA HAD faded after his first glass of Kentucky sourmash, was scribbling in a small spiral-bound notebook when he saw two familiar faces in the mirror behind the bar. He put away his pencil slowly, took a slower sip of Jack Daniel's, and slipped the notebook into his coat pocket. "Fallon, Hendrick," he said, turning toward the men with a welcoming smile. "Have we all made the same good guess, or the same bad one?"

Tom Fallon, of the *Post,* had the thick shoulders and flattened nose of a mediocre club fighter twenty years after leaving the ring. He recognized the rumpled little Russian first and made a comical face of surprise to Hendrick, the roly-poly veteran *Times* reporter. "Jeez, they'll let almost anybody drink in Atlanta," Fallon said, but slid onto the stool next to Melnik and clapped him on the shoulder as Hendrick took the next stool. "I've noticed you're a good guesser, Melnik. But are we guessing about the same thing?" He caught the bartender's eye. "Whatever he's having," he added, nodding at Melnik's glass.

"Sounds right to me," Hendrick added to the bartender in his lazy Midwest twang. "In the spirit of *glasnost,* Melnik: you guess first."

Melnik truly enjoyed the byplay of such men, all of them a bit jaded, all slightly cynical about human affairs—perhaps because he had become one of them. After a few years, hardened professional newsmen learned how to balance their natural love of competition against the virtues of shared information. If they had not both flown into Atlanta International on the trail of Black Stealth One, their editors would doubtless divert them to the story before long. If they *had* come for that, probably they had already done a bit of sharing. "I would guess," Melnik said, "that you are both trailing a lead about a stolen airplane, as I am. And because Delta and American have hubs in Atlanta, we will find it easier to catch other flights to—wherever rumor leads," he finished with an expansive wave.

Quickly, from Fallon: "Why not, say, Dallas?"

"A flip of the coin," Melnik shrugged charmingly. "You?"

Fallon glanced at Hendrick. "You, uh, probably have some pretty special sources. So do I; so does Hendrick. A quid pro quo might help us all. Sound good?"

"Why not?" Melnik's openhanded gesture seemed to invite a body search, but it was he who asked the next question. "What do you have so far?"

Fallon hesitated, but *glasnost* worked both ways and the little Sov had already admitted he was on the Spookplane story. Accepting his drink, Fallon sipped, blew a richly scented exhalation, and said, "There's a place called Monroe about forty miles east of here that's popular with glider nuts."

"Sailplane," Hendrick put in, without lowering his glass. "High performance glider's a sailplane." While he tended to ramble in writing a story, Hendrick seemed to make up for it with telegraphic speech.

"Ah," Melnik said as though it was important.

"Whatever," Fallon said. "The Georgia state cops came down on that little field at Monroe like acid rain on pantyhose a few hours ago. They practically ringed it with patrol cars, turned the police channels to mush arguing over what the hell they were after, and snagged a couple of guys out of a glider—awright, sailplane—that had just landed. The sailplane was clean, but it turns out that the cops had got a tip about a hush-hush government plane that'd been stolen up north and positively identified near Monroe by a flying cop. When somebody used the word, 'stealth,' the *Post* got wind of it and pulled me off something else I was bird-dogging in Nashville. When I got on the next flight to Atlanta, guess who was already on it." He jerked a thumb toward Hendrick.

"*Times* jerked me off a piece in Memphis, sent me here," Hendrick said.

"They're always jerkin' him off," Fallon put in. "He loves it." Sip; sidelong look at Hendrick.

Melnik frowned for a moment, searching his

mental file of American idioms, then smiled. "There has to be more to it," he urged.

"Governors of several states are loaning air guard planes to the feds," Hendrick went on, unfazed. "Flying search patterns for a stealth plane spotted near here, and the sky's full of everything they can muster. Plane's not a Lockheed stealth fighter, or the Northrop stealth bomber; a sailplane, like. May be a hostage onboard." He saw Melnik's face change and added, "May be, I said. *Times* has some people schmoozing weekend warriors in the guard to see what we can learn. But if it's a sailplane, it's slow. Could still be someplace near." He cocked his head, thought about it, then shrugged and sipped. "Now you."

Melnik saw no reason to explain how his sources might have certain very special information. The American newsmen had been in the business much too long to be naive about Soviet satellites and listening devices. Nevertheless, Yevgeni Melnik lowered his voice and studied his glass, speaking as if to himself. "Your military air arms are searching for an aircraft stolen from the National Security Agency," he began.

"NSA doesn't fly spook airplanes," Fallon objected, sensing a mistake. "They just massage the data from military and CIA."

"They have been flying this one," Melnik went on quietly, nodding at his sourmash. Then, quieter still: "They built it."

"Holy shit," Hendrick blurted. "A different kind of stealth plane, then. For CIA?"

Melnik remained silent for a moment, then shook his head. "I think you would call it interservice rivalry," he said, and finished his drink. He saw Fallon's hand move toward his jacket, then jerk down. *You fear I shall quit talking as soon as your pencils come out. And I might, to strengthen my credibility.*

"Bartender, hit us again," Hendrick said, and leaned both elbows on the bar. "This is heavy shit, Yevgeni."

Fallon, tapping his fingers with newly minted energy: "My God, you don't suppose the CIA stole it? Nah." He squinted in a fresh surmise. "More likely your guys, Melnik, I mean, wouldn't that figure?"

Melnik used his newest Americanism: "Cut me some slack, *tovarisch.* Why would I be following the story if I already knew the details?"

"Doesn't mean they didn't snatch it," said Hendrick. "Only means they didn't tell you."

"Possible," Melnik agreed equitably. "It would not be the first time I have had a story rewritten. And I have said too much out of friendship. Do not source me, I beg you."

"I hear you," Fallon grumbled. "Listen, we've got more than one story here, you know that?"

"Not yet we haven't," said Hendrick, "unless you're into filing on something this big with a single, unattributable source." Still, the *Times* man was already selecting a quarter from a palmful of change. "I'd better call in, see which way I chase the wild goose next."

And send others scurrying to ask acutely embarrassing questions of CIA, not to mention NSA, Melnik thought. *Long after the stealth aircraft has been forgotten, American spymasters will be busy trying to patch the shreds of their careers. That is the real story—and my real value.* Melnik only raised a hand like a Hollywood Indian.

"Yeah, me too. Hold the fort for us, Yevgeni," said Fallon, in an implied promise of return.

Melnik watched Fallon shuffle away, digging for change in his pocket as he followed Hendrick to the telephones. "Oh yes, you will return to the fort," Melnik muttered to himself in Russian. Those two were both solid professionals who would want confirmation of every detail by more than one source. But Western news media were strange entities, willing to go far beyond mere *glasnost,* openness, in search of a story. Fallon and Hendrick were picking, like Pandora, at the lock which would release an administration's most secret problems.

And if they knew that Melnik had told them for that very reason? Perhaps they did know; what mattered in the West was not the potential damage by the story, but only the story. Fallon and Hendrick saw their duty to the story first, and to their country second.

Melnik drew out his little notebook and began to scribble. If he failed to call in this item about a hostage in Black Stealth One, he would be in—he plucked the phrase from his growing repertoire—deep shit.

TWENTY-ONE

IT WAS LATE AFTERNOON WHEN PETRA SAW THE scrawl of multilane highway below, a broad ribbon that slashed through flat, unvarying leagues of forest leaving verges as wide as the highway itself. She welcomed this sight after watching the endless morass of Okefenokee cypress, with water gleaming up at her like hostile eyes through the rank foliage. She even welcomed the huge triple-tandem trucks that crawled along the ribbon because those nasty brutes only plied major arterials, and this one was a monster. She asked the question simply by pointing with her brows raised.

"Interstate Ten," Corbett nodded. "We've nursed this crate farther than I thought we could. Another ten gallons and we could've made it to Key West."

I'll bet he's headed for Cuba. What if I started

playing with the pixel program now, she thought. *Would anybody notice the buzzard that kept changing color? And if they did, would it help me? Corbett would catch on immediately.* She had not forgotten the hiding he'd given her early in the morning. It all came down to, "if I do, I get a whipping" or worse, and such punishments were new to Petra Leigh. She kept her hands where they were.

The altimeter told her they were ghosting along at eleven thousand feet, and she wondered just how accurate the fuel counter was because it read under six pounds, slightly less than a gallon. No wonder Corbett was studying the terrain with such intensity. To their left, the sun glistened and winked from far distant windows in a small town. To the right at roughly the same distance was a larger town. Like it or not, Corbett had come too far to go back to that god-awful, trackless swamp. And now there were farms below, and rundown cafes and service stations at road crossings. And plenty of people. Deep in Petra's soul, a bubble of optimism began to rise through her nagging fears.

The whisper of the rotary engine was so subdued, she did not notice when the pilot shut it down. She did realize they were losing altitude because the horizon tilted and the earth began to pivot in that dreamlike way which had frightened her so the first few times she had experienced it. How was it possible that you could grow accustomed to such things in a single day, even to—well—almost enjoy some parts of it? Someone, probably Jason in one of his Connecticut cowboy monologues, had drawled that a feller could even get to enjoy hanging if he did it long enough. By the fall term, she would be able to make the same crack about abduction. With maybe just the teensiest bit of truth in it? *The hell with THAT kind of thinking,* she told herself. Yes, it was exciting, in an oh-my-God sort of way; and yes, Kyle Corbett carried a kind of grizzled, overweight panache with him, the kind of man who, as Uncle Dar liked to put it, would put a feather in his cap and call it macaroni. You couldn't help a certain grudging admiration for a high-tech thug who declared solitary war on the CIA. But the man was holding her by brute force and threats, and whatever justifications he offered, he was prosecuting his own brand of war against the United States. Or at least against some elements of it. *Develop a soft spot for Corbett? Not likely!*

The two-lane road seemed to leap up from the flat, wooded landscape ahead. Petra spotted a roof of corrugated tin between trees, tried to keep herself oriented to it, failed as Black Stealth One banked and jittered. Corbett brought the aircraft lower, soaring on airspeed alone, but he cursed and banked sharply away from one field below. "Damn bean poles could damage a wing," he said curtly, restarting the engine when they were less than a thousand feet above the field. A minute or so later he set the engine idling and Petra saw the second field, an irregular polygon slashed out of the surrounding trees.

They banked lazily over the area, emulating a bird both in plumage and maneuver, moving no faster than an automobile. Corbett split his attention between high-gain infrared video and the real scene out of his bubble. "See anybody down there?"

□□□

Petra laughed in surprise. "Would I tell you if I did?"

He muttered, "Jee-zus, Kee-rist," craning his neck around as he said it, and then brought the great bird of passage down to where Petra could see the shiny green ovals of immature melons in the field. "Cinch up; you never know," he said, and began to manipulate throttle, stick, and pedals simultaneously.

The shadow of Black Stealth One paced them over a scatter of oak and cypress, dipped, and then the craft stalled a hundred feet above the ground in a maneuver that put Petra's stomach just below her chin. The rush of air from waste gates steadied the craft, let its nose drop until she could see the melon patch below. Then they were settling, as broad melon leaves whipped in the battering downdraft. She felt tentative contact through her rump, another faint motion, and watched fascinated as the engine whirr doppplered down, the lovely wings relaxing until they drooped, their tips nearly touching the melon vines.

"Uh-unh," he warned as she reached for the hatch, and his right hand was a steel clamp on her wrist. "Keep your hands on the armrests." She did, watching him release his harness, and sighed as he pulled that hated roll of tape from his bag, binding her left wrist to an armrest, ignoring her silent glare. Only then did he exit the cockpit, grunting, exercising his arms as he walked around to her side, scanning the treeline around the melon field with slow deliberation. Petra wondered why he shrugged into his old leather jacket in such muggy heat, until she realized it would hide the ugly little pistol and the shoulder holster.

□□□

When he had opened her hatch, he began to tape her other wrist down. "I know you don't like it," he growled as he attended to the wrist and then her ankles. The menace in his voice was unmistakable. It was as if they had not spent the entire day working together against deadly odds. "Can't help what you like. I'm going to do a little recon circuit among the trees around this field just to make sure before I go for fuel. If I find you're working against the tape, I'll come back and beat the hell out of you. But I won't tape your mouth unless that happens." He reached behind her seat and snapped something, stepping back, lowering her hatch. "So you behave, and worse things won't happen."

She might as well have saved her angry "Hah!" as he withdrew the plastic fuel bag and then lowered his hatch, stepping high as he moved down a furrow and out of sight behind her. But as soon as he disappeared, Petra began to test the bonds on her left wrist. She had sweated more than once since leaving West Virginia. Rolling her wrist side to side, she hoped perspiration would be her ally.

Ten minutes later, her left shoulder and arm ached from exertion. She dared not struggle with her right arm because it would be visible through the clear polymer bubble if he were watching. The tape loop was wrinkling a bit, but she could claim that was from ordinary movement. The cockpit was a stifling little greenhouse and she was sweating again, which should have helped, but even if the adhesive gum released her skin she could not pull her hand through the loop. Very gradually, watching the treeline for telltale movement, she began to bend forward and to the left. Petra had very good teeth.

☐☐☐

Yet she could not employ them against that damned tape. Her upper body harness normally let her move around a lot, so long as she did not jerk hard enough to engage the inertia lock. Now, however, Petra could only snarl at that tape. She realized then that Corbett had locked the inertia reel of her harness, and she ripped the air with her panted curses.

She was crying with frustration, relaxing against her headrest, when Corbett popped up from under the wing on her side, strands of his hair sweat-plastered on his forehead. Now, in addition to the plastic bag, he carried a bright red five-gallon metal fuel can, evidently bought or stolen from a gas station, and his shirt was sopping with sweat. It pleased Petra to see that his face almost matched the color of that metal canister.

He gazed in at her, looking her over, and something unreadable passed across his face as he raised her hatch. "Looks like you could use a little ventilation" was all he said as he moved around to lift the hatch bubble on his side. Petra did not respond. She knew that if she did, her voice would shake. *I won't give you the satisfaction,* she told him silently.

She could hear him grunting and wheezing as he decanted a few ounces of dark liquid from one of the bottles he had warned her not to drink. *Work yourself into a coronary, you old bastard,* she prayed silently.

Perhaps he was talking to himself, perhaps not. "Ninety-two octane may be good enough for these folks, but we need a little boost," he muttered. Petra could hear him slosh the fuel around but did not bother to watch. She could follow his progress well enough by hearing the filler cap release, his panting exertion, and the gurgle of fuel. As he replaced the filler cap he said, "They're going to wonder why I keep coming back. I can claim I spilled it once, but not twice. Well, maybe I'm fueling a boat. Or maybe I just let 'em wonder. I don't suppose you have any ideas."

"Only one. You don't want to hear it," she said, vehemence steadying her voice. "Listen, I have a back cramp. You might loosen my harness a little."

He said, "I might, but I won't," and then lowered the hatch bubbles, moving off again almost silently, the big sloped shoulders suggesting a tired man.

"Bastard," she cried, but he made no reply.

He had not been gone a half hour on his quest. Petra decided that either the gas station was very near, or he'd lied about making a circuit around the field. She spent several minutes trying to writhe loose from her upper torso restraint, growing sticky in the humid Florida air, and then gave it up. "Somebody he-e-elp me," she screamed, so loudly in the confines of the cockpit that it hurt her own ears.

She screamed a few more times before giving it up. The only effect, besides half deafening herself, was on the cottontail that scampered off after her last scream, the one that hurt her throat. Then she tried to free her other wrist, without success. Finally she simply lay back and watched the sun drop toward the trees, and thought up new curses.

The first tendrils of shadow lay across the cockpit bubble when Corbett showed up again. He did not exactly pop up this time; more like an erect backbend in slow motion, moving side to side as he lowered the fuel cans and opened her hatch. *Carrying something like eighty pounds,* she thought, closing her eyes as she luxuriated in the faint breeze.

When she opened them again, he was arching his back, kneading at it with his hands. His mop of graying hair now looked as if he'd combed it with an eggbeater, and he breathed like a man who'd forgotten how. When he saw her looking at him, he muttered, "So much for staying in shape," and tried to smile as he carried the fuel around to the filler opening.

He opened his hatch, perhaps to improve her ventilation—but *screw his little friendly touches,* she thought savagely. "You can't stay in shape with a beer gut like that," she said smugly.

"At my age it goes with the territory," he said, again measuring fuel additive in.

"You've got more territory than Alexander the Great," she returned, staring pointedly at his belt buckle.

"I do believe," he said mildly, starting to pour fuel into the aircraft, "I'll pop you one extra for that."

"What do you mean, 'extra'? I'm still taped up like a Christmas present," she protested.

"A booby prize," he corrected, coughing, turning his head to avoid fumes. "You think I'm blind? You've been working on that tape like a crazy woman. I warned you, kid."

"Don't call me 'kid,'" she screamed.

He seemed almost glad of her outburst, beginning to decant the second canister as he said, "One

□□□

more shout and the hatches come down, *and* tape goes over your big high society mouth—kid."

Somehow, this reminder of social difference made it easy for Petra to rein her temper in. The Leigh household had many ways of demonstrating the adage that "class will tell," and one of them was an overlay of cool disdain for the vulgar. No matter that Petra herself could play the vulgarian with the worst of them; she maintained a silence that she hoped was lofty, watching him climb into the cockpit again. *I might've known he'd turn into a gangster again the minute we landed,* she reflected.

He flicked switches, watched the fuel counter, and grunted his satisfaction before running his fingers experimentally along the tape on her left wrist. "Pretty good stuff," he said, climbing out again, lifting that fuel bag for stowage in the cockpit. It had perhaps two gallons of fuel in it. As if to himself he said, "I don't think I can risk another trip over there for a lousy three gallons," nodding absently to the rear of the aircraft. A sigh: "So near and yet so far; I don't relish falling around in those creepers again."

Laying the bag of food and tools between their seats, he moved to her side and released her ankles, then her right wrist. "You can take the other one off," he said. "I'm bushed." While she stripped off the offending stuff, he circled around the cockpit and removed his jacket, cramming it behind his seat. "Time for dinner. I can whale your ass for dessert," he promised. Not until he was climbing in did Petra, rubbing her wrists and glaring silently at him, notice that the shoulder holster was empty. She averted her gaze too quickly.

□□□

Poised halfway inside, he squinted at her, then slapped his right hand at his armpit. It put him off balance. "Oh, Christ," he said softly, and then lost his balance, the aircraft rocking as he fell backward into the melon field.

Petra heard him hit the ground heavily, heard him cry out, and scrambled into action without taking time to think about it. Her legs seemed half asleep but that did not prevent her from dropping to the ground, rolling away. She leaped up, sidling off, remembering he had gone north each time, not daring to run until she saw that Corbett could only stand on one leg.

"God damn you, don't you try to run from me," he shouted in sudden fury, hobbling toward her, falling again, stifling another cry of pain.

Petra turned her back on him then and sprinted, stepping high, scanning the shadowed furrows because she could easily slide off one of those hard melons and break an ankle herself. She did not look back until she plunged into the trees, ducking past vines the size of hawsers. By that time Corbett was dragging himself into the cockpit of Black Stealth One.

She simply could not take the time to be frightened of this damp and shadowed jungle, ducking vines, scrambling on hands and knees when necessary. Her first thought was to put as much distance as possible between herself and Corbett; but then, as she burst into a clearing, she realized the predicament Corbett must be facing. She trotted up the perimeter road which was hardly more than a pair of ruts, and thrust both arms aloft, howling her triumph: "Allll *riiiight!*"

To engage the waste gates for vertical takeoff,

□□□

Corbett needed two good ankles. And even if he got the hellbug aloft, he could not menace her without his pistol. With any luck she could find help fast enough to catch this overaged spy still trying to take off. "My turn now," she exulted, trotting steadily up the ruts toward a broad break in the trees. "Let's see who whales the hell out of who, asshole!"

Petra took care to pace herself as she would on a bike tour, easing off to catch her breath and to scan the gathering dusk for any sight of the hellbug. She felt like capering in circles to demonstrate her freedom, but every second counted if Corbett was to be taken while he was this vulnerable.

She trotted past a low ditch and found the blacktop road. Barely visible in the dusk to her left, less than a mile distant, winks of light throbbed among the trees lining the road. Petra ran a hundred steps, walked another hundred, ran again. Gradually the little store came into view. A dented yellow pickup truck stood near the two gas pumps, and from behind the edge of the white clapboard store protruded the prow of something dark that looked like a Firebird. Just below the roof corrugations and over a screen door stretched a weathered sign announcing "Olustee Gas, Grocery & Bait." All of it defied the gathering gloom with the help of a smaller sign, "BEER," surrounded by winking, low-wattage bulbs. The bulbs winked their last when Petra was still a quarter of a mile away.

She quickened her pace. When the driver of the pickup climbed into its cab, she shouted and waved her arms, hoping the vehicle would turn in her direction. Instead, it picked up momentum with the stately pace of a dowager and thrummed away.

She strode onto limestone gravel and up to the door of the place, breathing easily but deeply. Those little bulbs had given the place an air of cheer, of welcome. She heard no welcome in the scrunch of her shoes through gravel, and no response to her knock. The screen door was latched; the half-windowed wooden door behind it sported bars hammered from reinforcing rod. Squinting through screen and glass, she saw a single hooded overhead light above a wooden counter, a pendulum that moved less as she watched. Minutes before, someone had been inside. "Damn," she said aloud. Could the driver of that pickup have been the owner?

Somewhere near, but not near enough to be felt, a breeze hushed its way through the trees. Petra knocked again, harder, then walked back to stand on the blacktop. She might try breaking in; a telephone line swung down from a nearby pole to the roof. Or she might wait for the next car. Surely she would not need to wait long. As she stood on the cooling blacktop, listening to the self-pity of a whippoorwill and wishing for lights to appear in the distance, she heard something else. An animal noise, a clean tone rising and then falling, yet somehow familiar, and she knew it had been made by a human voice.

Petra held her breath. Presently she heard it again, and laughed aloud. It had to be a radio somewhere behind the store, playing that stupid "Oooooh, new Moxie" soft drink commercial. The Moxie people must have lured Yma Sumac out of retirement, she decided, just for that dumb commercial. She picked her way through the shadows, stepping over a stripped engine block, calling twice more. Nothing—except that now she could hear that radio a little better. It was playing some rockabilly ballad. Playing it loudly, she realized as she emerged behind the store.

The shed was no bigger than a one-car garage, separated from the store with only a rickety roof to connect them. Petra's hopes fell because she could see no light from the shed. Her optimism swelled again as she moved nearer, because now she could hear another voice faintly, under the ballad, and it was not singing but talking. Now two voices.

Of course; couple of mechanics putting in overtime with the damned radio on so loud they wouldn't hear it if somebody dragged the store away on skids, she told herself. She walked up to the door and banged on it with the heel of her hand, shouting, "Hey," as loud as she could. And then the cardboard slid crazily down from the inside of the door and she could see through the small panes very clearly.

Two young men were in the process of dropping out of sight behind a heavy worktable, lit by a bank of overhead fluorescents. On the table was a printer's paper shear, and near it lay a sheaf of paper pages, each sheet containing rows of some delicate imprint in red. Petra's shout was imperious: "Come on, it's important!"

She figured they must have pulled the radio's plug, the way it fell silent. "Hurry," she insisted, banging on the door again.

"You go first," she heard a querulous voice say.

□□□

"And don't blame me if there's black widders down there."

"Shut up, Bobby," came the reply in a deeper voice, and a sound of wood dragging on wood. "That's a woman."

"Ah seen her. What you waitin' for?"

"They don't use women, use your fuckin' head. Or go on throo the hole if you'd ruther."

Petra, almost dancing in her impatience, hit the door again. "Please hurry," she began, and then thought of a phrase that might galvanize them, "it's a matter of national security!"

"Bullshit," said the deep voice as its owner stood up. He was in his thirties, thickset with dark curly hair, in dirty overalls and T-shirt, and he stared hard at Petra as he moved quickly toward the door. His show of teeth at her as he twisted the door's lock was probably intended as a welcome, but he stepped past her, peering around. If he had washed recently, he had forgotten to include those overalls.

"I need a telephone right away," Petra explained.

"Who you with, little lady?" The stocky man showed his teeth again like a robot, still looking around, holding the door open for her.

"Nobody, I mean there's a man who kidnapped me but I got away," she said breathlessly, stepping inside, her eyes darting in search of a telephone. "He's in a stolen airplane and—look, can I please use a phone?" It occurred to her that some people might find her story hard to believe, and that she had stumbled onto a couple of those people.

Now another young man was standing behind the table, very tall and slender in tan work clothes, blinking sheepishly at her through cornshuck hair as he gathered the imprinted papers and turned them over. "Hey, Elbee, why not?" He did not seem to know what to do with his hands, and Petra saw that they were shaking. He looked at her, looked away. "Let 'er in front. No problem. Raght?" His tone was hopeful.

"C'mere, Bobby," said Elbee, clarifying it by waving two hairy fingers toward himself as he stepped inside and shut the door. To Petra he said, "You just stay raght there, little lady, everthang's gonna be oooh-kay." He spoke softly, soothingly, the way one might speak to a skittish horse.

"You're wasting time," said Petra, starting around Elbee toward the door without knowing exactly why.

"Raght there," he repeated, gripping her upper arm, shoving her back roughly, reacting to her stare of disbelief with still another display of dental work, though he did not really have the teeth for it. He watched Bobby approach, moving only his eyes until both men stood between Petra and the one door. Then Elbee said, "Bobby, she says she's by her lonesome. You better hope so. Now you stay here whal ah take a looksee. She don't get out, Bobby. *She seen us.*"

"What the hell is this?" Petra put hands on hips and stared Elbee down. "Sure I see you, so what? You're not supposed to be here? Go away then, but I've got to get to a telephone! I swear to you, it's government business."

"Ah bet it is," Elbee said, and nodded. "She *seen* us, Bobby. Now keep her here, ah'll be back."

With that, Elbee slid out the door. The interior lock was a good one, a heavy side-mounted brass fixture at chin height, and it latched with a click of terrifying finality. Petra waited for a count of ten, trading stares with Bobby who might have been her own age and was clearly unhappy with his role. In most circumstances, she decided, probably shy. "You don't want to get in trouble, Bobby," she said at last, and walked toward the door bearing a load of false confidence.

It was the wrong thing to say. "Durn raght," said Bobby, putting his back against the door. "And you seen us."

Petra turned on a smile that should have warmed the brass lock behind him. "Anybody can see anybody," she said. "What's the harm in that, Bobby?"

"Them fake revenue stamps," he explained.

She glanced over to the table, mystified. "Stamps?"

Bobby said, "They go on whiskey bottles; lordy, you don't know much. They get you on that, you ain't got a good lawyer, send you over to Gainesville fahv years or so."

God, I've done it again. "Bobby, I don't care about that, I didn't even see what you were doing." She took a deep breath and moved near him, making her face tragic, gazing gently up into his face. "I've been kidnapped by a man who is stealing a secret airplane. If you help me catch him, you can be a hero."

"A hero," he said, his eyes roaming her face.

I must look like hell but he doesn't seem to care. "To the whole country. And to me, too," she added. *Got him. You're such a bitch,* she told herself smugly.

"You go with me to the phone, so you can listen,"

□□□

she said, keeping the flow mellow as she brushed against him, reaching for the lock, nodding and smiling as he moved aside. "Come on, it's all right, you'll see," she said, and stepped outside. And heard the angry bellow of Elbee, saw him pounding toward her from the semidarkness, and then she gave in to her fear and ran.

The open plot behind the shed was only an acre of clearing with spindly corn and less identifiable plants fighting for survival. She pelted toward the darker gloom at the treeline, knowing that once into that ferocious tangle she was as good as gone, but she could hear other steps behind her, and other breath whistling close, and then she was screaming in the grasp of Bobby's long arms, flailing with her nails and feet, and she might have made it if not for Elbee, who jerked her upright and cuffed her half unconscious with his open hand.

It was Elbee who carried her over his shoulder to the shed, dropping her onto a cane-bottomed chair with no back.

"She was alone, awraght," Elbee said, puffing, wiping sweat from his face, and the look he turned on Petra made prickly heat slide up the nape of her neck. "Now ah don't know about you, Bobby, but ah cain't see lettin' this little lady loose, all this goop about guvment work, who knows what she's up to, not you and not me. Least that'll happen is strange folks with ties and forty-dollar shoes hangin' round here. You wanta sell out, move? Who'd buy the place?"

"We could be heroes," Bobby said, as if testing the sound of it.

"Who said that? Her? Shit for brains, she'd

promise to suck your cock. Maybe she did." Elbee looked from Bobby to Petra and this time his slow smile was genuine, and chilling. "Maybe she will, 'fore this naght is out."

Petra stood up and began backing toward the opposite end of the shed, feeling rough shelves against her arm, trying to identify something, anything, that she could swing as a weapon. Crossing his arms, the smile broadening, Elbee followed.

"Ah don't lahk it," Bobby said, rubbing a red welt across his forehead. "Ah got a sister her age, Elbee."

"So do ah," Elbee said.

"Ah know what you done to her, too," Bobby insisted.

"Well shit, so did you," Elbee said, watching Petra, leaping forward as she grabbed for the scissors that lay on the table. "Look at her blush, Bobby. Wonder which one of us she'd ruther have git 'er first."

Petra struggled, speechless, nearly overcome by the stench of the man who hugged her face against those coveralls.

Bobby moved nearer. "You thought about what she's gonna say later?"

"She ain't gonna say nuthin', Bobby. That's why you can do whatever you want." He held Petra away, his hands gripping her arms, smiling at her. "Get it? Now then: why don't you go first? Raght up on the table, whal ah hold her."

"Ah don't know," Bobby said, but he moved nearer, indecision in his voice, and Petra quit trying to control her stomach, trying instead to provoke the vomiting that seemed so near. She remembered that some women claimed they had

☐☐☐

stopped a rapist by vomiting, fouling themselves in any way they could. She tried, but nothing in her past had ever trained her to urinate while struggling against two strong males, and when she felt the thick pitiless grasp of Elbee's hands holding her ankles apart, and when Bobby at last got one of her hands forced behind her back, she began the wordless, mindless screaming.

TWENTY-TWO

CORBETT HAD WASTED NO TIME BRINGING THE ENgine up to speed after the girl fled, levitating the hellbug gradually until he could see above the treeline. The sun lay dying on his horizon as he lifted another hundred feet, putting the infrared sensors on full gain. He did not see the vague pinkish blot that was Petra until she had reached the blacktop road, which registered faintly with its residual heat.

He hovered before bringing the nose up, urging the craft backward as he spotted a light-colored pickup truck that slowly accelerated from sight, its exhaust a fading red dot on the scanner. From time to time he could see the girl through treetops, still making an athlete's time toward that little store. "Boy, she's a pistol," he said to the scanner, grinning.

□□□

He circled around then, gaining altitude gradually, increasing his distance so that he could barely see her above the trees. When she reached the store he had a good five hundred feet under him. He flipped a mock salute in her direction as he turned the hellbug's nose to the west and advanced the throttle.

Something's missing, his cautionary demon whispered. "Yeah, a hundred and twenty pounds of trouble," he told it and kept going until he identified the missing item: the lights in that tacky little sign. It was nearly dark now, and those two crackers running the store could have been in the pickup. If so, Petra would be alone in strange surroundings. *She'll make out. Why wouldn't she?*

He delayed his decision another few moments, cursing himself when he banked his great bird and began to retrace. He maintained a good margin of safety over the trees, using the scanner again, and as he swept toward the garden plot his scanner picked up two pink blots, one stationary and large enough to be two people, the smaller one closing on it. He engaged the waste gates, pivoting the craft on its left wingtip, staring down into the gathering dusk. What he saw in the garden enraged him beyond curses.

Corn could damage the skin; well, avoid it, stupid! Get this heap down and kill all systems. Not so fast, you could crack this thing like an egg. One of the men, the ape he had seen lashing Petra with his hand, disappeared into a shed carrying her. Following them was the lanky dimwit who had sold Corbett the gas can, or his twin, and there was simply no way to speed up a landing without a crash, one that might put Corbett himself out of action. In less than two minutes he slipped the craft beyond the last row of corn and felt the jolt of landing, his hands doing the right things of their own volition. He could hear the impeller spooling down as he vaulted from the cockpit, and nearly whacked himself senseless against the wing's leading edge as he began to run the hundred yards to the shed.

The screams began when he was still twenty yards away, and he could see through a triangular patch of windowpane when he was still three paces from the door, and found absolutely no reason to use its knob. His body slam laid his left arm and shoulder on the door face with a splintering crash. The lock held but the upper hinge flew into the room, and his kicks flung the door flat.

The tall one straddled Petra's thighs, one hand gripping the open top of her jeans. He jerked his head around, his jaw dropping, and saw Corbett's right hand come up. "Gawdamighty," he bawled, and fell from the table as Corbett snapped off his first shaky round, a clean miss, from the automatic. The muzzle blast was concussive in such close quarters.

The heavy man with the pale muscular arms had already released Petra's feet, backing away as he fumbled in a pocket, his big yellow teeth bared, blinking in dust that fell from the ceiling. "Get the fuck outa," he bellowed, interrupted by the second explosion. He stumbled, dropped an open switchblade, clutched his belly and fell on his side, his mouth working silently.

Corbett stalked forward, trembling, his face alight with a kind of madness. He saw that the other man had been scrabbling at a trapdoor behind the table, gasping in falsetto, flinging the wooden rectangle aside, and Corbett lifted the pistol again.

The tall man writhed onto his back, hyperventilating, clutching his chest, and what he saw in this stranger's face made him close his eyes as tightly as he could. Petra had drawn herself into a fetal crouch on the table, still sobbing. The tall man was crying too, now. Corbett wheeled, dropped to one knee, and placed his free hand palm-out just above his weapon as a splash guard, pulling the trigger when the muzzle was six inches from the wounded man's ear. Somehow it seemed right; not because the heavy man was the only one not crying, but because he was the one who had stood in that garden and repeatedly backhanded Petra.

Corbett blinked hot tears away, his ears ringing from the muzzle blasts, drawing deep, ragged breaths as his rage began to dwindle. The tall man, little more than a youth, clasped his hands together, perhaps begging, perhaps praying, his legs apart. When he opened his eyes, Corbett said, in almost a whisper, "Go on into the hole. I can't miss then." The sufferer only shook his head, narrow chest still heaving. "Roll onto your belly. If you look up, you'll see a bullet. *Now,*" Corbett said with a devastating kick.

Corbett had to roll the youth over, finally. He reseated the pistol and carefully, tenderly, placed his fingertips on the heaving shoulder of Petra Leigh. She gasped and screamed. "Petra," he said, his mouth near her ear. "It's okay," and touched her again. Another flinch, but no scream. He patted her shoulder, his gaze straying to the tall man,

□□□

wanting to empty his magazine into the halfwit, seeing the ruin of the stocky man's head in a kind of wonderment. *I did that? Yes. Damned shame he could only feel it once.*

"It's okay," he said to her again, spotting the radio with its loose cord. He moved away, retrieving the switchblade from the floor, and cut the radio's power cord. It was easy to rip it lengthwise into two rubber-sheathed cables, and the tall man did not object when Corbett bound his hands and feet.

When Corbett stood, Petra was sitting up facing away from him, heartbreakingly small with her legs dangling from the table, snapping her jeans. He moved nearer. "It's okay, kid," he said.

"Don't call me 'kid,'" she said, no longer quite sobbing.

"You'll live," he replied with a half smile.

"Are they dead? Did you kill them?"

"One is," he said. "Don't look if you're squeamish."

She stepped down, holding herself erect with her hands, and saw the dead man. "Not about him," she said, and surveyed the tall one. "Why not that one?"

"Because I missed the fucker from twenty feet is why," Corbett said, shaking his head. He drew the pistol and offered it to her, butt-first. "You can do it. Or I will if you like."

She started to shake her head, then put her hands to her face, her head shaking faster and faster until he put the weapon away and cradled her shoulders in his hands. She leaned into his chest, moaning, gulping hard. They remained there until her shudders passed.

□□□

He knew that Petra was truly resilient when, once her breathing had become steady, she mumbled against his shirt, "Oh, you son of a bitch, Corbett." She moved away, not abruptly but with renewed strength, and looked him up and down. "There's nothing wrong with your leg."

"Well, I sure thought it was broken," he said.

"You seem to have found your pistol, too."

"Funny thing; put it in my pocket and forgot."

"Sure you did." She gnawed her lip, squinting at him. "You are weird, mister."

"And he," Corbett said, nodding toward the tall youth, "is listening. Want me to put him in that hole?"

"There's black widders down there," said a muffled voice.

"Sounds good to me," Corbett said easily, with one lingering pat on Petra's arm as he moved to squat near his captive. "Tell you what, old-timer: we're going out for a while. You don't make a sound, or try to get loose, and I don't dump you down there gut-shot. If you do, I do."

A nod. "You wanta put the trapdoor back?"

"Don't," Petra spoke up. "Leave it open as a reminder."

Corbett got up and headed for the doorway. "Teach you not to screw around, old-timer," he called back. "A woman will keep you terrified all your life. All I'll do is kill you." He made an after-you-Alfonse gesture, and Petra walked out ahead of him toward the back door of the little store, which was not even locked. The place was silent but for the tick of a big, old spring-wound Westclox that squatted beside the cash register—the kind of clock that more or less keeps time but will do it until the blast of Gabriel.

By common consent, they found the toilet first, Petra cursing as she cleaned the filthy thing before she would park her rump on it. Then he used it, knowing that when he opened the door he might be alone. He heard a car go by on the blacktop, its tires sizzling a tone that rose and fell familiarly with its passing. *So she didn't flag it down,* he thought, only half surprised. He found her opening two cans of beer from the old refrigerator that squatted near the sales counter.

They gulped for a few moments. "You let me go, back there in the melon field," she said at last.

"No I didn't. You ran. I came looking for you, that's all." A devilish smile. "You sorry I did?"

"Don't joke about it, Corbett, I— Thanks, just thanks. Look, you were going to beat the daylights out of me. Well, weren't you?"

After a pause: "Yep. Petra, leave it alone. You're going to be interrogated in ways you never imagined." He put down the can, opened another.

"I can imagine hypnosis. I can imagine an injection, uh, what's that stuff?"

"Sodium pentothal," he replied, sighing.

"Whatever. And I keep seeing you offering me your little shooter so I could kill that poor pea-witted scarecrow who tried to rape me. I'm sorry, Kyle"—she smiled, and he realized that she had done things to freshen her appearance while in that neanderthal bathroom—"but you've already blown it."

"Shit; I did, didn't I?" He began to laugh, the near-silent *uh-uh* of near exhaustion. "Well, say I wasn't thinking straight."

□□□

"I can't imagine why," she said, softly now. "You put in a hard day kidnapping big-mouthed society girls yesterday, flew all night, flew all day today. I think," she said, and now she was laughing too, "I think you should take me to a dance tonight."

"That and a bicycle ride would kill me right now."

"I know that old joke," she said.

"I'm not surprised," he said, shaking his head ruefully, dragging up a stool he saw in the shadows. She spied a broken couch near the door and claimed it, shoving the tattered cushions onto the floor. When another car sizzled by she did not look up. Its lights swept past her face for a moment and made her, he decided, very beautiful.

It was she who prodded: "And now?"

"Now you make your call, there's the phone over by the cash register—unless you made it already," he said in sudden alarm.

"I didn't. Trust me, as my favorite kidnapper says. Listen, Kyle, are you on uppers? I don't see how you're on your feet as it is, let alone fly Black Stealth One to Cuba tonight. That *is* your idea, isn't it?"

He paused a long time before saying, "Forget Cuba. Doesn't matter, I'll make it. I think. Yeah, I took a pill earlier today. And I'm gonna crash if I don't take some more."

"Where are they?"

Longer pause. He laid his cheek on the counter, feeling the first buzz of the beer in his head. "In my bag. Out in the field." He wanted to add, "in the hellbug," but somehow it did not seem terribly important. When the girl went out the back door he stood up, knowing he had to stay alert, swung his arms, tried deep-breathing exercises as he rolled a fresh can of cold beer over his forehead and smoked a cigarette. Then he sat down on the couch. He was snoring heavily when Petra returned, the cigarette smoldering at his feet.

TWENTY-THREE

WITH A WEALTH OF LANDING SITES TO CHOOSE from, Ben Ullmer suggested Jacksonville Naval Air Station. Naval surveillance aircraft carried highly sophisticated hardware, and in answer to a wild surmise by Ullmer, the NSA computers had kicked out a surprising answer. Yes, NAS Jacksonville had not one but *three* special X-Band radars gathering dust in a hangar.

Dar Weston approved Jacksonville because they could duck newsmen, who lacked the required clearances. The story had hit evening papers and now, as the Learjet taxied away in gathering darkness, Dar wanted to use a scrambler to Terry Unruh. Instead, he stood in the hangar, loosening his tie and trying to understand the impenetrable thicket of terms as Ullmer swapped jargon with a spiffy naval officer who seemed too young for his oak leaves.

When the officer turned away to confer with three ratings, all electronics technicians, Dar caught Ullmer's eye. "Ben, if Black Stealth One is invisible to radar, what's the point in putting these sets in naval aircraft?"

Ullmer blinked, looked as if he were about to explode, then shook his head. "I keep forgetting you're a—uhm. Okay: aircraft use a certain band of frequencies to avoid collisions and so on. We call it 'C' Band; it ignores clouds and birds and locust swarms and a shitpot of other stuff that clutters your scope. I mean, if C Band reflected *everything* you'd have mostly clutter all over your video screen. With me so far?"

Another time, Dar would have given an icy response to Ullmer's blatantly patronizing tone. But Ben Ullmer was under stress too, Dar told himself, and it had been Ullmer who'd had the humanity to balk at shooting down an airplane with a hostage in it—even before he knew who that hostage was. "Go ahead," Dar said calmly.

"But there's an 'X' Band of radar too," Ullmer went on, darting glances toward the men who were trundling test equipment out. "X Band sees everything, Weston; it'll see the hellbug. It'll also see everything else, including dust and clear air turbulence, and all of it gets painted on the scope so you have to guess what's what by the way it acts. Result is clutter like you wouldn't believe. But if you're already within a mile or two of something like the hellbug, especially in good weather, you might pick it up on X Band and then *maybe* you could get an eyeball on it. You narrow the X-Band aperture and boost its transmission power, and ignore everything that isn't acting like an airplane. It'll see the airchine, all right; you just have to *recognize* what you see." His faint smile held less worry and more confidence than Dar had seen that day. "Some scope men can do it. It's an art."

Sheppard, back at Elmira, had endorsed the X-Band idea. There was little doubt in anyone's mind, now, that Kyle Corbett had flown at medium altitude through a swarm of military aircraft over Georgia without being spotted by anything but an unarmed Cessna. "When science fails," Dar said, "I suppose we turn to art." Then, seeing the officer's return, he said quickly, "What's the X-Band stuff doing here?"

The young officer, Hinshaw, heard the question. "We have gulls, sir. Googols of gulls. We've retrieved naval aircraft from the bay and found the jet intakes packed half full of gull bodies. So we had to study their behavior. We, uh," he seemed faintly embarrassed now. "We did some of those studies in P2V's in nice clear weather using X Band for the, uh, chase. Eglin and Pensacola have the same problem, but we've got the P2V's. Gulls are protected animals but can we help it if they fail to avoid a big propeller?"

Ben Ullmer nodded. "Gulls won't hurt those old Lockheed prop jobs much, Weston. But a Neptune could pretty much wipe out a few thousand gulls. Civilians call the P2V a Neptune."

"Got it," said Dar, "but what in God's name is a googol?"

"Ten to the hundredth power, sir," said Hinshaw. "It just means 'a lot.' I was exaggerating, sir." He spoke like a contrite college prankster.

□□□

It broke the tension for Dar, who clapped the young electronics expert on the back gently and managed a smile. "You're entitled; you're part of the solution, not the problem, and you're responding wonderfully. I suppose the next question is, will there be room in a Neptune for us?"

"Room for ten men and a googolplex of sandwiches," Hinshaw replied, his eyes sparkling. "A *whole* lot."

Ullmer: "They as loud as ever? I used to be Lockheed myself."

" 'Fraid so, but there's a head onboard, too. It's not too bad when a man can take a leak in comfort," Hinshaw replied. "Without jet pods on the wings a P2V will loiter for, I don't know, at least twelve hours. The flight crews will know, sir."

A deep rumble filled the hangar, and Dar saw the massive doors trundling aside. Slowly approaching the hangar from the concrete ramp was a tiny tractorlike vehicle, towing a dull blue behemoth from the past. Dar saw the twin engines with their tremendous propellers, remembered the mind-numbing drone of the wartime transport that had dropped him into Greece. It did not seem possible that they would be chasing down the most sophisticated aircraft on earth in these vintage brutes.

Ullmer was speaking to young Hinshaw again, not whispering but clearly not intending his words to carry.

"That's not my field either," said Hinshaw. "The P2V has a little bomb bay of sorts for antisub duty. Whether you could fit a pod of fifties on, I don't know. Some blue-suiters from Eglin are already waiting for you, sir."

□□□

As Dar listened, his depression returned. Eglin Air Force Base and its blue-clad weapon wizards could provide a stunning array of armaments, including some that were still under test at Eglin. Dar found himself hoping that the nastier Air Force stuff could not be quickly adapted to a naval aircraft.

Hinshaw turned toward his primary job and a dozen technicians after promising that the two operating X-Band sets would be installed in P2V's before dawn. The third set was an enigma, missing parts that might or might not be found.

Ben Ullmer's face was set in a way that would not reveal much. "We've got to see the weapons people. I hate it as much as you do, but both sightings had Corbett heading south." The second sighting, by an off-duty National Parks ranger twenty miles from Waycross, Georgia, had been a fluke. The ranger knew something about wildlife, and had called in an official query as to the possibility of a California condor loose near the Okefenokee. NSA listening devices had isolated his call; they were that good. Unruh, claiming to be a model airplane builder, had interviewed the ranger by telephone and realized what the man had seen without alerting him to its significance. Unruh was that good, too.

With every datum pointing to a southerly course by Black Stealth One, Bill Sheppard would be paying close attention to Dar's decisions. "You're a decent man, Ben," Dar said. "We'll do what we're supposed to do."

A tinny beep began to sound rhythmically at Ullmer's side. He raised his hand to reveal a second wristwatch, a modern type with all the latest functions. Ben punched a button, stopping the noise. "Fucking pills," he swore, and fumbled in his pockets as they began to walk to the offices at one side of the hangar.

He needs a high-tech watch, but he still wears that old windup thing too, thought Dar. *I guess a man can be high-tech and old-fashioned as well. Maybe you can't hang on to both sets of values without a kind of innate decency. And I wonder if I have enough of that to matter.*

The weapons people included three "bluesuiters" and two civilian experts from Eglin, one of whom Dar knew slightly. They had been briefed only on the target's basic capabilities. As to the unspoken details, an Air Force colonel observed dryly, "Tonight's story in the Atlanta *Constitution* about that missing stealth airplane with the hostage is, we can all agree, purest coincidence. Right?"

No one smiled or answered him aloud. Dar's silent answer was, *You only thought you were a career man, Colonel Koons.*

The mounting of machine guns would have taken too long; rocket pods even longer—to Dar's intense relief. It was Dar's civilian acquaintance, Ernie Evanchow, whose solution came from left field. Short and grizzled like Ullmer, but with a young man's quickness, Evanchow suddenly sat up straight after an hour of silent slouching. He spent a minute slashing feverishly on a piece of paper with a flowpen before holding up a sketch.

The sketch depicted a tiny parachute with a very long wire hanging beneath. "Hanging from the wire is United Technology's latest caper, gentlemen," Evanchow said, using the flowpen as a pointer. "The size of a rolled newspaper, mass about four kilos; sensor sets it off when it's thirty meters above the ground. They're air-dropped from a munition pod the size of a barrel, about a hundred to the pod. Antipersonnel, actually. We call it Project Buckshot and we've got four pods at Eglin. Each of these little rounds is actually a submunition; it fires steel cubes downward in a conic pattern. Best of all, the firing sensor is sonic. Even if your airplane is plastic, it should bounce an echo." He stopped, then said, as if passing on a tidbit of rare entertainment, "But the round wouldn't have to fire to bring down a light aircraft."

Only Ullmer got it at first. "You don't even have to energize the warheads," he said, "if the wire's long enough."

"Wire's two hundred meters long"—Evanchow nodded—"hundreds of feet of wire hanging down with the live round on one end and a little drag chute on the other. Anything that flies through a forest of those little beauties will end up dragging 'em along, chutes and all. Hell of a lot of drag, probably enough to bring the target mushing down pretty fast. If the pilot were good enough, he might manage a landing he could walk away from. Take us hours to disarm those warheads, though."

Dar: "How many hours?"

Evanchow, after a brief mental calculation: "Three, maybe four per pod. You don't want to rush that kind of work."

"I say, go to it," Dar announced.

Ben Ullmer, sitting next to Dar, spoke very softly into his ear. "This is the sticky point. Think about

□□□

Sheppard's reaction when he learns we've disarmed them all."

The others were pretending not to listen. "You know what I'm thinking about, Ben."

"So am I. So let's ask for twice as many Buckshot pods as they can disarm before dawn. We take both kinds. We try the disarmed type first, if we get Corbett where we want him."

And that was how it happened that each sturdy old P2V was loaded with one fully-armed Buckshot pod and one with disarmed rounds.

Before the supper he did not really want and the sterile room in officer quarters that he honestly dreaded as only a lonely man can, Dar checked in with Terry Unruh on a line that was both secure and scrambled. "You know where I'll be," he said after answering Unruh's first questions, "so don't hesitate to call me if anything breaks. I'll be airborne by seven A.M."

Unruh: "Only one more thing so far; a third sighting, I'm afraid."

Dar, elated: "Afraid, hell! When and where?"

"About six this evening, by a Florida state patrolman who was looking up at a Peterbilt cab when your man Corbett flew over, heading south. I interviewed him myself, Hornet. The man hunts, and he knows a vulture from an eagle, or claims he does. Says this wasn't anything he'd ever seen and its tail feathers didn't look right, which made him think of a bulletin he'd seen when he went on-shift. He said, and I quote, 'God damn if it didn't just pop into sight like a ghost, tryin' to look like a buzzard.' I suspect Corbett has found out how to use that chameleon mode; Sheppard's certain of it."

"Wonderful," Dar replied. "Where was it?"

□□□

"On I-10, about twelve miles east of Lake City. We've already got Navy and Air Force flying grids down the center of Florida, but NSA doesn't think they'll find anything."

"Wait a minute," Dar said, fumbling for pencil and paper.

"Let me save you the trouble," said Unruh, his voice dropping slightly. "It's just about equidistant between where you are, on the Atlantic coast, and the Gulf coast to the west. That makes it sixty miles to our shoreline either way you slice it, and a gentleman sitting across from me asked me to convey his deepest sympathy, with the reminder that the interagency agreement was seventy-five miles. I'm sorry to be the one who has to make it official, Hornet. Black Stealth One is now fair game for a kill, by whoever sees it first."

TWENTY-FOUR

CORBETT'S FIRST AWARENESS ON WAKING WAS OF dim light; his second, that it shouldn't be. He ruined an armrest shoving up from it and came within an inch of stepping on the legs of Petra Leigh. She lay sleeping on the floor beside the old couch, one arm flung across the dirty linoleum, his leather jacket folded under her head. He stepped over her carefully and consulted his watch: nearly seven in the morning. *Or the evening? Hard to tell.* He heard the distant racketing thunder of a jet aircraft, realized that Black Stealth One lay fully exposed to anyone flying a search pattern, and bolted from the little store unsteadily, making no allowances for the early-morning twinges that time had begun to sift into his joints.

The hellbug was in costume. From his view it was easy to see, but its surfaces were mottled to match the ill-tended truck garden as seen from above. He had shut down all systems on landing, he was certain of it, but someone had energized the pixel program, probably hours ago. "Kid, you are a pistol," he said aloud, then quietly stuck his head into the shed. Nasal masculine snores echoed softly in the little structure. Corbett returned to the store wondering why Petra had not shot the fool, yet somehow relieved. It took a lot of subtle gears to make the kid tick like that—*and keep telling yourself she's a kid,* he thought. *Isn't twenty-two still a kid? Isn't it?*

She was in the bathroom. "Why can't you just walk around like everybody else," she said, emerging freshly scrubbed and radiantly irritated. "Scare a person to death," she grumbled, and went straight to the upright cooler where she selected a quart of skim milk. She squatted before a wire rack then, studying the scant choices in cellophane-wrapped snacks.

Corbett shrugged and sought the bathroom himself, noting with some surprise that the pistol was still snug in his armpit. He used the throwaway razor lying at the sink, telling himself it was only to make himself feel refreshed, that it had nothing to do with Petra Leigh. Whatever her motives, she had taken charge while he slept, and he hadn't awakened with his own gun barrel in his ear. He found that fact strangely unsettling as he returned to her.

He strode past the counter, pausing to open the cash register under the scrutiny of the implacable old Westclox. Nothing lay inside but small change. He glanced at her as he was choosing a quart of buttermilk.

□□□

"Fifty-seven dollars," she said, patting her jeans. "Bobby owes me that much in wear and tear."

The hum of an engine filtered in from the road, and the hum was not rising in tone but falling. Corbett heard the faint squeal of brakes and ducked down into shadows, seeing Petra squat behind the counter. They waited silently, trading silent eye contact as they heard tires on gravel. The engine stopped. A horn demanded attention it was not going to get. After an interminable thirty seconds they heard a starter, the engine's thrumm, and then the vehicle pulled away again. Corbett eased up from the shadows, watching a Dodge van tow a flat-bottom aluminum boat out of sight. He rubbed his arms to rid himself of adrenaline and stepped over to the snack racks, swigging on buttermilk as he chose his breakfast. If she wasn't going to mention that van, he wouldn't either.

"Twinkies? Christ, how can you eat that stuff," he said, wrenching open a bag of Laura Scudder's potato chips.

"I was thinking the same thing about you." She gave him an imp's grin and opened another package of Twinkies.

He knew she was watching, waiting for him to start talking about important things as he nosed around, rummaging in shelves stocked for the Florida sportsman, hefting the twin of the five-gallon gas can he had bought the day before. Now she would be all right, no doubt about it. *How long will she wait after I'm gone before she uses that telephone? And how much credibility will she have, especially on the Cuba ploy?* Then he saw the coil of tubing with its fist-sized rubber bulb on a lower shelf, and began to chuckle as he brought it into the light. "Well I'm damned," he said, inspecting the rubber for cracks.

Around a mouthful of junk food she replied, "What else is new?"

"A fuel siphon," he said, elated. "I might just cobble up a—" Then he stopped. "Nothing. Petra, I don't know why you're still here. What's more, I don't want you to tell me. You're going to have to repeat it all later today. And your Uncle Dar might not be able to help you. He might not even want to; we're not playing high-school fuckaround games. For the record, I've got a gun and I'll use it if you try to go for help. I've already killed a man and that should've scared the hell out of you, maybe so scared you didn't dare run during the night for fear I was playing possum. Do you understand?"

"Perfectly," she said, wiping an urchin's rime of milk from her mouth. "After that scum attacked me, I was half crazy with fear." Her eyes grew round, serious. "I really was, Kyle. I'd been trying to get their help to catch you, but they were cutting counterfeit liquor stamps at the time." A pause, and a headshake. Then, "Were you just trying to get me back in the airplane?"

He said, "Yes," and saw that she did not believe him. "Why the hell else would I have landed?" She just looked at him, and then smiled the kind of smile that a younger man would fight dragons for. "God *dammit,* Petra, stop that! What do I have to do for a little credibility; beat up on you?"

"It wouldn't help," she said. "I saw you. You were so mad in that shed, you were crying."

"I give up," he snarled, snatching the fuel can

□□□

and unlocking the store's front door. "All I ask is, let me know before you use that phone."

He was back in seconds, searching the place for the switch that energized the gas pumps, finding it on the wall near the cash register. He filled the gas can, feeling a humid morning breeze on his face and wondering how he might route a slender siphon hose from the cockpit of Black Stealth One to the tank. Hurrying back into the store he noticed that the "BEER" sign was lighted, and slapped the pump switch off. Relocking the front door, he saw that the lights were off again. In the ensuing silence he heard the distant drone of an aircraft. If they hadn't spotted the hellbug yet, maybe they couldn't. He might have plenty of time for some modifications.

As he was on his way out the back door, Petra followed. "Let me take that hose thing," she offered.

"Don't help me, Petra. They'll make you sorry." He kept walking toward the garden.

She kept pace. "I'm afraid not to," she said, and took the siphon hose from him. "You might hurt me." She ignored his whispered, blunt response.

Corbett needed two minutes to locate the fat polymer tube curving down from the filler neck of Black Stealth One to its tank; another five minutes with his knife to make a hole through the upper surface of the tube because he had to peel a plastic panel away behind his headrest. At last he inserted the end of the siphon hose into the hole and taped it securely with strips of his duct tape. With Petra's help, he routed the hose so that the rubber bulb lay between the seats in easy reach, the hose's lower end submerged in the fuel can. He

□□□

tested the system by squeezing the bulb rapidly, listening to the faint sounds coming from behind his headrest. He topped off the plastic bag from the metal can and then made a preflight inspection, ignoring Petra until she walked back to the store alone. *When she gets the full treatment, they'll learn I have an extra ten gallons on board. Well, that'll convince 'em I can make Cuba easily, maybe Haiti. There's going to be airplanes over Key West wingtip to wingtip when they've wrung this poor kid out, God help her.*

When he had checked the aircraft over, he stood for a moment with folded arms staring at the thing he had helped to create. *They didn't have to change much. Battery location moved aft to counterbalance all that computer stuff; little wing strakes added. Hats off to you, Ullmer—and you too, Speedy.* It was not merely the Rolls Royce of aircraft: it was the Chaparral, the Ferrari prototype, the Le Mans winner of aircraft.

He felt gooseflesh then, knowing that Black Stealth One was the sole object in all his remaining life that he would risk dying for—and that it was his. Some people felt that way about homes or cars; a few, about certain boats. It was probably those few who could sail around the world alone, visit any exotic port, who might come nearest to understanding his affection for the hellbug. For him, however, there would be no port authorities or border police to hinder his comings and goings. His could be a godlike freedom unknown to any other person on earth. That was the entire point; not to smuggle this or that, but to wish himself at a place, and know that he could go there.

He'd need to install some wing tanks for that,

which implied several bases of operations. The very idea would have been solitary fantasy without the prospect of money. *I don't know where I'll keep the hellbug, but I do know I'll need enough money for hangars. And Speedy's going to help me surprise some folks who are holding a bundle of that. Without that money, I can't keep the hellbug. No choice but to take the risk. One thing sure: I'll destroy this beauty before I let anyone else have it. It's mine; it's my price, they owe it to me and when this is over we'll all be even.*

Or I'll be dead.

He stepped up into the cockpit and flicked switches, moving the throttle gently, hearing a hollow click and a sound that was almost the low growl of a big animal. "Oh, Christ," he said, flicking the switches again.

He did not look up until she was striding through the furrows toward him, calling. "Kyle, come quick! It's on TV."

He shuffled back to the store and followed her to the bedroom which smelled of sour sweat, a room no Mexican peasant would have allowed into such a scabrous condition. Two empty quart bottles of Old Sunny Brook—or perhaps a local product masquerading as Old Sunny Brook—lay beside a bedside table, and a nearly full bottle sat by a snuff glass that might, once upon a time, have been clean. At the moment it looked as if bait had escaped from it. Petra leaned against one wall because it was preferable to the bed, nodding toward the big color set with its audio subdued.

". . . released this morning," said a handsome, blow-dried gentleman holding a sheaf of pages in a studio. "National Security Agency spokesmen would not comment on the skyjacker's identity, but sources say military and state law enforcement agencies are in close cooperation in a manhunt stretching from the Canadian border to Florida. More on this story now from Ynga Lindermann in Monroe, Georgia."

Cut to a statuesque blonde holding a cordless mike while a breeze flickered in her hair. Behind her stood a small commercial hangar. A wind sock nodded near a runway, and Corbett recognized a Schweizer sailplane in the background. "The stealth aircraft stolen from NSA near Elmira, night before last, may have landed here yesterday afternoon outside Monroe. If it did, airport manager Mel Ryder says he did not see it. Neither did any of several sailplane enthusiasts at—"

Corbett laughed aloud. "I dug a hole and buried it," he informed the reporter.

"Shh!" Petra's glance was formidable.

". . . was positively identified eight thousand feet over Monroe by a Georgia state trooper, a sharp-eyed 'bear in the air' whose small Cessna could not keep pace with the super-secret military plane. Chase planes crisscrossed airspace near here for hours afterward, and at least two armed, propeller-driven assault aircraft made emergency landings for fuel at small civilian fields near Athens and Vidalia, both in Georgia."

The photogenic blonde pointed toward her horizon, giving millions a view of her profile, and continued: "Later in the evening, another reported sighting placed the stolen aircraft in northern Florida, but a trucker who watched this sighting with a highway patrolman claimed, in his words, 'I know a bird when I see one, and I saw one.' Federal authorities clamped down on further details, but at this hour it's common knowledge that airspace over the entire southeastern United States is filled with military aircraft of every possible description, including AWACS in-flight refueling tankers. Whatever they're looking for, they do not seem to have found it. Ynga Lindermann, in Monroe, Georgia, for CBS. Back to you, Chris."

Again, the unruffled gent in the studio: "And still no word on the identity of the hostage, pending certain identification by the Federal Bureau of Investigation. In other news, talks on reduction of tensions with the Mexican government are underway, although drug-enforcement agents . . ."

Corbett walked out, chuckling, leaving Petra to follow. "AWACS my ass," he chuckled. "KC one thirty-fives are for in-flight refueling, not radar surveillance. And the Feebs know who you are, for sure. Why don't TV people get things right?"

"They got one thing right. I heard several airplanes go over in the night," Petra said. "I went out and set the pixel program for you."

"I know you did," Corbett said. "It took a lot more out of the battery than I thought it would."

"Any problem with that?" Perhaps too defensively.

"No—except that there's not enough power to start the fucking engine."

She gasped; put a fist to her mouth, chewing at a knuckle. Then, accusingly: "You were going to leave without—without saying good-bye?"

He put his hands out, shaking them as though holding a two-foot cocktail shaker, and burst out, "All right: good-bye! *Bon voyage, adios, ciao,* for God's sake, I know you were trying to help. I'm sure you did, in fact, but pretty soon there won't be enough juice to keep the computer program going, or some friend of the guy I shot will come poking around, and," he caught himself, sighed, and went on more softly, "I've got to find some way to fire the hellbug up."

"Can you?"

"I don't know. Maybe, if I can find a pair of car batteries. The hellbug uses twenty-eight volts, one car battery won't do it."

"How about the car outside?"

"That's one, if it works. I'll see. You could scout around, see if there's another one anywhere on the premises." With that, he hurried out to the rusting Pontiac and checked under its hood.

When he returned, she showed him empty hands. "Never mind, the battery's all but dead out there," he said.

"What if I hitched a ride and bought a pair of good ones? I've got fifty-seven bucks," she said brightly.

"Of all the dumb ideas you ever had," he began, and sighed. "You have any idea what they'd do to you for that?"

"You saved my life last night, Kyle Corbett."

He cocked his head at her. "Is that your real reason?"

Hesitation. Then, "A lot of it, yes. Most of it." Passionately: "Stop cross-examining me! Do you want those batteries or don't you?"

"I've got to have 'em," he admitted, "unless— Look, I might be able to mill the impeller blades over by hand. But I'll need somebody in the cockpit to handle the ignition and throttle. It's a long shot."

□□□

"Longer than waiting for batteries?"

He thought of the constant drain on the system from the energy keeping the skin camouflaged. "Maybe not." He stood up, headed for the back door. "You want to help?"

"Yes. On one condition," she said hesitantly.

"Hunh! Short of giving up the hellbug, it's yours."

"Then I'll tell you later," she replied.

Corbett's small tool selection included a multiblade screwdriver, and its crosspoint tip was not quite too small for the filament-filled nylon screws securing the intake screens. He removed the screen on the passenger's side, a huge crescent of stiff plastic mesh, then let Petra sit in the pilot's seat while he coached her. "Remember to keep the pixel program off during startup; we need all the juice we can get," he finished. "Yes, we could be seen from the air, but it's a chance we have to take. If you hear an airplane, of course, give me a shout and hit the pixel program. Clear?"

"I think so; yes," she said, straightening her shoulders, nodding herself into belief. "Clear. Wait," she said as he began to ease himself into the intake. "Is this dangerous? For you in there, I mean."

"No. Shut up and deal," he growled, and resumed climbing in.

"Liar," he heard her say, and he grinned at the big carbon-boron impeller blades.

If it starts and she pours too much coal to it, this sucker is going to literally eat me, he thought, judging the strength of rigid airfoiled struts that radiated out to the big duct, just ahead of the blades. *Maybe one of these radial struts would stop me, or*

□□□

maybe not. Well— In the semidarkness, he wrestled his gloves on, trying to ignore the pinch of the duct where it narrowed under his hip. He grasped one of the blades near the hub, a hub at least two feet across with a bullet-shaped spinner protruding behind. It moved with relative ease.

He could reach the blades with only one hand, lying with his legs protruding from the maw of the great creature, but found that it might be enough. He heard subtle whirrs inside the fuselage skin near his chest, where the engine lay, as he grasped another blade and pulled, the impeller beginning to move fast enough to blur. That was only an illusion of high speed, he knew, because there were so many blades. He did not call out until the impeller was moving as fast as he could move it. Then: "Contact!"

He did not move away as he should have, but kept flicking his gloved hand out, trying to keep the blades moving. He heard a stutter of electric fuel pumps, then a chuff. He snatched for another blade, missed, got his knuckles rapped hard. Another chuff, and another, and then nothing but the *tick-tick* of fuel pumps. "Kill it," he called, and dragged himself out backward, all but collapsing on the dry ground.

She knelt beside him, watching as he drew off the glove and flexed his bruised knuckles. She held the hand briefly, gently, then stood up. "I'm going after those batteries."

"No! It could take hours. I have another idea," he said, grunting to his feet, donning the glove again. He began to refit the intake screen, working steadily, attaching all the screws loosely before snugging them tight.

□□□

Petra's voice came to him with hollow echoes because she was peering into the duct. "You crazy son of a bitch, Corbett, how did you think you could—?"

"It's the impeller blades," he explained, laying his tools aside, moving to the rear of the aircraft with its three-foot exhaust aperture. "They're angled forward, so I had to reach inside to the trailing edges. But if I can get in there from the tailpipe, I can grab the trailing edges easy. No sweat."

"Except that if it does start, it'll blow you out of there like, like," she waved her arms.

"Like shit through a tin horn," he finished for her, running a hand along the polished inside of the tailpipe. "It's smooth enough, and the exhaust is cool air. You just concentrate on keeping the rev counter below twenty percent, so you don't blow me clean through the wall of that shed."

"I wonder how our friend Bobby is, in there," she said, watching him remove his shoes.

"Counting sheep, or his many sins," Corbett replied, and began to wriggle inside. His voice reverberated through the fuselage: "Better get in, my weight's about to tip this bird on her tail."

He felt the gentle rocking of the craft, then eased himself forward, surprised at the roominess of the exhaust chamber. The waste gates lay flush in recesses, hiding the ducts that would yawn open when the tailpipe was closed, and he moved carefully because he could feel the duct skin flexing beneath his hands and legs. He could see, dimly, lettered decals on the big spinner that pointed bulletlike toward the rear. A good sign; it meant Ullmer intended someone to crawl in there now and then.

The impeller, over four feet in diameter, required a duct big enough to allow him to sit sideways. He noticed the engine exhaust vents, fed through curved radial vanes into the airstream, and realized he could get a lungful of fuel-rich exhaust. Finally, with stocking feet braced across the duct, he reached for an impeller blade. Here he could reach between the vanes and grab a blade near the outer tip, and with both hands. He began to breathe hard, deliberately hyperventilating, and pulled downward on a blade. He could feel it flex slightly, and shifted his fingers inward.

He grasped another blade, realizing that both hands made a huge difference, and pulled, now adjusting his fingers, now using his hands on different blades. He felt a tightening in his breast, puffed harder, spun harder.

"I hear an airplane," Petra called.

"Forget it," he bawled over the whine of mechanical friction, knowing that he would never have more strength than at this moment. "Now—or never; *contact!*"

The rattle of pumps, and a chuff; several more, and he kept clawing at the blades, turning his head to face the rear; and then a great outpouring of gray, greasy fumes that roiled around him as he went to his knees facing rearward, and a gentle push on his rump became a gale that hurled him like a cork from a long-necked bottle, turning him in a half flip, and then he was staring up from the ground into a bright morning sky, coughing so hard he could not get his breath.

His throat seared from fumes, he managed to

lurch up, grabbing his shoes, ducking under the wing, calling to Petra. "The pixel! Paint her," he gasped, and fell on his knees.

Petra did it, the dull gleam of gunmetal gray changing magically to mottled green and brown as he watched. He stood up, hawking and spitting, and leaned in to see the instrument cluster.

Petra, misjudging his reason, leaned down and clasped her hands onto his shoulders, and he felt a resounding kiss atop his head. "Nineteen percent on the tach," she said proudly. The skin of Black Stealth One purred softly as Corbett leaned against it and nodded. "Go to twenty-five," he said, gulping clean air. "Gotta build up the battery awhile."

He wished, watching her as she handled the throttle, that some woman, just once, had fondled his body the way Petra Leigh caressed those controls.

They left the craft with its engine idling, and Corbett did not understand at first why Petra wanted to cut their captive loose, or at least drag him to the road. They walked slowly toward the store until he asked, "Look, why can't you just point the guy out when the cops get here?"

"Because," she said firmly, "I'm going with you."

"You're—I'llbegod-damned if you are," he blurted, and stopped.

"And you're going to take me at gunpoint," she added.

"To fucking *Cuba?*"

"You're not going to Cuba. You let me go so that I'd send them off in the wrong direction." Not in questioning tones, but a flat declaration.

"Also," he said, "so you won't get killed if I make a mistake. I've made a few, you know."

"And what I know, they'll soon find out. Because I'll damned well tell them, Kyle, I'll tell them everything I can think of if you break your promise now!" She was almost shouting as she finished, eyes blazing, breast heaving wonderfully, he thought.

"What promise?"

"I said I'd help you on one condition. You said yes. The condition is that you take me as far as I want to go."

"That's it?"

"That's it. I thought about it a lot last night." She folded her arms.

"Would you mind telling me why?"

She hesitated, looking from him to the softly purring aircraft, back to him again. "I can't. Too many reasons. I—well, if I'm in trouble, after last night I can't make it any worse by another day. Are you really going to turn that incredible machine over to someone else?"

"And what if I do?"

"You're crazy. I wouldn't. Whatever you get for it, it couldn't be better than keeping it." She saw something in his face, perhaps a recognition of sorts, and added, "You know what I fantasize, while I'm on a damn bridge design project? That it's my spaceship. I can land it on the moon, or the asteroid Vesta. Don't laugh, it's a feeling that just fills me up to bursting, something that could lift me away from everyday things, of, of—"

"Freedom," he supplied.

"Yes! I know I'm taking awful risks, maybe freedom is always risky. But dammit, I've been secure for twenty-two years, and I know what I want. I know you have it, and you owe me a little piece

□□□

of it without treating me like a God-damned juvenile delinquent. At least for another day or so. Please, Kyle?"

He saw that she was fighting back tears. "I'm giving you the freedom to get yourself seriously killed; you know that."

"I'm of age, Kyle! If I wanted to drive a race car like my dad did, nobody could stop me."

"Why don't you?"

She thought about it a moment, wiped her eyes, and grinned. "Too many rules," she replied.

"Shit," he murmured.

"What's wrong?"

"I was born thirty years too soon," he said, and cocked his head. "Don't move," he cautioned. "Here it comes."

The next moment her eyes grew wide because she could hear its approach but she stood there immovable as the little Northrup F-5 howled overhead at perhaps two thousand feet, banking as it passed. Corbett looked up and waved for the few seconds it was in sight. "Don't worry," he said as his hands came down. "He'd need a mile of freeway to land that thing. We've got a few minutes, but if he takes up orbit over us, believe me, *you don't want to go.*"

"And if he doesn't, what do we do with loverboy?"

"I'll cut him loose and—no, he'd see the hellbug and his testimony might hurt you."

"I won't let you kill him, Kyle, I don't know why but—"

"I didn't intend to. Wait: in that bedroom there's a bottle of booze. I want you to stuff everything in the hellbug and wait for me. Don't forget toilet paper. And bring that damned old alarm clock near the cash register. I'm probably going to need it." He saw the elation in her face, tried to avoid thinking how that face would look after falling a mile, or taking a fifty-caliber incendiary slug.

As they separated inside the store she asked, "What are you going to do to Bobby?"

"I'm going to have a little drink with him. And he's going to have a big, big drink with me."

TWENTY-FIVE

THE MAN WHO HAD SHOWN A FINNISH PASSPORT and the name Einar Fredriks to a customs official could have seen treetops in Chapultepec Park from the triple-glazed high window of the Soviet Embassy in Mexico City. Instead, Karel Vins leaned back in the swivel chair and placed his bootheels on the desk before him. "How do you like the pattern, Jorge?" Vins had trained these men and his Spanish was excellent.

Jorge Ocampo's was better. Before the Soviets took him to Cuba he had been tenth-generation Mexican. His short, sturdy brown body and strong aquiline nose were pure *Indio,* though European stock had favored him with eyes that were not quite brown enough to be black. "May I sit?"

"Of course, of a certainty," Vins exclaimed, smiling at Jorge and at Mateo Carranza, the scarred veteran whose reddish hair marked him, a Cuban, with his Castilian extraction. A few kilos lighter than Ocampo and only slightly taller, Carranza did not carry himself like a fighter. It had been known to give him an edge—and all Carranza needed was an edge. Men of the usual stamp—say, KGB—would have automatically favored Mateo Carranza over the swarthy peasant, Jorge. Vins was not hampered by such bigotry; and besides, Jorge had stood his ground with a Kalashnikov to cover the escape of his revered Lobo after Vins, some years before, had been wounded near the Nicaraguan border. Mateo was more of a loner, and probably would have deserted military life for armed robbery years before, were it not for his aged mother in Matanzas. She, it seemed, had thought the world of Mateo. So, in his way, did Karel Vins, alias Vawlk, alias Lobo. Vins had known both men in rough times, and knew what they were made of. He had chosen them carefully. "Sit, sit," he urged, smiling. He snapped the edges of his bootsoles together. "What do you think of these?"

Mateo, whose slouching carriage and stolid face made him appear dull at times, was nothing of the sort. "I think they are yanqui boots," he said. Jorge merely looked and shrugged.

"Exactly right. You remember a surveillance school session after all this time?"

Mateo Carranza ran a forefinger under his nose to hide a smile. "No, but I remember how you think. To claim otherwise would be lying, Major."

Vins dropped his feet and leaned forward. "No more rank, Mateo. Not this time. I am your lobo, if you like, and you will follow me as always. But this time, I think, we must consider ourselves more as equals, even brothers." He let it sink in, knowing the two latinos were not close, that Jorge did not really trust a man like Mateo. "Mateo: you recall the bar in Camaguey?"

"He recalls many bars, many places," Jorge said.

"But you were with me too, Jorge," Vins said. "I was standing you drinks for saving my pelt in Nicaragua."

"Ay, Madre de Dios," Mateo said. "The money."

"The *marked* money," Vins insisted, one finger raised.

"Not here, if you please," said Mateo, looking around him.

Vins beamed and stood up, stepping over to rap a wall which was surfaced with padded canvas. "Why not here, *compadre?* This is not an ordinary embassy room. This is a GRU room. I control the ears here. It is, in fact, the only room in Ciudad Mexico where we can speak as we like"—he paused and released another smile, prefabricated but always useful—"of the things we like. So: I saw the roll you carried was marked. And I knew how you had gotten it."

"A man must eat," said Mateo, flushing. "His mother must eat, too."

"And is your mother well?" asked Vins, who knew exactly how she had fared.

"Among the saints in Heaven," said Mateo, crossing himself.

"Lo siento mucho, it is much regretted," Vins replied. Nothing tied Carranza to his home now, and their interchange had stressed the fact. "But I mention Camaguey only to refresh you on certain things we discussed that night."

□□□

"You burned the fucking money, is what you did," Jorge said, between awe and dismay.

"To protect my friend against his error," Vins reminded him, now beginning to pace the floor. The pacing was important; it brought watching men to higher alertness, more readiness to pledge a risk. "But what did I tell you both?"

"Something," said Jorge, "about the danger of a little money, and the safety of much money."

"I remember. I was not that drunk," Mateo said, prepared to argue the point. "We spoke of the ways a man gains that kind of safety. We seemed to be largely in agreement."

Vins stopped pacing and faced the two seated men, no longer smiling. "If you have lingering suspicions that this room has ears, listen now: how much money would it take for all of us to become disappeared ones, *desaparecidos,* on our own terms, with a villa and a complacent maid for the rest of our lives? But not, if we are wise, in Cuba."

Now Mateo and Jorge did look at each other, more in puzzlement than friendship. Then Jorge named a figure. Mateo waited and named a higher one, which would have made Vins smile if he had been watching through one-way glass.

"Then you would certainly do it for," he paused, and named a much higher figure. Jorge jumped. Mateo lost his slouch. Vins put his knuckled fists on the desk and leaned forward, letting the smile seem to arrive of its own volition. "The amount that could be yours is *ten times* as much."

Jorge closed his eyes, shook his head, opened them again.

Mateo, laconically: "And whom must we kill?"

"Perhaps one man, perhaps none," said Vins,

straightening, hands on hips, a commanding presence. "And it may turn out that we return empty-handed. It depends on some things we may not control—but each of us just may have the chance to retire among the anonymous rich. For a warrior, it is the opportunity of a lifetime."

"Ten lifetimes," Mateo said. "But you, *el lobo?* Why?"

Vins would not simply identify Maksimov by name, nor the power shifts initiated by the hated liberals of the Gorbachev regime. Too many "ifs" remained to talk politics with peons. But he could read a soldier's face, and he no longer doubted the wisdom of his choices for a team. "No man reaches the top by pushing; he must be pulled up."

"For that, a thousand thanks," said Jorge.

"For nothing, Jorge, but I was referring to myself. And what happens if the man who is pulling you up, finds himself pushed from behind?"

"He breaks his ass and so do you," said Mateo, making Jorge smile.

"And some men at the top actually jump," Vins told them. "And if another at the top even suspects he intends to jump, that other man will push him."

"There are too many pushers in this world and not enough pullers," Jorge observed.

"No man pushes me," said Vins, with the wolfish grin that had inspired his sobriquet. "The only question is: may I pull you both?"

Jorge was first, but Mateo stood too, both of them making a gesture Karel Vins had taught them as a part of esprit de corps, a very old gesture, older than Czars, as old as Caesars. They stood erect, proud, right fists clenched over their hearts.

□□□

"I have already told you, but I repeat it now, and we will not speak of this again until we are driving on the last leg of this mission," Vins said, just a shade more somber than threatening. "We have a mission, and it requires the movement of a great fortune. All this is approved, just as you were approved."

"As you, too, were approved," Mateo interrupted, smirking.

Vins caught his snarl inside and inverted it. "As I too was approved," he agreed, perfectly aware that Mateo Carranza was already beginning to test the notion of equality. *I may have to shoot this son of a whore yet,* he thought. "We will pursue the mission, pay the money to a man for a piece of military hardware, turn that hardware over to certain authorities—and try to recover the money. All approved; what is not sanctioned is what we just might do with the money afterward."

For all his faults, Mateo had his flashes of insight. "I do not see why, Lobo, if we control the money to begin with, we do not simply disappear immediately."

"The hardware it buys," said Jorge, surprised.

"Fuck the hardware," Mateo said with a smile.

"Because that hardware is an aircraft of absolutely crucial importance to world socialism and the Soviet Union," Vins said tersely. "You will bear in mind that I am a patriot." And this time his smile was unfeigned, lopsided, and a little sad. "But not the kind of patriot to have my ass broken for nothing."

TWENTY-SIX

A NIGHT IN MAZATLAN HAD NOT IMPROVED THE temper of Raoul Medina. He braced himself as Aleman, the driver of the Chevette, dodged another chuckhole on the winding road to Regocijo. The long bag with the tanks and flight helmet in Medina's side of the footwell slid again until he clamped it between his feet. To fly five thousand miles in a day and then trudge from a lagoon to a town at the end of the day lugging SCUBA tanks, only to be balked by want of a lousy car! "They should have known the rental places in Mazatlan wouldn't be open at night," he fumed. His Spanish was fluent, though a little rusty.

Rodrigues, sitting in back with his long legs stretched at a slant, flicked the butt of his Delicado still smoldering from the open window. "I might have told them if anyone had asked me," he said.

□□□

"Aleman, can't you punch this thing harder?"

"Not if we expect to get there on four wheels," said Aleman with a trace of brusqueness. On such a road, forty miles an hour was good time; fifty, suicidal. They had turned south from El Salto a half hour earlier and after that the road had become worse, the pounding on the Chevette's suspension more fierce than Medina remembered—but then, old Julio's grandson had not been driving as hard as Aleman. Then, *"Iglesia,"* said Medina, spotting the superstructure of the ancient church through the lacy shade of trees. "We're nearly there."

He directed Aleman through the dusty whitewashed town of Regocijo even though the village was not the kind a sober man could get himself lost in, taking it slowly enough to avoid the dogs and barefooted children, then urged the driver on to the south. "Fifteen kilometers or so now," he said.

"I understand miles, señor," said Aleman, easily wounded.

"Certainly; my regrets, Aleman." After a night with these two, Medina knew that Aleman was older than he seemed, college-trained and insufferably proud of it. The lank Rodrigues claimed he had got his training in the jungles of Honduras and was well disposed toward the yanquis who had schooled him. *Even better disposed toward the money,* Medina thought, having known mercenaries in other countries. Rodrigues seemed typical of most of the breed, essentially a lazy man but tireless when he had to be, and he knew how to hide an Ingram submachine gun under his windbreaker by a sling.

□□□

Aleman's similar weapon, as well as Medina's, lay beneath the hood, wrapped in oilcloth and strapped to the engine oil filter with the ubiquitous black electrical tape. Half of all Mexican transport was literally held together with the stuff, Aleman had said. "I don't think we need to go waving our Mac Tens under old Julio's nose," Medina said now, beginning to recognize landmarks near the airstrip. "He's a good guy."

"Mac Elevens," Rodrigues said. "Ingram Mac Eleven, señor." He snapped his weapon loose and popped its narrow, boxlike magazine down, displaying them separately as Medina craned his head to see.

"Jesu Christo," Medina breathed, "don't tell me they're different. I haven't fired one in years."

Rodrigues gazed fondly at the squarish, gray lines of the stubby weapon, with its wire stock folded so closely over its receiver that the entire murderous little brute could be slung between arm and rib cage with hardly a bulge. "This weighs less than a Ten, a little shorter. Less recoil. Safeties are the same."

"That's good," Medina said.

"It is unless you want to stop a man with one round," Aleman put in, always happy to show his technical expertise. "These are little short cartridges. Less energy."

Rodrigues shoved the magazine home and resnapped the weapon, grinning as he caught Medina's eye, and raised his voice. "Ever shoot anybody with one, Aleman?"

"I am happy to say I have not found it necessary," Aleman said, looking straight ahead.

"Relax," Medina cautioned. "It won't be necessary today either," he added, proving himself tragically lacking in the gift of prophecy.

"We should not linger here long," Rodrigues said. "It will take us hours to get to Llano Mojado. I do not think you want to arrive there before we do, Señor Medina."

"I won't. If I'm delayed here, just wait there. I'll be along when I can." *I can't hang around here waiting for Corbett more than two nights. I don't dare collect those gas canisters until he shows, either. If he doesn't show by tomorrow, I'll have to go without him. Ullmer and that cold-warrior Weston think I have to sell the Sovs a fake in a hurry, and I'll bet my ass they think the real Black Stealth One is on the way to the same rendezvous,* Medina told himself. What bothered him was that, the last time he'd talked with Ben Ullmer in San Diego, Ullmer was in a Learjet over Georgia—or said he was. And Ben wouldn't be there unless he had a good idea which direction to go. Was Corbett really bent on hiding the hellbug in Mexico? He seemed to be headed for the Gulf. It was a long watery way across, unless a man fueled up in southern Florida. Still a lot of miles—what, five hundred, six?—to the Yucatan. *Kyle, you solitary self-willed bastard, why didn't you tell me you intended to steal the hellbug?*

And where would Corbett get his fuel? Medina could almost hear the gravelly voice say, as it had so many times during design forums, "A secondary concern. The primary question is, can it be done?" *Well, can it? With luck, maybe. I could do it if tailwinds were with me. And if I could do it, that hardnosed old fucker could do it too . . .*

Which raised a spectre that Raoul Medina

loathed and feared. What if Kyle Corbett really *did* intend to sell Black Stealth One to the Other Side? Maybe you couldn't much blame him, but you couldn't let him, either. It had not occurred to Medina, when he got himself into this fucking mess, that Corbett was actually capable of such a thing; or, worse, that Corbett might already have the KGB as a steady source of income. It was occurring to him now. *Take the hellbug to Mexico and fiddle with it; crash it, burn it, fly it into the Langley parking lot, but don't let me down, Corbett.*

Medina realized that Aleman was repeating a question. "Oh, uh, if I get there first I can loiter overhead. Just tie a sleeve of your windbreaker on your radio antenna, and park where I can see the car from above," Medina advised the driver. "I'll be swimming in, maybe an hour after I ditch. And I'll walk north. Don't go within two miles of that landing strip."

Aleman nodded. Medina looked back and saw Rodrigues nod as he lit another Delicado. *He's starting to chain-smoke now,* Medina thought. *Not as cool as he acts. I'll have to watch him with that goddamn Ingram of his, until they leave.*

Presently Medina placed a hand out, patting the air. "Slow down, now, and watch for ruts toward the left." Aleman found them soon, shifting into low, growling along for nearly a mile before they rounded a hill and saw the airfield.

"Why are we stopping?" Medina asked.

"The guns, señor," said Aleman.

Medina sighed. "You really think we need them for a friendly old caretaker?"

"I only think it is the thing we are paid to do," was Aleman's reply. "If I am your backup," he added, using the English word, "then I must do it properly."

"I suppose so," Medina said. He watched Aleman stop and pull his gloves on, precise and careful as he maneuvered the cloth-wrapped bundle from the engine compartment, and Medina accepted his own weapon without comment. Then they were lurching forward again toward the disused blacktop strip with tufts of grass that sprouted from surface cracks, and the wooden hangar that had not been painted in fifteen years. *With a souped-up airchine and a nice girl in the next town, a man could live in a place like this,* he thought idly. It was warm, peaceful; Corbett probably lived in some place like this. *But if you sell my country out, Kyle, I'll find you,* he said silently, *if it takes me the rest of my life.*

Medina stepped from the Chevette and glanced at the small personnel door at one end of the hangar, wondering why it and the hangar doors were partly open, shaking the kinks from his legs, hauling his helmet from the bag and waiting for the others. He slung the stubby Ingram so that it hung at his back and realized that, of his two backups, Rodrigues seemed much the more threatening. "Aleman, you come with me," he said. "Rodrigues can keep watch, he's very experienced at surveillance in the wild." Rodrigues made an "if you say so" face, satisfied with the reason, and leaned against a fender, scanning the open spaces as he lit up another cigarette.

Medina went through first, getting a nice little buzz of elation as he saw Blue Sky Three crouched in its three-wheeled stance, the same way he and Julio had left it, noticing the coat of dust with mild dismay. No wonder the door was ajar—it was stiflingly hot and a faint acrid tang stung his nostrils. Well, the old man had a trickle-charge going on the battery, at least, and it wouldn't take long to wipe the bird down. Aleman was looking around him, his Mac Eleven slung but near to hand, and his eyes kept straying to the aircraft with its slender wings and sinister charcoal-black paint job.

"Julio," Medina called, making echoes. *"Hola, mi viejo,* old friend," he said, smiling, striding toward the set of small office rooms that lined the rear of the building. He remembered it was cooler there.

"Hola, amigo," responded from the second office, the one Medina recalled with its windows intact. But the voice was not Julio's, nor the face, alertly smiling as the man stepped from the office. Medium height, late thirties, in good gabardines and a sportshirt with a bright print pattern in reds and yellows. Recent haircut, plastered neatly with goo; something of a dandy, Medina decided, one who carried himself as though he was worth carrying. "You must be hunting elephants," the man said, still smiling, with a nod toward Aleman's weapon.

"My apologies," Medina said. "I expected my friend Julio, who understands these necessities."

"He is indisposed," said the man, and stuck his hand out in the yanqui fashion. "I am Comal, cousin of Julio. He wished me to stay here, I cannot say why. We have waited a long time."

A cousin, thirty years younger? Fairly common around here, I guess. But who is "we"? Medina shook the hand briefly. "A thousand thanks, Comal, you do not have to say why. I am the pilot who flew this aircraft. I must take it away now, if you will help us open the hangar."

But Comal was turning away, beckoning. That damned smile was beginning to look like a permanent fixture. "Come and share my tequila, then. If you are the pilot, I must tell you why the aircraft cannot be flown."

"Ahh, shit," Medina said, wondering what it could be, whether it meant going for fuel or another battery. If it was a stuck hangar door they would rip the fucking thing off. He stepped forward into the doorway and then the man turned, *still* smiling, and Medina never quite figured out where that revolver came from but suddenly it was sticking into his belly as he stood in the doorway, blocking Aleman's view.

"Tell your man to put his weapon down, or we will kill you both," said Comal.

Medina swallowed. "Aleman, did you hear him?"

"Oh, Mother of God," Aleman said softly. Medina dared not turn his head but it sounded as if Aleman had shuffled off to one side.

Comal's smile had, mercifully, come unglued and slipped away now, but Medina did not much like the nervous glances that replaced it. "Tell him," Comal insisted, shoving with the barrel of the revolver.

"I don't think he will, whatever I say," Medina said. It seemed that Comal was a man who wanted talk, and Raoul Medina was happy to comply. "He's not my man, I'm, uh, only a pilot, as I said. But you're not Julio's cousin."

"Hands up, but first lower that strange gun to the floor. Do not move from the doorway." As Medina obeyed, he kept hearing Aleman's breathing behind him. Comal, or whoever he really was, had not been smart to stand so close. Medina had seen men who could actually disarm a gunman positioned this way—but Medina was not one of them, at least not today. Too far from a hospital, and a terrible risk even for fucking Bruce Lee.

"I am a man who takes great interest in strange happenings," said Comal, still nervous, using one foot to scrape the Mac Eleven to one side. "I can fly an airplane. I heard about the old man who guarded something wonderfully strange here," he said, the smile threatening to reappear. "And so I asked my friend, 'Why, if this strange thing is on my land, should I not investigate it, perhaps fly it?' And so we investigated. Imagine my surprise when the place filled with mist that makes one breathless and took two days to clear."

"It's not your land," Medina bluffed. Aleman's breathing was no longer audible. Standing in the doorway, Medina could hear things that Comal might not; and it sounded as if Aleman was easing into the next room but the wall facing that room was piled with metal bins and spare lumber.

"Perhaps it might be," said Comal, shrugging, "given enough money."

"Who's going to give it to you? I haven't got it. Look, take our car, take the damned gun if you want to," Medina said, and heard a foot scrape echo faintly in the hangar. He spoke louder now. "You think you can fly this airplane away?"

"I have studied it carefully. It is no heavier than the Piper and the Aeronca I have flown, and it has two seats so that you could teach me its manners. Yes, with a teacher I think I can. I have told my friend that I can. And so I will," said Comal, with the finality of a man who will fulfill a boast or go to hell trying.

Though Raoul Medina's mouth was dry as Melba toast, he had to keep talking to cover the sounds he heard behind him. "I'm telling you, this isn't an ordinary airplane."

"That was my thought," said Comal judiciously. "By the way, tell your man that if he keeps his weapon, my friend will kill him instantly."

"I'll do that," said Medina, realizing that it was probably another bluff but, all the same, something for Aleman to keep in mind. And maybe if he said it loudly enough, Rodrigues would hear. He started to shout the warning, but Comal silenced him with a backhand across the face. "Quietly. He can hear you. Did you think we did not see the three of you approaching?"

Medina called out more softly then, wondering why Rodrigues hadn't become suspicious of the long silence. Licking blood from the edge of his lip, he said, exasperated, "You would kill yourself in that airplane the first time you tried to land it," and then he realized that the truth was more awesome than any lie. "It's a *chingada CIA* airplane! I fly it for the CIA," he burst out, jerking a thumb downward at himself. "You take this airplane and they'll get you, they'll get your family, they'll get your friends, they'll get your whole damn town!" He saw a shadow of credulity in Comal's face as he broadened the exaggeration, realizing that to many latinos the Company was synonymous with Satan and perhaps more powerful as a bogeyman of the here and now.

"Where do you think we get weapons and airplanes like these, Comal? We're big, the biggest thing you ever saw! We're so big, we could erase your town so nobody would ever know it had existed."

Then a sort of disappointment crossed Comal's features. Whatever belief he had entertained, he was discarding it as he spoke. "They are big. Yet here you are, only three men, not in three helicopters but in a small Chevrolet. Not to fly an airplane of steel but one of wood. Not guarded by an army in a new building, but by stinking smoke and an old fool in a firetrap." He snarled, perhaps infuriated by his moment of obvious indecision, and moved to pistol-whip this liar claiming to be CIA, but to do it he turned the revolver sideways.

Medina grabbed for the pistol with both hands and kicked Comal as hard as he could, aiming for the kneecap but connecting with a shin. Comal was already twisting, snatching the pistol out of reach, and the kick whirled him around so that he fell on his face away from Medina, whose sense of timing said that Comal would shoot him before he could grab the Ingram and cycle a round into its firing chamber.

Medina leaped out into the hangar and ducked behind a low-slung rudder of Blue Sky Three. "Aleman," he shouted, "get him as he comes out!" Then, with every decibel at his command: "Rodrigues! Help me!" He began to back away farther, realizing that he might get shot by his own man if he made it through that side door. The man who trotted from the next small room was not Aleman but an unkempt stranger in the shabby garb of a farmer. He carried a machete in one hand and a shotgun in the other, and the machete glistened with fresh blood.

Comal, limping into the hangar with both revolver and Ingram, saw the other man too. "Where is your man?" he barked.

"He did not put down his gun, so I carried out your promise," said the farmer, showing the blade of the machete. "He never saw me."

At that moment, Medina saw a shadow fill the rectangle of light at the side door. "Take them, Rodrigues, they got Aleman," he called, but the farmer's machete clattered to the concrete, and as Rodrigues showed his head for a fast glimpse inside, the shotgun bellowed. A portion of the door's upper half disintegrated, leaving a hole the size of a kitchen sink. Medina, who had reached the seam between the big hangar doors and was trying to slide one of them open, could see the farmer sliding the shotgun's pump but could not hear it among the echoes. Comal stuck the revolver in his belt and swung the Ingram up, aiming toward the side door, and then began to shake the weapon in a frenzy when it refused to fire. It had been Medina's idea to dart outside to safety but that big half-open door moved easily and Comal obviously did not know how to cycle the Ingram's bolt. Medina kept hauling the hangar door wider, watching the men inside, ready to plaster himself against the outside of the doorframe.

Rodrigues, who knew better than to stand guard without a round in the chamber, had no problem with his own Mac Eleven. His first spray, a half-dozen rounds, ricocheted from the concrete in front of Comal who bent double and dropped the useless weapon. Another blast from the shotgun ripped the doorframe near Rodrigues as Medina hurled himself against the opposite hangar door in the effort to slide it wide open. Reeling from a wall, Comal ducked into the office in time to avoid the next stuttering burst from Rodrigues.

The farmer spun to face Medina as sunlight flooded the hangar, and knelt to get a clear shot beneath the nose of Blue Sky Three. Medina stumbled and fell, and wood splintered over his head as shotgun pellets perforated the hangar door.

"I need that one; he is harmless," Comal shouted, squatting near the doorway, and risked a shot with the revolver as he peered around the office door. The long burst from Rodrigues sent hunks of old wood flying in the doorway, and Comal rolled into the hangar, his head thudding against concrete as his body twitched.

The farmer sent another of his thunderous rounds in the direction of Rodrigues, then ran in a crouch toward the room where he had dispatched Aleman, and Medina did not pause to think it out but dashed to the open battery panel near the cockpit of Blue Sky Three. *I spent too many months helping build this bird to let some fucking bandit destroy her,* he told himself, and flung the battery charger clips aside with one thought: *she's not that heavy, I can roll her outside before that maniac blows her full of holes.* Filled with this suicidal optimism, he began to hope that the shotgunner had fled through the broken back windows.

Rodrigues stepped into the hangar. "Aleman! Medina! Let me hear you," he barked.

"Aleman's dead," Medina called, slapping the battery panel closed as he ducked under the wing to kick a wheel chock aside. Then, because his view opened directly into the little rooms and sunlight had replaced shadows, Medina saw the shotgunner finish reloading. "I'm here under the," he said, and dived for the other wheel as the man aimed directly toward him.

The blast of buckshot shredded the wing skin of Blue Sky Three and carried away most of the wing's main spar, and the next round tore through the landing gear mount, and it was the failure of the mount that sealed Medina's fate. Raoul Medina still had his hand on a wheel chock in a heroic effort to salvage his mission when the landing gear collapsed on him, the wing smashing him against concrete, spearing him with jagged ends of spruce as the damaged main spar failed. Fuel was already running from a punctured tank when the battery charger clips, still energized and sideswiped by debris, clicked together.

Rodrigues heard the chuff of ignition, sidestepped fast around the aircraft still facing his enemy, emptied his magazine into the little room. Though four seconds are good time for reloading an Ingram, Rodrigues managed it in three, and snapped off more rounds before he squatted next to Medina, whose inert head and shoulders protruded pathetically from beneath the shattered wing.

When Rodrigues saw the flow of viscous crimson from under Medina, and felt the heat of the blaze from the fuselage, he staggered back and set his weapon for semiautomatic fire, sending his single rounds into the open door of the room in a maneuver the yanquis called "suppression fire." It seemed to be working because he could no longer see the shotgunner, but he found no good

□□□

reason to remain. What did one more bandit matter to him, with pilot and compatriot both dead and the aircraft ablaze? Still pumping single rounds into that little room, Rodrigues sidled out the ruined door and ran for the Chevette.

Five minutes later, Rodrigues parked near the ruts of the Regocijo road and squinted back toward the hangar. He saw smoke, but no actual flames. He could stow his weapon as poor Aleman had done, but if Mexican federal agents stopped him they would find it sooner or later. Better to remove all traces of his employment and report this savagely failed mission from the safety of Mazatlan. He hurled the little Ingram as far into the grass as he could, dumped the now-useless SCUBA gear in a ditch, and used Aleman's oilcloth to wipe down the car. The Chevette was rented in his own name, so he would not have to abandon it, but Aleman and the foolishly unprepared Medina had left fingerprints all over it. Those prints had to be removed before anyone stopped him.

When at last Rodrigues stood up after wiping down the front passenger's seat and windowsill, he glanced again toward the distant hangar. He swore because the flames now rose higher than the hangar roof and a tendril of smoke arrowed straight into the sky, a signal of disaster that would soon be visible for many kilometers. He leaped back into the Chevette and turned it toward Regocijo. He saw no telephone lines flanking the road; it was still possible that he might outrun detection.

TWENTY-SEVEN

"NO, HE ISN'T GOING TO MAKE TROUBLE. WHEN he works his hands loose, Bobby will dump his pal in that hidey-hole with a bag of quicklime and forget about the whole thing," said Corbett, who was heartily sick of the whole argument after a half hour in the air.

Petra, holding a sectional chart across her knees, placed her finger over a spot on the chart and leaned her forehead against the window canopy, gazing downward. "You don't have enough appreciation for the habits of stupid people, Kyle. Someone shoots your friend; you call the police and demand justice—when you sober up," she amended, and then began to sing: "Wayyy down upon the Swan*eee* river . . ."

When she stopped, with an expectant glance toward him, he said, "I hope you don't expect me to sing, young lady."

"No, I was just commemorating it. The Suwanee River; it empties into the Gulf just ahead, according to this map."

He shook his head in mock dismay and peered past the nose of Black Stealth One. At twelve thousand feet, they could see the gradual curl of the Mexican Gulf which indented the Florida coast ahead. He glanced at her chart quickly, then back at his console. "That puts us dead on course, due south," he said after a moment.

"Kyle, where are we headed, really?"

"Dry Tortugas, at the moment. Just run your finger straight south down the eighty-three degree line. It's out in the Gulf, west of the Keys."

She refolded the chart and, after a moment, said, "Aha—but what's there?"

"I don't know; don't much care. I said we're headed there, but we aren't going there."

She wrinkled the heavy paper in frustration. "Please don't play these damn games with me."

"Sorry," he said, "I suppose I'm pretending you're in a search plane, and I'm trying to throw you off."

"Well, I'm not," she said emphatically. "So talk to me."

"You mean, you're in this for the adventure, not the puzzle."

"If you want to put it that way," she sighed. "Adventure is fun, but puzzles worry me. I've worried enough."

Now the green of savannah growth below had given way to the blue of the Mexican Gulf, the Florida coastline stretching away southward on their left. In the far distance overland, a condensation trail stretched across the lower edge of the stratosphere. "Let's paint the bird for that guy, he's heading in our general direction," Corbett said. He kibitzed as Petra called up the pixel program, using Black Stealth One's infrared sensors to locate the searcher's coordinates.

When she had finished, she looked at him for approval. "Very nice," he said. "Petra, the TV news makes it clear that we've been seen. We can be invisible only to a single viewpoint, and we can't know when some guy with a fishing pole will glance up."

"We probably won't even notice him," she agreed. "You can only fool some of the people some of the time, hm?"

"Yeah. Well, anybody on land who saw us this morning saw us heading south. But there aren't nearly as many people looking up from boats. I'm betting we can turn west in a couple of minutes, and *nobody* will see that."

Petra nodded, a sly smile lifting the corners of her mouth. "That's what you intended all along."

"Sure." *She's still going to face interrogation sooner or later. I've got to use that against them.* "We're going to Nevada while half the world's airplanes patrol the airspace between here and Cuba."

"On my say-so, if you'd had your way," she prodded.

"Partly. I've made a hell of a long detour to put that idea across." He moved the control stick and watched the readout on the compass as Black Stealth One banked westward. "Check the video now; let's see if the program is still following the

IR signature of that guy." He nodded to their left where the contrail, now an intermittent scrawl, extended almost parallel to their course.

"It's still locked on him," she said presently. "Would it, if he had flown through clouds?"

"Beats me. I doubt it," he admitted.

They fell silent; he relaxed at the controls, while she watched the hypnotic motion of whitecaps far below. After a time he said, "Your question about staying locked on after clouds have passed? That's pretty sophisticated thinking. Score one for good old Brown U."

"Has it crossed your mind," she said, "that in twenty-two years I may have learned a few things *you* don't know, Mister Hotshot?" Her voice was as soft and cool as crushed ice.

Corbett gave her an openmouthed, studious frown, a parody of astonishment. "You know, it never has. I mean, how could I go on living with such shame?" He saw that his joke was not received well, and smiled. "Come on, Petra. You keep surprising me, that's all. Think of it as a compliment; you're not exactly the average, uh . . ."

"Airhead," she said. "Would it surprise you to know I've had a lover who was much older than you?"

"Damn right," he said. "Would you believe I've bedded girls as young as you?"

"Why not," she shrugged, indifferent to the idea.

"Of course that was thirty years ago," he went on, grinning, then laughing outright as she slapped his arm; but he sobered quickly. "Why would you have a lover older than fifty-three, Petra?"

□□□

"Fifty-six," she stated. "You're fifty-three? I thought you were prematurely, well, you know."

"I know you're changing the subject on me."

She folded her arms and closed her eyes, her head cradled on the headrest, and she spoke as if the topic were tiring. "He was a professor at a school I went to, a veddy posh place; great school, really, but I wanted to go to Brown and my parents wouldn't let me at first. I was eighteen, and I was full of resentment, and Lydell, well—he was there, I guess."

"Um," he said, mulling it over, sparing time to watch the contrail that slowly crossed some miles off, above and ahead of them. "Hell, that's not a jet," he said. "It's a twin prop job. Must be some cold air up there to give him such a trail. They get weird weather over the Gulf. I believe I'll tune in and see about it." He clamped his mini-tel over his left ear, tuning the receiver as he went on: "So tell me about good old Lydell: all tweeds and pipe smoke, looking for one last fling?"

"Pipe, yes; tweeds, no, and if he'd ever had a fling before, it sure didn't teach him much." Petra giggled, shook her head, tried to be serious. "He was married, really very sweet and tentative and shy." Another giggle: "I practically jumped his bones."

"Every time?" Corbett's lifted eyebrow said he heard more than he believed.

"There were only a few times and no, not every time. Believe it or not, some men think I have enough charm to respond to." She waited for him to reply.

Dangerous ground, he told himself, and began silently to fine-tune the radio, avoiding her gaze.

□□□

Suddenly, with a bright brittleness that tried too hard to be bantering, she asked, "Kyle Corbett, are you one of those macho men who prefer the company of other men?"

"What?"

"Are you gay, Corbett?" Her smile was wide and, he decided, altogether false.

"Not very," he said. "I tend to get subdued when I'm flying a carbon-fiber toothpick and weather builds up ahead of me." He pointed to the low blanket of gray cotton that stretched across the horizon to the west. He waited until she opened her mouth, then said, "And stop that shit, Petra. I get a hard-on for no man and, if you want the truth, not many women." He made manual adjustments, throttling back, and watched their sink rate as he added, "I'm not passion's slave. Just because I notice you have great knockers, doesn't mean I have to grab 'em."

"Ninnies. We say ninnies in high society," she said, straight-faced.

"God, but you're a pistol," he said, chuckling.

"But not one you want to grab," she said. "I'm not being provocative, Kyle, I'm just—curious."

He nodded. Presently he said, "You have to understand how I live, Petra. I learned to get along without strong ties to other people before you were born. In some ways, a hobby can take the place of relationships. Some hobbies get to be your whole life."

"I think that's very sad," she murmured.

"Easy for you to say, but it really can plug the gap; I mean, you may be alone, but often you're having too much fun to be lonesome." He studied her keenly. "Ever wonder why your dad spent so much time racing cars?"

She returned his gaze. "But he had Mother, and—me," she said slowly. "I don't want to think about it that way."

Phil Leigh might have felt like a father, if Dar hadn't been constantly on hand to remind everybody of the facts. Maybe he did anyway, how the hell would I know? "Suit yourself. For me, airplanes plugged that gap. Let me tell you, a sortie over China in an SR-71 is just about the most fun you can have without risking AIDS."

"That's the fast one, isn't it?"

"It's a rifle bullet. The only reason the pilots aren't jerking off, up there, is that it's too much trouble in a flight suit." He laughed softly, wistfully. "Besides, you don't have to, the airplane does it for you. I guess you'd have to be there," he said, making it an apology.

Another long silence followed, penetrated only by the whirr of the engine. Corbett had almost forgotten their last exchange when Petra said, "You're telling me that hot pilots don't really crave sex, after all the stories we hear?"

"I don't know about other guys. And I knew plenty of pretty ladies, Petra. It was simply easier to avoid letting any one of them get to be a habit. I traveled a lot. Why get attached to someone when you know it can't last?" *And I won't talk about the last few years in Mexico. When you can't trust the condoms, things can get pretty grim . . .*

"It's still sad," she said, and then brightened. "You got attached to my uncle. But you're going to say that was different."

"Fuckin' A," he said, an ancient curse for an ancient memory. "Never had a pretty lady stick a time bomb in my fuel tank; now, there's one friend in a million. You *will* tell him, won't you? That I kept all his secrets, every one of them."

"I'll tell him," she promised. "I'm certain I'll be telling him more than you want me to decipher; but I'll tell him."

"What makes you say that?"

"You won't understand, Kyle. You've kept yourself aloof from relationships so long, you don't even realize how people can read each other. I know it's important to you that I say that to Uncle Dar. I know it's more than business. And I don't have to know what it is."

"Jesus Christ," he said.

"Now do you see why I think it's sad to alienate yourself?"

"I guess. Only, what's so great about reading people?"

"Nothing, unless you're close. Then it can be," she faltered, and he saw tears welling in her eyes. "It can be wonderful while it lasts. I don't know why I'm crying," she said, laughing as she wiped her tears away.

He intended it to be droll: "Maybe you miss old Lydell."

She refused to look at him, staring to her right, toward the Gulf coast on the far horizon. "Maybe I do. He's the only man I ever slept with who cared about more than my—my parts."

"And you're much more than the sum of your parts," he said, studying the shadows of clouds on seawater as the aircraft sank gradually lower.

"It's not funny. It's true," she sniffled.

□□□

"I wasn't being funny, Petra. I know it's true for me."

"Imagine that: the man is human. And why are we going down below the clouds," she said as their world darkened abruptly.

He tapped his right ear. "Cloud cover is building, and I want to keep the coast in sight. I think we can make it as far as the Texas coast," he said, "with this in-flight refueling system."

"Pretty smart," she said, giving him a smile.

"Not too shabby," he winked, and when he looked back through the windshield the little parachute was there, as though it had winked into existence, and Corbett needed time to check his depth perception because it had passed his left wingtip almost before it registered in his mind, so it had to be smaller than a drogue chute, perhaps two feet across, and then he saw something else ahead, several somethings in fact, small metal canisters sliding down the sky. "Hang on," he said, but she had already gasped.

It takes time to deflect a huge moving mass of air, and before he had moved the nose waste gate for reverse thrust they had passed so near to one of the tiny canisters that Corbett saw the thin trailing wire as it fell. Farther to their left, the damned things were fairly raining from the clouds. The one that they hit came down to the right of the cockpit, and the wire might have slid along the wing's backswept leading edge to release them if Corbett had not tried to bank away. The right elevon, the hinged rearmost portion of the wing, responded to his movement on the stick and his forward speed was still too great.

The wire whipped back across the wing, slid into

the crevice between the wing and its canted elevon. Corbett thought, *Somebody else is getting smarter than I am,* as Black Stealth One bucked and fought its tether, sliding toward the water.

TWENTY-EIGHT

DAR WESTON FOUND HIMSELF SHAKING AS HE watched the radar operator, who seemed continually unsatisfied with the yellowish clutter on his scope inside the droning old Neptune. *Probably that strong coffee,* he told himself, thankful that the borrowed flight suit over his civvies made him too bulky for those shakes to be obvious to the radar operator beside him. Across the narrow aisle from them were the duty stations for the radioman and Ben Ullmer. The electronic consoles inside the craft appeared to be the latest equipment, though the interior smells were strictly World War II.

Ullmer's flight suit enveloped him comically but there was nothing funny about the chill inside the aircraft. Ullmer blew on his fingers, refusing his gloves because they impeded his use of his own console with its special frequencies.

Dar felt a tug on his sleeve and saw Ullmer motioning toward his headset, which boasted ovoids the size of earmuffs. To be heard over the steady roar of the Wright Cyclone radials, which made the entire airframe buzz with vibration, Ullmer raised his voice. "Elmira on the horn."

Dar snugged his earpieces tighter. It was Unruh, calling on their special mission frequency. When Dar and Ullmer had both responded, Unruh proceeded, sounding as brisk and fresh as if he had stolen a full night's sleep though Dar knew better. "FBI just called in from a general store near Lake City, Florida. They've got a body and a drunk, and evidence that Black Stealth One was sitting in a garden plot exactly as that F-5 pilot reported, even though the pilot retracted his claim when he came down for a low pass a minute later. It was there, all right, he just couldn't see it anymore. Indentations of landing casters, and positive makes on prints of both the perpetrator and the hostage inside the store. Those guys are working fast, and—"

"Whose body?" Dar rapped out, his entire body suddenly cold with apprehension.

"Forgive me, Hornet." Unruh's voice said he had just realized his gaffe. "White male adult, name Lyndon Baines Beacham. His friend the drunk wasn't too drunk to reach a telephone operator, but they say he is now; he's the store owner, name Bobby Clegg. According to him, a regular gorilla of a man tore a door down and shot Beacham dead. Feebs won't be sure of the details until Bobby sobers up, so they're shooting him full of B vitamins. Bobby's idea seems to be that Corbett shot Beacham and tied Bobby up. But the Feebs say Beacham and Clegg were engaged in certain felonious activities. Beacham died of gunshot wounds at close range, probably over twelve hours ago."

"So Corbett stayed there all night?" Dar clamped down on his visions of Petra in the hands of a vengeful murderer, at night in an isolated store.

"From the F-5 pilot's sighting, he must have, Hornet. We show an envelope here that could put him below Tampa, possibly nearing the Everglades by now. Isn't that roughly your position?"

"That's a roger," said Ullmer, "crossing from Vero Beach to Sarasota at twenty-three thousand feet. Our other X-Band aircraft is patrolling the Gulf between Tampa and Tallahassee, as, uh, Killer Bee wanted," he added, invoking Sheppard's code name. "We'll orbit farther south until we're over the Keys, and hope Corbett won't be able to sneak through all the pickets we have flying around there now."

"Stand by," Unruh said. After a moment he went on: "Killer Bee wants to know how the aircraft got from West Virginia to Lake City without refueling."

"Probably did refuel somewhere," Ullmer replied.

Dar: "See if you can get an open line so you can tape the drunk—Bobby?—when the Feebs interrogate him again. You never know what you might hear. Pentothal might help."

"Roger, Hornet. Don't get your hopes up, the word on Bobby is that if IQ were octane, he couldn't run a lawnmower."

"Do what you can; I have all confidence in you,"

Dar replied, noticing the radioman's bid for attention. "Stand by."

The radioman's signal, crossing two fingers followed by those fingers upraised and separated, meant an incoming call from their sister aircraft, dubbed "Cyclops Two" for the mission. With only one set of the special NSA frequency hardware in Ullmer's possession for Cyclops One, they had decided to use standard frequencies between the two aircraft, although Dar and Ben Ullmer could also talk directly to Elmira.

Ullmer switched, and Dar heard the Neptune pilot acknowledge its sister ship to the northwest. "Go ahead, Cyclops Two," Ullmer said tightly.

"We have a blip proceeding due west at eighty-four degrees fifty minutes by twenty-nine degrees twenty minutes," said the pilot in carefully noncommittal tones, "but no visual sighting. And we should have one unless it's invisible. Our magician says it's a big blip, but not a dense one."

"Try to duck into clouds if you have any," said Ullmer. "He may know how to lock his IR scanner onto you, but that should unlock him."

"Negative, Cyclops One, it's CAVU here but there's a mass of low stuff to the west. I'll nip over there without making any sharp course corrections and make a return run."

"How fast is your blip?" Ullmer asked.

"Hundred knots or so. Too big to be invisible to the eye, but it is."

"Stand by," said Ullmer, and looked toward Dar. "Why would he come this far south and then turn toward New Orleans?" he asked.

"Maybe all the sorties have done it," Dar said,

□□□

groping, "or maybe that F-5 changed his mind. Maybe he's low on fuel."

Ullmer switched channels. "Elmira, do the Feebs at that store know whether Corbett was able to refuel?"

"Damn, I should've asked," said Terry Unruh. "I've got an open line; wait one."

Dar, to Ullmer: "Aircraft fuel at a grocery store?"

Ullmer: "Just covering all the bases."

Unruh came back on-line with, "They sell gas there. He might have refueled, if he could use ordinary gas."

"Fucking Corbett," Ullmer snarled. "I'll bet you my gout pills he's carrying additives; it's what I'd do. Have 'em check the pump for prints, and get back to—"

"Excuse me, Wasp," said Unruh. "FBI chopper has spotted a metal gas can in a field less than a mile from the store. They'll check that out, too."

"Let us know," said Ullmer. "Wasp out." He switched channels again. "Cyclops One to Cyclops Two, we have reason to believe the aircraft may be fully fueled, so there's less reason to think your blip is the one we're after. If you can—"

"Cyclops Two to Cyclops One, I have our ghost blip on visual," said the voice, no longer dry or bored. "And he's for real. Dropping toward low cloud cover but it's a flying wing, all right. Short fuselage bulge, big intake scoops, paint job like ocean waves. That's really something for the books; he's still hard to see."

Dar and Ben Ullmer shared a half-second stare. "Turn this thing around," Dar shouted, letting protocol go to hell, and snatched at the wrinkled chart that lay clipped to a writing surface near him.

□□□

"That's him," said Ullmer into his microphone. "You know what to do, Cyclops Two. But listen: don't drop your live rounds until you've tried to snare him with the others. You know you've got a hostage there."

"Wilco, Cyclops One, banking now for a run. He's trying to get under cloud cover but he hasn't made a course deviation since we picked him up. We'll try to snag him."

"They could wait for us," Dar said, his face tortured.

"No they can't," Ben Ullmer replied, suddenly looking very old, "and we both know it."

The lurch of the big Neptune as it banked was a heavy drag at Dar's shoulders. "Ben, put the word out," he said. "We'll want all those picket aircraft pulled back toward Tallahassee."

"I'm going to alert Air-Sea Rescue too," said Ullmer. "The hellbug should float like a cork, Dar. There's still hope for the girl."

Ullmer was redirecting the aerial armada off the tip of Florida when the radioman, monitoring the standard frequencies, called it out for all to hear: "Commander Openshaw in Cyclops Two reports munitions away!"

TWENTY-NINE

THEY HAD LOST HUNDREDS OF FEET IN ALTITUDE before Corbett found the cure for the downward spiral: he brought the aircraft to a stop with the waste gates, steering with the nose jet, and hovered. "Okay, I've got it," he said, hoping to calm Petra. "I can't see your wingtip, but something's fouling that elevon. Can you describe it?"

Petra, whose features were pinched with fright, swallowed hard and twisted her body, loosening her harness with reluctance. "I can't see through the wing. There's a wire hanging down from the tip."

"The *tip?*"

"Well, six or eight feet from it. Two wires, actually. One hangs straight down; the other one slants a little."

"Makes a big difference," he said sharply.

□□□

"Wire's got to be caught at the inboard hinge of the elevon. I think there's a little drag chute on one end of the wire; a breeze must be pulling it. Christ knows what's on the other end. Look, this is going to take muscle. See the pin clipped to the control stick down between your feet? Slip it in so your stick is engaged."

She did so, with a glance at him that reeked of doubt.

"Now," he said, "we know the right elevon is stuck in the 'up' position because the control sticks are stuck sloping to the right."

"Wait a minute," she said, her eyes shut in concentration. "Okay, I can see it. In here," she tapped her forehead. "Also because we were sort of spinning down to the right before you got it stabilized."

"Don't try to understand it all, for God's sake, there could be another skyful of those things coming down any minute." A sigh, as he wrapped himself with intense calm. "Now, we're going to try and force the elevon the other way, but with both of us horsing on it too hard, we could snap a filament cable."

"In which case?"

"Don't ask. Just lean into it, that's right, I want you to preload it before I put my shoulders into it. Okay, I can feel it," he said, and felt the control stick begin to come upright when he had put half of his power behind it.

"OH GOD, KYLE," she screamed, staring ahead, recoiling.

The Neptune had turned after its pass, dropping down beneath the clouds, and some sharp-eyed aviator must have seen Black Stealth One immediately because the heavy reconnaissance plane thundered in, boring straight toward them, the twin scythes of its props perfect blurred circles, closing a gap of less than a quarter mile at a hundred yards a second. Corbett had no option save one: he firewalled the throttle and levitated Black Stealth One straight up, seeking the clouds that he knew he could not reach in time.

He bared his teeth as he saw the Neptune respond, realizing that the naval pilot could shred a wingtip with his propellers or simply slice through it with the far stronger wing of the Neptune. But, though the hellbug's downblast of air lacked the great power of a true jet engine, it did accelerate the gossamer craft and in an eyeblink the big Neptune had passed scant yards beneath them, with a shattering roar and two distinctly separate results on Black Stealth One. Corbett felt a faint tug from the right wing, then a tremendous buffet as the Neptune's slipstream tossed them, sucked them down, spun them in almost a half circle as the bonded structure of the hellbug groaned and creaked.

"It's free," he exulted, realizing that the P2V had somehow torn the wire clear. A whirling prop could have wound that wire up, or cut it; but no matter. The hellbug was floundering but apparently still intact, trying to right itself as Corbett sought the clouds again. He did not look back at Petra until they were surrounded in grayness, moving ahead under maximum power. Some half-perceived cog in his mental clock reminded him that every minute, at this pace, brought them two miles closer to the Texas coast.

She breathed long shaky breaths as she watched

him. "I'm sorry I screamed," she said, rubbing her cheek.

"You know why I didn't? Too damn scared," he said.

"If you grin and wink I will get out and walk," she said, her mouth trembling into a shape that imitated a smile.

"There's blood on your teeth, honey," he said.

"Too late for sweet talk now," she muttered to the video console, and explored her mouth with her tongue. "Wow, the side of my face is numb; I wasn't cinched up tight when we did that whirligig."

"It could happen again," he warned, easing ever upward until they soared atop the cloud layer. The sky was innocent of any other aircraft. Blinking in the sunlight, he asked, "What're you doing?"

"Running an IR scan," she said as if surprised that he needed to ask. "I don't want one of those big bozos to surprise us again. And what's so damned funny?"

"The way you adapt, I guess," he said. "If everybody your age learns as fast as you do, Petra, old farts like me might as well pack it in right now."

The girl seemed unwilling to believe him, though he had been perfectly candid. Most experienced copilots would have adapted faster to the physical part of flying this craft but few, he decided, could have picked up utterly new and abstract techniques any more quickly than Petra Leigh. He began toying with different frequencies again, while mentally reviewing the attack of that P2V.

It had been no fluke; they were ready with some kind of aerial tripwire that he had never heard of.

□□□

That recon plane had somehow penetrated their chameleon disguise from afar, picking them out of an otherwise empty sky. *But how could they pick us up at all? Maybe something's wrong with the pixel skin, but it was okay this morning. If Ullmer's guys had buried some kind of transceiver in this crate, they'd have nailed me last night. Even the harness attachments are glass-filled nylon, there's not ten pounds of metal in the hellbug. Except for the fat, five-gallon steel gas can at my elbow!* "Oh, lord, but I can be stupid," he said, and checked the fuel tank readout. "Petra, take the cap off the gas can and feed the end of that hose into it. Just squeeze the bulb, like you were milking a cow, and keep pumping as fast as you can 'til I tell you to stop."

According to the readout, they had used up nearly four gallons from the main tank. When Petra had refilled the tank, roughly a gallon would have to go over the side with that can, which had probably quintupled their signature on any kind of search radar, even X Band. He cudgeled his memory on C Band, X Band, side-looking, doppler, every kind of radar he could remember. Some radars were particularly good against low-flying aircraft, but he remembered an NSA memo from Sheppard to the effect that Black Stealth One would be all but invisible to that stuff. Trying still another radio frequency, he felt gooseflesh flood his limbs.

". . . rendezvous in four-zero minutes," rumbled a southern-fried voice in his ear. He had known and liked and, yes, sometimes feared that voice, once. Ben Ullmer, or someone who could fool

Ben's wife. "Will you make a second run, Cyclops Two?"

A soft, almost boyish reply: "Not without a visual sighting, but we've scrambled everything from Pensacola to Keesler and this airspace ought to be popping any minute."

That's all I need: those bases are right over there on the Gulf coast, practically on our right-hand horizon, Corbett fumed. He checked the fuel readout again, reached over to take the bulb from Petra. "Just giving you a rest," he told her, unwilling to mention his eavesdropping until he knew what to do about it. He squeezed hard and repeatedly on the bulb and continued listening.

". . . certain he was tangled in your munition, Cyclops Two?"

"Affirmative, my copilot tells me we probably cut the wire when we tried to nibble at him with a head-on pass. You should've told me he could jink straight up."

And now Corbett's eyes slitted because the next voice was one he knew even better. "You attempted a midair collision? That's foolhardy with a hostage onboard," said Dar Weston.

"Our orders are pretty clear, sir," countered the younger man in Cyclops Two. "That thing is supposed to come down, and in our briefing you said a little damage could do it. The aircraft was going down in a tight spiral when we banked for our next pass, so I'd say we did something right. Sir."

Ben Ullmer again: "Any sign of wreckage in the water? Have you sent the coordinates to Air-Sea Rescue?"

"We're searching now, sir, in a tight orbit; and

affirmative, the choppers are coming. *Everything* is coming."

"So are we," said Ullmer. "Cyclops One out."

Corbett saw that the main tank registered full. *Well, Cyclops One, alias Uncle's puzzle palace and spook show, let's see if we can give you something to puzzle over when you get here,* he thought, starting a brisk descent through the clouds as he checked his heading. "Petra, as soon as we break out of this stuff I want you to set the IR scan behind us. That guy who tried to ram us should be a few miles back, and you've got to lock onto him so he can't possibly spot us when we come down."

She began to punch the keyboard. "Exactly what do you mean by 'come down'?"

"Enough to hover and drop something into the water," he said, chuckling. He moved the hose from the gas can to the full plastic bladder, lifted the metal can by its homely baling-wire handle and shook it, satisfied with the slosh.

They broke clear of the clouds with small, even whitecaps perhaps a mile below. Almost immediately Petra said, "Locked on. How'd you know he'd be there?"

"Tell you later," he said, spotting contrails far to the right as jet interceptors rocketed high, much too high to be a threat, up from the Gulf coast. He watched the airspeed indicator climb as Black Stealth One neared one hundred and eighty knots, a speed possible only because he had it in a shallow dive toward the water and an ambitious gamble. "Find me a piece of cloth I can use to plug the spout on this can. A sock; anything. In fact, take out a dress, or shirt, a whatchacallit . . ."

"Blouse?"

□□□

"You choose," he waved a hand helplessly. "Something else you don't mind dropping in the water. And, ah, if your mouth is still bleeding, chew on the blouse a little. Won't hurt at all if it has a little blood on it."

"My mother gave me this yellow silk blouse. I thought I'd be seeing her this weekend. It wrinkles like tinfoil and I've waited for years for a reason to ditch it," she said, with a spiteful look at the bright garment. "I look pale as a vampire in yellow."

"Another time, all right?"

"My, but we're touchy," she said. Corbett rocked with déjà vu; he had heard Andrea Leigh use that phrase when Petra was no more than a waist-high pixie. *Maybe foster parents are as real as any,* he thought. *I hope so. Phil Leigh sure raised a pistol. Ten minutes ago she was yelling her head off, and no wonder . . .*

As she rummaged through her little overnight bag for a sock, he considered the engineering problems involved, and their solutions. "*Damn* I hate this, but my stuff's probably helping give us a radar echo too. Take my tools out of my bag, all the metal things. Wait! Not the clock or those little cardboard tubes; they stay. What'll go into this gas can, put it in for ballast. What won't, tape it to the bottom of the can." He fumbled into his pocket, wondering if he had managed to lose his cigarette lighter.

"What about your gun?"

"Like hell. A Glock is mostly plastic anyway. I'll keep it."

□□□

Dropping an expensive adjustable socket wrench into the gas can, she said, "I wish I knew what I'm doing."

"Later," he replied. "For now, just do it."

THIRTY

CYCLOPS ONE LOITERED THREE THOUSAND FEET over Gulf waters as the big Sikorsky Sea King helicopter, two miles away and hovering just above the water, winched the last wetsuited man aboard. Dar Weston, his forehead pressed against Plexiglas, continued to scan the waves for any sign of debris that would mark, without question, the end of Black Stealth One. A badly scorched five-gallon canister and a woman's bright blouse floating close together were, as proofs, highly suspect.

Because you don't want to believe it, he argued silently. *You'd rather believe Kyle is still alive?* He knew the answer. No irony could be more complete, more against the principles he had held inviolate throughout his career, than this: better to have Corbett alive than Petra dead. *So much for the man I thought I was; the man my father thought I was.*

But if Black Stealth One was still aloft, it was still his job to help track and bring it down. There was a pedant's word for that, he mused, still alert for floating wreckage he did not want to see. The word was "antinomy," a naming of opposites; two equally valid principles locked in combat.

Dar felt the tap on his shoulder and turned. "You're going to love this," said Ben Ullmer, lowering his headset around his throat like a necklace. "That fuel canister had mechanic's tools inside, and more taped under it. A piece of a burnt sock came out of it. Pretty clear evidence to me."

"A decoy, you mean?"

"Sure." Ben Ullmer's face held animation, almost glee. "Corbett set it on fire and dropped it on purpose. With a little smoke and a hard IR signature, he knew there was a good chance someone would spot it. The blouse too, to make us think they'd sunk. An old submariner's trick, setting their clothes afloat to fake a sinking." Ullmer squinted out of the portal, gnawing his lip. "He's still up here, Dar, somewhere. We have to believe that—not just on a personal level, but at the mission level."

"All right." Dar replied without vigor, lost for the moment in a waking dream. He imagined for a harrowing instant that Petra, exhausted and in shark-infested waters, lay somewhere below, seeing them, swallowing salt water as she screamed for help. "Look, we have to leave a couple of those choppers here for a while, just in case, while we take up the search again."

"Sure we can," said Ullmer, with a callused hand

on Dar's shoulder. Ullmer toggled the onboard communication channel and instructed the pilot, studying a coastal chart as they conferred.

When he was finished, Ullmer leaned near Dar to avoid shouting over the drone of the engines. "I know what you're thinking. Listen, even if he's that kind of man—and I don't think he is—Kyle Corbett wouldn't push the girl out, knowing we might get a closer visual sighting now. He thinks she's his ticket out of this, but only if we can see her."

Dar moved back to his seat and cinched his lap belt. "Even if we do," he said, arguing against hope, "he's not going to come down unless we knock him down."

"He comes down when he's out of fuel, just like anybody else," Ullmer insisted, jabbing a forefinger into his open palm. "We can stay aloft longer than he can, even if he started out with an extra five gallons. If anyone spots him again, we know how to keep him in sight."

"You've lost me."

"He can't fool more than one searcher at a time! If we can spot him and surround him with several widely spaced chase planes, at least one can keep him *visually* targeted at all times. We just follow him until he runs out of fuel."

"And hope that doesn't happen over open sea," Dar said.

"He's not nuts. Fact is, that gas can could mean he's found a way to refuel in flight. I'll bet he doesn't get far from the coast the whole trip."

Dar selected another chart, cursed, grabbed for another. "I think he will. Taking the worst case, if he wasn't heading for Cuba it might be Nicaragua.

I'm trying to find a goddamn map," he said, furiously refolding a chart, "that shows Central America."

Eventually, they borrowed a North American route chart from the pilot of the P2V. It revealed the tip of Mexico's Yucatan peninsula, and brought an educated guess from Ullmer. "He just might stretch it to the Yucatan, with five extra gallons. Only he didn't have a full five, 'cause he burned some of it for that decoy. Dirty, smart bastard," he went on, apparently to himself. "And because he *is* smart, he's got a sleeve full of aces; and he isn't gonna start off from Florida toward New Orleans and then turn south when his fuel is iffy." Ullmer looked up and saw Dar's gaze. "Unless that attack panicked him."

"He's not the type," Dar said, with a strong headshake. "Did you ever see his psychological profile?"

"Why would I? NSA doesn't rely as much on that crap as you people do," Ullmer said with some pride.

"Touché," Dar said, unsmiling. "Well, the Company does, and I defend it. Kyle Corbett used to get some sticky missions back in the sixties because he's the kind that doesn't know how to panic. I've seen him after missions that might as well have been designed for panic responses." *Shaking and sobbing off in a corner somewhere, where no one but me could see him, and then a cold shower and after that enough alcohol to bank his fires again, and no one but me the wiser.*

Ullmer was waiting. "Yeah?"

Dar shook his head. "A little subdued after the mission," he said, "but no panic under pressure that I ever heard of. And I used to listen to his voice tapes. It was my job." *And I hated it, because I admired Corbett, perhaps loved him as we are taught to love our heroes. But I listened to the tapes of that man in mortal danger in the name of national security, the same flag I spread over myself when I had to kill him, all for the higher good. And see what all my high-flown motives have brought me. . . .* "No, Ben, he wouldn't panic."

"He's not heading for the Yucatan," Ullmer said with sudden conviction. "And he never was."

Dar stared blindly down at the charts, remembering the kind of man Corbett was, the way he thought, the kind of counsel he had given in more innocent days. At last he began to nod, looking up at Ullmer. "He never was," Dar echoed. "I think he intended us to know he was in Florida, else he'd have taken more care to avoid leaving prints in that store."

"Which means that right-angle turn toward New Orleans was a planned maneuver." Ullmer saw another slow nod from Dar, chose and unfolded a long sectional chart, then moved forward in the narrow passageway to talk with the P2V's youthful navigator.

He returned presently, lurching as the big airplane began to bank in another of its endless—and thus far, fruitless—sweeps. "We're out here, south of Pascagoula, Mississippi," Ullmer said while making a circle with his finger. He moved that finger to the left, toward mauve and yellow markings that represented navigation beacons and townships. "When last seen, Corbett was heading toward, oh, roughly New Orleans."

He flipped the chart over and spread his fingers

across a spatter of irregular shapes that sported little mauve and less yellow. "This is bayou and island country, south of New Orleans," Ullmer went on. "It's beginning to look like Corbett does *not* have fuel dumps waiting. He's taking it as it comes."

"Implying that he doesn't have any big organization working with him," Dar said, carefully noncommittal.

"Uh, yeah, I guess it does. We'll run all this past Elmira pretty soon but right now—if he can pick anyplace he wants to get fuel, there must be a thousand mom and pop gas stations here in Cajun country. He's done it once already and left a corpse, maybe to make sure we knew it."

"Why wouldn't he keep going to Texas? He used to like the place, learned to fly there."

"Because the son of a bitch may know how to stretch a gallon of fuel but he's not God almighty. Even with twenty-five gallons, he couldn't get there. No mountains in the Gulf to soar off of, and no onboard oxygen to let him fly high enough to catch a jetstream, even if there was one. The hellbug's engine isn't carbureted for it anyway. Nope; he can't get to Texas on twenty-five gallons."

"What if he had thirty gallons?"

"Shit, make it fifty," Ullmer exclaimed angrily. "If you change the rules enough he could fly straight to Nicaragua!"

"You're right," Dar said, rubbing his temples. "So what do you suggest we recommend?"

"That we pour on the coal to both these Neptunes, get ahead of the hellbug, and set up a new picket line along the Louisiana coastal islands. Even if he *were* trying to reach Texas we might pick him up on his way; we'll probably pass him. Hell, if we're fanned out, say, fifteen miles apart he can't use that chameleon mode against everybody at once."

"Sounds good," Dar replied with cautious optimism. "And if we're to rely on visual sightings, why not bring more aircraft with us instead of all this interservice chaos? We could be spaced five miles apart and at several altitudes."

"There's something to be said for chaos, but I agree. He seems to like flying between eight and ten thousand feet, so we'll do it too. We commit to the best gamble and cross our fingers."

"All right," Dar said briskly. "Call Elmira, and you carry the ball. Sheppard will like it more from you, Ben."

"If it works, he will," Ullmer said, with one of his rare grins. "Don't you go shy on endorsing the idea."

Dar's gaze went flat for an instant. "You call him. I'll pretend I didn't hear that."

THIRTY-ONE

PETRA STARED WITH WORRIED FASCINATION AT the whitecaps that sparkled and marched, rank after rank of them, ten feet below her. Corbett's course had finally taken them west of the cloud-bank, and he had pumped the plastic fuel bladder dry before they emerged into bright early afternoon sunshine. After two hours at wavetop altitude, with its greater sensation of high speed, Petra had learned the dizzying result when she gazed straight down. Speaking around one last mouthful of canned meat, she said, "I hope there's a good reason for this."

"The best," Corbett replied, checking his fuel counter and wristwatch. "It's working." He took a bite of cheese and a swallow of water, then handed the water bottle back. He noticed that Petra no longer bothered to drink from a separate container; one of many signs that both warmed and disturbed him. "If you're through, stow all that stuff. I really hate a messy cockpit."

"If that's a straight line, I think I'll leave it alone," she said with a smile, and repacked their food before zipping his leather bag. She sucked her fingers before setting the IR scanner for a complete sweep. "I still don't understand why we're practically kissing the water or why it's working. Something I'm not supposed to know?"

"Nope. There are two advantages to skimming the waves, Petra. One, it defeats even the kinds of radar that might pick the hellbug up, if I remember correctly. But better still, it lets us use ground effect."

"Show me some ground, Kyle. All I see is water."

"It works with water, too; over any flat surface, you can save a hell of a lot of fuel by skimming. It's called 'ground effect'; when the air's caught between the wing and the ground surface, the wing gets extra lift. The closer the better; right now I'm throttled back so much we're stretching our fuel nearly thirty percent. That's an extra hundred and fifty miles for us."

"Then we won't even have to stop for fuel in Louisi—uh-oh," she broke off, swinging the video monitor to give Corbett a better view. She keyed the scanner again. "I'm locking onto that guy. Okay?"

"Yep, paint us for him." Corbett studied the fast-approaching blip and saw another faint blip approach on the same course, a few miles from the first. He had swung the hellbug's nose a few points southward to avoid the Louisiana coastline entirely. The infrared scanner proved that this region of coastline, beyond their horizon only because they flitted so near the water, was thickly patrolled. *Almost as if they knew where I'd intended to refuel. Sure, Ullmer would know what I've got to do; the old fart may have guessed what I'm doing now, but he can't know which direction—can he?*

Switching among military radio frequencies, he divided his attention between the crosstalk of pilots and those blips approaching at ten thousand feet, one of them nearly overhead by now. It might be any of several twin-engined types, though the radio messages seemed to emanate from many aircraft. ". . . a roger, Poker Three, turning on eastern leg at three-zero thousand . . ." No problem there; probably a flight of Air Force interceptors much too high to worry about. Then, "Red leader, try Bravo channel," said a voice on another channel, so Corbett tried it too.

". . . shadow on the water," said a youthful male voice which Corbett recognized, "at your two o'clock low. It does cast a shadow, right?"

"Roger, Cyclops Two," Ben Ullmer's voice assured. "We get nothing on the scopes yet, and no visuals. He could be locking onto us. We'll orbit at this altitude; you might sortie down for a better look."

Corbett could see them clearly, two dark silhouettes at ten thousand feet, too low to have contrails, too slow for jets. As he watched, the most distant aircraft began to drop from the sky and he decided it must be a P2V, maybe one of the Cyclops team carrying Weston and Ullmer. "Bandit at four o'clock high, Petra, ah, over your right shoulder. I'm going for a tight pullup. You've got two blips; lock onto the other one but wait 'til I tell you. And tighten your harness."

Through the clear polymer bubble over his head, Corbett studied the unlovely lines of the P2V as it passed almost directly above. Visual sightings were always a problem directly below most aircraft, and Corbett firewalled his throttle to gain maximum level speed before he urged Black Stealth One into an abrupt climb, then turned to follow the wind. "Lock onto the other one now," he said calmly.

And grinned to himself as he heard, ". . . steep climb, banking toward me. Hell's fire, he's disappeared! Shadow's still there; ready munitions," said the young commander with grim self-assurance.

For a moment, Corbett did not recognize the voice of Dar Weston. "Cyclops Two, wait for us to . . ."

"Munitions away," said the pilot, barreling along at over three hundred miles an hour, flashing across the sky a thousand feet above and ahead of Black Stealth One. Corbett knew then that he had grinned too soon.

He had never even wondered how the hellbug would respond to full power to the waste gates while engaged in an inside loop, and he did not think about it as he tried it; the long string of dots that appeared from the Neptune's belly were already becoming a train of tiny parachutes as Black Stealth One responded, the combination of forward speed and diverted thrust hauling the craft up and over within a few hundred feet, now upside down as Corbett released the waste gates. He felt the drag of inertia on his body, judging that the air-

□□□

craft was straining under a four-G load, instinctively aware that he must cut back on power and roll the hellbug out of this inverted position.

His rollout completed a classic "Immelmann," half of a loop followed by a half roll. Petra yelped as loose hardware bounced off the canopy, the leather bag landing in her lap. Corbett found the siphon hose draped across his shoulder and shoved it aside, guiding the hellbug into a downward sideslip to gain more distance from those weighted parachutes.

At the end of the maneuver, Black Stealth One was again skimming near the waves while, a hundred yards to the right, a long train of munitions began to explode as each "buckshot" pod neared the water. Several of the explosions were deafeningly near. Corbett, accelerating again, kept waiting for the sizzle and thump that would tell him a hunk of shrapnel had struck the hellbug, unaware that buckshot munitions had been designed to hurl all their slugs downward in a lethal conic spray.

As the voices in his mini-tel generated a kind of chaos, Corbett glanced at his passenger. "You okay?"

"A shame to lose my lunch," she said, pale and gasping, as she shoved the leather bag behind her knees.

"Can you still work the pixel program?"

"I can try," she said, struggling to sit straighter.

"Those fuckers are chasing our shadow; we can't paint that, but we can sure hide it if we get low enough," he said, watching the two Neptunes as they circled with the obvious intention of a return pass. He banked again, moving with the wind—

□□□

and with the ranks of whitecaps. "Now, do what we tried yesterday, to fool something infinitely high," he said. "There's no real bogey to lock on to—"

"Right, right," she said, her fingers racing. Then she sat back, still taking long breaths to quell her nausea. "Now tell me why—and I hope you can see that damned airplane coming at us again on your left front."

"My ten o'clock," he nodded, throttling back. "I see him, but if he sees us we're in deep shit. Listen, uh—now that it's empty, the plastic fuel bag will keep you afloat a long time. We're about thirty miles south of land but we're headed northwest toward it. If you're not used to keeping your bearings by the sun's position, better start now."

"What are you saying?" Her voice was very small.

"Just in case we wind up in the water," he said, staring at the aircraft that approached, slowly now, so slowly that its big wing flaps slanted down as if for landing. "Now hush so I can hear what they're up to." He slowed as much as he dared, using the waste gates to hover at the same pace as the wavetops, now so near the waters of the Gulf that he expected to feel the slap of salt water against the fuselage.

". . . wreckage on the water," said the gruff voice of Ben Ullmer. "It'll be gray. Wait one." A pause. The big patrol plane droned overhead and Corbett saw what might have been the head and shoulders of a man in the nose bubble of the Neptune. Ullmer again: "Cyclops Two, we're dropping a dye marker." As he spoke, something fell from the Neptune's open belly hatch into the sea in a long,

□□□

steepening curve. "Navigator reports a Plexiglas bubble with two occupants in the water. They're not moving. Could be part of the fuselage. On your pass, please drop a rescue raft, ah, five hundred yards southwest of our marker."

"Wilco, Cyclops One." Corbett spotted the second patrol plane again, closing from two miles off. It banked toward a stain of orange, bright against blue water, that was now spreading to the right of Black Stealth One.

Flying the hellbug so near the water that it hid its own shadow from the noonday sun, its skin a near-perfect imitation of the moving lines of whitecaps, Corbett shoved the throttle forward and cursed the clear shining Plexiglas of the canopy around him. There was not one damned thing he could do about that canopy and the glassy reflections it could provide in bright sunlight. He could only flee at top speed, and hope that the orange dye stain across the water would become the focus of the Cyclops team. He waited another few seconds and then firewalled the throttle.

These guys are too good, Corbett thought, as the airspeed indicator crawled toward a hundred and forty knots. *But I wonder if Dar has just started to learn what a conflict of interest is all about? He didn't want 'em to drop those 'chute bombs, that's for sure. Can't blame you, Dar, old buddy, you murderous bastard. I've had the same problem ever since your kid showed me what she's made of.* He risked an instant's glance at Petra, noting the gleam of sunlight in her hair as she studied the video monitor with steady concentration. *Reminds me of an ad for pasteurized milk; lord, she's lovely. At a time like this, I want to kiss a college girl? One thing I don't want to do, is tell her Dar Weston's in one of those goddamn Neptunes.*

Judging by the crosstalk, Corbett realized that the Cyclops team—perhaps including Weston, who was apparently in the same aircraft—had succumbed to a seductive belief in the thing most desired: Black Stealth One shot down, with survivors. The navigator's eyesight might be excellent, but it had registered only the clear canopy and its occupants, virtually on the water amid the image of whitecaps endlessly repeated to the horizon. But some of those whitecaps were electronic, rolling back across the skin of Black Stealth One as it whispered northwest.

Two minutes later, Corbett intercepted a rendezvous message from a Navy Grumman Hawkeye and another from a flight of Marine Broncos, all converging on that dye marker. He never saw the Hawkeye but the three Broncos, twin-engined loiter craft with prominent gun pods, passed at low altitude no more than a mile to the left of the hellbug. He held his breath over that one; any one of those close-support gunships could have churned Black Stealth One into floating fragments.

When Corbett heard the Air-Sea Rescue choppers respond en route from some place called Grand Isle, he was within sight of islands off the Louisiana coast. He pointed the hellbug westward and, to Petra's profound relief, put five yards of safe air beneath the fuselage. "I think we've squeezed through," he told her as he listened to a fruitless rescue operation on Bravo channel.

"I have never been so scared in my life," Petra replied, "except maybe for last night. It's really strange how safe I feel with you."

□□□

He uttered a snort of astonishment. "Well, you weren't. You still aren't."

"I know it. Maybe 'safe' isn't the word." She yawned and stretched, flexing her fingers, gazing at him reflectively. "Like just before a design competition, or a game against Yale. Very special things are going to happen but even if you take some lumps, you enjoy it; oh, I don't know." She shrugged, unsatisfied with her own explanation.

"Try this, from a guy who took some lumps," he said: " 'I do not regret the journey. We took risks; we knew we took them. Things have come out against us. Therefore, we have no cause for complaint.' That pretty much sum it up?"

Now her look was sidelong. "Not quite, but close. It's beautiful, and a little scary."

"Yeah. It was one of the last lines Captain Scott wrote as he sat freezing to death in the Antarctic."

A long silence. Then: "You really know how to make a woman feel good, Corbett."

"I want you to know how *I* feel. Of all the dumb fucking things I ever did in my life, to take you along today! Petra, you talked your way into the hellbug this morning because you thought it would be fun. I don't think you have any clear picture of what it's like to get yourself killed."

"Who does, except those who die?" She began as if voicing a mild objection, but developed a strong cadence, as if marching toward an objective clearly seen. "Some of the men flying those airplanes, trying to kill us, are probably younger than I am. Don't tell me it's different, I won't buy it. When a young man dies for his country, do you think he joined up to die? I'll bet you've forgotten, Kyle. I'll bet he joined thinking of the *fun!* Of course it's a risk; so is riding a bike in Providence traffic.

"But you don't think I know what it's like to hurt. Hey, ever get kicked in the head by a soccer forward who's a head taller than you are? I woke up with a molar missing and would have slide-tackled that bitch into the middle of next week, only the game had been over an hour when I woke up. Listen, you want to loop this fucking thing again? I might panic the first time, but I learn fast, and I've learned to go with the experts, so I trust you. Go ahead, try me; wring the sucker out."

Her eyes blazed with internal light, her jaw knotted, her challenge unequivocal. Corbett decided she was the finest-looking thing he had ever seen. *Not just her appearance, it's a way of thinking. You consider the risk and then you go for broke, like Medina. Sure I do it. Dar did it a hundred times, God damn him to hell. And Petra is truly his child, and it's no longer a matter of my turning her loose. Damn if she hasn't captured me . . .* "Some other time, maybe I'll teach you aerobatics. Right now we're conserving fuel."

"Suit yourself," she replied. "I'll be ready."

"I believe it, but it'll have to wait. It's still a long way to the Texas barrier islands." He jabbed a thumb toward the monitor. "You might keep an eye on the IR scanner."

She nodded and began to key the device, and was encouraged by the clean scope. "I meant what I said about experts, Kyle," she said, her tone friendly again. "I've known you for two days, but there are some things I trust you with. And if it's not asking too much, how on earth did you get

□□□

away from those airplanes? I mean, what was the key?"

Corbett laughed aloud; shook his head, knowing there was only one honest answer. "We hid our shadow, and pulled maneuvers I didn't know the hellbug could manage, and painted this bird just right. Now, you want a translation with the ego strained out?"

"That would be nice."

"We had a shithouse full of luck," he said.

THIRTY-TWO

NEW ORLEANS NAVAL AIR STATION IS NOT IN NEW Orleans proper, but adjoins the suburb of Belle Chasse some miles to the south. NAS New Orleans sprawled so near the half-mile-wide Mississippi River that Dar Weston, holding a ham sandwich with one bite missing as he stared out the window, could see barges traverse the great waterway in evening shadows. He had been sitting there, with telephones at his elbow, ten minutes earlier when Ben Ullmer had left the room. Dar was still sitting with the same bite filling his cheek when Ullmer returned. He did not react when Ben placed a fresh cup of coffee before him and sighed into a nearby chair.

Ullmer was a man who had spent his life coaxing special tricks from inert materials. He had never claimed expertise with people, certainly not with a mature man whose depression made him forget a perfectly good bite of ham. "Eat," said Ullmer, nibbling a chocolate chip cookie. "You look like a fuckin' hamster."

Dar blinked, looked around, and began to chew. When he had swallowed, he put the sandwich down and faced Ullmer. "She's alive. I'd know if she weren't."

"Then they'll find her," Ullmer assured him. "I've been over it with the navigator 'til the poor kid is dizzy, and he's a trained observer, and he sticks to the same image. He only saw 'em for a second or two, Dar, but nobody had told him the pilot had dark hair and the hostage was blonde, and that's what he saw. He still says the cockpit was sitting in the water, moving with the wave motion which can't be over a few knots. I just wish I knew whether the hellbug could do it."

"Do what?"

"Land and take off on water. Now don't get all antsy," he said, watching Dar's face, "you heard me talking to Sheppard about it. Sure, the hellbug will float like a cork but without some kind of pontoons—oh, we considered 'em, but never built 'em—there'd be water in the exhaust plenum and the nose thrust diverter and I'd stake my rep that nobody, not even Kyle fucking Corbett, could take the hellbug off from water. But Corbett might have landed with minor damage. And if the structure doesn't break up with wave motion, they could be floating toward shore right now. Almost intact, maybe. Wouldn't that be something?"

Dar stood up. "Then why aren't we checking on currents and overflying the area?"

"There's five thousand men doin' that right now,

better than we could in a P2V. They've got a whole squadron of Marine Harriers coming in as well, with IFR capability."

Dar nodded, thinking about the redoubtable Harriers. With IFR, in-flight refueling, a Harrier could approach near-sonic speeds or hover motionless, for hours. "So the rescue operation is full-bore?"

"They'll be out there all night in boats, choppers, air-cushion vehicles, you name it. And we've pulled in the picket aircraft from Corpus Christi to Florida, to help. Weren't you listening?"

"I suppose not," Dar said, slowly resuming his seat. "And that doesn't say much for my stamina, does it?"

"That stuff isn't your specialty, all you had to do was nod. And you did a lot of that," Ullmer added, trying for a joke. "There are a couple of things you *can* do this evening, if you feel up to it."

Dar wiped his hands down his face, picked up the coffee cup. "Whatever."

"The naval exec for Public Affairs has a shitpot of news people on his hands here, howling for a statement. The Navy would like it if somebody faced the cameras for a few minutes and said something the reporters can use, maybe answer a question or two, so they'll get out of everybody's hair. I'm no goddamn good at that, but it's time we said something."

"And nobody's saying anything at Elmira?"

"I have a copy of Sheppard's statement," Ullmer said, pushing a folded page across the table.

"Right," Dar said as if to himself, reading it, "and Elmira is there and these media people are here, and I wish the Company were as good as the media at getting information."

"It could be if you had their budget and their manpower. And we'd have a police state," Ullmer shrugged, clearly not enchanted with the idea.

Dar took a small gold automatic pencil from his pocket, turned the Elmira statement over, and began printing in neat block capitals. Some people could compose a statement on paper while talking about something else, and Dar was one of them. "I won't add much to this; no point in giving Bill Sheppard a coronary. You know that every step of the way, Ben, you and I have our butts bare."

"Mooning the world. I'd like to show my ass to the whole Puzzle Palace when this is over," Ullmer grumbled. "So many decisions at the top are plain fuckin' stupid, but when you tell 'em what they're doin' is worse than nothing, they just smile and keep you doin' it. Now we've lost Black Stealth One."

As if he had lost a child, Dar thought, making a deletion, continuing to print. *And I can't even tell him that the hostage in that damned airplane is my own child.* "When you spread the power base in a democracy, Ben, committee decisions are what you get."

"That's what Dernza is for," Ullmer growled, "and your Director, and the President."

Now Dar looked up and smiled. "Still a committee, isn't it?"

"Yeah, now that you mention it. And it still makes dumb fucking decisions."

"Well, we cope the best we can. Take a look at this," said Dar, proffering the printed statement as he stood up.

□□□

"I'll read it on the way," Ullmer said, pointing toward the hallway. "There's a staff car already waiting to take us to pubic affairs."

Dar smiled at Ullmer's pun. "I believe you said there were two things I could do."

"Oh, yeah. Well, that exec said he'd be grateful for the statement, and I said how grateful, and, uh—how would you like a free ride and a free meal? The exec promised he'd have a beeper on him, in case something turns up while we're eating in the French Quarter."

Dar's smile returned. "I'll be rotten company, under the circumstances, but I couldn't face a BOQ room right now. Where did you have in mind: Antoine's?"

"Better. Brennan's, they don't give a shit about ties and ceremony, and they used to have a filet with some kind of wine sauce that would kill my doctor if I told him, so I won't tell him."

Dar fell silent again during the ride to the public affairs hall near the edge of the sprawling naval base, dealing with guilt the best way he could. *How can you go to a fine restaurant while your only daughter is floating in a derelict aircraft? Easily; you consider your options, and you realize that slashing your wrists in a solitary room is more a real option right now than you ever thought it could be; and you remind yourself that a message of reprieve could come flashing in at any time, and when it does, these people will get it to you. The system works, for the most part. Ben Ullmer is right about the bad committee decisions, but a remarkable number of decisions are good ones. Who decides? Who plays God? Someone has to.*

The executive officer, a full commander, looked

like a physically fit leprechaun and his walk was almost a dance. "The media is primed, Mr. Weston," he said as he led the way. "But when they show up here, they always are."

"Is the Navy prepared to pay our price?" asked Dar, with a fresh stab of guilt that this kind of badinage could lift his spirits.

"The price is Brennan's, and slow down," Ullmer complained as he explained.

"It's in the budget," the exec bubbled, and led Dar into a room in which media bodies and Kleig lights had begun to overwhelm the air-conditioning. Ben Ullmer melted away, unwilling to mount the podium, let alone stand at a lectern.

There must have been a hundred people present. Some, carrying network television cameras, dressed like stevedores in T-shirts; others, hoping to stand before those cameras, patted moisture from their brows as they stood in blow-dried perfection and thousand-dollar jackets. Most, like the tanned little man in the wrinkled trousers with his tie askew, had their hands full with tape recorders and notepads.

The Commander asked for quiet, asked again, folded his arms comfortably as though prepared to wait until doomsday, and waited until the hubbub dwindled. Reading from a card, he introduced Dar as James D. Weston, Deputy Director for Science and Technology in the Central Intelligence Agency. "Mr. Weston led a task force over the Gulf today in a Naval surveillance aircraft; I'm sure you already know why. He has agreed to make a brief statement for the press, but this will not be a full-fledged press conference. Mr. Weston?"

Dar opened the sheet of paper and began, "A

classified experimental aircraft under the cognizance of the Department of Defense was stolen two nights ago from a government test facility in New York State. The aircraft was unarmed in the military sense, but the pilot was believed to be armed. He took one hostage, believed to be a young woman, whose identity is—is being withheld at present.

"The military services, using means that are also highly classified, tracked and finally intercepted the aircraft as it was flying west over the Gulf of Mexico at approximately one-fifteen P.M., Central Daylight Time today. Though the experimental craft was forced down, every precaution was taken to protect the life of the hostage. The stolen aircraft was seen briefly after crash-landing in the Gulf, but we have not yet recovered the wreckage nor—nor the occupants. We do have reason to think that the occupants were forced down unhurt; I repeat, unhurt, thanks to razor-sharp precision by naval aviators." *There, Commander, I've paid for dinner at Brennan's.*

"At this hour we are making every possible effort to recover the aircraft and its passengers. The rescue and recovery mission will continue through the night. I have nothing more to report at this time," Dar ended. The place was bedlam before the last word was out of his mouth: waving hands, shouts, flashbulbs.

As Dar folded the paper and began to turn away, the noise increased as suddenly as in a sports stadium. He faced them again and pointed to a tall, plain-faced woman who looked as if she might be there for better reasons than television cosmetics.

"Louise Gardner, Atlanta *Constitution,* Mr. Weston. Would you comment on the report that the stolen airplane is actually a new type of stealth weapon system or a CIA airplane like the U-2?"

Some sensation here, but not enough to suggest the idea was new to most of them. "It is not a military stealth aircraft, Ms. Gardner. It is a civilian research craft, something along the lines of NASA's 'X' series which studied flight regimes of interest to the Department of Defense. It was not designed to carry weapons, and it is not a CIA project. Our major concern is for the hostage, not for an ultralight experimental airplane." Judging that he had dodged that one nicely, he pointed to another hand.

A young man in rimless glasses, with sweat pouring into his eyes, called, "What can you tell us about the hijacker?"

Dar knew that his face betrayed him then. He pretended his reaction was frustration and not hostility. "We simply don't know enough yet. He used identification of a man known to be deceased; not a very imaginative tactic. But it's obvious that he was no young thrill-seeker." As an attempt at wry humor, that last sally failed. Dar pointed toward an exquisite creature with an Asiatic face and an NBC cameraman at her shoulder, but his gesture was misinterpreted by a pale old veteran newsman next to her—probably by intent.

"Garrison Pyle, Denver *Post,*" said the veteran in a voice like a bullhorn. "We hear the hostage is close kin to someone very high in U.S. intelligence. Care to confirm or deny?"

Dar gave himself a long breath. Then, "I've heard it too, Mr. Pyle. No comment at this time." He chose one of the beautiful people next; this one

□□□

happened to be male. "Jeremy Cotton, for WWL: can you tell us why the hijacker shot and killed a grocery clerk near Lake City, Florida?"

This has the earmarks of a man who knows less than he shows, Dar thought. Media reporters, like trial attorneys, often phrased questions as "fishing expeditions"; as if they had knowledge, when they had only surmises. "I wasn't there, Mr. Cotton; I can't even say with assurance if the hijacker shot anyone." Though Jeremy Cotton seemed ready to revise his question, Dar had already looked elsewhere. "Time for one more question, ladies and gentlemen, it's been a long day. You, sir, with the tan I envy. And the loose tie. Yes," he nodded, doing his best to charm a roomful of ferrets. Maybe he had swivel-hipped his way through this without adding to the Company's troubles.

Yevgeni Melnik did not identify himself. After all, it was not a formal press conference. "If the aircraft belongs to the Department of Defense, but is not military; and if you are well positioned in science and technology; and if this stealth craft is not CIA: then who *did* build it, and why did they not trust the CIA to do what it did so well with the U-2 and SR-71?"

In the ensuing hush, Dar heard himself swallow. *There it is,* he admitted. *That swarthy little jerk even reminded everybody of my position; so if I say I don't know, everyone concludes I'm either lying or incompetent, which is the Company man's classic dilemma. Well, I haven't forgotten how to dodge behind an organization chart, buddy.* "I'm only one of several deputies. And other divisions work with different government agencies. No reason why the answers would come to my desk until that aircraft was operational." A lie, but not a palpable one.

"It seems to have operated very well," said the little man, getting a laugh.

"Not as well as our detection systems," Dar replied evenly, aware that he was at that moment as much a spreader of disinformation as the Soviets, who invented the word. "Thank you," he said then, and strode from the room, ignoring the entreaties of fifty other people. *I should've asked that little fellow what kind of accent he had,* Dar thought, now that the time for such a riposte had irretrievably passed. *I think I know, and I'm sure he would've lied, but he was inviting those other people to go for this country's throat. At least our media hotshots should get a hint, now and then, who's issuing the invitations.*

THIRTY-THREE

AS LONG AS THEY FLEW STRAIGHT INTO SUN DAZzle, its hard brilliance was only an irritant; but after they veered southwest, keeping the endless sandy worm of Matagorda Island off their right wingtip, the sun dominated the horizon in regal splendor, imperceptibly shading to orange as it slid down the sky. Petra allowed—welcomed!—the sense of wonderment that began to steal over her as she floated between sky and sea in virtual silence. *A lovely sense of power; no, of freedom, as if I might fly into the sun itself if I chose. Perhaps I'm beginning to understand this man, perhaps he has no intention of turning this magical gossamer beast over to anyone, ever.* There was only one thing missing—well, perhaps two. "Kyle, would you mind if I flew it for a few minutes?"

He had not spoken for a long time, restlessly

checking digital readouts, using the scanner in an empty sky, tempting fate in his efforts to hug the water. "What for?"

"You were happy enough for me to do it yesterday, when you were trying to—"

"I'm not objecting, Petra," he rumbled lazily, and from his tone she wondered if he was feeling the same magical timeless sense of peace. "Just asking why." He pulled up to fifty-foot altitude, checking their fuel counter for the umpteenth time.

"I want to. Humor me, dammit." She beamed when she saw him nod.

"Steady on," he said as she pinned her control stick into place. "You've got a throttle there, but don't goose it too much. We're down to twenty pounds of fuel."

She knew he watched with a critical eye as she eased the throttle forward but not too briskly, moving the stick, feeling the vast wings respond as Black Stealth One swung to and fro, a stately waltz for a dying sun. Then she eased back, felt the craft settle, and presently realized that if she wanted to come down any nearer to the water, she would have to cut back further on power or force the hellbug's nose down. "This is ground effect?"

Arms folded, grinning, he nodded. "You're good, k—uh, cadet."

"You were going to say 'kid,' " she accused, seeing him wipe the new stubble on his chin and knowing it was to hide his needless chagrin. "I don't care, now that I know *you* know better." She leaned her head back, feeling the tightness of sunburn on her face, perfectly at peace as the great orb of light sank into the Texas plains. "You can take it back now. There is no way I can possibly thank you, Kyle. Whatever happens for the rest of my days, I have flown Black Stealth One down a Texas-sized island on a warm summer evening." She paused a long moment. "That's *FUN,"* she said.

"That's fun," he agreed and, after another pause, added, "You were right, some kinds of fun are worth whatever risk it takes. Wup, see those lights on the horizon? Rockport, I think. That's a risk we don't have to take," he added, and swung the hell-bug's nose inland to the north of the township, ignoring an airport nearby. "Paint us like a big-assed bird," he suggested. "That should work from above or below."

As she complied, Petra said, "I think you've been without much fun for so long, you want to call it something else."

"Something more dignified," he said, almost comically defensive, "at least when you're risking your buns for it."

Staring into the sliver of remaining sun as they drifted over a bay toward land, Petra murmured, "My mother's tombstone should have 'dignity' on it. My father's too, but with a little parenthesis below that says, 'fun.' How about yours?"

"I'd have to die—and I have other plans," he chuckled.

"Play the game," she urged. "Mine will say 'fun' in big letters, and maybe 'usefulness' below. Now you."

After a long silence, ghosting across a clean beach toward another expanse of water, he said, "Vengeance. Maybe 'fun' below, maybe not."

"Wonderful," she muttered. "You've really picked my spirits up, Kyle. I've cast my lot with

□□□

a man who wants to be remembered for his most negative quality."

"Sorry. I might have a different answer next week, or next month."

She gazed at him earnestly. "Will I be able to ask you then?"

"Probably not," he admitted, then returned her gaze and smiled. "But anything's possible. You never know when I might need a copilot."

She decided then that whatever his motives, he did not intend to relinquish Black Stealth One. Unless, of course, he was carefully laying down a network of lies as he had lied previously, using her as he had tried to use her before, as an agent of misdirection. "Well, you'll know where to find me," she said, jiggling her eyebrows, flicking an imaginary cigar in her best Groucho imitation.

"Yeah, in a federal hoosegow if you're not careful." He had guided Black Stealth One higher with the gradual rise of the land, revealing a solid coastline beyond the bay with a forest of oil pumps that spread for miles, some of the pumps bobbing slowly like the heads of great birds. A few miles off, an acre-wide cylindrical tank squatted, growing monstrously large as Corbett approached it. "Nobody on the ground could spot us up there," he chuckled, swinging wide as he approached the storage tank. Petra noticed lights both to the north and south, defining two more townships. Headlights gleamed in gathering dusk on a highway between the towns.

They saw no lingering workers, no headlights in their immediate area, and Corbett lowered the hellbug gently until it touched down in a gauze of dust atop the curve of the tank dome. The tank, she saw, was truly awesome in size; so vast that a craft with much greater wingspread than Black Stealth One could have perched there without protruding. He checked the fuel readout one last time before snapping off the electrical power. "A little more than a gallon—and the battery reads full-charge, in case you're interested."

"And we're a hundred feet in the air," Petra reminded him. "Don't tell me the engine will take crude oil straight from this tank."

"I made sure there's a ladder and no, it won't take Texas crude or ordinary fuel either, and I've used up most of my additive. What I need is green," he sighed. "One hundred, one-thirty octane avgas." He unfolded one of his maps, holding it up at arm's length in the dusk. "Shit," he muttered, and produced his tiny Maglite, adjusting its beam-spread to study the map.

"You've still got a whole bottle of additive," she reminded him, "and we could siphon gas from cars with your gadget."

"Gotta keep that for later," he replied without elaborating, still studying the map. "We're between Refugio and Woodsboro, and there's an airport a half hour's walk away, right about—there," he finished, pointing midway between the nearby towns.

"No beacon?"

"Some do, some don't," he said, clearly preoccupied now, and grunted as he climbed out of the cockpit taking the fuel bladder with him.

Petra scrambled out onto the metal dome, stretching, learning to walk softly because she did not enjoy the low, ghostly echoes of her footfalls

□□□

from the tank below her. "God, this feels weird," she said, laughing at her own discomfort.

The curl of a steel ladder stood in the dusk, fifty feet away. They walked to it and grasped its rails, scanning the ground several stories below. The distance to the nearest pump unit was hundreds of yards, she noted. He must have been thinking about those wide-open spaces too. "Long walk, ma'am, but you're not coming anyhow. Does this height make you woozy?"

"Not anymore," she said, laughing, and ran her arms around the barrel of his rib cage before she lost her nerve for it. She felt him start to pull back, hesitate, then clasp her roughly in a hug. He kissed the top of her head. "On the scalp doesn't count," she murmured, looking up at him. "Give me a real smack before you go." *I know you wouldn't if I called it a kiss,* she thought.

He kissed her with the tender diffidence of a boy but held her as if he meant it, then gave her shoulder a squeeze and turned, tossing the fuel bladder over the side of the tank. "Gotta go fuel up," he muttered, and climbed over the edge.

"I've still got good ole Bobby's money," she said. "And how are you going to get twenty gallons in that plastic thing?"

"One thing I have is money," he said, starting down. "And I'm going to improvise like hell. I'm a crop duster who's out of gas like a damn fool; half of those guys are nuts anyhow. I'll think of something," he added, his voice diminishing in the faint pungent breeze.

She watched him as far as she could see him in the deepening night, reluctant to move, still savoring the kiss they had shared, even if she'd had to demand it and absorb the tingle of whiskers in the process. *I've known freshmen who understood more about romance,* she told herself, feeling the flush of sunburn on her cheeks as she smiled into the breeze. *But I don't love him with that dizzy kind of rapture I felt for the others. In fact, do I love him at all?*

She noticed her first star of the evening and, feeling foolish as she did it, whispered an old formula. ". . . wish I might, have the wish I wish tonight. I wish—that Kyle would get beyond vengeance and find me waiting. Okay, star, that's two wishes; if I get the first, maybe the second will follow. And as for you, Corbett, you old bastard, don't screw up and make me waste the first unselfish wish I've had in years."

It was that unselfishness that pricked her intuition. *Oh yes, I'm in love with him, twit that I am, and maybe I should not be dissecting it like a problem in stress analysis. But why not? Maybe because I'll have to admit that it isn't all unselfish. Uncle Dar used to laugh and say that Kyle Corbett led a wild life, and he said it with plain envy, which seemed strange to me at the time because my uncle is the most sober-sided responsible man in the world. But he envied Kyle; maybe enough to kill him? I can't accept that. And the one thing I'll never learn from Brown University is how to live with Corbett's kind of decisive abandon. Could I become a pro in my field and still find his kind of damn-your-eyes freedom? Could anybody?*

"You'd tell me no," she said into the night, speaking to the departed Corbett. "But you've done it yourself. Even though you got pushed into some of it. And then you pushed me," she said, laughing at him, and at herself.

An hour later she was sitting at the ladder with one leg through a steel rung, nibbling a Hi Ho and enjoying the breeze, when she saw headlights swing in her direction a mile away. She moved back and hunkered down. *A night watchman? Please, God, let him keep going!* But the old pickup truck stopped near the ladder. A moment later she heard scrapings and soft echoes in the tank, and realized that someone was climbing the ladder.

Heart beating wildly, she made her decision and swung onto the ladder. "Don't shoot, I'm coming down," she called.

"What the hell for?" he called back. Corbett!

She scrambled back up and did not wait for him to reach the top. "My God, I thought you were a watchman or something," she said, laughing, placing a hand over her hammering heart.

He swung over the top, puffing with exertion. "Then why give yourself away, dummy?"

With some heat she said, "So he wouldn't come up here and see the hellbug, *dummy.*"

Starlight was a poor guide, but he must have seen her fairly well because, after he laughed, he kissed her. It was a frustrating moment for Petra because she had no time to gear herself for a really promising response. "Don't worry," he said with a kind of manic elation, throwing an arm over her shoulder, "I kiss all my copilots. Well, I finally had something go right; a guy was pulling an overhaul at Rooke Field. He offered to loan me his pickup when he heard my sad story. You know, I'm dusting crops and run out of fuel but I land okay, and I'm gonna get fired if I don't get this leased AgriCat back, and I'd rather not have to show my ID to this guy or tell him where I put the duster down if that's okay with him.

"And he's your typical small-town Texan who'll give you the bandanna off his neck if you don't sneer at him, or talk about the size of Alaska." Petra wondered if he had been drinking, because this expansive yarn-spinner was not the Kyle Corbett she knew. He was a Corbett flushed with quick success; and she found that she liked him even better this way as he continued, "Only there's no spare tank around, and it's against the law to put avgas into a car, so the guy keeps filling my plastic tank, helping all he can without actually breaking a law, and I go around the edge of the hangar and pour it into the pickup's tank, which was nearly empty but I promised to bring it back full of unleaded because he wouldn't take the pair of twenties I tried to give him. And here I am," he said.

During this spiel he had led her to the looming bulk of Black Stealth One, and now he crawled in. "C'mon, I'm gonna take it down below and do the siphon routine," he said, patting the copilot's seat.

She started to comply and then stopped. "I'll go down the ladder," she told him.

"What's wrong?"

"Nothing; but I've never actually seen this airplane fly when I wasn't in it. It's not something I want to miss."

He flicked switches, and began to spool the big impeller over. "You won't see much tonight either, honey."

Her heart leaped. *Honey! But that's just high spirits talking,* she thought. "I'll cope. You go on." She gave him plenty of room, squinting as dust teased her eyes, and watched him levitate the craft, seeing him faintly limned by reflection from instruments as he lifted like a creature of fantasy. *It's a UFO,* she realized with a thrill of gooseflesh, *a real one to everybody but us, probably the only one in this corner of our galaxy. How long before I can help build newer ones?*

She watched its progress as much by its occlusion of stars as by direct light, and was ravished again by the graceful sweep of its wings. Presently she moved to the ladder, refusing to think about the distance. She counted over eighty rungs before she reached the ground and realized only when she brushed his shoulder with her rump that Corbett was patiently waiting there, perhaps to break her fall if she had slipped.

She found other purchases in the pickup's bed: the plastic bag was full of ordinary gasoline, and the same Exxon station had boasted the kind of cheap tasseled blankets only a tourist, desperate for mementoes, would crave. Wrapped in each of the two thin blankets were cans of Classic Coke. After he backed the pickup into place, they made the fuel transfer directly using the siphon and pressure bulb. He pumped the pickup dry, topped off the tank of Black Stealth One with ordinary fuel, then poured one of the two remaining two gallons of ordinary gasoline into the pickup.

"You're really going to drive the guy's pickup back?" she asked.

"A deal's a deal. Besides, I don't want him calling the cops," Corbett replied. "One thing about a cover story, Petra: you can't just give it, you've got to live it."

He stowed the almost empty plastic bladder into

□□□

the hellbug and, with Petra beside him, had soon settled the craft in its eyrie atop the huge oil tank. "You can make our pallets," he said, heading for the ladder by starlight. "Mosquitoes shouldn't be bad up here."

"I wish I could go with you," she said wistfully as he swung onto the ladder.

"So do I. Don't wait dinner, this'll take a while," he said, and left her. She watched the pickup's lights until they faded from sight.

THIRTY-FOUR

AFTER CORBETT RETURNED AFOOT, COMPLAINING of sore feet, they had feasted under starlight, belching Coca Cola fumes tinged with cheese. Now they lay on the pallets she had placed together under a wing of Black Stealth One, feeling residual warmth of the dome on their backs through the thin blankets. "You know," she said dreamily, "even if I told the truth about this experience, my family would absolutely not believe it. My uncle, maybe; probably not even him."

Corbett yawned and put his hands under his head, feeling her arm against his, comfortable with it. "Why not?" *You're just putting off what you have to tell her. But you're assuming she wants to keep going and she just might have had an attack of good sense after today . . .*

□□□

"They wouldn't be able to reconcile it with what they think I am."

He asked it in all seriousness: "And what are you?"

"Oh—I want it all. Pleasure without consequences, I guess. And don't think you can't, if you're little and cute, and never forget anything or admit anything."

"Sounds like a real sandbagging little shit. I hope I never meet you," he chuckled.

"You already have," she said darkly, "but I'll turn your question back to you. What are you, Kyle? All I know about you are the most important things."

He sighed and shifted position. "I won't give you that crap about there not being much to tell. Let's see: I grew up in Manhattan Beach, California; surfed a lot, got into things that fly because my dad was an engineer with North American—Rockwell, to you. He helped me make boomerangs, kites, gliders, all that stuff. I got through high school without cracking a book but nobody told me how bone lazy I was until I damned near washed out of cadet training."

"Gee, I always enjoyed studying," she said, turning over, her face so near that he could feel the warmth of her breath.

"Yeah, but you're a natural nerd."

"You know what a nerd is," she said, "a nerd is the guy you make fun of all the way through college, and he owns your whole town when he's thirty-five."

"There's something in that," he laughed. "But all I ever wanted to own was the sky. Did a tour of duty in F-104's, took a bunch of engineering courses because I wanted to build better airplanes, married a girl who thought I was going to be a nice, steady, rich airline pilot."

"Lord, I know better than that already. Why would she get that idea?"

"Because I told her so," he shrugged. "But I was wrong. I got a chance at something really wild and woolly to fly so I stayed in, and that's when she started packing. Then in 'sixty-five I climbed into a Blackbird, an SR-71, at Beale Air Force Base." He sighed. "That's where all the engineering paid off; I figured it would. Boy, that thing is—well, the only thing I'd rather have is parked right here. It's a different kind of freedom. Found out, a year later, that I could resign from the service and still fly a Blackbird. Of course, I flew 'em for CIA, but I had some freedom too. Stationed in a place called Tak Le in Thailand, sometimes flying out of Kadena in Okinawa. I met Dar Weston over there; flew recon during the Tet Offensive in 'sixty-eight in another kind of plane, a Lockheed Quietship. The Q-ship could be hairy as a bear. The hellbug is kind of like a Q-ship gone to heaven.

"Eventually I picked up a fungus over there, practically grew moss in my ear. Inner ear infection can put you right out of the flying business. But Dar pulled a string or two for me with another spook agency: NSA. I thought it was just a fill-in job, until I realized I might be building things that fly. With some, uh, occasional test flights, I was pretty happy there until one weekend when I went on a fishing trip with an old buddy. And you know how that turned out. I can't tell you what I've done since then. Mostly soak up desert sun," he said. He

□□□

had said "Nevada" to her once; twice would be overkill.

For a moment, from her regular breathing, he thought that she had fallen asleep. But, "What was she like?" Petra asked suddenly.

Somehow he knew instantly, as a gazelle knows in open country, that he was being stalked. To his own surprise, he enjoyed it, perhaps because Petra Leigh did a very nice job of stalking. Or maybe just because she was such a spectacular little stalker. "My wife, you mean."

"No, your ear infection; *yes,* your wife," she said, the tone making her sarcasm unmistakable.

He knew that she would resent him if he laughed. "Blond, tall as I am in heels," he said, "and dynamite in a garter belt."

"Stop it," she said, low in her throat. "Not how she looked; what was she like?"

"That's what she was like," he said, "image was everything for Peggy. What she could see reflected in other people's eyes was all that counted."

Petra surprised him again with her giggle. "I thought she'd be smart, but I'm losing interest already."

"She was valedictorian at Torrance," he objected.

"Sure, if that was all that counted for her at the time. At Brown we call it 'barfback'; she can feed back what she's been given. Trained memory but retarded at the analytical level. I'll bet you a really good kiss I can tell you something about her that you haven't mentioned."

"You're on," he said without thinking.

"She never, ever *once* did anything inventive or original," she said. "And she probably never will."

□□□

He fell silent a moment, then began to laugh. "That's right."

"Well, didn't that bother you?"

Her tone became more urgent, almost pleading. "Didn't you ever wish she'd come up with something new, something uncanny and maybe useful?"

"I may have," he said. *Yes. Sure, a hundred times, but then she wouldn't have been Peggy.* "It was a long time ago, Petra. She could be a gray-haired old woman by now."

"Barfbacks are born old," she said.

Rolling onto his side toward her, his head propped on one hand, he said, "Sounds like you've given it a lot of thought."

"You bet I have. And it may be too soon to tell, but I'm developing some very definite ideas about you."

He reached a hand out, felt the softness of her hair, caressed it down to her chin and left it there. "I know that, Petra; I'm not a completely insensitive clod. But you're probably wrong about me, and there's something I must . . ."

"Why don't you just shut up and kiss me as if you meant it, and let *me* decide whether I'm right or wrong," she urged, turning toward him.

He found her mouth with his own, gently, and tasted Classic Coke and felt the firm softness of her lips, parted in acceptance and, gradually, with increasing desire. Then her hand was in his hair in a gentle caress, more sensual than insistent, and now he tasted only her femaleness, and they moved together until she was lying supine, her breasts swelling wonderfully beneath his arm, his tongue evidently with a mind of its own, she accepting that too and responding in kind, and her breath filled his lungs, an almost-forgotten sense of sharing for him. He lifted his head then, knowing she must feel his erection growing against her hip, and rolled away with a manful attempt to quell his impulses.

She moved again to face him and uttered a sigh that was almost a moan. "Marvelous," she whispered, her fingers blindly tracing down his arm. "For such a muscular devil you can be awfully tender, Kyle."

He had his breathing under control, enough to say, "To think I've been calling you 'kid.' "

A giggle. "We're even, then; I started out thinking of you as a hardened old bastard." She eased an arm around his chest and placed her face in the hollow of his throat and then murmured, "Well, listen, old bastard, we were both wrong."

He put a hand up to her hair, stroking lightly, turning to kiss her forehead, and then she lifted her face and initiated a kiss that began in tenderness but soon became a long, lingering wonderment for him as he flung his caution aside, his tongue tracing her lips, kissing her throat as she held his head cradled in her arms.

And when he lifted his head again, she was unbuttoning her blouse for him, and for herself. "Must I tell you 'yes,' Kyle? This is why yesses were invented."

"No," he said, suddenly, almost truculently, sitting up, leaning forearms on knees, staring into the starlit sky. "This is fucking crazy," he muttered.

"Sounds good to me," she teased, sitting up too, her chin on her knees.

□□□

"Stop it," he growled, and faced her. "Listen, you: I didn't think a woman could bother me, let alone get me questioning my own motives, anymore. I like you, Petra, a hell of a lot, but—"

"I could get to be almost lovable," she murmured.

He laughed helplessly, and snapped his fingers. "Like that," he agreed. "That's why I won't make love to you for the wrong reason. You said vengeance was my worst quality, and you were right."

"Ah," she said, and fell silent. After a long pause she said, "And you've only been making me fall in love with you for revenge. On my uncle," she accused.

He raised his hands and shook them. "Don't— make it sound like I've done it on purpose. But revenge is the last passion remaining to old men, and it has crossed my mind that nothing could possibly even my score with that uncle of yours more than for him to know I raped you before I let you go."

"I can think of something worse," she said. "If I told him I raped *you!* Wouldn't be far off the mark, either."

He began to chuckle, his shoulders shaking with it. Then, "God, it's ingenious. You'd do that?"

"No. I could say 'yes' if all I wanted was to get laid tonight, but, Kyle, I think we feel the same. I'm not certain I could fall in love with anyone on such short acquaintance, but I like you, I really, really do," she said, massaging his upper arm with gentle fingers. "I know you're twice my age, I know when I'm forty you'll be Methuselah. But that's a long time from now. Maybe I wouldn't care then, either."

□□□

He did not move away from her fingers because, simply, it felt so damned good. "Born thirty years too soon! I need reading glasses already, and I can't see in the dark anymore," he grouched. "But it's more than that. There's a thing that often happens to people after they're captured, taken over. They flip their allegiances inside out, find a kind of glamor in giving themselves to their captors. A week from now, you'll be realizing this self-control on my part is the only unselfish thing I've—"

"Unselfish. I'm glad you told me that," she said with tenderness he could not fathom. "Do you truly imagine that I'm another Patty Hearst?"

"I doubt it, but I don't know. She went for the outlaw glamor."

He could not tell whether anger or determination was foremost in her reply. "It would take me a lot longer than a couple of days to snap like that, mister. As for glamor—have you taken a look at yourself lately? You're overweight, your whiskers are sandpapering my goddamn sunburn, and you smell like gasoline! I hate to burst your bubble, Kyle, but I'm not just gaga over your glamor."

After a moment she said, more gently, "On the other hand, this incredible airplane *is* glamor. But I don't feel like making love to it. By and large, glamor sucks."

He grunted softly; she was massaging his shoulders now from behind, her feet touching his thighs, her position more companionable than sexual. "But for Black Stealth One, you'll make an exception," he said.

"Sure. If you have any glamor, Kyle, any social status in my eyes, it's in this airplane and what you did to get it. Not so much because you *have* it; but because you helped *create* it. Any muttonhead with money can have a nice house or car or airplane, but how many can build one?"

He sighed in contentment, leaning back, letting her rest her chin on his shoulder. *I've been waiting all my life for a woman who understood that, but I didn't know it until this moment. And if I don't tell her the bad news now, I might weaken.* "Petra, you'll have a lot of time to consider what we've said before you hear from me again. I can't take you any farther now."

Quickly, as if she'd been expecting something of the sort: "Don't say that."

"It's said, all the same. I just can't do it."

"Of course you can; you mean you don't want to."

He could feel the tension in her body and knew that she still hoped, with all the naïveté of youth, to somehow argue her way through. "Have it your way, then," he said, implacable. "I don't want to, and I damned well don't intend to, least of all now that I care what happens to you. Period, end of argument."

"But you promised—"

"Consider it broken. I'd break any promise rather than put you at risks you have no conception of. You wouldn't be a help, you'd probably get me killed, and I can't tell you why. I'm going alone tomorrow. Period."

She sat up straight and breathed very slowly and deeply, several times, before sliding her arms around his chest from behind him, her chin snug against his cheek. "But I will hear from you again. I'll hold you to that," she murmured.

□□□

"If I'm still in one piece," he said gruffly. "If you don't hear from me in, oh, say when the leaves turn this fall, you can figure you're not going to."

She shivered against him, despite the warm breeze. "Could we just hold one another?"

He turned, straightened his pallet, then lay with her, fingers linked, faces nearly touching. "I should go at first light," he said, very softly.

"God, I'm going to miss you," she whispered. "I think we'd be good for each other. And if it turned out otherwise—call it a no-fault love affair."

"Don't say that"—he chuckled—"until you know what kind of lover I am."

"I was working on it. I—I guess I knew you'd leave me tomorrow." And with a simple earnestness that held no sexuality she added, "I just wanted you to leave knowing I'm really a terrific lay, Kyle."

"I suppose I'm so-so," he rumbled grudgingly.

"I've felt your so-so," she said, giggling again, and touched her forehead to his, and then she snuggled down against him, her hands cupped together as if she were protecting something of great value, and slept, bathing his face in the candid scents of woman. For a time, he entertained an idea he would have thought laughable only days before. It was, he knew, unworkable. He had committed himself to his original plan, and if Medina was still willing when they met at Regocijo, they would use both aircraft to complete that plan.

Content in his ignorance of the Regocijo disaster, Kyle Corbett kissed his captive gently, and then he slept.

THIRTY-FIVE

"I'M NOT EVEN ASKING FOR ULLMER," DAR SAID into one of the Navy's scrambler phones. "He's waiting for a Lear to return him to Elmira already, Abe. . . . Certainly I know," he replied to the CIA Director after a pause. "In the past two days, Ben Ullmer's had so many trained observers say they've seen something they couldn't have seen, he simply doesn't believe tonight's sightings from a couple of frightened civilians. He believes Black Stealth One is down in the Gulf."

It was after midnight at NAS New Orleans, and as he listened, Dar sipped his third cup of bitter coffee. He had consumed only two ales and an aperitif at Brennan's. He would have consumed more, perhaps, had the Commander's beeper not started the train of events that electrified Dar,

□□□

made him dizzy with hope and sober with resolve as they sped back to the naval base.

He picked up his cup, but when he had it halfway to his lips, he forgot the steaming brew. "I'll tell you why, because those two sightings were in line from Corbett's last known course, and the time fits the parameters we know, and the descriptions fit too, if you bear in mind that they thought it was some kind of feathered monster. All of the other recent reports failed one or another of those criteria, especially the descriptions, everything from lights in the sky to little green men.

"What? I don't know the exact number; Unruh simply told me they had logged over three *hundred* reports, thanks to all the media coverage."

Now Dar had time to sip, injecting a "yes" at one point. But he kept shaking his head and finally cut in: "Ullmer says the airplane could not possibly get that far on the fuel it carries. I say it is foolhardy to underestimate what Kyle Corbett can do in an airplane. . . . Ullmer is, naturally; but *I* have expertise with the *man.*"

Again, Dar checked his impulse toward a headlong passionate plea, loath to risk losing the support of the man who could allow or forbid his pursuit of his own daughter. Abe Randolph, he knew, mistrusted too much passion in his people.

He waited until the DCI had finished, this time. "Absolutely no personal conflict between us; none from my end, at least. I have only the highest regard for Ben Ullmer as a man and as a professional, and I will so state in writing." Dar let his voice slide from formal tones into the more habitual way in which he spoke with Abraham Randolph. "Frankly, I'd say Ben is in mourning for that airplane of theirs. For your ears only, Abe, I think he means to resign. . . . No, Sheppard canceled NSA's end of this thing because our man called the bad news in from Mazatlan; they feel, quite rightly, that they've lost our whole damned joint operation in Mexico, their pilot and the aircraft included. They're just hoping the Mexican Federales don't learn about Regocijo for a week or so. Give us all time to build a cover of plausible denials. The blunt truth is, from here on it's purely a CIA operation—or none. I say we still have a chance."

He sipped this time as he listened, jotting cryptic notes in his personal shorthand. Then: "I certainly have, it's only midnight here and all I need is your blessing to proceed. And Unruh, of course, to screen any fresh reports and coordinate the possibilities with me." Pause. "A fisherman on Matagorda Island and a teenager in his dune buggy, a few miles northwest of a coastal town called Rockport. Black Stealth One may be damaged because they both reported a hundred-foot bird practically skimming the surface. Scared the hell out of them both."

Dar drew a long breath of relief at Randolph's reply and began to itemize the jottings before him. "We should have a press release from your end, announcing we've canceled the interagency operation, which we have. Citing solid evidence that the fugitive aircraft was forced down in the Gulf. Meanwhile, I need your recommendation to the Secretary of Defense that I get every rotary-wing and hovering fixed-wing aircraft in the region. I can fly the back seat of a Harrier. . . . Yes, I checked, they're right here on the base and a cou-

☐☐☐

ple are two-seaters for training. . . . We fly east of San Antonio, refuel at Chase Naval Air Station nearby, and re-form before dawn in a line from Padre Island to Freer. Then we start a very slow sweep, converging toward the coast at Rockport."

A grim smile twitched at his jaw. "Well, he can't hide that cockpit, you saw it yourself in Elmira; it's how we spotted him in the Gulf and I intend us to be several squadrons strong, virtually touching wingtips within a thousand feet of the ground by the end of that sweep. He won't get past me this time, Abe."

Dar set the empty cup down and stood up as he heard his director's penultimate words. He replied, "If he's flying at night, yes; I could miss him, assuming he manages to get fuel nearby. But he didn't fly last night, and I think he could be overconfident. Say again? . . . I know that, Abe; I'll be happy to resign if I'm wrong, but this time we'll bring overwhelming force to a small area, and we can force him down by sheer numbers of hovercraft. This time," he announced, "I'm going to get the son of a bitch."

THIRTY-SIX

HE HAD FORGOTTEN TO SET HIS WATCH ALARM, BUT no matter: the dry-hinge squeal of a gull waked Corbett while the sun was little more than an exuberant promise on the eastern horizon. The sky was cloudless, still star-flecked above and to the west. *Probably no cloud cover all the way to Mexico,* he thought. He would have kissed the young woman who slept at his side, but chose not to wake her as he gentled his arm from hers, flexing those familiar early-morning twinges of pain from his joints as he stood.

He used his seven-dollar blanket to wipe dew and bug remains from the canopy of Black Stealth One, taking his time to avoid scratching the polymer bubble, with no intuitive concern for anything that might be building low across the sky like a metal stormline, miles away. He hefted his roll of duct tape with mild astonishment, reflecting that he had used almost the entire roll of the stuff in a trail stretching from New York to Texas. He decided he might have enough of it left to make Petra's bonds look convincing.

She awoke as he knelt beside her to rub her arms, beginning to stretch before she opened her eyes, then opening them wide as memory and recognition flooded her face. She flung her arms around him with the hug of a small, sleek bear. Her "Good morning" was as intimate as foreplay, and as full of promise.

"Hi, little pistol," he said, hugging her with one arm. "Ready for your morning bondage?"

She saw the roll of tape, realized that it was necessary, and grinned, pretending to misunderstand. "I've never tried it, but I might like it." By the time she stood up to tuck her blouse in, Petra's face had clouded. "I wish," she said, and bit her lip. "You know what I wish. God, I'm starting to miss you and you're still here! Dammit, Kyle! I just hope you leave before I start crying."

He pulled her into an embrace, sharing a long and fervent kiss before she pushed him away. "Hey, dirty old men need love too," he joked.

"Go on, get it over with. I intend to be absolutely furious with you before I climb down from here for help," she said glumly.

He taped her ankles first, then unwrapped his handiwork and did it again. "I taped you up when I went for fuel last night, remember that," he said, and read her frown correctly. "Well, logically I would've had to. You think they won't analyze the stuff to see how often it's been used? Never underestimate them," he said, in unconscious irony.

□□□

He rewrapped her wrists too, making certain that she could reach the torn edge with her teeth, and then carried her to the ladder. "Don't forget the dust the hellbug raises," he said, pausing on one knee. "If you worry that tape loose before I'm gone, it'll get all dusty and they'll wonder about that."

"Don't forget to write," she replied solemnly, and he saw that her mouth was trembling. He kissed it, longingly, gently, and then walked to the cockpit. "And for God's sake be careful," she added suddenly, raising her voice in virtual panic.

He gave her a high-sign, then grinned and winked as the hellbug's engine cleared its throat.

"I hate that macho shit, I *hate* it! Go on," she yelled, drumming her feet on the tank dome in a brief frenzy, but once he closed the canopy he could not hear past the hellbug's subtle stirrings, and it might have been his imagination when he glanced at her for the last time, her eyes closed but her mouth forming, *I love you, Corbett,* as he lifted.

He set the hellbug's nose directly toward Beeville, remembering that this entire region was a training ground for Air Force cadets. *I'd like to paint this thing as a bird and go high, but I'd best use ground effect to save fuel,* he decided, calling up the pixel program to paint his craft for high-flying searchers, then checking the IR display. Five minutes later, as the sun's first direct light hardened shadows in the cockpit, he could no longer see the oil tank. Black Stealth One wheeled southwest, in the general direction of Laredo and the Mexican border a hundred miles distant.

Corbett had not flown across this piece of country for years, but he remembered how suddenly

□□□

the land changed from creek-veined arable acreage to sere, dry ranchland fit only for oil derricks and forced irrigation. "Derricks," he said aloud. There might not be many in his way, but those few probably would not show on his scope. *Hell of a note, to get wiped out against a damn abandoned derrick over a dry hole. Pull up to two hundred feet? No ground effect there, I might as well be at twelve thousand. Well, keep your bloody eyes open,* he commanded himself.

He knew a reasonable chance existed that he would be seen, but at this hour most Texans would be pulling on boots about the time he crossed the border. And whatever they saw, he imagined that he would be in another country's airspace in less than an hour. Considering the current political climate, he did not worry much about the Mexican Air Force.

He first suspected that he was not going to make it while skimming thirty feet above the lazy waters of a miles-long reservoir. The IR scanner dutifully registered the exhaust of a ferryboat—and then showed him a dotted line of pink on the horizon. The line lay directly in his path. *Power line reflection?* But he knew that power lines did not stretch a hundred feet above this prairie and as he watched, the dots became more distinct on his scanner though still too distant for a visual check. He banked to the west. That line still stretched to the horizon, and it was not stationary, but approaching fast.

He tuned for military frequencies and found two of them fully occupied, the transmissions strong and getting stronger. ". . . lagging, Broom Five; form on me," urged one commanding baritone, and "Mop Bravo group, close it in," said another, with brief acknowledgments—some of them using jargon that Corbett had almost forgotten, not Air Force but Army. The guys flying Bell "Huey" helicopters had sounded like that over the jungles of Vietnam. And judging from their terse comments, the Broom group had to be Navy or Marine, because the Air Force referred to rear-seat observers as "gibs," guys in back. Corbett felt an instant of cold trepidation as he glanced at the scanner and saw more blips than he could easily count, forty or fifty of them, low on the horizon. And now he was too close to risk a steep climb because, as he had learned the previous day, that gleaming canopy would not remain totally invisible this close to such a far-flung set of eyes, and his rate of climb was comparatively sedate.

"Broom leader to Broom Two and Broom Seven, sortie again on present heading and re-form in five minutes, over."

"Ah, wilco, Broom leader, warn the slicks so they don't sweep me up on my way back" was one response. "Slick" was a generic military term for a helicopter. Corbett saw a sun glint as one of the dots ahead and to his left began to rise out of formation, picking up speed. He locked the pixel program onto that dot, saw it become a bulbous, ungainly swept-wing brute as it accelerated. Evidently the other sortie craft was so far down the line that Corbett could not spot it. But he recognized the aircraft with icy dread. *Oh, my God: they've got a squadron of Harriers!*

Mop and broom; it's a major sweep, Army "slick" choppers and those goddamn Harriers! And they're sending a pair of Harriers ahead to see if they can

□□□

flush me, he realized, slowing, dropping nearer to the hard-baked soil. He knew by now that Broom was the Harrier code word, and stayed on Broom's frequency as he kept one eye on the blue-and-gray camouflage of what was obviously a Marine Harrier. It passed a mile to his left at four hundred knots and gave no indication of spotting him, but Corbett knew that he was more nearly invisible when motionless on the ground than while his gleaming canopy bubble skated above the surface. He planted his legs hard, employing the waste gates in an attempt to land almost instantly in one of the many broad depressions of the scrub-dotted landscape.

The line of sweepers, AV-8B Harriers interspersed with Army helicopters flying behind and even lower, was clearly visible now, a vast armada of machines all capable of hovering, and of outrunning him. Someone had worked out an unlikely but fearsome combination, the sinister Harriers flying so slowly that their thrust diverters flung mighty downdrafts of jet exhaust toward the ground. That line trailed a virtual dust storm behind it, the product of their downdrafts. Corbett did not remember until too late that, painted skin or not, the hellbug's diverted air sent a huge spurt of dust flying as it touched down. And the dust storm raised by the searchers was probably no accident; even a pixel-covered skin might stand out as a distinct outline in such a soup of flying particles.

Corbett had hardly felt the grazing thump of hardpan when one of the Harrier pilots in a line approaching at perhaps a hundred miles an hour and so near that Corbett could see their flaps extended broke in with, "Broom leader, your ten o'clock on the deck! Canopy in a circle of dust!"

Corbett firewalled his throttle; the impeller was still revving respectably and as he cleared the ground, the sweep line was almost directly overhead, slowing in response to the sighting. But an aircraft of the Harrier's fourteen-ton mass does not maneuver well at such low speeds, and though they were spaced over four hundred yards apart, they used precious seconds in their attempts to maneuver in midair without colliding. Meanwhile, Corbett skimmed tumbleweeds as he plunged Black Stealth One's nose into that dust cloud.

Eighty knots would not have been enough for most light craft to crab sideways, dead-level, in a pall of dust without losing a wingtip. Corbett managed it using partial waste-gate power, virtually skidding, the right wing swinging fast until he was moving almost parallel to the dust pall. But one of the Hueys must have seen his canopy too, and Corbett knew it only when he saw the earth before him erupt as if a land mine had detonated.

If Corbett had been in doubt about the Hueys' armament, he knew now. Though some military helicopters carried rockets and cannon, this one had loosed a burst from its chin turret, a minigun firing as many rounds as six machine guns. Corbett veered right, now moving at a hundred knots, passing under the Huey before it could swing to keep him in its sights. He saw the bulk of a Harrier swing sluggishly into place ahead of him, sinking, and no more than fifty feet above.

The tremendous downblast of the Harrier's superheated jet exhaust, so close above, would have

□□□

slammed the delicate hellbug into the ground had Corbett flown into it. Instead, he judged that the Harrier was slowing and killed most of his own forward speed by a sharp, almost vertical climb, then nosing over. He ended directly above the Harrier, slamming the waste gates open, and found himself riding a few yards above the brute, its rudder an upswept scimitar scant feet from the hellbug's wing root.

The Broom channel was simply chaos. Two of the monsters had apparently collided, one of them damaged enough to force an emergency landing. A Huey circled, clearly unwilling to risk hurling a wall of lead so near a "friendly," but Corbett could see the shining ellipses of other Huey rotor blades as the choppers converged. He wasted no time trying to reprogram the hellbug's skin, knowing the bird plumage would be useless and too many warriors were converging from too many points to let him fool more than one.

Corbett could see the pilot below him as the man twisted in search of the hellbug, revealing his head-up display screen. The HUD might reduce a Harrier pilot's workload, but it was little use against a fugitive hanging overhead. The Harrier pilot did not take time to consider his choice, so he did what attack pilots like to do: he began to accelerate.

Corbett grinned fiercely, though he knew he could not keep forward pace with the Harrier for more than a few seconds. Had its pilot simply landed then and there, Corbett would have been an easy target for those Huey slicks the instant he moved away at fifty miles per hour. The pilot had a definite agenda, however, with darted glances at

□□□

the rearview mirror on the upper left side of his canopy. Corbett saw him try to use his rudder like a cleaver through the hellbug's wing and rocked that wing upward, as if to bank in one direction. Then, failing to match the Harrier's pace above a hundred knots, Corbett jinked upward and banked the other way.

The main rotor of the following Huey almost cut his wingtip off. It could not have missed the hellbug by more than an arm's span and its tail rotor did not quite miss, ripping a chunk the size of a man's hand from the wing trailing edge; and the hellbug's trailing edge was tough stuff, developed from the same filament-loaded aramid polymers used in bulletproof vests. The Huey's small tail rotor, its tips shredded unevenly, set up a hellish vibration as it began to come apart.

Corbett saw the Huey go down, spinning madly around its main rotor axis, and took the time to "check his six," using the scanner to show him who might be closing on him from his six o'clock position, directly behind. There were three of them, a Harrier and two Hueys, and Corbett heard the Marine pilot warn the Hueys aside as he readied his rocket pods. *Good, I'm more worried about them than about you,* Corbett thought, and saw the two smaller blips on his rearview screen move well aside. That was when he yawed the hellbug to place himself directly between his pursuer and the Harrier he had used as a shield before. It was completing an ungainly turn ahead of him.

His pursuer loosed one salvo anyway, the pencil-slim rockets glinting harmlessly past the hellbug's wingtip like huge needles, and Corbett was nearing top speed as he flew directly toward that turning Harrier which now approached head-on. Both of the Harrier pilots announced, one of them with short Anglo-Saxon comments, their plight: they would be firing toward each other. And while their rockets were no thicker than a man's wrist, one of those little warheads could equal one Marine airchine. Broom leader evidently forgot which channel he was on as he demanded side passes by the Hueys.

Corbett realized that the aircraft approaching him would be more dangerous if its pilot jinked upward to catch the hellbug in his exhaust, so Corbett did it first, again using the nose diverter to help flick the nose upward so suddenly that G forces nearly dragged his head down. Then he was over and past the Harrier, darting quick glances in search of enemies, which were plentiful, and cover, which was nonexistent.

The almost silent shuddering from his left wing made his decision for him; four neat holes had punched a straight pattern between leading and trailing edges. Corbett had penciled the line that defined the main spar of Black Stealth One, and he knew where that crucial structure lay under the hellbug's skin. One of the Huey slugs had missed it by less than six inches. Corbett rolled his aircraft onto that wing from an altitude of three hundred feet, seeing the rotors of two Hueys flash as they moved in from that side, seeing other flashes from a chin turret.

And ahead, cutting into the hardpan soil like angular fingers, lay one branch of a ravine that deepened and broadened as it stretched away to the southeast. More than one cadet had made of himself a flesh and metal marmalade by playing in these arroyos with fast, heavy airplanes. Corbett kept his left wing down, knifing toward the ground like a broad arrowhead in a long sideslip that brushed shrubs at the right-hand lip of the ravine.

Typically, the lip of a Texas ravine is an absolutely vertical cliff, abruptly becoming a slope that is not curved, but angled, toward the bottom. The wider that ravine, in general, the deeper—and the longer that vertical drop at its lip.

No airplane falling in a sideslip at nearly two hundred miles an hour could maneuver abruptly enough to avoid careening into the opposite slope of this ravine, without thrust diverters beneath its wing and nose. Among the excited voices clamoring in Corbett's ear was one that said, "Scratch one bogey." As Corbett let the hellbug's diverted thrust align him, now angling his right wing down, perfectly parallel with the ravine's left-hand slope and no more than a man's height above jumbled stone, he knew that his abrupt disappearance must have looked like a hopeless fall into destruction.

Ravines do not simply quit. They issue either into flat lower plains or bigger ravines. In his haste and bedeviled by G forces, Corbett punched a wrong instruction, erased it, then punched the right one into the pixel program while keeping the hellbug's belly mere yards above the slope that was leading him downward toward a blind bend. Virtually the only real curve associated with such a ravine is the graceful bend that changes its horizontal direction. If he could only reach that bend ahead, and bank tightly around it before one of them saw him, he could . . .

"Bogey in the ravine, Broom leader," called the only voice that did not sound perplexed. "Still taking evasive action but that canopy sparkles like a diamond ring. Broom nine pursuing," it went on, and Corbett cursed. *I had to polish the goddamn canopy, didn't I? Should've left it dirty.* A fragment of his mind said it would not have mattered. They would have borne him down like this anyway, sheer numbers overwhelming Black Stealth One's bag of tricks.

Corbett was already committed to a tightly curved bank to negotiate the bend but, as he swept through it, saw that the ravine was only an arm of a broader depression. Eastward, to his left, the glitter of whirling blades peeled over the ravine's lip a mile distant. Almost immediately he saw the Huey crabbing toward him, winks of light almost a steady gleam from its chin turret. Corbett dropped lower, following the slope contour, and saw what appeared to be a small volcanic eruption halfway up the slope across from him. It was a small area of ravine disintegrating in a solid hail of minigun fire, and the pattern seemed to be moving only up and down slightly, as if some huge beast were writhing just beneath the rocks.

The bastard doesn't see me, he's just keeping up a curtain of fire, Corbett realized. But he locked the scanner onto that Huey anyway and hoped that his canopy would not give him away again until he had flashed below that steady withering blast. Corbett actually heard the ricochets humming like bees in hell as he passed two hundred yards from that disintegrating rubble, beneath the line of gunfire.

He found himself pointed toward the mouth of another ravine, shadowed in early light, and swung into it even though he knew it would become shallower, not deeper, as he flew up its gullet. Another voice, then two, announced that he had been seen before his canopy ducked into the ravine's shadow. Twenty seconds later, as he climbed over the lip and dropped near the brushy plain again, a series of small explosions flung debris into the air three hundred yards ahead. He jinked upward to miss any stray hunks of rock that might still be raining down; he had not even noticed the rocket salvo, but it had missed by a fair margin.

Then, before darting down to ground level again, he saw the next ravine, less than a mile ahead. If his eyes were still perfect, it was a wide one—therefore probably deep. If his parallax perception was off, he could soon be a smear mixed with plastic. Two big, strong blips on his rearview were closing hard, and patiently settling into that ravine ahead to wait, four Hueys dipped below Corbett's sight.

Boxed. Trailing those two Harriers on his tail were other blips, flying higher as cover and, in a final, almost certainly suicidal ploy, Corbett prepared an appropriate exit. *How do you get out of a box? Same way you got in. Or not at all,* he decided, taking five precious seconds to tighten his harness and reset the pixel program. Not to fool anyone watching his upper surfaces: to fool anyone watching the hellbug's *belly.*

He could not see those waiting Hueys until he had nosed over at the ravine lip, and they were there, all right, blasting away as he judged the depth of the ravine and risked tearing the wastegate controls loose. He hauled the stick into his gut, pouring full emergency power into the nose

□□□

diverter, and started the first part of a loop. This time it would not become an Immelmann.

He had judged himself no more than five seconds ahead of the pursuing Harriers, but he was wrong: they were still approaching the ravine lip as the hellbug swept up above the ravine, upside down, and he leveled off that way. Inverted, ten feet above the plain at full tilt, Kyle Corbett flew out of the ravine and almost directly below the Marine craft. His pixel program painted not the top, but the bottom of Corbett's aircraft, and his canopy was completely hidden as he arrowed away, still inverted.

He took another risk, yawing slightly to change course, switching to the Huey channel. One of them had seen his maneuver and was bellowing it out as hard as he could, giving chase although, the Huey pilot admitted a moment later, he had "—no joy." He too had lost sight of Black Stealth One, and hanging upside down while gasoline trickled from his plastic bag into the cockpit, Corbett set the scanner to show him where the rest of his enemies were.

Coughing, eyes streaming with gasoline fumes, Corbett passed beneath the last of the covering Hueys without provoking a shout of recognition. He could not remember how long that experimental rotary engine behind him was supposed to run inverted, but the hell with it, he had enough velocity now to gain a little altitude and roll rightside up, if his engine seized. He kept waiting for signs of engine trouble, and blinking gasoline fumes from his eyes for a five-minute eternity as he streaked toward the border near Laredo. And he

□□□

listened with joy to the Mop and Broom channels for even longer than that, until he had righted the hellbug and cracked his canopy door to flush the worst of the fumes out.

THIRTY-SEVEN

THE AIR FORCE MEDICAL EXAMINER, A LIGHT COLonel with no appreciable bedside manner, ambled into his office and handed a sheaf of Xeroxed pages to Dar Weston with obvious relief. "We don't get many requirements of this sort, Mr. Weston; the Texas U. med center is just across San Antonio. It would have been a better venue for a workup like this."

Dar, after a perfunctory glance at the findings of Brooks Aerospace Medical Center, realized it would take him an hour to puzzle through it all. "But you were closer and Brooks is more secure, Doctor. We're deeply grateful. Could you summarize her condition for me? Her—father is flying in. What can I tell him?"

"That's a bizarre question from you people," said the Colonel. Dar saw the flicker of distaste in the man's eyes. Not an unusual reaction, even in the military: CIA had very few friends. "But apart from a few minor contusions and abrasions I'd say Miss Leigh has not suffered much physical abuse."

"And mentally?"

A shrug. "Difficult to predict over the long haul. No profound depression or confusion; she's a bit suspicious and angry, but that's to be expected. Perfect strangers have been poking her and asking questions for"—he checked his wrist—"what, ten hours or so? Her chief complaints seem to be mild sunburn and a desire, as she put it, to 'get the hell out of here.' Believe me, that would suit us very nicely," he added.

You're used to patients who have to salute, Dar reflected, shaking the man's hand. "I'll tell her," he said. "Where is she?"

"Staff lounge," was the reply. "That's where the junk food is."

Dar paused at the lounge entrance, then saw Petra at a corner table with one of the Company debriefing experts, a marvelously benign old tub of lard named Rogers whose gentle manner could have drawn a moray from its lair. Rogers was among the best men with naive civilians. He had flown portal to portal from Langley in four hours flat, after the Huey had spotted Petra atop that storage tank. After their reunion, Dar scrambling from the back seat of a Harrier to the belly of a helicopter so that he could hold tight to the daughter he had feared lost forever, they had flown straight to Brooks, on the southern edge of San Antonio's urban sprawl. Now, as he viewed those straight little shoulders and heard the barely contained impatience in her voice, Dar began to feel

□□□

his own body sag. He had stolen very little sleep the past few nights.

". . . no idea where he was going," said Petra as Dar, stepping up behind her, patted her shoulder. She jumped. "Please don't do tha—oh, Uncle Dar," she ended, rising to embrace him. Into his chest she said, "You can do it as much as you like."

He kissed the top of her head, feeling the warmth of his daughter like a long-sought benediction. He let his raised brows make a silent query to Rogers, who raised an open palm in response, then made it into a circled thumb and forefinger. Murmuring into her hair, he said, "I love you, Pets. These past days, I've realized I never said that to you as often as I should. By the way, we fished your yellow blouse out of the Gulf."

"Mother will be ecstatic about that blouse," she replied through a gulp that was half laugh, half sob, still holding him. "When will she and Dad get here?"

"Andrea is at home under sedation, but Phil should be here by now."

"Then can we please, *please* wind this up? I've got some summer exams coming up and I don't want to think about that damned skyjacker anymore," Petra said.

"I think it can be arranged."

"How about a few quarters for a Hershey? I've used all of his," she said, and indicated the smiling Rogers.

He found three quarters and smaller change for her and, as she moved off toward the line of vending machines, said, "How about it, Rogers? Get as much as you want?"

"Never enough," Rogers sighed. "She can't tell

us where the man is headed, and she swears he wasn't in radio contact with anyone. He could have telephoned from that place in Florida. No NSA confirmation on it, though."

"How did he treat her? She might not tell me the worst."

"You already know about her escape and recapture," Rogers said. "He roughed her up, but he also stopped a rape attempt." He released a Kris Kringle smile. "After two days in that airplane, I think the young lady's in love."

Dar only mouthed, *What?* but could not keep his face from contorting.

"With the airplane," Rogers went on, unperturbed. "Every time she mentions it, she gives herself away. I suppose there's no accounting for women engineers."

Dar let a long breath go, watching Petra tear the wrapper from a candy bar. "But there's nothing more you have to cover?"

"Nothing we can't go over some other time," Rogers said, feeling inside his coat, doubtless to shut off the recorder. "Section head may want a bit of light therapy in a few days."

That buzzword, "therapy," usually meant hypnosis or even a polygraph. *The sort of thing you do to field operatives who've been out of touch so long they might be compromised. And you can claim it's not all that intrusive but this is my daughter you're meddling with and, by God, she has been through enough already.* "Tell him," said Dar with blued steel in his glance, "that might not be necessary, nor politically expedient. Her father is Philip Leigh, a man who has already invoked the blessings of two senators and an undersecretary to get here. I don't think he'd let *me* do a deep interrogation, much less anyone else. Her family has too many media connections; they'd have a field day, Rogers."

Rogers cocked his head. "You're family, aren't you?"

"Yes, but it's not I who would sic the media on my own people. It's Phil Leigh you'd be dealing with."

Rogers beamed a smile that said he understood perfectly. "Well," he said, "if we have any follow-up questions, perhaps you could do the honors."

"Of course," Dar nodded, holding out his arm, letting Petra walk into a hug. She offered him a bite of Hershey, which he declined with a smile.

Rogers made his departure with handshakes, and Petra watched him go with unfeigned satisfaction. "I hope that's the last of that," she said.

"Probably not, but I can smooth it for you," Dar replied. Intuition made him ask, "Was there more that you didn't tell him?"

She slid into a chair and he sat too, facing her, holding her small tanned hand in his big, pale one. Her face showed signs of exhaustion, but also of a lively earnestness. "Yes. Corbett wanted me to tell you something."

"Something you didn't tell Rogers or the others?"

"I gather it was personal."

He withdrew his hand, folding his arms, sliding back in his chair as if steadying himself for a blow. "Well?"

"He said to tell you he kept the secrets. All of them," she said, adding, "whatever that meant."

"That was God-damned decent of him," he said

in savage sarcasm. *Then she's not play-acting for me; she still doesn't know. And why didn't he tell her?*

"He's not a monster, Uncle Dar," Petra said softly, quickening her pace as she added, "not that I think he's Mister Nice Guy; whatever he gets, he has coming to him. But in a way, I think he loves you. At least he did once."

Who the hell do you think you are, Kyle, to make me feel this guilty, this inferior? "Where'd you get that idea?"

"Because he couldn't hate you so much otherwise." Caught by the steadiness of her gaze, Dar Weston dared not look away. "He told me it was a fishing trip that made him do what he's done."

"Makes no sense to me," he said.

"He told so many lies about where we were going, I think I know when he was lying. I don't think he was lying about the bomb in the fuel tank. Why did you do it, Uncle Dar?"

He made a great effort to avoid swallowing, or changing the pace of his breathing. "Did you ask Rogers that question?" *If she did, there will be no way I can protect her in the future.*

Her glance held a trace of scorn. "Give me a break! I'd have that guy underfoot for a week if I stepped into such a can of worms. In fact, I withdraw the question. You wouldn't have done it if you didn't think it was right."

"It was a matter of crucial importance to national security, Pets," he said with soft intensity. "And unless you want to be hounded in ways I couldn't control, you're going to have to accept what I've said, and try to forget about it."

□□□

Now her look carried more compassion. "Is that what you did?"

"If only it were that easy; but my job is remembering, not forgetting. I have very few outstanding regrets about my life, but Corbett is one of them. I can't tell you any more than this: it had to be done."

"For the higher good, no doubt."

"There was no doubt at the time," he said. "Corbett was—is a man who puts no one's decisions above his own."

Petra vented a small "hunh" of wry amusement. "Tell me about it," she said, with sarcasm that implied "don't tell me about it."

"And his decisions aren't always in the country's best interest, Pets. Do you need any more proof beyond what he's done? Including the airplane, the search, and damages, he's probably cost the taxpayers a billion dollars."

"Wow." Petra stared at nothing for a moment. "That ought to make him happy. He said revenge was the last passion of old men."

"He said that, did he? The son of a bitch."

"Funny, that's just how he speaks of you," said Petra, now with an impudent smile. She must have seen his jaw twitch because she grabbed him again with that exuberant hug that he often drove hundreds of miles to experience. "But you're my son of a bitch, and I love you."

He blinked hard, hoping that she would not look up and see the tears welling in his eyes. To keep from breaking down completely, he said into her hair, playfully, "Rogers thinks I'm not the only thing you love."

□□□

He felt her stiffen. She did not look up. "I can't imagine what he meant," she said.

"Black Stealth One," said Dar. "He thinks you've fallen for a piece of machinery."

"He's very perceptive," she said, relaxing.

THIRTY-EIGHT

WITHIN TWENTY-FOUR HOURS OF THE GIRL'S RElease from Brooks, a score of middle-echelon men in both CIA and NSA knew many details of the Black Stealth One fiasco. Ivan the Terrible, his nose buried in a tin of Chicken of the Sea, did not even look up from his feast as Sasha said, "You know, Ivan, I never thought I would *add* a name to the list of possibles."

Sasha had added Kyle Corbett to his list of possible decoys after realizing the man had broken Snake Pit security well in advance of the theft—perhaps years before. It did not matter so much where the man had been hiding since the false report of his death. What mattered most was that Corbett's record went back a long way, and he had proven himself adept at espionage.

"What a joke if the KGB has been running him

all this time, Ivan," murmured Saŝha, giving the cat a languid scratch on the rump. Ivan lifted his sleek hindquarters in response, but continued to pursue a morsel of tuna inside the tin. "But if the man had gone over, it's probably old Pyotr what'shisname, Karotkin, who'd have handled him. And those people are no slouches at wringing a man dry of information." Karotkin, and the men who made his policies, would not have waited for years to make use of Corbett's intelligence; that much was certain.

"So it's most likely that Mr. Kyle Corbett is running loose with his own agenda. As you do, Ivan." Now the cat looked up. "And as I do," Sasha went on, giving the cat a scratch between the ears. "I need not care about his motive unless he's waited until now so that he could go over to the Other Side with the airplane. That would be good news and bad news, and it's certainly possible." But so long as the mysterious Corbett remained a loose cannon after his rolling rampage through U.S. security, he might still have a close connection within the intelligence community somewhere, and he might pop up almost anywhere. Sasha mulled those implications over until the cat's nose emerged from a perfectly clean tuna can.

Ivan commenced an elaborate ritual, licking a paw, then using it to remove the last traces of tuna oil from his face. "Oh, you can get clean"—Sasha smiled at the cat—"but Corbett can't. He would be a more credible Sasha than I am. And even if he is finally caught, who would believe his denials?"

The loss of Black Stealth One was already having its effect on all those who had endorsed the false ransom operation. Men at the very top would

□□□

have their sacrificial victims chosen; men near the top would be wise to prepare for early retirement. *And that could cut the decoy list in half.* "Well, no matter," Sasha said. He had a new decoy, returned from the dead as it were, who would serve nicely. The point might well be moot; Sasha himself might never again perform a service of any great importance.

It suddenly occurred to Sasha that his own survival and that of the evasive Mr. Corbett were tightly intertwined, an irony as broad and as deep as espionage itself. Sasha began to laugh so abruptly that Ivan bolted from the table.

THIRTY-NINE

CORBETT HAD CROSSED THE RIO GRANDE AT FOURteen thousand feet because a lot of armed, frustrated airmen were looking for him lower, and even though blessed with his barrel chest he could not fly higher in an unpressurized cockpit without some loss of alertness. It was barely possible that the Mexican Air Force would be waiting in their ancient T-33's, despite the political invective hurled back and forth across the border.

Living in Mexico, Corbett had watched those hostilities build. The torture and murder of a U.S. drug agent named Camarena, in Mexico, had lifted the edge from a blanket of Mexican deceit. Evidently the same government officials pledged to stop international drug traffic were, themselves, peso billionaires because of that traffic. The Mexicans had now replaced many of their top people within the federal judicial police but some of those changes seemed, to the yanquis, mostly cosmetic. And Mexican complaints of yanqui meddling into affairs of state had escalated into a national clamor against the colossus to the north. American tourists now faced a stronger likelihood of trouble than a fleeing American skyjacker. Still, Corbett knew he could not afford to relax. He could resume skimming the surface, however, to stretch his range.

Under ideal conditions he might have reached Hidalgo del Parral without stopping for fuel. The city was more than halfway across Mexico, beyond the sun-blasted hell of western Coahuila in a region more mountainous, but also more hospitable. He knew a man there who would ask no questions about his fuel requirements as long as that man did not see the hellbug itself. Even among the shadowy folk who prospered by making themselves useful to smugglers of all kinds, Black Stealth One was worth a few questions.

But conditions were rotten, and Hidalgo del Parral was out of the question. Corbett had squandered fuel with a lunatic's abandon during his escape in Texas—though only a lunatic would have pulled half an inside loop in a ravine, and nothing less could have saved him. Some of his extra fuel had splashed around the cockpit, and the two quarts remaining in his plastic container proved a bitch to chase down with that siphon hose while flying the airplane in choppy winds. Skimming low through the state of Nuevo Leon, with the hellbug in its buzzard's plumage, he knew he had been seen at least twice. On one occasion he saw a farmer cross himself frantically, fifty yards away. On the other a goatherd who might have been ten years old waved a hefty stick to ward off this vast predator. By that time Corbett knew that his only assured source of fuel would be Torreon, on the Durango-Coahuila border.

Torreon, enriched by a nearby network of canals that were the envy of many a Mexican farmer and perhaps a sign of hope in a drought-blighted nation, could be a tough town. Corbett had spent a week there overhauling a Cessna for the friend of a friend, in 'eighty-seven. Some of the hangar loungers might remember him and his German surname which had become as acceptable to him as the one he was born with. That might help, but familiarity had its drawbacks: old acquaintances, especially Mexicans in the flying business, might virtually drag him home for a small informal fiesta.

He might cope with that by claiming urgent business. His more serious problem in the Torreon vicinity was the lack of dense cover, where a man might step down from a sixty-foot bird without having to explain himself to curious strangers who could be friendly, or lethally unfriendly, but it was always the friendly ones who liked to gossip. No, he would have to make certain he arrived in darkness. If the little commercial strip outside Torreon was as he remembered it, he could land in high grass near the strip and portage his fuel as he'd done before. Unless, of course, someone had harvested the grass, or started a goddamn junkyard there, or—

The answer to all these surmises was a pass at medium altitude while watching the scanner for anyone who might be sharing his airspace. Corbett made that pass shortly after three in the afternoon to find the Torreon strip unchanged. He chose primary and alternate landing spots, then flew east again. From a dry spot in the marshes beyond Tacubaya it was only thirty miles to Torreon, and here he could wait for dusk in splendid isolation. No sensible Mexican would waste time in such a dismal place as that.

He endured mosquitoes of prodigious size and smoked his last cigarette to dissuade them. He lifted off at dusk, and in the last glow of light beyond the Sierra Madre range, he let the hellbug settle near the Torreon airstrip into wild grass so high that a man on stilts could not have seen over it, high enough to hide the canopy, the wingtips flexing downward as he cut the engine. Corbett fought his way through a grassy thicket and found himself at the edge of the runway. Ten minutes later he found that luck was with him, in the person of one Elfego Velarde. It was young Velarde who had cleaned parts on that Cessna engine, and the tale of a downed crop duster worked again. Velarde laughed at the sight of the plastic bladder, but he had seen old *cerveza* bottles employed for the same purpose. In Mexico, a man made do with what he had.

Best of all, Velarde could lay his hands on the keys to *el patron*'s Volkswagen van, the kind with a truncated pickup bed behind. Roughly once a month, said the young man, they had to bring fuel to someone in Corbett's situation. That situation, Velarde implied, was often one beyond the law. Velarde even helped wrestle a half-filled drum of avgas onto the van, and accepted enough American dollars to buy himself a few hours of flight in-

□□□

struction. It was with some difficulty that Corbett talked Velarde out of going along to help him refuel, though he accepted a half pack of cigarettes and matches. He drove a half mile before dousing his lights and cutting across stubble toward the runway.

Without his little Maglite, Corbett would have been hopelessly lost once he stepped out of the van onto stubble, and while wondering how a man could lose a sixty-foot airplane in a few acres of grass, he bumped against a wingtip. The rusty old pump on the fuel drum had a long rotary handle that squealed like a terrified animal with each rotation, but it filled that plastic bladder in less than sixty seconds and Corbett fell only once while wallowing through the grass. In a half hour he had filled the main tank and the spare bladder and was jouncing the Volkswagen van back to Velarde. He had grass cuts on both forearms and he would have burned like a torch with the spillage on his clothes. Young Velarde aimed him toward a shower which, astonishingly, even produced hot water.

Kyle Corbett washed off a twenty-five-hundred-mile accumulation of grime outside Torreon before donning his filthy clothes again. He pressed another twenty dollars on Elfego Velarde and had to refuse the young man's offer of a ride three times.

He followed his swath to the hellbug and found some comfort with his jacket bundled behind his neck, thinking not so much about the next day's tactics as about his friends. After years of enforced isolation, focused on machines that could provide a certain sense of accomplishment, a man might convince himself that things were more important than people. *Yet here's Velarde, who knows I'm a gringo but doesn't let flags obscure a casual friendship. And Medina, good ol' Speedy, who trusts me more than he does the whole spook hierarchy. God, what a copilot he'd be in Black Stealth One! If he doesn't get nailed for his part in this.* He considered the possibility that Raoul Medina might go behind bars. No worse possibility occurred to him.

And then there's Petra. If she had any sense, she'd stick with a nice safe life and design New England bridges, but Petra doesn't run on what they call good sense, she runs on a passion for living and learning. To hell with what "they" call it. What could be more sensible than that?

He chuckled in the darkness. *She says I'll be Methuselah when she's forty, and she's right. If I have any sense I'll write this little episode off. Only I have more passion than sense too, and not just for revenge. There's got to be something in genetics because she has the best of Dar Weston, the things I loved him for, the son of a bitch. And she might turn against me the same way.*

And it might be worth it, he decided, with a smile that lingered as he began to snore.

FORTY

MATEO CARRANZA LEANED AGAINST A CORNER post of the sheet-tin shed to escape midmorning sun. Karel Vins thought that he seemed more comfortable lolling in dirt than sitting in one of the two Ford Escort rentals that were parked under the salt-corroded metal roof. "I might as well be on garrison duty," Mateo muttered.

Vins, leaning against the blue Ford Escort, lowered his newspaper and leveled an emotionless gaze on the man. *And you were always troublesome when idle in a garrison,* he thought. "If you were, I would have you cleaning the trash out of here."

Mateo turned his idle gaze toward the empty oil cans, the faded and torn cardboard boxes, the ancient fragments of doped fabric that men had discarded during emergency repairs, perhaps years before. "The next contrabandistas who use this miserable hovel will only leave more," he said, yawning.

Vins knew that it was true. Corrugated cardboard remnants lay pressed between the noses of their Fords and the decayed sheet-tin siding. In another few years the accumulation of trash would make it impossible even to park a small car inside, let alone a damaged aircraft. The amazing thing was that the shed had lasted this long, eaten by salt air, sandblasted by storms, its corner posts sunk into dirt that was itself half sand. *Most likely,* he thought, *the roof will meet the garbage halfway.* "You need not keep me company, Mateo. Our cover is as fishermen," he said. "You might consider actually fishing, as Jorge does. We will soon grow tired of canned food, and we bought more fishing tackle than three men will need."

Mateo pushed up the bill on his baseball cap and stared indolently toward the salt marsh, half a kilometer distant. "Have you ever eaten a marsh fish, lobo? They are not called bonefish for nothing."

"For all I know there may be none of those here on the Pacific side," Vins replied, folding the paper. "And I do not intend any of us to leave this miserable excuse for an airstrip, for food or anything else, until our man arrives. You may crave fresh fish soon, if he is delayed." He tapped a third-page headline on his day-old Mazatlan newspaper.

Mateo, whose taste in reading ran to a particularly virulent sort of comic book, leaned back and tilted the bill of his cap over his eyes again. "What does it say?"

"That his hostage has been recovered in Texas, and also it implies that Señor Medina falsified his identity very nicely before stealing the airplane. The yanquis believe him to be some other man. Or so they say; who believes the news anymore?" *I believe this: Medina and his airplane must be true* boyevaya *to escape the kind of gauntlet the Americans seem to have put in the air.* Aloud, but softly as befitted a hunter near the end of a stalk: "We must not underestimate a man of Medina's determination, Mateo."

Mateo stood up abruptly, brushed dirt from his trousers, and walked outside to relieve himself, urinating onto the sandy soil. Over his shoulder he remarked, "What I do not understand is how this Medina expects to simply disappear afoot from here with fifteen kilos of money."

That had bothered Karel Vins too. They had covered several square kilometers nearby, the latinos afoot and he in one of their rented cars, searching for—a hidden car, motorbike, boat, anything. Aside from the ancient Chevrolet rusting into debris near the road, they had found nothing. *I would have sunk a small boat in the shallows somewhere, not readily found by accident and not too near this primitive dirt landing strip or its sheet-tin shed. And if I were Raoul Medina, I would arrive at sundown. Or I would radio confederates who could show up in a most unlikely way. Perhaps by air,* thought Vins, *and certainly armed.*

Mateo buttoned his fly, gazing past the low, stunted trees to landward and then scanning the scraps of cirrus that rode the stratosphere winds. It was not so much his question as his insolent air that set the *vawlk*'s teeth on edge: "Well? What do we do, Lobo, when a carload of his friends arrive?"

You're scum, but you aren't stupid, Vins thought.

"We welcome them, offer them chocolate, and kill them. All but one—it does not matter which one," Vins said evenly, putting the paper down at last. "He will take the money, and we must catch him later. We could have several days to recover the money and become *desaparecidos* before a search is mounted for us."

But Mateo's mind ran in more direct channels. "It seems to me we could merely bury him immediately and then tell your superiors we are chasing him," he said, sliding down that corner post until his rump reached dirt.

"Mateo, it is impossible for us to know all the ways that my superiors might employ to check on our progress here," said Vins with a sigh. "They could have been watching you from orbit as you pissed into the sand. They may have another team well hidden, perhaps frogmen, checking the number of Medina's friends as they arrive. *If* such friends arrive. So, we must release one man with the money. He is our reason for disappearing."

"And then he escapes," Mateo said sullenly. "And we get to be poverty-stricken heroes."

"Not if we are on our toes," Vins replied. "I have means of signaling that we have succeeded in ransoming that airplane. The money itself is bugged, and we have direction-finders. You two will follow our quarry, but not too closely. The moment I am relieved here, I will set out after you in the other car. With our radios, and our training, we should have no difficulty."

"If he wants to buy one of the cars?"

"They are not for sale," Vins shrugged. "And if he leaves on foot, he can be followed on foot."

□□□

Lazily, almost dreamily, as if Mateo did not really care: "Then why did we rent two cars?"

"*Callate,* shut up," Vins spat, "enough of your cross-examination. If he has a vehicle nearby that we have not discovered, that question will answer itself, yes?"

"So much for our brotherhood of equals," Mateo said cynically, scratching his armpit.

We are still far from soviet man, the perfect, selfless product of world revolution, Vins told himself as he regained his poise. *But at least I will satisfy my country before I satisfy myself.* "My apologies, Mateo; my temper grows short as the time grows near. Do you have any further questions?" His tone conveyed, nonetheless, that he would tolerate very few more such questions.

Mateo Carranza grunted and waved a languid hand to acknowledge the apology. Then, "I know something of the way your GRU works, Lobo. And unlike that poor fool Jorge Ocampo, I have given this much thought. It seems to me they would not weep if they arrived here for the airplane and found the pilot dead. I should think they would insist on it. And then they would demand the money."

"And if that happens, we must give it to them," Vins said. "That could be a part of the plan they kept from me, and that is another reason why I will not take one step out of line until the airplane is secure in the proper hands. But I think it is not part of their plan, because it is the Soviet Navy, not the GRU, which will take that airplane from us. The GRU may have a man on that team, but most naval men are a different breed, Mateo; they are not trained for wet work like ours. It would not be good for their morale if they knew some of the things we must do."

"So," Mateo said, with a grunting that could have been laughter, "we must appear to deal fairly with a turncoat thief, because your sailors think of themselves as honorable men."

Now Vins stood up and stretched, scanning the edge of the marsh for Jorge Ocampo. "You may ask them if you like," he said with easy sarcasm.

"I would rather count the money again," said Mateo Carranza.

"You have counted it twice already," Vins said, and strode toward the marsh where Jorge was dutifully plying his cover with a fishing rod. He did not see Jorge for several minutes and, when he did, for an instant he did not recognize the swarthy little man with the battered hat and saltwater lures festooning it. *It really might have been someone else,* he admitted silently as his heart settled down to its usual steady rhythm.

It might have been Sretsvah, or some young captain I have not met, sent to keep tabs on me. There may be one hiding nearby, and it is barely possible that Maksimov sent him. But he would not show himself so openly. And if I found him, would I kill him? More to the point, would he beat me to it? A man does lose his muscle tone, given enough years. I will be well out of this business, and the sooner, the better. Right after we chase down our rabbit, and I kill my two hounds.

When Jorge Ocampo turned toward him, el lobo was doing deep knee bends.

FORTY-ONE

GROUND-EFFECT SKIMMING WOULD HAVE BEEN sheer suicide for a man in an ultralight aircraft crossing Mexico's jagged spine, the Sierra Madre Occidental Range, with its violent downdrafts and uncharted wilderness where, some said, men still fired weapons with crude black powder and raised pre-Columbian crops, and sacrificed to gods that Hernan Cortez only thought he had vanquished. Corbett fell back on his other tactic for fuel economy, far older than those gods, as old as the condor itself, searching out the updrafts that skirted the ten-thousand-foot peaks, gradually working his way south down the state of Durango. But a soaring sailplane moves at a stately pace, and Black Stealth One did not reach Regocijo until after noon, though its fuel bladder was still full.

No hurry, he told himself, with a control movement that sent the hellbug wheeling in an upward spiral, buoyed by a thermal current. *This is why you took the risks, beyond any notion of revenge. And if you can't come out of this mess with a king's ransom, you won't be able to afford the hangar and the maintenance the hellbug demands. So why not spend a day playing with your new toy? It might be the last day you'll ever see.*

Medina had said the "Bulgarian" looked like a tough, smart customer. Chances were, he wasn't Bulgarian at all; KGB, most likely, and he wouldn't be alone. After the old switcheroo at Regocijo, taking Blue Sky Three from there to a rigged crash near Llano Mojado, did Medina really expect them just to assume he drowned? *You'll have to get cute; check the area for signs of ambush. We'll have to talk it over, Speedy.* With only a set of map coordinates for the Llano Mojado strip and no previous landings there, Medina would need eyes in the back of his head once he waded ashore.

But Corbett cursed, those plans forgotten instantly, after he soared past Regocijo and spotted the old deactivated spook airstrip. Its hangar had been a big structure of dry old wood, now only a smear of blackened debris collapsed in on the concrete floor. Corbett, his throat dry as toast, made three successively lower passes over it, the last into the wind at a trifling speed less than fifty feet above charred timbers, before he knew that someone had died in that ruin.

His passage might have been noiseless to a man, but not to the sharper senses of vultures, and to the gaunt coyote that burst out of the wreckage and skulked off at a lope. Corbett saw three buzzards hopping across smoke-blackened concrete like gargoyles in a frantic effort to take off with full bellies, and he got a glimpse of what had drawn their attention. Sickened, he climbed a hundred yards before using the IR scanner.

The burned-out hangar showed no trace of residual heat, not even as much as the coyote which had not skulked far off. Corbett's eye traced the outlines of something that had once been a graceful craft of wood and plastic, now ash and glistening filament, partially covered by sections of burnt roof.

He wanted to land, because a careful foray into the debris might tell him more. But, *Got a bad feeling about that,* he thought. *Uncle Sugar sure didn't do this, and if the Sovs did, how do you know they haven't booby-trapped the fucking place? There's not a soul here and that in itself is suspicious—but then, this is mañana land. Wonder whose remains those are next to the airplane. The old caretaker, probably. Shit! This means you have to ransom the hellbug itself if you want that money. And you haven't got Medina now; nor those gas cartridges either.*

With one final slow, skimming pass over the wreckage, he assured himself that the remains had been human. *Whoever did this, they wouldn't be Americans and they've killed somebody already. The odds are, those same people are waiting at Llano Mojado. In fact, maybe this was their way of saying, "We know about your clever switch, and this is what we think of it; we want Black Stealth One, or nothing." Yeah, that figures.*

He sent the hellbug climbing, fully aware that temporary safety lay within reach, near San Luis Potosi. The place had become his home and maybe

□ □ □

he would simply *have* to trust someone to keep his secret there. *And what a load of shit that is; if you believe that, you'd believe anything! Hiding near San Luis as a man with modest means and this mind-bending airplane simply isn't an option, so put it out of your head. The question now, is whether you go on to Llano Mojado and try to flimflam the people who invented flimflam.*

But by the time he reached cruise altitude he had cut through his rationalizations; knew that possession of *only* Black Stealth One, or *only* the money, would leave him forever embittered at his own failure, not the failure to win but the failure to try. The question of confronting that Sov paymaster was not, and never had been, a matter of "whether." The only question was "how."

FORTY-TWO

JORGE OCAMPO, SQUINTING AGAINST THE AFTERNOON sun, shoved his battered hat onto the back of his head and leaned his fishing rod against the shed wall. *El lobo has spent much of this day sending us on childish errands. And some of them no longer make sense,* he reflected when Vins had finished giving new orders. Aloud, Jorge asked, "Are we searching for a boat, or a man?"

"Either," Vins assured him, "or both. Perhaps more than one man."

Mateo Carranza, spooning beans directly from a can onto a tortilla, said, "We have searched for men already, Lobo. It sounds as if you know something you have not told us."

My thought exactly, thought Jorge. *This Russian is not the same man I knew, and perhaps the money has changed him. He gives us no credit for brains; leads us here and there like burros. If he has brought us here as sacrifices, I shall put a bullet in him.*

Vins stood up, brushing crumbs from his thighs, and folded his arms as he let his gaze sweep the marshlands. "It is only a suspicion, a feeling I have. And I have learned to trust my suspicions. If this man Medina is cunning enough to put an airplane in our hands, he is not so stupid as to arrive without some kind of support. So," he said, and waved both hands to indicate the countryside. "Where is that support?"

Jorge's eyes followed the wave. "He must be so cunning that we will not see it until the man wishes us to," he shrugged, and rolled himself a bean sandwich.

"I will not accept that," Vins said. "We simply must be more cunning than he is." He chose a key and unlocked the trunk of the blue Ford. "Something is out here. I know it. We have only to find it."

Jorge chewed as he looked into that trunk, looking not at the submachine guns ranked inside, nor the direction-finder units with loop antennae for tracking money, but at the three net bags of paper money el lobo had let them count into almost equal piles, and then he swallowed, though he did not taste the *frijoles.* He was tasting the money.

Jorge accepted a stubby little Uzi from Vins without a word and watched Mateo take one as well. The short, wire-stocked Israeli weapon was heavier than an American M16 and had a shorter range, but three of them could be hidden in a single piece of luggage and the Uzi's reliability was a legend. *You keep the weapons inside a locked trunk in between patrols. Why, Lobo? I know why; and a man who no longer trusts his squad is a man I no longer trust. With all this money lying about, you have become more coyote than wolf.*

Still, it was clear that Vins had lost none of his shrewdness. "Mateo, you will see the water's edge with fresh eyes because you have not investigated it. Look carefully for signs of a boat, probably not within sight of the runway. We meet back here at dusk; sooner if the airplane arrives. Jorge, you and I will move out from a central point in the brush. He who finds a vehicle, shoot once to signal."

Mateo: "And he who finds a man?"

Vins: "Shoot to kill. We do not want more than one man to chase, later." He motioned for Jorge, who fell in step as they marched toward the scrub.

They had not walked thirty paces when Mateo called, "And what if the man is one of your own? You said it was possible."

"I have only two men," Vins called back. "If you shoot anyone else's, it is their problem."

Jorge did not often hear Karel Vins chuckle to himself as he did now, striding into the brush. *You say you are a patriot, yet you would willingly shoot a man from your own country, a man like yourself,* thought Jorge. *Me, I think perhaps you do not like men like yourself.* And then Jorge understood. "A dead GRU man would be one fewer to chase us. Correct?"

Vins did not reply, but his heavy-lidded glance endorsed the notion. Presently, Vins made a hand gesture as if patting an invisible dog, commanding silence as he turned away. Jorge watched him for a moment, in grudging admiration. Coyote or lobo, Vins knew how to move through brush with no sound that would carry more than a few yards, watching where he stepped, avoiding branches when he could, holding and releasing them with silent hands when avoidance was impossible. *I would not want to be the man you hunt,* Jorge thought as he began his own reconnaissance. *And you turned your back on my Uzi, Lobo. Perhaps you can be trusted after all.*

Jorge tried to think like a sniper, skirting every likely hummock and thicket, checking each one thoroughly and taking his time to do it right. Now and then he paused, as el lobo had taught him in earlier campaigns, squatting to listen. He did not want to hear a Ford Escort engine because that would mean Karel Vins had doubled back, after all his talk of patriotism, to take the money and leave alone. In fact, he did not want to think about it, and so he could not help thinking about it. Jorge did a lot of listening in the next hour or so.

But with perhaps two hours of sun left, Jorge had also covered a broad swath of the sparse sandy landscape, some two kilometers of it, dodging cactus as well as less hostile shrubbery. He was wondering whether Mateo had taken his work seriously, also wondering whether he had gone too far to hear a gunshot, when he saw a shadow cross a hummock ahead of him. The shadow was far too vast to portend any living thing. Jorge looked up and saw the monster bird instantly, no more than a hundred feet above him.

It was a creature so stunning, so terrifyingly enormous, that Jorge Ocampo simply stared with his jaw agape. But it produced a sound like a soft wind though its wings did not beat as it wheeled almost overhead, and when it came still lower something happened to its plumage. It was no longer plumage at all, but a dull gray with faint glitters of late sun from a million points on its hide, and now that he saw that the thing was an airplane, Jorge's eyes picked out the faint outline of a cockpit bubble. *I must have imagined that it wore a bird's plumage; the error of a poor observer, and one not to be mentioned.* Jorge began to run in a steady trot toward the landing strip long before he heard a single gunshot, multiplied by faint, flat echoes.

There had been a time when such a run would not have winded him, but Jorge arrived at the strip breathless. He had seen the airplane's first slow, floating passage down the length of the landing strip, and its second pass somewhat higher as it crossed over the shed, continuing low over the scrub until it disappeared. El lobo was already standing on the strip's grassy verge, peering at a gray, creased placard of some sort, and Mateo approached with his trousers wet to the thighs.

Jorge, with forced breathing to flood his oxygen-starved tissues, heard the rumble of Russian curses as he realized Karel Vins was reading from the inner face of a flimsy cardboard container. "I saw nothing on my patrol but that monster airplane," Jorge reported. "Me, I think the man is truly alone."

Vins glanced at Mateo, who only offered an elaborate shrug by way of a patrol report. "You may be right," Vins muttered. "He must have seen me wave; he dropped this on his second pass. Certainly not the message of a man who came prepared."

□□□

Jorge saw the scribbles penciled onto the gray cardboard. "What does it say?"

"It is in English," Vins replied. "He demands that we place the money one hundred meters from the far end of the strip, and stand together at this end until he has landed to take the ransom. He must think we are fools."

Mateo: "But if he is afoot, Lobo—"

"That airplane, I am told, can rise like a helicopter gunship. He could fly off with the money before we could get within gunshot range. No, thank you."

"Ahh," Jorge said. El lobo had explained much in few words, for any airplane that could do such wondrous things might indeed be worth such a ransom. "So what do we do? Shoot him down?"

Vins held his silence for a long moment, sweeping the horizon with his gaze, before answering as if to himself. "We must take the aircraft intact. This man Medina is improvising now. I think, if he sees the money through those net sacks, his greed will make him land—even if I am standing next to the money. Yes, that is what we shall do. We can assume he is armed, and he must have seen my Uzi. I shall place it far out of reach on the dirt. You two, go to the other end of the strip and wait."

Jorge: "You will face him unarmed?"

"I am never unarmed," Vins said with his wolf's grin. Jorge nodded. He had not seen el lobo's sidearm during the entire mission, but of course the man would keep one. He watched Vins select a key, open the trunk of the blue Ford, and lift out the bags of cheap jute net full of Swiss banknotes.

□□□

Then Jorge walked toward the end of the dirt strip with the laconic Mateo Carranza.

Jorge saw the thing come out of the sun five minutes later, settling low over the water, awesome in its silence. El lobo stood waving. This time the vast wings seemed almost to flap as the aircraft banked away in a long, slow circle over the marsh, returning a minute later, passing almost over Karel Vins who seemed to be shading his eyes before he ran forward toward something that fluttered to the ground after the monster began to climb into the heavens.

It seemed to Jorge that this whole operation was turning to muck under his feet. He thought perhaps el lobo had begun to hold the same opinion when Vins, trudging back like a peon with the ransom of a king over one shoulder, whistled a familiar old call. He did not feel much like taking any more orders but, *"A sus ordenes,* Lobo," he said as he and Mateo reached the shed.

Vins flashed another piece of torn cardboard, brightly colored on one side, gray on the other. On the gray side were four letters: a single word. "He wishes us to wait," Vins grumbled in Spanish, dropping the money into the car's trunk and slamming the lid.

Now Mateo spoke up. "He will return, then."

The eyes of el lobo searched the sky. "I am certain he saw the money; who would not return for that? But he has turned very, very cautious for a man who has dared so much. He could force a change in our tactics. And our tactics may depend on just how long we have to wait." Jorge studied the Russian's face and saw no duplicity there, but simple frustration.

FORTY-THREE

CORBETT'S FACE REMAINED IMPASSIVE UNTIL HE had studied the terrain thoroughly from three thousand feet, but once he had made his choice, the corners of his mouth began to develop smile lines as he pursued his stratagem. Some of that grass in the salt marshes stood higher than a man could reach, thick as cattails and sharp-edged enough to slice a man's skin unless he moved carefully. To go touring through that stuff, a man had to be highly motivated. The grass was capable of supporting a very light load if it were well distributed—across, say, sixty feet of ultralight wing. It would compress a bit. Well, so much the better, up to a point. He wafted Black Stealth One in its pixel mode over the protective sandbar, almost grazing the surface, keeping a dunelike rise of ground between himself and the distant landing strip. The

□□□

hellbug nosed deep into dense marsh grass less than a hundred feet from shore, roughly a mile from that scabrous little landing strip.

He reasoned that the man his IR scanner had picked up out in the scrub would probably be the Russki's ace in the hole, maybe a sniper. He'd been on the other side of the landing strip, though, on foot; certainly not in a position to see the hellbug slide into its grassy nest.

The Russians had two small cars in that shed. Corbett had seen two other cars within a few miles of this spot, one an abandoned hulk close by near the road, the other a windowless old VW a mile or so out in the scrub, perhaps dumped years before from the look of it. He had hoped for, but not really expected, one or two men; if more than three or four, the risk would have been unacceptable. *So quit worrying about what you might've done; too many ifs and you might chicken out. This bunch puts your chances on the very margin of sweet reason.* The access road stretched away to his left, and the vintage Chevy lay just beyond the road. From the distant shed, a man would not be able to see the old car unless he walked to a nearby rise of sandy turf. Without that obscuring rise, Corbett would have had only the dry brush for cover.

He feared at first that the hellbug's nose would settle too far, and if the forward exhaust diverter entered the water he was in serious trouble. *But with nobody aboard, I could cut brush and shove it beneath to free the diverter.* Still he held his breath as the impeller spooled down, waiting for a jolting slap into salt water. When that did not happen, he set the pixel program to fool a watcher

☐☐☐

from near the road, and smiled at the result. Amid this thicket, the chameleon effect was startlingly good.

He took the old Westclox and two small wire-filled cardboard tubes from his bag, rewinding the clock, then smashing the cover glass. He removed the minute hand because it would only get in the way. He slipped folded bundles of insulated wire from the protective cardboard tubes, working quickly because he did not want time to regret what he was doing, and uncovered pencil-thin copper dynamite caps from inside the wire bundles. One cap, marked for a two-second delay, he placed behind his seat track. The other, which would detonate with no delay, he wedged between the base of the fuel tank and the flexible cockpit housing after he broke its wires off to the lengths he needed. It was always possible that the first cap would split the tank without igniting its fuel, but the second would detonate into a mist of fuel and fumes. The devastation that would follow was not an event Corbett wanted to think about.

After trimming the wire ends, he spliced the cap wires together and wrapped one long lead gently around the clock's hour hand so that the bare end would move imperceptibly with each stolid tick of the clock. Then, using spare wire he had broken off, he jammed one wire end into the energized side of the circuitbreaker panel and routed its other end to the clock, which he shoved carefully beneath the copilot's seat. The final adjustment of that energized wire was not a thing to be done until he was ready to leave the hellbug. He decided that three hours would be enough. Whatever hap-

□□□

pened, no damned Russian would ever find more than debris from Black Stealth One.

The cockpit had not been designed to let a man remove his shoes, socks, and trousers, but he managed. He had a moment of near-panic when, after counting four mauled but serviceable cigarettes in their packet, he could not at first locate the paper matches Elfego Velarde had given him. Finally he found them, stuffed everything into his leather bag, but left his wallet. He gave special thought to his ammunition, dropping one round into each jacket pocket because Dar Weston had once recounted field agent tricks to him. *The Weston giveth, and the Weston taketh away. The son of a bitch.*

He placed the leather bag and his plastic fuel bladder in the footwell, made a final placement of the energized wire with utmost caution, then eased himself down outside to avoid grass cuts on his naked legs, the hellbug rocking gently. Silted water lapped at his knees, and the patina of gray salt on grass stalks told him this was not high tide. *Christ, that's all you need, to have this thing float out to the sandbar,* he thought. *One thing you never thought you'd need was a bloody boat anchor.*

He solved his problem with most of his remaining duct tape, begrudging every inch he had to use. Torn lengthwise and spliced, it reached from the thrust diverter pivot to a group of stalks he bound together as a living anchor. It did not look any too dependable to Corbett. From this point onward, life itself would not be all that dependable.

He reached over the cockpit sill and retrieved the bag, then the fuel-filled bladder, using them to shield his face as he moved to shore. A tuft of the

□□□

rattan-stiff grass made a passable broom, sweeping away his footprints at the water's verge. *Yeah, but it still looks funny.* However, from a hundred feet away the hellbug itself was visible only as a vagrant gleam of canopy, which might have been water reflection, and outlines that appeared as wire-thin dotted lines among the luxuriant growth of marsh grass.

Within minutes his legs had dried, and he donned his trousers. He brushed away his tracks again one-handed as he moved steadily toward hummocks topped by lower, stiff beach grass. Once there, he put on his socks and shoes, then looked himself over. *This is not a man who has waded ashore,* he decided, and moved from hummock to driftwood to hummock until he reached turf that did not accept a footprint.

The twin-rutted path of the road curved around the shoulder of the rise of dunelike mounds that lay between him and the landing strip. Moving cautiously forward, sweating with his thirty-pound fuel load, he began to hunker down when he saw the outlines of the long-abandoned Chevrolet near the road. The bad news was that its seats were gone. The good news lay in the ceiling and rear seatback upholstery, strips and tufts of stuff that he could gather with ease.

Best of all, the Chevy's fuel tank did not leak as he poured a few cupfuls of fuel in. He could see fumes rising from the sunbaked tank as he began moving away from the hulk, strewing bits of upholstery below the spiny underbrush, trying to follow the outline of a swept, sixty-foot wing. Much of the brush was crackling dry, and that would help too. Before dousing that same area with his remaining gasoline, he sat down and built his timers.

He tore the paper match packet into two roughly equal packets, laying one match aside, then bent the protective covers backward, each lower flap standing edge-on against the heads of the matches. When he grasped each pack by its striker strip, match heads downward, the outline of each was a perfect numeral 4 in cardboard. He did not use the spare match to light cigarettes yet, but spent two minutes feverishly dousing all the shreds of upholstery and leafy shrubs in a shallow, sixty-foot V. He wanted a half-hour to circle around the airstrip but knew the cigarettes would burn down in less time than that.

Placing a small pile of cloth shreds on the Chevy's trunk near the tank opening, he wetted them thoroughly, cursing as he waved to dry a splash of fuel from one hand. Then he moved away with his figure-4 timers, lit two cigarettes, and wedged the unlit ends between the match-heads and the impinging covers. He approached from upwind, then, setting the deadly little timers within inches of the fuel-soaked detritus so that the cigarettes pointed toward the sky. One timer, he knew, was 90 percent certain. Two provided extra assurance. While a cigarette's glow rarely ignited liquid fuels, the sudden flare of a dozen paper matches almost always did.

Corbett did not realize he had been trembling until he began to run, bent almost double, through the thorny brush. More than once he stopped, then stood up slowly and carefully to check his position with respect to the distant shed. Sudden move-

□□□

ment on his part when standing erect, he knew, might be disastrous.

When he was still a half-mile from the shed, he saw that the little team was leaving it, spreading out into the brush on recon. Evidently they were more interested in the sky than their immediate surroundings, for the blond man stopped several times as he moved off in the general direction of the shoreline, shading his eyes, scanning the heavens as he disappeared into the underbrush. *Getting nervous, pal? Wondering if the bird will make another pass? Making just one more little patrol? Well, you just keep going while I have a look around.*

Corbett had lost sight of the other men long before and realized that they must all be out of touch with each other. *Another five minutes,* he begged, already nearer that shed than any of them—but his own diversion put an end to that, when the old Chevy's gas tank went up with a mighty, subterranean cough that was not quite an explosion.

Almost instantly, he saw the lick of flames above heavy brush and heard someone whistle once, twice. He began moving directly toward the shed now, hoping to see men converging toward the distant flames that grew more smoky as he watched. He froze in dismay and astonishment, then dropped to a squat, as he heard footsteps and heavy breathing very near and getting nearer by the second. The man was running hard, his gaze on the smoke, and he held an Uzi before him to sweep branches from his face as he appeared. Intent on his horizon, the lean, swarthy man burst into Corbett's view only five paces away. He must have seen Corbett squatting because he tried to snap the Uzi around as Kyle Corbett leaped into him in a dusty collision.

Any gunfire now would be a pointed announcement and Corbett battered at the man's temple with the barrel of his sidearm, tearing the man's trigger hand from the Uzi with his free hand. Both men went down, the lean latino grunting as Corbett's elbow slammed into his diaphragm. The Uzi clattered onto sandy soil and, now using both hands, Corbett rained punishment against the man's head. Corbett finally connected with a clean, unimpeded blow on the point of the man's chin and then watched him lapse from consciousness.

He had no time for niceties, kneeling within a hundred yards of the shed. The man's bootlaces took an infernally long time coming out, but they were sturdy enough to bind wrists and ankles. Corbett wrenched one of the loose boots off, then a sock that had seen better days, and stuffed that sock into the man's mouth. When Corbett moved forward to scan the airstrip again, he could see the blond man standing in the open, calling orders in Spanish and waving his assault rifle toward the distant smoke with an air of command. Corbett did not see another man at first, but finally spotted a small figure on the other side of the airstrip in the edge of the brush as it set off toward the flames at a dead run.

The blond still seemed preoccupied with the sky but did not take Corbett's diversionary bait himself, moving instead until he was striding back and forth in front of the shed as if unconsciously guarding a command post. *Well, I'll just have to come to you,* Corbett decided, tucking the Glock

□□□

away, holding the Uzi at his side as he moved around to keep the shed between himself and the sentry. He needed precious minutes to cover the distance without snapping a branch, but as he stepped to the rear of the shed's salt-corroded tin wall, he heard the blond curse aloud, not in Spanish or English. The man took several paces toward the airstrip, shading his eyes with one hand, an Uzi cradled across his chest as he turned his back to the shed.

Corbett said it in Spanish because the blond had given orders in the same tongue: "If you move, you are a dead man."

The blond moved, but only to flinch, his shoulders drooping slightly. He did not look around. "I should have known," he replied in Spanish.

Corbett stayed behind the shed, stepping into shadow, knowing that at any moment the man investigating the fire might come within sight. "Hold the gun by its barrel and put it over your shoulder," he demanded. "No whistles, no sudden moves." As the blond obeyed, Corbett could see him trying to eyeball his captor from the edge of his vision. "No, look toward the fire. And show me the money."

The blond shrugged. "It is on the runway, where your pilot could see it," he said.

"How far?"

"Four hundred meters."

Corbett hesitated. He needed a car for an immediate escape, but he would have to pass at least one armed man who could shoot from cover. And the instant a car started up, the sound could be as revealing as gunfire. Better if he collected the money before that happened, but only an idiot would ex-

□□□

pect this stalwart blond to simply go and retrieve the money for him. "Put your gun down by its barrel. I'm going to walk with you to the money, and you're going to stay between me and that smoke." As the blond eased the rifle down, placing it flat on a tuft of grass, Corbett came forward, holding his own rifle in a way that might not seem threatening to a distant watcher.

As the blond began to walk toward the airstrip, Corbett strode two paces wide of him, cradling the rifle so that he need only move it slightly to bear on his captive. "And where is my team now?" the blond asked rhetorically, glumly.

"They're around," Corbett said. "Walk faster. If you get me into a gunfight you'll be the first one to go down." The pace picked up. Corbett's eyesight was as good as any man's but he could not see a telltale lump that might be cash among the dirt and wiry tuftgrass ahead. Presently, when they had covered three hundred paces: "Point to the money, damn you," he insisted.

The blond hesitated, then pointed ahead. "There, I think," he said, not sounding any too certain. "Near the end of the runway. It would be obvious from the air," he added and then, in genuine anxiety: "Did your pilot crash the aircraft?"

"Maybe, maybe not," Corbett said. "I'm the pilot. I'm the guy who dropped those notes on the cardboard from a box of Hi Ho's. Medina had a little trouble. What the fuck do you care? What you'd better care about is that it's getting late, and I'm getting jumpy, and I don't see the goddamn money."

"All this is unnecessary," said the blond, "if you

□□□

have the aircraft. I expect you to take the money. It is planned," he insisted.

"You bet it is," Corbett said. After another minute he quit walking. "Stop right here." Unbidden, the blond turned to face Corbett with a gaze of frank assessment. Corbett's accusation was equally frank: "The money isn't out here."

"Maybe it is," shrugged the blond in a way that was almost pure Mexican.

The man's feet were planted just so, and Corbett judged the moment correctly. "Don't. I'd just as soon kill you as not," he warned.

The man released a carefree sort of smile. "The money must be somewhere out here," he said, seeming to relax as he turned away. From somewhere in the distance a thin, two-note whistle floated on the breeze.

"You're too damned sure of yourself," said Corbett. "Put your thumbs in the back of your belt and keep looking away." As the blond did it, Corbett unholstered the Glock and put down the Uzi. He stuck the sidearm's muzzle into the man's ribs and began to pat him down; sleeves, jacket pockets, beltline, trouser pockets. No firearms. "Well, you sure keep up a cheerful front, I'll give you that much," Corbett said. "Now get back to those cars on the double." *I slipped up, this fucker was just buying time. But I did see the money out here! Shit, shit, shit . . .*

They were three hundred paces from the cars when two figures stumbled from the brush behind the shed. Only one was armed. The blond cursed and began to limp, Corbett falling in line behind him, doing his own cursing in English. The blond staggered and fell on hands and knees, Corbett

□□□

dropping to a crouch because it was now obvious that he needed a hostage.

"Twisted it," grunted the blond, sitting now, rubbing an ankle.

"Stay right there," Corbett snarled. "Tell those men to walk away with their hands in the air or I'll kill you. I mean it."

"I am sure you do," said the blond, turning, an ugly little snub-nosed revolver coming out of its ankle holster like a melon seed pressed between fingers. "But in dying, I could not miss you."

Corbett said nothing at all, but continued to point the Uzi. Without refocusing his eyes he could see two men fanning away from the shed in a flanking maneuver, and now they both carried weapons.

"You were already in place," said the blond, "when that diversion went off. And since you are the pilot, it was not an airplane crash."

"Tell them to stop or I'll blow you away," Corbett said tightly.

"And if I only wound you, still you must deal with my veterans," the blond said, very quietly, not moving. "No wounded man could do that." Then, in tightly controlled passion, "It is *expected* that you take the money! You are throwing your life away, second by second."

Why doesn't the bastard shoot, if he's lying? Because I'd kill him too. But he's right about one thing, I don't have a prayer out here in the open. Still Corbett cudgeled his mind for another option, the seconds ticking away.

As if to endorse Corbett's thoughts: "I could have fired already, if that were my intent," said the blond. "I am going to tell my men to hold their fire," he added, the little revolver with the big muzzle unwavering on Corbett's breast. He raised his free hand; waved it, still not turning from Corbett. "Do not fire unless he fires first," he called. "This is the man who must take the money!"

It was the sight of the approaching men that made Corbett's decision for him; that, and a feeling that the blond truly wanted to hand the money over for reasons that might become clear, if he lived long enough to hear them. *Die right now in the next thirty seconds, taking a Russian with me, or live from moment to moment and hope they fumble worse than I do. Either way, they aren't getting the hellbug.* "Tell them if anybody fires, you get it," he said, his mouth dry.

"You are not a man for panic," said the blond, with a nod that was almost admiring. "Well, do we shoot each other after all?"

Corbett knew that he had just come as near to panic as he ever would. "The time for that is past, and you know it," he said, and lowered the Uzi.

As the two latinos approached Corbett stood up, hands at his sides, and watched the blond reseat his revolver in its astonishingly small ankle holster. The blond stood, then, and retrieved the Uzi, with a perfunctory glance at its receiver. He looked into Corbett's face as he reached into the jacket and withdrew the Glock pistol, sticking it into his belt. Then he hefted the Uzi. "This is yours, Mateo," he said, and exchanged weapons with the taller of the two men. "I see he did not take it without a fight."

The lean man stared hard at Corbett, a vein pulsing in his forehead next to a fat blue bruise. "An ambush, Lobo," said Mateo, and swept the barrel

□□□

of his weapon in a slashing blow toward Corbett's head.

"Stop that," commanded the blond. "He is necessary!"

Corbett, who had ducked away from the full force of the blow, reached up to feel the torn cartilage at his earlobe. The third man shook his head as if to distance himself from such things.

At a gesture from the blond they called Lobo, the men fell in behind Corbett, the four of them walking toward the shed, Mateo grumbling in boots that flopped without laces. Lobo turned his attention to the small man: "What of the fire, Jorge? Did you find an aircraft?"

"No aircraft," said the little man, evidently surprised at the question. "Greasewood and that relic of a car. And when I circled back through the brush, our friend Mateo grunting and flopping like a trussed pig. He made enough noise for ten."

"You did not have to cut my laces, you son of a whore," Mateo grated in return.

Despite the blond's pointed disapproval of their wrangling, the two were still at it when they reached the shed. The lank Mateo strode away from the shed, unzipping his pants as he went. "I will want that shoulder holster now," said the blond wolf; "it pleases me. You will not need it when you take us to the aircraft. We could find the aircraft anyway, of course, because it cannot be far away."

Corbett removed his jacket, dropped it atop a pile of trash, and shrugged out of his holster straps, handing the leather rig over. "You'll find the airplane booby-trapped if you ever find it at all."

□□□

"That, I believe. You have done much for a man alone," said the wolf, pulling keys from a pocket. "But after you have counted what is here, you may wish to disarm your handiwork."

What I'll do is try to stay alive until dark, Corbett decided, as little Jorge slung his Uzi over a shoulder. *If I can't get away within a couple of hours, there'll be a real explosion for them to deal with. Christ, maybe I can swim to the hellbug in the dark,* he was thinking, furiously working on some vestige of a new and workable scenario, unwilling to embrace utter failure, when the blond lifted the trunk lid.

The man stood perfectly still for a count of two and then, with motions so fluid they seemed almost unhurried, pointed his Uzi at little Jorge's stomach. "Put down your weapon, Jorge," he said calmly.

Jorge frowned, glanced at the open trunk, and Corbett thought the man's eyes seemed to glaze. He leaned his weapon against a tire and the blond kicked it under the car. "Sit facing the wall," he said in a soft snarl. "Both of you. If either of you moves or speaks I will kill you here and now."

The little man met Corbett's gaze, shrugged, and lowered himself to the dirt, Corbett imitating him. A long moment later, Corbett heard the flop of loose boots, then a rapid command in Spanish and a burst of curses from Mateo. Blessed with a fighter pilot's peripheral vision, Corbett watched as the blond used his weapon to prod the man forward. In a voice tight with contained rage, the blond rasped, "Which of you ladrones took the money?"

"Hijo de puta," Mateo hissed, and without an in-

stant's hesitation fell on the little man at Corbett's side, beginning with a kick that must have broken a few ribs.

In an instant the two latinos were grappling, the smaller man already in obvious pain as they fell against Corbett, who scrambled aside, coming to his feet with his hands in the air.

The blond stepped forward, grasped Corbett's collar, hauled him aside, then fired a burst through the shed wall just over the heads of the struggling pair. Corbett rolled and came to his feet, then backed against the wall of the tin shed. One of the combatants made a sound that seemed less than human, half bleat, half sigh. Their leader snarled, "Stop it, Mateo! How will we know where he put it?" He began to lash at the lean Mateo with the barrel of his weapon.

"Ay, caray," said Mateo, still holding onto the little man's hair with one hand as his other hand appeared holding a thin-bladed knife. As Mateo's gaze fixed on Corbett's face, his eyes grew round and unfocused, a man filled with furies suddenly unleashed toward all comers.

Corbett grabbed his leather jacket by one sleeve; used it as a flail to whip the maddened Mateo away, without effect. The man simply lowered his head and charged, snatching at the jacket with one hand, slashing with the knife in the other. The warning shouts of the blond seemed to go unheard as Mateo bore Corbett backward, slamming him against a corner post.

Corbett caught the knife hand, not at the wrist but with his own left fist literally covering the other man's right, going down beneath the cursing latino, feeling the blade flick like a tongue through

□□□

his shirt collar. With his free right hand he found Mateo's coarse hair, hauled back, then snapped his own wrist forward, the top of his head pounding against Mateo's nose. He felt the thin blade against the edge of his chin and arched his back, then put his entire left shoulder into a single, short upward blow of his left fist, still holding Mateo's knife hand in it.

The latino's wrist failed, his hand twisting to the side, and Corbett saw the razorlike blade make its brief passage through the straining throat of Mateo. For an eyeblink of time, only the pink and darker than pink of a sudden incision showed, and then a warm cascade of crimson flooded onto Corbett's arm.

Someone was shouting, pummeling the shoulders of Mateo, who now began to slide away, jerking and gasping, Corbett still holding on to that knife hand as long as it quivered. The slashing blow of an Uzi's metal stock caught him at the juncture of neck and shoulder, driving him once more against the wooden post.

"Get up," commanded the blond, taking two paces back, his weapon aimed point-blank at Corbett's torso.

It took Corbett two swallows before he could say, as he struggled away from the gory mess, "The bastard would have killed me."

The blond cursed again. "Yes. Hotheaded fool, it may have been he who took the money after all. Now we will have a devil of a time finding it." Motioning Corbett further away, the man felt for pulses in both his men. He did not seem pleased at his findings, but with more plain disgust than sadness.

□□□

Corbett felt his chin and realized for the first time that it had been punctured. "So one of those guys stole the cash?"

"It cannot be far away," said the blond lobo. "I am sure it was Mateo, now. Jorge was not the kind of man who would learn to pick a lock."

A late splash of direct sunlight, penetrating far into the shed, highlighted the body of the little man, who lay with legs drawn up, his head lying in trash, one hand clutching the side of his chest where blood had seeped from between the dead fingers. His lifeless eyes seemed to be studying the sand in fixed concentration. "Mateo fooled me," said the blond, once more taking keys from his pocket. "He killed Jorge to make me believe he was furious at another man's treachery."

"Why did he come at me, then? I sure as hell wasn't a suspect," Corbett fumed, trying to wipe blood from his chin.

"Who justifies a madman?" For a moment the blond held the Uzi indecisively, then pulled Corbett's weapon from his belt and dropped the larger weapon onto an old fragment of doped fabric.

That shit would burn like wildfire, Corbett thought. *That's the time to go for this guy.* "You wouldn't have a cigarette."

"No. Get in the car. You will take me to the airplane before dark."

"Why not wait until tomor—" Corbett began, but grunted as the blond drove a fist into his face.

"Because of you, everything has changed," the blond growled as Corbett sagged against the nearest car. "You want me to delay and delay, but I will not. I know my people can find Black Stealth One, no matter how well you have hidden it. But if you show it to me—" He seemed lost in thought, chewing his lip, then nodding as if to himself. "I can and will let you go. It is expected."

"With the money." Corbett's tone was rich with insinuation.

A backhand slapped Corbett's head against the car, leaving a bloody smear. "Yes! Shut your mouth and get in the car."

"Only you don't have the money anymore," said Corbett, rising unsteadily on knees that did not want to straighten. "And Black Stealth One has intruder systems, pal. Very high-tech. It goes up like an ammo dump if I don't give the right password."

"Then you will give it," said the blond, breathing through his nose now, and no longer steadily. "Or I will kill you out of hand. Now, today, as the sun sets."

"Go fuck yourself," Corbett replied. "Money or no money, you borscht-swilling asshole, I'd never let you lay a hand on—"

The man moved as if to pistol-whip Corbett and then, as Corbett threw up his hands, kicked him in the groin with appalling accuracy.

Corbett staggered back and fell into a two-foot mound of trash with the gasp of a child with croup, doubled over in agony.

"I will simply have to do without you," said the blond wolf, raising Corbett's own handgun.

The burst of gunfire spun the man half around, flung him backward as he fell. He lay on his side, firing aimlessly until Corbett, on hands and knees, managed to stop that flailing arm.

The blond, wheezing through sucking wounds in his chest, licked his lips and stared up at Corbett, their faces two feet apart, lit by a saffron sunset. "One man? One damned American?" His eyes seemed to be begging for a denial, or for absolution.

Corbett gave it: "No. Your luck just ran out, that's all." He took his pistol from the dying hand. "There's some honor in you, mister," he added, trying to get to his feet, and only then did Corbett fully understand that a man had risen from the pile of corrugated cardboard between the noses of the two automobiles, holding a mud-ugly automatic weapon in his hands.

Corbett's arms failed; he fell back on his rump, staring at the man with the Ingram. He managed only to say, "I guess I owe you one, Speedy."

FORTY-FOUR

CORBETT NEEDED HIS FRIEND'S HELP TO RISE. HE sat sideways, doubled over in the driver's seat of the little Escort. "So it was you I took for a Russian sniper out in the brush," he said, his voice still husky with pain.

"I hope so," said Raoul Medina, glancing off toward the shrubbery. "I hot-wired a dead Mexican's old VW to get here from Regocijo, left it a mile or two out in the boondocks."

"I saw it," Corbett said, unable to keep his hands from massaging his groin, though it only hurt worse when he did.

"Looks like a wreck, and it is," Medina muttered, holding the Ingram ready. "You too."

Corbett looked up, saw behind Medina's dry commentary, into his sympathetic gaze. Corbett fingered the ragged edge of his earlobe. It too was beginning to hurt, now. "I flew over Regocijo today. What happened out there?"

Medina outlined the Regocijo disaster, adding, "Fucking frito bandidos severed a hydraulic line when the main landing gear collapsed. Damn red hydraulic fluid all over me, I looked worse than you do. Cancel that, nothin' looks worse than you do, man. I'm a little beat myself, still got some spruce splinters in my shoulder. By the time I came to and crawled out from beneath the wing there were three bodies lying around, the place was an inferno, and my only help had taken off in his car. Probably thought I was dead. All I salvaged was this little Ingram. And the VW at poor old Julio's, a mile away."

"You knew I was coming," Corbett said, staring at Medina. "Why didn't you just wait?"

It was Medina who looked away first. "I didn't know if you'd make it. And if you did, I wasn't sure you'd come to Regocijo. That's the long and short of it, Kyle."

Corbett shifted against the pain still radiating from his groin, tugged at the crotch of his trousers, then managed a smile. "You really think I'd hand the hellbug over for money, Speedy?"

"Not after I took the stuff out of the trunk while those assholes were beating the bushes," Medina replied, saying volumes by what he had not said. "That little fucker in the corner? He nearly caught me out there. I watched this Russki hotshot, or whatever he was, lug the money back after your last pass, and I heard the trunk slam. They went out on recon again when you didn't come back, so I nipped inside. I hit the trunk release down there under your busted balls, but I didn't have time to

□□□

scoot back into the brush. Had to stuff the cash in that garbage in front of the other car."

"So you had a ringside seat for all this."

"No choice," Medina shrugged. "That Russki would've seen me for sure, so I burrowed under the crap in front of the cars and tried not to breathe." He fell silent for a moment, gazing at the body of Karel Vins. "You know what I think?"

"I've given up trying," Corbett grunted, supporting himself on an open door as he tried to stand erect. "Oh, man; this has been one rough trip on the family jewels."

"I think those guys didn't know about the inside trunk release on an Escort. Not even the Russki," Medina said. "He sure didn't trust 'em. Listen, Kyle, we've got to clean up this mess and clear out of here fast. Are you in shape to bring the hellbug here?"

Corbett's grin was wry. "Yeah, and I'd rather you didn't see just how primitive my booby trap really is. You sure you trust me not to just keep going?"

"With the hand I'm holding, I'd bet millions on it," Medina cracked. "I'm wearing gloves, but you aren't, man. I can wipe down the car, remove your prints. Make this look like a falling out of thieves."

Corbett essayed a step, then another. "That means we'll have to hide one body." He interpreted Medina's frown as perplexity. "One guy has to be missing, Speedy; he's the one they'll be looking for in every whorehouse in Acapulco."

Medina's headshake was a tribute. "I'm too goddamn new at this, man," he said. "You know I can't go back, don't you." Not a question; a flat statement.

"Yeah. They'd turn you inside out," Corbett

agreed. "They already think you're dead, you said. Look, we gotta talk this out, Speedy, and I can help. It'll cost you half that bundle. You earned the rest."

"Damned decent of you, man, seeing as how I stole it fair and square already." Medina moved around the nearest Escort, kicking corrugated debris aside, lifting the bags of money with a grunting effort. He dropped it all into the dirt at Corbett's feet, toeing it roughly, and grinned. "Ain't that a bitch, treating our spookers so rough?"

Corbett nodded. "I'll give odds the stuff is marked, or bugged somehow. That's one of the things we have to check before we leave here. And I don't know where we can go."

Pause. Then, suddenly: "I do," from Medina. "That old guy, Julio, had a little place on a creek, a mile from the Regocijo hangar. He got zapped; that's his VW I drove. The Russki seemed to think the guy you killed was the sneaky type, so he's the one we should hide."

"Yeah?" Corbett's heavy shoulders shook faintly with amusement. *"Yeah?* Try this: we hide the Russian. Somebody was depending on him, Speedy, and so on up the line. Fuck 'em all," he said, and winked.

"All the way back to the Kremlin," Medina nodded, his eyes alight. "Jesus, I'm glad you're on my side." He saw Corbett turning his hand over in a "maybe yes, maybe no" gesture, and laughed. "You fly him to Regocijo and I'll drive the VW there."

"You and the money," Corbett said.

"Fuckin' A," Medina said. "And it's only fifty miles by air but if you don't get your ass in gear, it'll be dark before you could make Regocijo. Don't land at the strip; look for a thatch-roof place a mile to the north, by the creek. It's got a pasture big enough for you." Then, with a sigh: "Shit, I'll be driving half the night. But at least I know the way, and you'd never make it with your balls the size of punching bags."

Corbett picked up his pistol, wiped it down and thrust it into his jacket, took a half-dozen steps, then turned. "You still have that modified airchine you were building?"

"The Imp? Sure, hangared under false ID outside Binghamton. I'm not holding out on you, man."

"Didn't think you were, Speedy. I'm just reminding you: you've got your airchine. I've got mine. I won't object to a little trading around now and then, but—"

Medina drew a long breath. A muscle twitched in his cheek. "Yeah, what's mine is mine, and what belongs to the fucking NSA is yours. Is that all? You through setting terms and conditions, ole buddy? Maybe you'd rather just take the money and let *me* lug that fucking deader in a VW that might conk out on the streets of Mazatlan when I'm halfway to Regocijo, huh? Seems I heard you say you owed me one, and that was damn straight, Kyle; you do."

Corbett raised a conciliatory hand. "Dead right on all counts. I'm just giving all the bad news up front, Speedy. I'm not holding anything out on you either. We have a lot of planning to do. We need to buy spreads from Canada to Chile where we can build hangars, a couple of dead dropout ID changes for you, stuff you may not have worked out. The good news is, I can lay it out for you, step by step."

"Not if you don't quit talking and get moving," Medina said gruffly, reaching into a net bag as if it were full of scorpions. He popped the seal from a bundle of banknotes, dropped the money, and held the paper tape toward the sun which was now within a hand's breadth of the horizon. "Well, how about that," he said, "circuitry printed into the tape. We're not the only high-tech spooks in the game."

"Nope; just the best," Corbett replied as Medina began to remove more tape wrappers.

EPILOGU

THE JAVELIN'S TIRES HUMMED A SONG OF GRAY slush and skittishness as Dar Weston wheeled from the beltway toward Potomac and a fireplace that needed only a match to make the afternoon absolutely perfect. *That and hot chocolate with brandy,* he amended. She had loved the stuff since the days when it was forbidden. Tires like these were definitely not for January weather, but Dar had not expected his retirement to feature many trips, certainly not a jaunt to and from Baltimore on a moment's notice. A block from the house, he made a turn just a few degrees too tight and felt the Javelin's rear end slip before straightening. He glanced at his passenger.

"Don't mind me, I'll just eat my knuckles," Petra said brightly. Her tone said that a little fishtailing

□□□

was of no concern. Then, looking ahead: "What on earth happened to the edge of your carport?"

Dar turned in at his driveway. "Don't ask," he said. "Been meaning to fix it, but somehow I never seem to get around to it. And don't imagine I did it, Pets, I may be retired but I'm not senile enough yet to collide with my own carport."

He would have taken her two small overnight bags inside but neither of them would be staying the night. When she had called, she'd given him choices: pick her up at the Greyhound station in Baltimore and take her to Dulles in hopes of a flight to Hartford, or spend the balance of the day with her at his home in Potomac and then drive her to Old Lyme that night. Or let her continue by bus. *That,* thought Dar, *was never a likely choice and, bless her, she knows it. She also wants me to help her take some heat from Phil and Andrea when she gets home. And I will, and she knows that too.*

"You'll never be old, Uncle Dar," said the young woman, sliding her arm around his waist in a hug too powerful for most women her size. The hug made him miss the keyhole in the kitchen door, but Dar did not complain.

She skipped up the three steps into the kitchen, snapping on the light without looking, as if she owned the place—*which might as well be true,* Dar thought. *I need no higher compliment.* In the light, Petra's tanned features radiated health that seemed a reproach to other women. "Been skiing, have you?"

"No," she said, touched her sun-bleached hair, and laughed. "Looks like it, huh? The truth is, I feel an awful slut for taking off like this over Christmas holidays when Mother and Dad expected me, but—I'll be starting winter term knee-deep in snow, Uncle Dar! This is a beach tan, I'll have you know." She strolled with him to the living room, a place of lounge chairs and incongruously modern lamps, made untidy by the scatter of books. She returned his smile. As he knelt to light the crumpled paper beneath oak logs, she stood behind him, fingertips touching his shoulders. More seriously, now: "Tell me it's okay with Mom and Dad—but tell me the truth."

He laughed into the growing blaze, then stood up and hugged her to him. "The truth," he said gently, "is that it's not okay yet. But it will be, a half hour after you kiss Andrea hello." He released her and pointed to one of his recliner chairs, taking the other. "The greater truth is that the right thing to do isn't always the thing people recommend."

She flopped into the chair like a child. "That sounds funny, coming from you. Tell me honestly: would you have said that before—you know."

She doesn't want to say, "before you were canned." "Probably not, Pets. But I knew it, all the same."

The blaze had caught nicely now, licking up through the smaller split pieces, searing into oak bark that hissed in protest. "If it bothers you to talk about it," she said with some hesitation.

He waved her reticence away, staring at the flame as if mesmerized. "Truthfully? A little, Pets, but sometimes you have to talk to someone." His voice lowered, the words falling from his reverie as if from a great height: "And there is no one I would rather talk with than you."

□□□

"I feel the same way. Always did," she said. "I wonder why, Uncle Dar."

"You're the daughter I never had," he said. *Ah, God, the day Andrea's will is read, she will remember this moment. I hope she forgives us all when that day comes.*

There was no irony in her murmured, "Yeah, I guess. You remember our truth game, back when my waist and hips and boobs were all the same measurement? No fudging, and tough questions, and promise to love each other no matter what the answers?"

"I seem to recall it," he said. *Could I forget? I lied to you in those days, reassuring you that the world was a nicer place than it is.*

"I need to play it again."

"Why?"

She grinned and stuck her tongue out. "Let that be your first question, then."

He laughed outright. "Okay, then it is. Why?"

She held her grin, but Dar could see that beneath the surface lay fear. "Because I need to understand how much I owe you."

She knows, he thought, holding her gaze. *She is going to ask me about her real mother. And God help us both, I will tell her.* "Good enough. Now your question."

"Dad thinks you sacrificed your career to try and save my life last summer. How much truth is in that?"

"Some," he nodded, feeling his heart leap because she could still retain a fragment of innocence in a world full of deceit and, worse yet, stupidity. She would not cry, he knew. He knew because he had seen her this way before, denying

□□□

tears of regret. He went on quickly, to help her. "You have to understand, Pets, it was a thing that I did without regret. Not then; not now. It may have been the first entirely right thing I'd done for—oh—twenty years or so.

"And there were other factors involved, decisions that had nothing to do with you. Right is a hard thing to know, honey. You think you've done it, and you find out you were wrong. The utter and total truth is, I'm glad it all worked out this way. Now, for my next question," he said, and cleared his throat importantly, earning her full attention. "I know you wouldn't go hurtling off to some sun-baked hell by yourself." She began to smile again. "So what's he like? And if you tell me what *they* are like, or *she* is like, I intend to throw myself into the fireplace."

Her turn to laugh, his to feel relief. "He's—maybe more mature than the other guys I've known. In some ways he's probably a little like you. He makes me laugh. He's a gentle thug, a little overweight, and he loves me and no, I don't intend to marry him yet. Maybe not ever. And God, do we have fun!"

"Any money?"

"Quite a bit," she said. "International trade. That's two questions, but I'm big-hearted. Now: I know who the people are who tell me to do things I think I shouldn't do. Maybe you don't want to name names, exactly; but what people told you what kinds of things that made you defy them? I didn't put that very well, I know."

He leaned back, eyes closed. "I think it started with Eisenhower," he said.

□□□

"Jesus freeze us! I was thinking more like family stuff."

"No, I did a lot of stupid things in the name of family; probably should have defied them. But I didn't. I was raised with noblesse oblige in my pablum, Pets. This country is a lot of shitty things, but not as shitty as all the other countries. Anything that threatens the American way of life—with all its damnfoolishness—was something to fight against."

Petra's astonishment bordered on awe. "You fought President Eisenhower?"

"No. But I should have, when he did things I knew were dangerous to all of us." He opened his eyes again, turned toward her. "It's no secret that people like me are valued for something called 'balance.' But the same folks who value us for it, sometimes set courses that would upset that big, tippy balance we call peace. Our leaders think they're right, of course. Usually they are. But what do you do when you know they aren't? When they undermine that delicate balance, risk pulling down a nuclear curtain over us all to gain some little edge that isn't worth that risk? The so-called correct answer is, you're a warrior; you obey orders. And I did, generally."

"That's not defiance."

"Not openly. Sometimes I raised hell, though." *And now I'm holding back with weaselwords like "generally." God almighty, what else should I do in this child's game?* "Now, my question: where'd you go for your holiday?"

"Oh, shit," she said, coloring under her tan. "That's not fair. Would you believe Cabo San Lucas?"

□□□

He simply stared at her, a smile beginning to lay around his mouth. "As in Baja?" She nodded. You didn't take a goddamn bus to the tip of Baja," e said. "You must've flown."

"He has his own plane," she said, so offhandedly hat he knew it was important to her.

"Must be a jet," he said.

"No, just a single-engined something or other. ley, what're the chances of getting some—"

"Hot chocolate," he finished for her. "I've aleady made it. In the fridge."

She was already up, moving to the kitchen. That's not what I call hot."

"It is after two minutes in the microwave. Nuke ne a cup too; the brandy's in here."

"Ohh, great," she said, rummaging unseen in the itchen. He heard her cluttering among his old ups and relaxed in the simple joy of hearing his laughter amuse herself. "Well hello there, you old panhandler," she said, still in the kitchen. "I suppose you want some too. Well, tough; but here's ome half-and-half. Been keeping out of trouble? Not if I know you, you old fart." The microwave oven began to hum. Calling over it, she said, Uncle Dar? I know this is way out of line, but are you really and truly retired? I mean, are you ever ikely to go back?"

"That's your last question. Yes, I am completely and irrevocably retired. I can't imagine anyone wanting to drag me out of retirement and if they lid, I wouldn't."

The ping of the microwave oven gave him an audible exclamation point. She bustled into the room carrying mugs, each with a marshmallow melting nto foam atop pungent hot chocolate. "I'm glad you're out of it. Oh-oh, look who's followed me. thought I'd bought him off with a saucer o cream." She sat down carefully, patted her lap a Dar hauled the brandy bottle from behind a book The cat jumped into her lap and fixed its fatuou gaze on her marshmallow.

Dar poured, replaced the bottle, claimed hi seat. "So here's my last question, Pets: when do get to meet this man of yours?"

She sipped, he decided, to buy time. "He know a little about you. I don't know, I'll ask him abou it sometime."

Dar sipped, watching her carefully. "Pets through no fault of your own you are privy tc some things that no young woman should know I can't express too strongly the fact that you mus never—*never*—talk to anyone about the things you went through last summer. Just how much do you know about this man of yours?"

"Enough to know he's not interested in pumping me for information," she said evenly. "I know what you're getting at. He's not some Russian spy."

I know he's not. I know exactly who he is, the dirty, dirty son of a bitch. International trade, hm? Single-engined something, hm? Well, our people think the Sovs got Black Stealth One, and the Sovs think we snookered them, and the GRU is chasing its tail over lost money. And Corbett has my daughter; I wish I knew how it feels to have a cup that full. I guess it is time to play the man, Master Weston, and know when you're beaten. "However much you trust him, whoever he is, Pets, there are some things you must never discuss with anyone, just as sure as you love me."

"Such as?"

□□□

"Oh, things Kyle Corbett told you. The mere ention of such things could still cause me"—he aused to compose an immense understatement— certain amount of discomfort."

Her smile was warm, sympathetic. "Do you ean to say my uncle actually regrets a decision nough to deny it?"

He studied the fire for moments before he re- lied. "My country, or my best friend: regret is de- gned into decisions like that, Petra. I imagined at I could opt for my country with a clear con- cience. Wrong; that decision haunted me for ears." *And I will pay for it forever now, it seems.* only knew that Kyle became curious about— omething; someone. Something as silly as imita- on shrubs, actually. Someone learned what was ot to be learned, and Kyle was one of the people ue to be interrogated about it. He would have an- wered honestly. And that would have been a di- aster. He never underwent that interrogation."

"What's wrong with just answering honest," she egan, but stopped when she saw his expression, look that combat troops call the thousand-yard tare.

"It would have taken a crucial player out of ac- ion. It would have certainly disturbed that bal- nce I was talking about, a balance that two undred and forty million Americans depend on whether they know it or not." *And I still believe hat Sasha kept the balance! I must believe it, Kyle . . .*

"If that was your reason, I should think you ould live with it. Nobody's right every time," she aid gently. "Except God. Were you playing God?"

□□□

"Somebody has to do it," he said, "but not forever."

"Well, the guy survived it. Ironic, huh?"

He tried to smile without showing the pain. "Ironies beyond measure. Pets, mine was an error you must never discuss, not even with me after this. Promise?"

"Cross my heart," she said, gesturing to seal the oath. She took a dollop of marshmallow foam on a finger; offered it to the cat. "Better than mice, hm?"

The cat licked her finger, and Dar Weston's smile broadened. "It won't keep him from hunting them, though. Birds, too. I probably should get him fixed."

"No-o," said Petra, nuzzling the tiger-striped tom. "Then he'd just be plain Ivan, and not your Ivan the Terrible."